CW00351478

IT CALLS FROM THE FOREST
VOLUME TWO

AN EERIE RIVER PUBLISHING ANTHOLOGY

IT CALLS FROM THE FOREST
VOLUME TWO

Paperback ISBN: 978-1-7772750-0-6
Hardcover ISBN: 978-1-7772750-1-3
Digital ISBN: 978-1-7770410-9-0

Edited by Alanna Robertson-Webb
Cover design by Michelle River
Book Formatting by Michelle River
Title page art by Sebastian Zunino

When you are finished reading this collection of stories please take a moment and review it on Amazon, Goodreads, and/or BookBub.

ALSO AVAILABLE FROM
EERIE RIVER PUBLISHING

NOVELS
Storming Area 51: Horror At the Gate

SHORT STORY ANTHOLOGIES
Don't Look: 12 Stories of Bite Sized Horror
It Calls From The Forest: Volume I
It Calls From The Forest: Volume II
Darkness Reclaimed

DRABBLE COLLECTIONS
Forgotten Ones: Drabbles of Myth and Legend

COMING SOON
It Calls From The Sky
It Calls From The Sea
With Blood and Ash

This book is dedicated to all of our family and friends. Those that cheer us on, support us through the up and downs of writing and bring us coffee without us even asking. We hope you enjoy.

Contents

Foreword

We want to take a moment and thank you for purchasing this book, for supporting Eerie River Publishing and for experiencing the talented authors we've featured.

It is in our nature to seek the wild. We yearn for it, we crave it within the essence of our souls. We clamour out of cities to search it out, this fleeting promise of peace and solitude within nature.

There are dangers that lurk within the boundaries of trees and soil, where fresh air and meandering streams are not the only things that whisper our names.

Inside this anthology of the dark and twisted, you will read original stories from award-winning authors that have dared to take this journey. Let them weave you tales of the hidden, secrets within plain sight. Stories of beasts, both human and not, and of unspeakable horrors dwelling amid the trees.

May you be forever entertained,
Eerie River Publishing

I Speak for the Trees
Donna J. W. Munro

On the hill that rose above Grickle Grove evergreens grew thick, brushing the clouds into wisps with needles pink and soft. Grickle Grove's men worked in lumber, and they had built the first log and daub cabin that sat in the crook of Grockle Creek. Two hundred souls made their home in the valley, taking only the trees they needed and replacing what they took.

The oldest resident, Unc, had built the road, carrying stones from the creek bed and from the rockslides that came off the craggy cliffside. He led without appointment, deciding where to cull the trees and how many replacements to plant.

Unc was the head for the prayers that wove through the humming song of Grickle Creek. His voice would sing, low and sweet, "I speak for the trees, for the trees have no tongues. The trees, the fish and the birds are our kin. I speak for this hill, our mother, from where we take what we need. We take no more."

The rest murmur along, grumbling beneath his song.

And they prospered.

Only Unc ever led the prayer, and only he climbed the cliff to bring the bundle of soft, pink needles to the cave where the Grickle lived. Only Unc ever went to Grickle and looked into his yellow eyes, but he told the others about the creature's long teeth and spindle-bone legs.

Unc promised that any night wanderer on the hill would feel those teeth in the soft flesh for their throat, and that those long claws were allowed to tear at their skin. This was for the peace of Grickle Grove, which was negotiated and renewed each year by Unc and the Grickle among all the needle offerings.

Unc could not live forever though, could he?

Jacob Barbelot, the fifth child of Unc's granddaughter Sara, didn't think so.

"Unc, how old are you?" Jacob asked as they gathered the apples from the trees, taking what was needed and leaving the rest to tumble to the ground by the tree roots. Those were for the birds, and for the Grickle.

"As old as the grove," Unc said, his hands full of apples. He turned his full attention to Jacob. "I speak for the trees, and they give me life. As long as these woods live so shall I."

Jacob nodded, though inside he seethed. Why should Unc live forever, while the rest of the Barbelot family passed like dandelion seeds in a spring wind?

When the warrior woman stumbled into the village,

Jacob's anger found a kindred soul.

He'd found her, Captain Oncer, with moss growing on the scales of her armor. She'd laid her sword down to greedily drink from Grickle Creek, scooping the sparkling water by handfuls. A warrior from the plain, the kind who Jacob's mother had depicted. Sara had wandered in her youth, returning with recollections of the fierce warriors. Of course she sang out with disdain at the brutality she'd found, but Jacob had heard the words between. How exciting the battles were, how life and death were decided by the skill of your arm and the strength of your comrades.

He'd wanted to leave, to wander as his mother had, but Sara had forbidden it. The Barbelot family needed a male to sit in the circle next to her, one to give Unc their annual offerings, and Jacob was the only male. Maybe now, with the arrival of this warrior woman, things could change.

As Jacob approached the new arrival she spun on her boot heel, grabbing her sword and challenging him, "Back off!"

Jacob raised his hands, palms out. "Peace, sister. You look tired, and I can offer you food and rest."

The warrior didn't drop her guard, but her features grew quizzical. "For what in return?"

"Words. Just words, about the world outside of this place."

She stared at him, locked in the rigid stance of a soldier. Eventually she lowered her sword, cautiously following Jacob to his cabin. He maneuvered his pot of soup further onto the fireplace, stirring the banked peat lumps until the flames licked up the side. She sat at the table, sword next to her right hand.

The silence stretched, and Jacob's stirring didn't drown out the humming of Grickle Creek. He watched her out of the corner of his eye, her gaze shifting as she took in the cabin.

"Don't have much, eh boy?"

"Jacob."

"Jacob then." Captain Oncer grabbed a hunk of bread from the bowl and bit the rough dough, chewing slowly. "You live in the midst of plenty, yet you have this little hut and rough bread. How many days has that soup been simmering?"

He glanced around, ashamed, though it wasn't for the first time. He'd been raised in Grickle Grove's poverty, and had always struggled with the facts of it compared to what Sara had said of the outside world. Now, even with dirt and moss encrusting it, pieces of the woman's silver armor shone in the flickering light of the fireplace. It was worth more than all of his possessions combined.

Ladeling a bowl full of the three-day-old soup he merely grunted in response, then set the meager fare in front of her.

"Even in camp, we soldiers eat meat with our meal." She stirred the apples in the spiced water. "You have fish and fowl, so why not eat those?"

"It isn't allowed."

"*Allowed?* If I were to go out and kill one of those fat

birds in the trees would you really stop me?"

Jacob shook his head.

"Why do you burn peat, when you have so many trees?"

"We only take trees when we have to for winter, or when they fall and then we must replace – "

"Why?" She crushed the crusty bread in her clenched fist. "Who makes you?"

He shook his head. How could she understand?

"Unc is our leader. He keeps us safe, and we follow the rules." Jacob filled his own bowl, sitting next to her. As he spooned the thin soup into his mouth he shamefully noted that it had never tasted so bitter before.

"If my army had these trees, that clear water and those fat fish, we'd win our war. You fools don't even know what you have! This Unc, is he a strong man that he holds you with such dedication?"

Jacob shook his head. "He's the chosen one of Grickle. He speaks for the trees, because…"

She scoffed. "Trees are things to be used, Jacob. I'm going to lead my troops back here. There's money for you to make from the use of your resources –"

"I don't want money! I want to be a soldier, like you."

At his outburst she laughed, holding out a hand. Jacob grasped it happily. "Then I'll train you. Come Jacob, let us bring the army."

…

Two evenings later, as the sun sank behind the grove,

the army crested the far hill. It made its way down to Grickle Creek, bands breaking off to chop down the pink pines or to spear the geese squaking fearfully between the fallen tree trunks. The residents of Grickle Creek didn't come to stop them, as Jacob had thought they would. In his shiny new armor, and standing next to Captain Oncer, he had hoped his mother Sara and his sisters could see how he'd changed.

He wanted them to see how much stronger he was under the army's care, but only Unc came out of his hut. He walked without pause to Captain Oncer, easily recognizing someone who held power. As he passed Jacob he spared him a sorrowful glance, but not a word.

His low, sweet voice rang out in the dusk. "I speak for the trees, for the trees have no tongues. The trees, the fish and the birds are our kin. I speak for this hill, our mother, from where we take what we need. We take no more, so you take what you have and leave before it is too late."

Captain Oncer dismounted from her horse, drawing her sword in a fluid motion. "Old fool! Get out of my way."

She shoved Unc, laughing at the old man, but –

He didn't fall.

The last of the daylight died in that moment, and Jacob's jaw tightened as he watched Unc stand like stone.

"I speak for the trees, who have no tongues." The words stretched in his throat and, strangely, so did Unc's body. His eyes melted in his sockets, burned out by the bright-yellow light shining from deep within him. He grew upwards and out of his skin, stretching on bones tall and thin. The tips of his elongated claws scrambled in the dirt among the fallen, pink evergreens. His skull was now half buck and half wolf, with teeth longer than Captain Oncer's sword.

The soldiers stopped chopping and spearing. They were frozen in horror as they took in the sight of Unc, took in the sight of the Grickle, slobbering over their Captain.

"You will replace what you take," the Grickle rasped.

The warriors screamed as one. Their armor was ripping, metallic crunches filling the air as their bodies lengthened. All of them threw their heads back and stretched their arms out, branches breaking through their skin. Their flesh transformed from soft, pink skin into the ridged, hard skin of the pink evergreens. Metal scales sloughed off as their toes stretched into the earth, and the pink needles spiraled out from every branch and finger.

The Grickle raised its claws, clicking the tips, calling the tongues out from the mouths of the dying soldiers. The meaty organs snaked out from between lips, pink and shining wetly. Soldiers gurgled as their tongues ripped from them, the body parts flying to the Grickle. It popped the saliva-coated meat into its jaws, chewing it into mush that disappeared behind his gnashing teeth.

The Grickle repeated, "Trees have no tongues."

Without the screaming the humming of the creek filled the space between Jacob and the Grickle. Its lamp-like eyes shone in the dark, glinting off of Jacob's shiny new armor.

"Forgive me, Grandfather. I didn't know they

would…"

The monster listened to the echoes of Jacob's lie bounce among the new stand of trees. It bent over the speared birds and pulled the death out of their wounds, releasing black clouds into the air.

"Jacob Barbelot, my little traitor…" The words rolled in the beast's bone windpipe. "You let them in, you led them back. I thought, maybe someday, you might -"

"Please Grandfather, I'm sorry!"

The Grickle crept forward on long spindle legs, teeth shining red in the brightness of the moon.

"I can't make you a tree, my child, because you didn't protect them. I can't make you into a fish or a bird, because you watched them die. No, I'll make you part of me. This way I'll know you'll never hurt them again."

Jacob opened his mouth to protest, but the Grickle caged him with its bony arms and long claws. It peeled Jacob's skin, spilling blood on the roots of the new, pink-needled trees. He dropped hunks of skin over the bird's wings, making them longer with each strip. The muscles and organs he tossed to the fish, who gobbled each piece up.

Jacob felt each injury, even once he was only bones.

And then the Grickle, humming with the creek, wove Jacob's bones in with his, latching them on as they clacked and melded together. It made itself stronger.

Then it breathed out life in a white cloud, which wove around the bones and pulled them together back into the shape of Unc. Jacob's bones ached to speak, but he had no breath. Unc laughed and patted his distended belly, Jacob's bones like a shield on the inside, and walked through the grickle grass toward town, breathing in the slow, sour scent of blood on the wind as he greeted the laughing crows.

DONNA J. W. MUNRO
ABOUT THE AUTHOR

Donna J. W. Munro's pieces are published in Dark Moon Digest # 34, Flash Fiction Magazine, Astounding Outpost, Nothing's Sacred Magazine IV and V, Corvid Queen, Hazard Yet Forward (2012), Enter the Apocalypse (2017), Beautiful Lies, Painful Truths II (2018), Terror Politico (2019), Burning Love, Bleeding Hearts (2020), and others. Her upcoming novel, Revelations: Poppet Cycle 1, will be published by Omnium Gatherum in 2020. Contact her at https://www.donnajwmunro.com or @DonnaJWMunro on Twitter.

THE THOUSAND EYED-STAG
SYD RICHARDSON

O n this night the air is crisp and bitterly cold, and they stand together somewhat huddled in a small group, made quiet and contemplative by the weather. Reflecting against the fresh snow, the brilliant stars and full moon almost provide enough light for him to extinguish the tiny, burning lantern that he holds in his fingers. But he and the other men have reached the clearing before the deep wood, and he peers into the canopy constructed by redwood and birch trees whose tops scrape the sky; it is dark and jagged, like looking into the maw of an animal. It is like looking into eternity itself.

It is pitch black, as far as he can see. Nothing moves, except the leaves that sway and shake in the bitter wind. He looks into the forest, at the gun enclosed in his mitten-covered left hand, and at the lantern in his right. A frigid arrow, colder than the snow, pierces his heart; fear. The fire swaying in the howling wind is pathetic, and

Micah thinks helplessly:

What will this little flame do, against a darkness such as this?

"There's something in those woods," Douglas Feldecker points a gloved hand at the forest, teeth chattering with such intensity that the others have a difficult time understanding him. He pauses, racking his head for the right words on this dark, long night, "in this forest…it took him. It took my boy."

He starts to shake harder, his normally bright-red face flushed pale white. *Like a corpse*, Micah thinks, and Douglas' mouth is set in a frown. Though he is addressing the group of men directly in front of him his kind eyes seem hard, distant, as his mind replays the events leading up to the search party. It is a loop that never seems to cease. His brown coat is stained, with something that looks like dirt.

Micah thought that, if the man could cry without the tears freezing instantly, he would be. Within the span of mere minutes Douglas, a bright, big man with a wide smile and a demeanor that reminded Micah of a golden retriever—kind, easy to please, not all that bright, but equipped with a ceaseless, ferocious loyalty—was absent, and he suspected that this part of Douglas would never come back. It went with his son as he was dragged off into the deep woods.

Douglas and Cassy, his wife, had heard the distressed braying of the cows in the barn. The Folsom folk know the sound of braying is a sure sign that the beast was taking its meal. Then, to their horror, the high shrieks of their son

Wilson reached them. By the time Douglas ripped through the front door Wilson had been long gone—except for the seemingly never-ending trail of frozen blood and gore that had been left in his wake. Almost comically, though Micah could not find much humor in it, there sits a long trail of red, like a path of bricks, leading through the break in the trees in front of which they group. It reminds him of a tongue, almost.

"It has been terrorizing us for weeks now," Douglas continued, "first my animals, and now…now my family. My boy."

He quivered; the awful events of this night having reduced him to nothing more than a child in an adult's skin. Micah knew it by the look in his eye. His mortal personage, attempting to process the rapidly progressing events, strained. Less than an hour ago he had been laying with his belly full, thinking about menial tasks to be done the next day as he lay next to his wife. The men waited for Douglas to continue, shuffling from foot to foot; waiting for the okay to do at least some searching that night. None of them wanted to step foot in those woods willingly, and Douglas said nothing. It was impossible for him to say anything more, and a line of drool dangled from his mouth to his chin before freezing there.

Micah finally yielded as someone put a gloved hand on his shoulder, pushing him out of the way softly and without any hard feelings. With the man's back turned he looked no different from the seven or eight of them all dressed in brown or black coats, but Micah knew that swagger. He recognized the assured stride in his walk anywhere; it was their trapper Graham McTaggert, the son of one of the richest families in Folsom. The McTaggert family had made their fortune by selling pelts, and meat, from animals. Animals were their possessions, and they took pride in being able to fatten up their livestock. They thrived on their cows and horses and chickens, and the old running joke around the town was that the animals on the McTaggert farm were faring much better than many of the Folsom folk.

The beast that stalked Folsom was especially insulting to Graham and his family; they had awoken many nights to blood in the stalls where animals once stood and slept and shit. Their sprawling farm was a popular target for the carnivore, and from what Micah understood it had taken several of their prized livestock. Not eaten, per se, but taken. No matter how fast one of the McTaggert clan, or anyone else, had come sprinting out of their houses to the screams of livestock only a spray of blood had ever been left at the scene.

And each time they searched around the perimeter of the forest, the only place that such a beast could hide on a low-land area such as Folsom, not a drop of blood or a discarded bone was found. Not even a tuft of horsehair or dog fur. It was like the animal was devoured neatly by one huge maw, swallowed snout to toes, and nothing was spit back out.

Graham pushed to the head of the group, laying a heavy hand on Douglas' shoulder. He turned to the small party of able-bodied Folsom men, seven in all. Once dawn broke, and the morning sun lit the forest safely, there would be more hands to assist with the search party. But the trail was newly made, and if Wilson wasn't dead from blood loss by now he would be after a long night in the freezing cold.

"Gentlemen," Graham began, and all eyes turned raptly towards him; Graham had some sort of innate likability about him, with his easy smile and handsome, rugged face. "Douglas is correct. It may be bitterly cold, and it's late in the night, but we have a fresh trail to follow. If we make it in time, there is a chance we can find him. We can find Wilson, and find the thing that has been destroying us."

There were a few murmurs of agreement, some nodding of heads, but the freezing cold had simmered some of the fire in them. They looked at the entrance of the woods skeptically, Micah included. He wanted to find Wilson as badly as any of the others, if only to spite the perpetrator and bring some semblance of happiness back to old Douglas Feldecker's homely face, but the forest outside of Folsom was unyielding and unforgiving and extremely unwelcoming to guests.

"'Sum'n evil in them woods, Mister McTaggert," Sunny Richardson spoke up finally. He was a vegetable farmer, and the town mailman, not a skilled hunter. His voice cut through the silence and the howling wind. He shook his head, eyeing the forest as if it had half a mind to rear up and bite off his fingers.

"Dougie, sorry 'bout your boy, real sorry. Wilson was

a fine lad," Micah looked down, unnerved how Sunny was already speaking about Wilson in the past tense, "But you could not get me in them woods, 'specially at night, even for fifty silver coins."

Douglas, worn out wholly by the hit to his livelihood and family, ducked his head in silence, sobbing quietly. Micah suddenly had a roaring, searing hatred for the foul thing that made them come to this haunted wood in the middle of the night, and he despised how it made a gentle giant come undone. Graham, however, looked like he was not to be deterred; he eyed the party silently, grey eyes jumping from one harried Folsom man to the other, stroking his chin softly as he did so. After a beat of silence he looked the sullen Sunny Richardson in the eyes.

"How about a hundred silver coins?" He challenged. The men looked up at him, made tired and quiet by the cold, but their interest was peaked.

"A hundred silver coins for the man who can catch this foul thing!" Graham suddenly yelled out against the wind, snapping them back to attention. The promise of money upped the stakes, and Micah watched, still floored by the sudden turn of events, as a couple of men hoisted their guns to the ready. Even Douglas had looked up in sedated shock.

"A hundred coins," he repeated, "from my family and I personally. I want it found, gentlemen! But, most importantly," he cocked the gun held in his right hand for emphasis, "I want it dead. It has taken so much from all of us, and I would like to take something from it now."

Micah had also been wronged by the thing from the woods; a bachelor and childless himself, thankfully he had no family that the beast could threaten, but he was not much different from the other good folks that had settled in Folsom. Micah had inherited a farm from his father, the late Gregory Sloane, who bred the best milking cows this side of Pennsylvania.

They kept their three milking cows—Bessie, Bertie and Gertie—in the barn alongside the house. Those three, along with their two oxen for ploughing the fields and four horses, were bedded down with a couple of goats and a handful of chickens, though the fowl usually made their home in the henhouse not three feet away from the barn.

One night Micah listened to the high, shrieking wind. In his hands was a novel of poems. He had never been much of a reader; he found the little words imprinted on scratchy paper a touch intimidating, and sometimes they blurred together and reminded him of ants crawling on parchment.

It was on a night such as this, when the wind whistled through the breaks in the wooden walls that comprised his cabin, that Micah Sloane looked up from his book. He heard a peculiar noise coming from outside the cabin and, with the recent slew of missing animals, he had his gun readied in the corner within reaching distance should he ever need to jump from bed and run towards the barn.

He heard no sounds of animals in distress. The night was quiet, and sometimes the wind would howl, but he could feel it; the hairs on the back of his neck stood to attention, and his breaths came out in inconsistent, quick shudders. Something was standing outside. Someone was breathing, breathing slowly. He heard it above the shrieking wind; something with a huge mouth was pressed to the exterior of the cabin, teeth scraping up against the wood. Micah slowly reached for the gun, cursing the house's floors for groaning in agony at every one of his soft footsteps.

Outside the thing, if it could hear him, seemed to pay him no mind. On and on it breathed, obscenely even, as if a creature on the verge of climax. Micah readied the gun, but he found it shaking in his unsteady hands as he pointed at the door. Should the thing come in he would shoot it, but there would be nothing on God's Earth that could ever get him out of his house.

In time the huge thing bumbled away, but not before Micah heard the high, eerily human shrieking of a goat. It had taken not one, but two of his animals that night alone; the passing days saw cows, sheep and a handful of chickens disappeared by the creature's hand. Always a shock of blood, on the hay or the inner wall of the barn, with nothing else to signify that the animals had been taken.

They broke through the tree-line, McTaggert and Sloane in first, with Feldecker taking up the rear. The forest swallowed them without a single sound.

...

They walked and walked, the snow crunching under thick work boots was the only sound other than the occasional breeze that made the dry sticks and branches crackle. Swaying and bobbing his tired body through the near-impenetrable barrage of trees, Micah felt akin to a clumsy dancer with an unforgiving, impressively good partner. He fell in step next to Graham, who was trying to suppress a shiver under his thick parka.

"What do you think it is?" Micah asked softly. He was certain the party behind them were listening.

"I saw it one night," at the raising of Micah's eyebrows in disbelief, Graham quickly corrected himself, "a glimpse of it. It got into the horse's stables, and I shot at it before it could run off into the woods. Wounded it a little, I think. Could not see the head, but it's hind legs..." He trailed off, and Micah decided not to press him on it. The band of men trudged on through the forest, and he made sure not to step in the trail of Wilson's blood underfoot.

"It looked like a deer." Graham finished suddenly.

"You are saying a deer did this?" Micah was unable to hide the utter disbelief that crept onto his face. A deer! Spiriting off with tens, if not hundreds of Folsom animals and now, and one Folsom boy? A deer, causing all this havoc on their tiny town?

"I am saying that whatever did this looked like a deer, biggest deer I have ever seen."

Micah looked at Graham, "So, what do you think? Was it a deer, or not?"

Graham opened his mouth to reply when he suddenly looked down, stopping so quickly that Larry Abes did not look in time and bumped into him.

The trail simply…ended. It was like Wilson had been dragged, bleeding and screaming, and then suddenly his broken body disappeared. Or something ate him whole, thought Micah, and he swallowed the thought down. A fat drop of snow plopped on his head, sliding down his hat and onto his face where it froze.

"Where did it take him?" Douglas inquired in a high, reedy voice.

"We are going to find out. Men, I think it best to split up and check what area of the forest we can. Sloane, you are with me. Richardson and Lockheed, go Eastward. Feldecker—"

Something wet, likely melting snow or ice, slid down Micah's woolen hat; he only paid it heed when he looked down and saw his light grey mittens spattered with blood. He craned his eyes upward.

Blood dripped from branches that chittered in the wind overhead. Something had managed to splatter blood, *Wilson's blood*, Micah thought, several feet above them. He tapped Graham on the arm, and spoke his name quietly, "Graham, Graham, look," still looking up, and he heard the sharp intake of breath by one of the others in the search party. Graham looked, his brown eyes wide in the moon-light. When he turned his head back down, he eyed the meager search party.

"We will meet back here in exactly ten minutes. Whatever is moving in these trees that is not one of us, shoot it."

"Wilson's blood in the trees," Micah and Graham

trudged through the thick snow, past branches sharp enough with cold to cut. They moved through the under-brush, weaving their way past oaks and redwoods, "how do you think it did that?"

They had been walking in silence, listening for any-thing else besides the sounds of a dead forest in the middle of winter.

Graham peered at him, his face set in grim, exhausted curiosity, "How do you mean?"

"It was…what, at least four, five feet over us? There is no possible way a deer, no matter how tall, could reach up that high."

"Maybe whatever it was swung his body around. Splattered the blood in the trees."

"My point being, Graham, that a deer would abscond with a child and mangle his bloodied body."

His companion considered this quietly, eyes swim-ming with some contemplative look that Micah knew as memory. Beside him Graham replayed in his mind's eye what he had witnessed that night, trying to recall even the most scant or hazy of details, and after a beat of silence he said once more, "It looked like a deer."

Micah bit his lip to suppress a loopy grin. Though brought to fruition by exhaustion and fright, it seemed inappropriate due to the circumstances of their little romp in the woods. "That still does not bring me much comfort."

They came across a little clearing. Trees towered on every side, and nearby sat a shallow brook that wove through the trunks, still and silent and frozen. In the dead of winter, in this deep forest where the sun itself could not penetrate the canopy of leaves, the snow threatened to eat up his boots. Both of them looked around, and the silence was almost too much for Micah to bear; he bit down on his lip to stop himself from asking Graham a question. Gram held a palm up to the open air, stiff as a board, a hunter locked on to the scent of prey.

"Do you hear that?" Graham cocked his head, an obedient hunting dog listening for the ducks.

Micah frowned, puzzled. He heard nothing out of the ordinary, nothing besides the wind whistling and branches scraping, and when he opened his mouth to voice this to Graham, something moved. He heard it then, long before he could see it.

The sound of crunching, fresh snow under the paws of a large animal. Graham pulled him by his coat behind a tree, a thick oak surrounded by underbrush, and the thorns of the bush pulled at their clothing and scratched their faces as they tried to stay hidden.

Micah did not speak—he was suddenly too afraid to. He was gripped by an unyielding, impending sense of wrongness, and though in his mind he said over and over again *'Bear, it is just a bear, or maybe a moose or a deer, some kind of big animal...'* he knew, in some primal part of his brain, that while it was a big animal it was not a moose. A moose did not drag a bleeding child through the woods.

The scent of meat assaulted his nose first—of rotting, stinking carrion, permeated with sickly-sweet notes that made him fight the urge to vomit the contents of his late dinner. The reek of it brought tears to his eyes, though they froze instantly in the oppressive cold.

From the trees, from a place neither of the men could see from their mediocre hiding spot, came the unmistakable, inquisitive bleating of a sheep. Soft *baa-baas*, questioning, as if it had become detached from the herd and was looking for it's kin.

Micah and Graham locked eyes; he could see Graham's breath coming from his nostrils in uneven pants, like a spooked horse. Micah wondered how a sheep could stray so far from home and still be alive in this weather, when the sound ended as quickly as it had started.

He began to rise from the hiding spot when Graham pulled him back down, shaking his head furiously, one palm exposed to the air as if to say 'Wait'. In the silence of the sheep came the loud braying of a donkey, which nearly startled Micah and Graham out of their thick winter coats.

Then, when the donkey stopped, it was quickly replaced with the noise of whinnying horses. Then there were the cries of cows and goats, and occasionally the howling of a dog. The cries became an amalgamation of animal noises that overlapped, and the sound was louder than any farm to ever exist. Micah fought the urge to clamp his hands firmly over his ears to drown out the incessant noise, and Graham had the gun cocked and was ready to fire if whatever was making the cries came for them.

Did it bring all of the animals from town here, somewhere? He thought. But still, eyeing the clearing in terror, he did not see the sheep. Nor was there the donkey, nor the horse or the dogs. Everything was white and frozen, picturesque. Nothing moved, and the forest fell silent for a moment.

"*Helb me.*"

He doubled over behind the thick underbrush, arms wrapped around his own body as tightly as he could manage. Graham gasped, his eyes open wide as the finest china plates, mouth positioned in a perfect circle.

He only tore his eyes away from the clearing to lay a heavy hand on Micah's shoulder, and whispered in his ear, "I am going to get the men, I am going to find the men," only in a high, frightened voice that was very unlike the valiant and brave Graham, and off he went. He cut through the underbrush and ran in the opposite direction of the creature, bearing west for the nearest duo of men.

"*Helb me,*" the voice called from out of Micah's line of sight, as if it were testing the waters. It was seeing who would come out and check first.

It was him, Micah was positive it was him. That was Wilson, Douglas' first and only boy, speaking from somewhere behind the trees. He was trying to call for help, but it sounded like his tongue had been ripped from the root and his teeth plucked out, only to be haphazardly pushed back into his black cavity of a mouth. Something was terribly wrong here. And, doubled over in sheer terror, Micah kicked himself for ever venturing out into this thing's territory without the protection of the sun.

"*Helb me,*" he said over and over, through a mouth that sounded like it was full of blood and spittle, "*Helb me, helb me..."*

Under the weight of the beast something huge, like the fallen, thick branch of an oak, crunched in its wake.

Beside him, close to his hiding spot of bushes, somewhere outside in the clearing where it could be seen Micha heard the sticks on the forest floor break, and he held his frozen fingers over his mouth to silence a scream.

"Hello?"

Oh. Douglas, it was just Douglas. He appeared so suddenly, with his dark brown jacket, walking unsurely past him. How terribly he wanted to shriek out, to tell that kind, old man to get the fuck out of there, to run and never come back into these woods and to forget about his son. Yet he stood still with his gloves around his forearms, made silent and cowardly by cold, made silent by terror.

He watched through the brush with wide eyes as the creature spoke again, unable to hide the mirth in its voice:

"Helb me."

Micah knew it; this time, the thing was smiling. The old man raised his head slowly, his breath hitched in disbelief and terror as he heard his son speak from behind a thick canopy of trees.

"...Wilson? Willie? Isaat you?"

Douglas reached his hands out towards the trees, beckoning to his son, his only boy. He beckoned to the light of his life, but when it emerged from the blackness of the forest it gave Douglas just a fraction of a second to scream.

From his hiding place behind flimsy brush, Micah

saw the Wilson-thing emerge from a black clearing on too many legs to count, scuttling like an insect. Micah saw now how Graham could have mistaken it for a deer, but only for a moment; it slithered like a millipede, but instead of a thousand little black legs it had a thousand hooves. Atop its head the crown of antlers was sharpened to the tip, like a bull's horns, and they were decorated with frozen blood.

And God, dear God, Micah wondered what, in his final moments, horrified Douglas more; the demon plucked straight from the foulest pits of Hell that was clutching him in a clenched fist, or the fact that it had the face of his son Wilson.

It had Douglas gripped by the old man's neck, with sharp, long fingers. With a speed unmatched by any animal on God's green earth it opened a gaping, reeking maw and tore off the lower part of Douglas' jaw. It bit through the man's face like a piece of wet bread, and, behind Wilson's front rows of teeth, he saw two more, then four more after that.

Micah stumbled back through the bush, and some of the eyes on its body rolled in his direction, looking back at him hatefully. There was the sheep and the horse and the cow; only they were clumped together on its body as they moaned and screamed in agony.

And, through all the chaos of its body, Micah saw it; Wilson Feldecker's upside-down face, clumps of blonde hair still clinging to his forehead. A waterfall of black tar and blood streamed from his mouth, and, when he opened his jaw to swallow the rest of his late father's head, it unhinged wide enough to swallow it whole.

Micah turned, tripped over a tree root in front of him, and then ran.

His heart roared in his ears, and the lamplight was extinguished completely; he followed the light from the full moon that he could still see through the thick trees. Behind him came the sound of running hooves, of footsteps, and the smell of ripe, dead meat. To look back now would mean his death, and so he sprinted for the tree-line, and only stopped once he burst out from the edge of the forest, showered in moonlight.

Micah hit the show hard, the blood that had rushed into his face during his retreat turned frigid by the fallen slow. Up ahead the shadow of Folsom greeted him like an old friend, and he took a couple unsteady steps towards the town, his town, when he heard the chuffing behind him.

He turned around.

It was no more than four feet away from him. It followed him from the clearing, though it had stopped at the edge of the forest. One hoof stuck out into the snow, as if it was unsure if it should take the final step needed to end Micah's short, miserable existence early, but it moved no closer.

Trembling, he craned his head and looked at it.

All he could see, its body obscured by the creeping darkness of the trees, was Wilson's blanched-white face, teeth pulled back without his lips. He looked at Micah gleefully, mouthing words he could not understand as it retreated into the woods.

Micah stumbled back, scanning the tree line in case the beast returned. In the deathly silent snow, and the deep fright that coursed through his body, Micah managed to vomit up the remains of his late dinner. He crumpled to the ground suddenly, and sleep took him within seconds.

...

He awoke to the glaring sunlight and a maid attempting to unthaw his lips with warm water. Micah Sloane awoke as many do, in a deep-inner peace bordering on confusion as the brain and body recollect the events and actions of the previous day. And, like many, this state of nirvana only lasted about ten seconds for Micah.

The events of the night before came back to him in stunning detail. Wilson's face, Douglas, and the thing scuttling on too many legs. He could visualize the creature created of many other creatures, and a soft wail escaped his chapped lips. After a moment his mind settled, and he saw Graham's face, outlined by a ring of soft, morning light.

"Where am I?" he managed, the words burning Micah's sore throat. A cold would be fast approaching, if it was not there already.

"In my house. I am sorry, I tried to find your key but it was not—"

"Douglas," Micah rasped. The events came to him rapidly, far too fast to keep up with his lagging mouth, "Douglas, did you see—"

"Yes. We think he got lost somewhere in the woods," said Graham, eyebrows furrowed in confusion, "we heard him wailing all night."

He touched his swollen fingertips to Graham's forearm, and his mouth began to form words, a warning of what horrors were to come, but Micah's eyes suddenly swam. Within seconds he had slipped back into unconsciousness. Sleep had demanded its dues, and Micah could do nothing but oblige it.

In a few hours night would descend on the decent folks of Folsom, and Micah suspected that they would be seeing Douglas and his son again very soon, and with them would come scuttling the stag with a thousand legs.

Syd Richardson
About the Author

Syd is a thing made of spite, who consumes nothing but chai lattes; their favorite pastime includes buying cheap 90's horror paperbacks on e-bay and watching films like Five-Headed Shark Attack on Syfy. You can find them and their bad takes @sydyendys. sometimes they post things at chatterteeth.blog or jogboy.com

A DEBT OWED
KIMBERLY REI

I was a story-teller once, in an age when such a skill mattered and held power. Back then my home was a small cottage made of wood planks, with little more than spells and dreams to keep the cold out. But it was mine. It was treasured, until the forest came to reclaim its own.

Had I been less comfortable I may have had more warning; at least I like to think so. I like to think I am a skilled enough hedge witch to recognize such harbingers, but life was good and I was happy. Too many witches are feared or outright persecuted. I was needed. I had my garden and my woodland friends. People would come to me for advice and enchantments for their daily lives. The villagers brought me chickens and bread, and my loom was never without a project. I had no need for a man, but neither did I want for company.

I have had a great deal of time to look back, to rebuild events. I should have known something was amiss when the birds stopped visiting. They are the first to feel a disturbance. A wise witch, a title I can no longer claim, learns to speak with them. In my foolishness I had simply assumed a new predator was in the area, so I tightened the door on the chicken coop and went about my life.

The garden always needed tending, and as I was often injuring myself in one way or another I thought nothing of it that early spring day when I drove a thorn deep into my thumb. It took a visit to the blacksmith and his tongs to pull it free. The blacksmith, a burly fellow named Ian, cringed as he tugged.

"Aye, that has got it, but the tip busted off. Still in yer thumb, it is."

I smiled, as though it were nothing. I acted as if the pain was not blinding me, "It will work itself out. A small poultice will do the trick. How is your daughter? Her time is near, yes?"

That distracted him, and I was soon home to finish tending the wound. But the herbal salve didn't help. I spent the rest of the Spring fighting my own body. First it swelled, red and angry, then it wept. Then it just hurt. By the start of summer and the flurry of festivals, I was protecting my entire left arm.

Ian scolded me when I attended his grandson's birth. My arm was no longer red, but the skin had taken on an almost bark-like texture. It itched constantly, so I kept it covered in sheep fat and wrapped in clean cloth.

The child was born healthy and wailing, but Ian took him from me a little too quickly for my liking. His wife pulled a cloth over the new mother, both shielding her from view and my touch.

Ian settled the child by the fire and tucked his hands behind his back, "We are right grateful to ye, ma'am. It has been a tough time for Ellie, and you saw her through it. Right grateful. But we can take care of her now. I shall send payment 'round in the morn."

As simple as that, I was dismissed. I wanted to argue. It was just a rash, after all. Nothing to fret over, and certainly nothing to ostracize me for, but that is exactly what happened. It took time. The winter winds were stirring by the time I had no visitors at all. My village was not entirely heartless; baskets of bread would show up on my porch, and random chickens appeared with my own flock. There was even a pig delivery, complete with a new pen built for it. I assumed that was Ian, as gossip had it that the entire family was thriving and the new babe was well-blessed.

By then I could barely walk. My entire left side was stiff and useless. When I had the energy to tend chores I did so with the help of an oak stick, dragging my leg behind me. Rowan would have been better for protection, for I was certain this was a curse, but oak for endurance would have to suffice.

My dreams were haunted by darkness and shadow, with a surety that monsters and curses were waiting. In those journeys I could walk. I was whole, at least in the beginning. As my restless sleep progressed the forest moved. Shifted. Closed in around me until I could only risk taking a step by sacrificing flesh. No mere scratches from these branches, no. These were gouges and thorn strikes, which felt like fangs. I woke from each of these dreams thrashing as best as I could, my heart screaming for respite.

Ian showed up one bright morning. I was on the porch, soaking in the sun. I did not much care for bread or meat anymore. Milk nor mead, either. Water was like wine, and the sunlight felt like a feast. My limbs were too heavy to lift in greeting, but I managed a smile to see him.

He stopped at the gate to my land, eyes widening with alarm. My smile deepened to show him I was still the witch he knew. I parted my lips to speak, but only a rustling sound emerged. I do not know when words fled, for when you live alone you do not use them often.

I saw a tear slide down his cheek as he approached, "Ah, Henny. My old friend, what has happened to ye?"

I tried to shrug, but my shoulders creaked in protest.

"I borrowed a looking glass. None of us know how to help ye, Henny. Ye have to see for yerself so ye can guide us."

He held out the mirror, a battered, silver thing. It had been passed around more than the harvest's first brew, and dropped just as much. I wish I could say I was surprised by my reflection, but that would be a lie beyond forgiveness. Water in a glass offers enough of a view.

My face was no longer my own. The form was there, the shape was familiar, but I had become a mask crafted of wood and bark. Sorrow swept over me as I pushed slowly to my feet. Ian flinched, but may the spirits guide his soul he held steadfast. I turned with the effort of the ages and motioned vaguely to my cabin.

It took focus, but I found I had not lost my words entirely.

"You, Ian, helped build my home. You crafted my fence. Raised my small barn." I paused for breath. Everything took so much out of me. I could see the trees moving now. Slow. We did everything slowly, but inexorably.

Fear flickered in his gaze. He held steady, perhaps remembering those days and giving me the benefit of a long friendship. He did not move, not even when my hand gripped his wrist with surprising strength and speed.

"We forgot, Ian, we all forgot. If you take from the forest, you must give back."

Branches closed in around us, and as I felt my legs sink into the porch my feet burrowed into earth. I heard his screams.

KIMBERLY REI
ABOUT THE AUTHOR

When Kimberly Rei was five years old, her parents gifted her with a set of Children's Classics that she had no hope of reading. Yet. Sitting at the Christmas tree, surrounded by dozens of beautiful hardcovers, she was giddy with the potential of one day diving into the pages. That love of words and hunger for stories has never wavered.

Kimberly has been featured in more than a dozen anthologies. Her tales lean creepy and aim to leave you with an unsettling urge to look over your shoulder. She is, like most authors, working on a novel, but an addiction to micro-fiction is keeping her on her literary toes, chasing paper dragons.

Always seeking new ways to make words dance, she has taught workshops and edited novels for Authors You May Recognize.

Kimberly currently lives in Tampa Bay, Florida, with her bladesmith wife, a circle of creative friends, and an abundance of gorgeous beaches to explore. Life is good!

http://tales.studiorei.org/

https://www.facebook.com/ReiTales/

https://twitter.com/SeersDaughter

https://www.instagram.com/theseersdaughter/

THE BOG FEEDERS
ERYN HISCOCK

Mafa raised the straw blind of her thatched hut; moonlight wedged through the darkness, illuminating the shape of her sleeping husband Ofu nestled under straw mats and woven wool. Mafa paced their hut, shivering in the late autumn's midnight chill. She was not trying to be quiet, and she did not mind whether she disturbed Ofu, since he always slept like a dead man.

Ofu told Mafa her suspicions were wrong, but she could not shake them: they whispered in her ear, their voices louder and louder. She was well familiar with their fevered pitch from times past, when their community gathered round the raging fire well after midnight, their weapons raised.

Times when the bog needed feeding.

Fudir and Osoln were the last to be sacrificed. That was some harvests ago, before the first snows fell and after the wild dogs quieted their nightly howls. The moon was almost scythe-like that night, as it was again, and Mafa could not stop thinking about Fudir and Osoln because they were of her heart. She had once returned to the bog, slyly and alone, to float a votive anklet she had secretly woven in Fudir's beloved name. It was a parting gift, a way to remember her loved ones.

On a lazy sunny afternoon, when the other villagers were deep in the forest foraging for low-ground berries, Mafa's eyes had followed the braided circlet as it drifted along the bog's surface. It was moved by gentle breezes, the wool catching occasionally on peat before finally yielding to the weighty, murky water's fathomless blackness. She wondered, if she looked hard enough and far enough into the bog's bottomless depths, if she would see Fudir's pale, forgiving face.

Ofu had delivered the first ritual blow upon his brother, Osoln, when his time had come. Cracking Osoln's skull open had pained Ofu, naturally. He did not want to do it, but to save face before their people he had to.

Osoln, bound with his wife Fudir by his side, had pled for their lives. Together they spoke a prayer in unison, appealing to the Gods and their fellow villagers for mercy. Mafa wished she could mouth the words of the savior's prayers along with them, but she did not dare with everyone watching.

Ofu raised his blade, bringing it down hard on Osoln's head. There was a pause of shocked stillness and frozen silence, as always after the inaugural blow, and everyone watched the skin of Osoln's skull split like a seam; crimson humors gushed forth, splattering and trickling from his weeping scalp. At the smell and sight of blood the villagers moved in to claim their sacred part in this ritual massacre.

Fudir's body shook with fear and unbearable grief throughout the ritual. She recited prayers, trying to drown her husband's cries with chanted blessings. He grunted after every blow and thrust, alternating between whimpers and shrieks before finally fading into groaning softly. He moaned Fudir's name a final time, and then, at last, there was nothing.

Ofu proffered his blade to Mafa, still scarlet with Osoln's blood. He gathered some fresh blood with his thumb, ritualistically smearing it over his cheekbones and along his temples. A shudder passed through Mafa, rattling as a shock current when Ofu handed the weapon over. She turned to watch her people tie a noose around Osoln's neck, dragging his corpse away from his weeping wife. They had hogtied him, hanging him head-down from one of the ancient trees. They drained his blood into the soil beneath it, so that his sterile existence could no longer curse their impotent fields. Then, once he was bled dry, they offered his broken, battered body to the starving bog.

Mafa wished to do her part quickly. She closed her eyes, so that she would not have to look at Fudir, and she intoned the ritual blessing. Raising the blade high over-head she opened her eyes, waiting until the last second just to ensure dead aim. She brought the blade down smack in the centre of her beloved friend's skull, splitting it as neatly as a splintered log.

The moment she finished Mafa had backed away, letting the horde dive forth. She returned her husband's blade so that he could set upon Fudir, and she continued to utter ritual syllables. Mafa found a large rock, squirming her way into their huddle, but she mostly just clashed rocks with others to make it look as though she was doing her duty. She watched Elder Hespence shatter Fudir's leg with an iron sledge, surprised that the ancient hump-back still harnessed enough energy in her stooped body. Mafa turned away as soon as she could, busying herself with gathering anchoring stones and sticks to be arranged into burial crosses. They would float above their dearest friend's submerging bodies as they sank down. Down, down, down into the very bottom of the bog.

Now they were next. Of that, Mafa was certain. They were the only remaining couple in their settlement unblessed by offspring, and the last harvest had been disastrous.

The signs were all there: she and Ofu were no longer included in hushed conversations, and Mafa seemed to be an interruption when she came upon their whispered huddles. Whether she was passing by them in the forest, gathering food or transporting baskets of necessities to and fro they would all smile innocently, as if no bog-feedings were in the offing.

Mafa knew differently.

She watched them sharpen their blades, testing their keenness, and hammering boulders to see whether their irons were fit for bone-splitting—of beasts, of course, they said—only beasts—like those massive wild boars snuffling their way through the forest.

Mafa searched for a way out, walking farther and farther along the woodland paths each day. She tried to convince Ofu to come with her when the time came, but he was resigned to their fate. It was God's will, he said.

Mafa disagreed; If bog feedings were God's will then she no longer wished to please Him. She watched the moon closely, and once its shadow had cannibalized its own bony skull down to a sliver she stuffed two sacks with food. Then she woke Ofu, explaining she was leaving and he must come. She claimed to see the fire of distant torches moving toward their hut, and felt certain they were in mortal danger.

Their fellow villagers were coming to feed the bog.

After a moment's indecision Ofu rose from their straw bed, hurriedly layering on all his clothes and following Mafa into the night.

Shaking the sleep from his head as they moved through the soft, leafy darkness, Ofu told her God would punish them severely for this. Mafa retorted that she imagined far worse punishment if they stayed. He mentioned a settlement he had traded with some sunrises away, one where people had not fed their bog in many years, and he suggested that perhaps it was God's will they settle there.

"Yes, it is God's will," Mafa replied. "Let us go there!"

"Let Him show us the way," Ofu said.

She motioned for him to hurry. Mafa would say anything to keep Ofu following her as she led him down the winding, deepening forest path. She had filled her pockets with small pebbles and stones, using them to mark their trail with as they moved deeper into uncharted areas of the forest. At least they would be able to retrace their steps if they got too turned around.

Passing the bog Ofu waved his torch for one last look at the moonlit, unbroken surface. This might have been their eternal resting place, were it not for some greater power's deliverance this night.

In the northwest corner, right by a jutting peninsula that extended into the bog's center, Ofu peered intently along the water as Mafa checked through shadowed trees for advancing torches. Moving his torch around the circumference of the bog, Ofu spotted two clothed heaps bobbing in the murky water. He gasped, motioning to Mafa, who shone her light upon two forms near shore where the heaps were harpooned by reeds. Under the brighter light of both torches Mafa and Ofu recognized the bloated, copper-tinged bodies of their dearest friends, Osoln and Fudir.

Fear rose in Mafa's throat, cutting off her words as she was dumbstruck by the ghastly vision.

After years of submersion their rusty garments were washed clean of the fountains of blood Mafa and Ofu last remembered. How could either Mafa or Ofu ever forget the stream of blood? Blood, endless blood, which had gushed, sprayed, and splattered from their friend's wounds—wounds that had been inflicted by the people they trusted and loved the most.

How could Ofu and Mafa's hands ever be clean again? They could never wash the blood away from their flesh, bones, or memories, not after what they had done. No matter how many times they bathed, cleansed, or self-baptized, the blood would still stain their souls. Had it been worth saving their own skins, just to live in this constant state of remorse and torment?

Before the utter horror marring their final hours with their friends there had been nothing but a lifetime of shared memories, fond companionship and laughter. The group had taken multiple odysseys and long treks together, or sometimes in pairs. There had been days when Ofu and Osoln had journeyed away from their thatched dwellings in the village, venturing out in search of greater prosperity while Fudir and Mafa guarded their homes. The women spent that time repairing huts, weaving garments and woolly coverings, foraging in the forest, climbing trees to gather what fruit they could find that season and spending hours talking and laughing.

Mafa missed those days.

Ofu waved his torch around the bog to examine Osoln's headless torso, as if in some torturous attempt to absolutely, positively identify his oldest, dearest friend. He could still damn well remember Osoln's last horrified, betrayed look. It was that final vision which flashed before Ofu's eyes as he slipped fitfully into a tormented, night-mare-filled sleep every night since.

Fudir's corpse bobbed alongside her beheaded husband's torso; her head grotesquely present and accounted for. Both bodies appeared amazingly well-preserved. Fudir's glorious eyes, which were once so blue and crystal-clear, used to catch the sunlight like the deep, clean sea. Her glance was once so captivating that any person beheld by her living gaze felt blessed—those same, beautiful eyes were now rolled up into her head with only the whites showing. Her lips were pursed and open, as if to speak.

Mafa was filled with dread to hear whatever her friend now had to say, yet she was sadistically willed by some unseen, undeniable force greater than her own to listen. Mafa turned to Ofu, "She speaks; let us hear."

They found a long stick to maneuver Fudir closer to shore. The stick kept sinking through her body, as if all the meat within her was so soft, so unstable, that to prop her corpse upright against gravity would tear the loosening flesh too easily from her soggy bones.

After much effort, and after having to submerge themselves in the steely bog's shallows to assist in their endeavor, they managed to heave Fudir's ponderous, grotesquely disjointed corpse held upright by the stick. They both felt the lifeless chill of Fudir's aqueous flesh, like a jolt of lightening to their marrow, and then she awoke.

Fudir inhaled a long, cosmic gasp, as if drawing breath to new life. She flung her sopping, stringy hair around, bog water spraying wildly. Her neck bones creaked disconcertingly due to multiple fractures, and Ofu and Mafa's numbing hands struggled to grip her slippery, waterlogged body. They were trying to keep their nostrils from inhaling her foul, polluted stench too deeply, and Mafa thought how it was utterly repellent to be this close to a corpse. It was even worse to touch her.

What will, what compulsion, drove their hideous, morbid curiosity to hear her words? Mafa asked this of herself, while still standing in the frigid bog. The spreading chill, which had begun in their legs and feet, was seemingly contagious as it rose through their bodies.

Syllables gurgled from Fudir's decaying throat, which Mafa and Ofu strained to hear. In her new, yet ancient-sounding crone's croak, it seemed as if Fudir whispered, "Come, come." This new tone was nothing like her once-soft, living voice had been.

Her corpse beckoned with skeletal fingers, gripping Ofu's biceps as she wrapped her arms around his back. She seductively caressed him with bony fingertips, her white eyes gazing hideously at Mafa as she batted coppery lashes.

Before they could react, before they could collect themselves well enough for Ofu to throw her off and make a mad dash for the shore, he was toppled from the shallows into the deep bog waters by the weight of Fudir's embrace.

He shot pleading eyes at Mafa as he splashed down, a look that screamed Rescue me! as it's intensity sent piercing daggers through Mafa's heart. Ofu howled, gulping turbid bog water, his cries gurgling as he vanished beneath the bog's shadowy surface and into the coal-black depths.

Mafa shrieked in agony, as if something vital to her survival had been torn from her. She splashed around for Ofu, reaching down as she tried to grasp his hands, his wrists, any part of him. If only she could pull him from the water using the sheer force of her will. She tried and tried, searching and searching for those terrified eyes. His last, gurgling screams echoed in her mind, resonant, reverberating, looping through her skull. But Ofu had sunk too far below, down to where icy water would flow through his body and became one with him, marrying him with his old friends and the generations of earlier villagers who had met similarly ghastly ends.

All bones sank like anchors to the bottom of the bog, until tonight.

Mafa was not designed to accept defeat. She rushed to shore, splashing past Osoln's headless corpse and the gory pulp of his neck. She ignored the jutting cervical vertebrae, the trailing rope of the unwinding noose still about his neck. Her once-beloved friend's body parts bobbed grotesquely around her, but she only thought of Ofu.

Reaching the shore Mafa grabbed a stick, the one they had used earlier to prop Fudir's body upright. Rushing back to where she'd last seen Ofu, with the torch still blazing in Mafa's other hand, she stuck the stick down as far as she could without losing her grip. Ofu could, if God was willing, see it from his sinking swan dive into the black hole of the bog's bottomless deep and grasp it. Mafa prayed that, hope against hope, he would surface again and take one long, deep, revitalizing, life-giving breath so he could return among the living. Mafa shimmied the stick right to the ends of her fingertips, until it finally slipped from her numbing digits and sank away.

Mafa could not give up. She waded deeper and deeper into the bog, waving her torch over the black water, searching desperately for her dearly beloved's face. Somehow, some way, however far down he had sank, she would follow him. She would follow him to the pits of Hell.

With her mind distracted by these frantic thoughts, and her body anesthetized by the bog's frigid water, Mafa hardly noticed that she had slipped further and further away from shore. She was now toward the bog's centre, treading water and holding her torch over the dark surface as she stayed on the lookout for Ofu. Could he hold his breath for so long? Could he break free from Fudir's death grip?

Mafa did not notice Osoln's headless torso bobbing closer and closer with each gentle sway of the bog's rocking current. His noose uncoiled from his mushy neck-stump, the snaking rope trailing after his body through the water.

Mafa first felt a tickling around her legs which she took to be a water snake. She tried to shake it off, but the relentless serpent kept coming. It wound its steely, tentacle-like body higher around Mafa's kicking legs as she fought to pry the reptile away, but like a strangling python it squeezed harder and harder. It coiled higher and higher, shimmying from Mafa's calves to her thighs, then to her waist. The constricting creature was squeezing the chilled air from her shriveling lungs, leaving her near-breathless.

She raised her torch to take one last look for any signs of Ofu. Mafa was now firmly hitched to the noose, which was still looped around the stump of Osoln's neck. She could feel it dragging her down, and she sucked in a massive breath just before plunging deeply. She was weighed down by his headless corpse, and they sank together into the dark, cold, pulsing heart of the bog. The deathly snake-noose still encircled her body, constricting, constricting, tying her up, keeping her legs from kicking and her body from surfacing. The hard cable of the sinewy length cracked Mafa's ribs as it wrung out her lungs; she felt the agonizing pain of her vital organs being crushed like smashed insects.

With her vision fading Mafa faintly detected a constellation near the surface, recognizing it as the villager's torches circling above. They, having arrived to feed the bog, were unable to find quarry to appease their sadistic tendencies.

Their flames faintly flickered, dimming like extinguishing stars as Mafa sank deeper and deeper and further and further away from them, until she was all the way at the bottom of the bog.

ERYN HISCOCK
ABOUT THE AUTHOR

Eryn grew up in a housing project in the east end of Toronto, raised, along with her siblings, by a single mother. She read Edgar Allan Poe as a child and remembers how struck she was that his stories evoked such fascination and fear. She's been preoccupied with writing her own strange tales ever since.

Today, she is a poet and author of both fiction and non-fiction published in numerous literary journals and various anthologies. Recently, she worked as an entertainment and pop culture content contributor for an online publication where her articles earned 15+ million views within one year.

Although she dabbles in many styles and genres, Eryn feels most at home when crafting weird, chilling and out-there tales. She's currently immersed in two ongoing speculative fiction novel manuscripts, going back and forth between them so when she hits a snag with one, she can turn to the other.

THOSE THINGS WE CANNOT SEE
LEX VRANICK

The waning sun weaves threads of gold between the branches of the trees. Their warm light is deceptive; the air's autumn chill edges closer to winter as November draws to a quiet close. There have been clouds rolling in since the morning and, soon, if the wind does not thaw, there will be snow.

Asphalt roads turn to gravel, then gravel turns to dirt. The windows are rolled down; the heat inside cranked high. With one gloved hand on the wheel Mae pulls the zipper of her track jacket up to her chin. She scans the tree line as she drives, her German shepherd pacing the length of the backseat. She goes from one window to the other, sniffing all the way. Each time the dog pauses Mae pumps the breaks. She waits, the dog juts her nose out the open window, and then she whines as she pulls back into the car. When she resumes her pacing, Mae keeps driving. They repeat this two times, three times, four - and then the dog barks.

"Here?" Mae asks. The dog barks again, and Mae jerks to a stop.

They are on a dirt road in the thick of the woods. Goliath trees tower over them on both sides, their leaves mostly gone; instead of hanging above them, they form a carpet of oranges and reds and browns on the ground. The dog whines and paws at the window. She bumps Mae with her nose, then barks again.

It is 3:56pm, and it will be dark soon. The colors of the sky, obscured by large clouds, are already fading to dull, pale purples. Mae watches the quiet forest. Even with so many bald branches, there are deep shadows beyond the tree line. Mae's breath lights off her lips like a ghost as it rises up and off into the cold. Mae checks the temperature gauge on the dashboard, noting that it is 40 degrees and dropping rapidly.

Static erupts from the small, hand-held radio sitting in the cupholder.

"It's getting late," a crackled voice says. The dog barks again. Mae grabs the radio.

"Stella's got something," she says.

"You sure?" the voice asks. It belongs to Jack Tompkins. He sounds as tired as Mae feels. Mae looks over her shoulder. The dog, Stella, is whining now. She's facing the passenger-side window and pawing at the door, and when she notices Mae looking she barks a third time.

"She's sure," Mae says.

"We have your coordinates," Jack says. "How sure

is she?"

Mae presses down on the transmitter so that Jack can hear Stella's pleas.

"Pretty sure," she says when she is satisfied. "We're going to take a walk."

"We're on standby," Jack says. "If it gets dark-"

"-come home," Mae finishes. "I know."

"Tompkins, out," Jack says procedurally.

The radio static dulls, then ceases altogether. Stella's insistence is louder with it gone.

"Okay," Mae says. She turns off the engine. Stella lopes in tight circles when Mae gets out of the car and leaps onto the ground when Mae opens the door. "Easy," Mae says. She produces a read leash from her pocket. SEARCH & RESCUE is embroidered on it in white thread, and she clips it to Stella's matching collar. At the same time she produces a balled-up tee shirt from her pocket, holding it to Stella's nose. Stella sniffs, then barks. "Okay," Mae tells her. "Let's go."

Stella doesn't hesitate. She tugs at the leash, and Mae follows her into the dense trees. There's a cleared path, patted down by thousands of hikers and joggers and cyclists, that Stella follows for about ten feet. She comes to a stop. She sniffs at the ground, veering one way and then the other, before pulling Mae off the trail.

The radio is clipped to Mae's jeans. It bounces against her hip as she navigates the uneven terrain. Occasionally it crackles to life, and disjointed voices break through the static. Fallen leaves crunch beneath Mae's boots; twigs snap with every footfall. Stella is unperturbed, and she doesn't even seem to notice the rustling leaves or static storms. She drives ever forward, her nose down and her tail up.

Mae hears the same story over and over again: So-and-so went out on the trails this morning. So-and-so is an avid hiker. So-and-so always comes home after insert-your-preferred-increment-of-time-here, but so-and-so is not back yet, and this is extremely unlike so-and-so, so something must have happened.

The story has been relayed by tearful mothers, worried fathers and concerned friends all plugging in the names of their lost loved ones. Brady Wilson's story came from his girlfriend. Rachel Powell had been jittery, and she hsd wrung her hands as she spoke.

"Brady's training for the Appalachian Trail," she'd said. "He's been doing long training hikes, but he's never been gone so long before. He said that today would be quick. He was supposed to be taking it easy, because he hurt his ankle last week, and he left early this morning. He should have been back hours ago."

Mae had filed away the basic information. Brady Wilson is six-foot-one and athletically built. He was wearing cargo shorts and a black shirt. He kept a hydration belt in his car, which he may or may not have worn on his hike. He normally starts at the central trailhead at Silver Falls Park and follows the blue diamond markers north. Rachel had given Mae one of Brady's shirts from the laundry hamper. Now Mae keeps one hand tucked into her pocket, where that same shirt sits, Brady Wilson's scent embedded into the Pink Floyd logo.

Stella follows that same scent deeper and deeper into the woods. Her leash is taut, and she hasn't been this intent all day so Mae thinks they must be close. Stella quickens her pace, and Mae does too. The sky above them continues to darken, but Stella isn't bothered. When Mae looks up she thinks the clouds must have gotten thicker, and she's already seen a snowflake or two drift from their bulbous bottoms.

"Tompkins to Fox." Jack's voice bursts through the radio chatter. Mae scrambles for her radio, nearly dropping it once, then twice, as she catches it in mid-air. Stella doesn't take any notice, stopping only briefly to sniff hard at the ground before charging forward once more. Mae is breathless by the time she gets a good grip on her handheld.

"Go for Fox," she says.

"We've got snow coming in fast," Tompkins.

As if on cue, a fat snowflake lands right on Mae's nose.

"Yeah," she says. "I see that."

"Can you turn in?" Jack asks.

"I think we're close," Mae says.

"How close?" Jack asks.

It's as though Jack's inquiries are stage directions, orchestrating a production around Mae. The moment he asks his question Stella pauses, her ears flicking back and then forward. She barks. Mae looks left and then right, seeing nothing but trees; rows upon rows of them, stretched out far in every direction. She checks her pedometer, which shows they've traveled two miles into the wilderness. Stella barks again, and again, and again. She bounces on her front paws, throwing her head back in what Mae has come to call her Jackpot Bark. It means, Mae has learned, that she's found what she's been searching for.

"Brady?" Mae calls. She's caught up with Stella by now, and rests a hand on Stella's back. Stella's hair is lifted up in a ridge toward her wagging tail, and she stops barking the moment Mae touches her. Instead, she whines and nudges Mae with her nose. "Good girl," Mae mutters, though she's not looking at her dog. She steps forward, turning in a slow circle.

No one is there.

Mae pulls Brady Wilson's shirt from her pocket, holding it out to Stella, but Stella backs away.

"Fox?" Jack's voice crackles through the radio speaker. "Fox, are –u th-re?"

"What's wrong?" Mae asks Stella. "Come on."

She thrusts the shirt toward Stella's nose. Stella bumps it, then barks again.

"Fox?" Jack repeats.

Stella keeps barking, and now she's stomping her paws. Mae looks around again, but still sees nothing.

"Mae?" Jack says. "What's going on?"

"Something's wrong," Mae says.

"Yo-'re br---ing up," Jack says. The signal jumps and starts.

"Something's wrong," Mae repeats.

"Wh—is -it?"

"I don't - " Mae starts, but she pauses. She's distracted, and she thinks that she's seen something dart past her on the right. Stella sees it too, and she stops barking. Her ears turn toward the moving shadows. Mae squints in the deepening dark, but she doesn't see anything. "Brady?" she says. There's the sound of leaves on the ground, of branches striking each other, and Mae can't tell if it's from something moving, or if it's just the wind.

"Mae?" Jack is saying, over and over beneath the pops of white noise. "Mae?"

It's snowing now; a light dusting settles over Stella's back and around her paws. Flakes melt on the sleeves of Mae's jacket as she straightens herself, moving toward the strange shadows. Stella doesn't follow. She whimpers and steps backward, tugging Mae in the opposite direction.

"You said he's here," Mae says to Stella who sits, refusing to budge. "What's up with you?" Mae asks. Stella barks as something moves in the shadows behind her, making Mae tense. She moves toward the shadows, but Stella steps in front of her just as the radio crackles.

"Mae, can y—hea—m-?"

"Brady?" Mae calls. "Brady Wilson?"

The shadows move, or something moves in them. It's quick, slinking to one side and then the other, dancing behind Stella's head as it slides back and forth. It's as if it was taunting Mae. Stella's ears twitch, and she whines. Mae rests a hand on Stella's head. The moment she moves the thing in the shadows does too, darting to the right and vanishing upwards. Mae follows it with her eyes, tilting her chin up so she can spot it when it makes its harsh, vertical descent. She shields her eyes from the dying sunlight and the falling the snow, and—

Mae screams.

At least she tries to, but the sound gets caught in her throat. It emerges as a strangled sort of gasp that makes Stella jump up. She begins barking in earnest, circling around Mae. Mae doesn't look at her, doesn't acknowledge her, and she wouldn't have remembered the dog was there had Stella not bumped against her legs.

Up in the sky, trapped in the bare branches of an oak tree, is Brady Wilson, and there's something perched above him.

"Oh, my God," Mae breathes. "Oh, my God."

She can't tell what the something is, but it looks like a shadow come to life; large and black and looming. She can't find its eyes; she doesn't know if it has eyes, but she knows that it's watching her. She can feel it. Mae thinks it has talons, great big ones that curl around the thick bark of the uppermost branch of the tree, but it doesn't look like a bird. She's seen vultures and eagles and falcons, hawks and ospreys, owls and buzzards, but she's never seen a bird quite as big as the thing in the tree.

Below this monstrous being Brady Wilson hangs precariously between the branches.

Mae can see blood dripping down his face, streaks of red smeared over his bare arms. His shirt is torn, and the cloth appears caught on the sharp end of a broken branch.

Stella is still barking, and she bumps Mae's hand with her nose. Mae glances down, blinking. Stella whines and nudges her again, and it's then that Mae is reminded of the weight resting in her palm. She raises the radio to her mouth. Jack Thompkins is in the middle of saying something, his voice loud and worried, and Mae steps on his transmission.

"Backup," she says. "Now."

"Di—you f—d-"

"I found him," Mae says, though she doesn't know if she's even hit the button. She looks back up.

The monster is gone.

Brady Wilson lifts his head, a painful breath wheezing out.

"He's alive," Mae breathes. She drops her radio into her pocket. "Brady! Brady Wilson!"

Brady blinks. He looks about as dazed and confused as Mae feels. It's dark now, truly dark, but she can see his eyes glisten in the navy blue of the sky. The snow falls all around and on him, and it catches in Mae's hair. Her breath escapes in quick, white puffs as she looks for the creature, but she can't find it.

Was there even a creature? Now, Mae isn't sure. Perhaps the changing light had played a trick on her. She's tired, and she's edgy. Stella is too, which is why she's acting strangely. It has to be. Mae shakes her head to clear it, focusing her attention on Brady Wilson up in the tree.

How had he gotten up there? She can't waste time wondering.

"Brady," she says, and she grits her teeth at the tremble in her voice. "I'm Mae Fox. I'm here to help you, and Rachel sent me to look for you. Let me know if you can hear me."

"I can," Brady croaks. His breath is labored, and she can see it spill out of his mouth in a stuttered stream of white as he wraps his arms tight around one tree branch. "I think-" he starts, and he tries to lift himself up. "I think...I think I can get down."

"Relax," Mae tells him. "I've got an ambulance on the way."

"Is-" Brady starts. "Is it still here?"

Mae feels a pang in her chest. "What?"

"That...that thing," Brady says.

"I don't-" Mae says, but she stops herself. She can't lie to this man, and she can't lie to herself. Stella whines beside her as she goes to jump onto the tree trunk, her nose up in the air, and she barks her victory bark. "Good girl," Mae assures her.

A rustling behind her grabs Mae's attention. She swings around, but is greeted with nothing except shadows and snow. She listens, hearing nothing, and when she turns back around Brady Wilson is attempting his descent.

"Woah! Woah, woah," Mae says. "Take it easy."

"I'm fine," Brady insists. He gets his belly flat against one large branch, his arms and legs tightened around it. He inches forward, getting himself close to the trunk, when something darts out of the dark. Brady screams, as does Mae. Stella barks as Brady starts to fall.

Mae stumbles backwards, falling flat on her ass. Stella trots around her, growling and barking in turn, her sharp nose pointed up at the sky.

Brady hits the ground with a hard thud. Mae scrambles to her hands and knees, crawling toward him, but before she can get to him the thing swoops back around. It shoots between them, leaving long, dragging claw marks in the fresh snow before veering back into the sky. Mae moves forward, but again and again the thing comes back. Stella lunges at it, her jaws snapping, and a few black feathers catch between her teeth before the thing is gone again.

Fear and frustration boil in Mae's chest. Hot tears well in her eyes, and she tries her damnedest to keep them from falling. She begins to crawl forward once more, and her hand lands on one of the fallen feathers that Stella has spat onto the ground. It's wet with Stella's saliva, and the whole thing is bigger than Mae's hand. Hell, it might be longer than her arm. She shakes it away, and makes another move toward Brady. The thing doesn't come back this time, though a watchful Stella circles around Mae, snarling as she follows Mae toward Brady.

"Brady," Mae says. She reaches out to touch him, and this is when the beast returns.

Mae hits the ground, holding her hands over her head. Something cuts through her gloves and slices her skin, and she can feel the warm blood pooling in the open gash. A light spray of blood flies onto the snow when she dares to lift her head.

"What the fuck," she cries.

Stella's barking, and there's new feathers spread out over the show. Mae tries to look up, but all she can see is snow. It falls down peacefully, beautifully, calm and bright. Mae's heart hammers in her chest; She thinks it might snap her ribs. Stella keeps barking.

"Stella," Mae snaps. Stella doesn't stop. Without raising her body Mae reaches to Stella's neck, unclipping her leash from her collar. Stella pauses, her whole body tense. She looks to Mae. "Go," Mae tells her. "Go meet Jack. Go!"

Stella nudges Mae with her nose, licks her cheek, then begins to run.

Mae isn't a religious woman, and she hasn't set foot in a church since the sixth grade. She doesn't remember any of the words to Hail Mary, or the Our Father prayer; these are relics of Sunday morning lessons with a nun named Sister Stephen. But now, watching Stella race between the trees, seeing her turn to a dot in the evening dark, Mae prays. She prays hard.

Stella disappears.

Mae lifts her head. "Brady?" she whispers. Brady doesn't answer.

Mae waits. She listens, then her arm crawls toward Brady. She grabs one of his hands, and his fingers weakly twitch against her skin. He's alive, he's still alive.

This is the last thought Mae has before she's swept from the ground.

She tries to scream, but she can't. There's something wrapped like a vice around her body. She hears crunching and cracking, and she prays that it's not her bones breaking. She squirms and struggles, her fists beating against the great talons holding her.

Her ears ring, and then they pop.

The snow catches in her hair and on her eyelashes. She can't see. She can't breathe.

And then, she falls.

Mae doesn't know how high up she is when the thing drops her, and she doesn't know how far she falls before it catches her. Those talons, those massive claws, close around her again and pull her up and up and up. And then, a second time, she's dropped down. This thing, Mae realizes, is playing with her.

She tries to cross her arms around her face to protect it, hitting branches on her way down. She waits for the thing to grab her again, to toss her like a tennis ball, but it doesn't. It lets her fall.

It lets her hit the ground.

…

Mae Fox wakes to a harsh, white light.

Her head is pounding, and her ribs ache. She can't move her arms. She looks at her right hand and sees a large slit cut down the back of it, then she looks to her left and finds an intravenous line threaded through her veins. A slow and steady beeping thuds rhythmically in her ear. There's a shadow over her, and when Mae sees it the beeping quickens.

"Easy," a voice says.

Jack Thompkins, sans the radio static. Mae blinks, squinting up into the light. Jack's face is soft at the edges, fuzzy at first, and it's slow to come into focus.

"Take it easy," he says.

"Brady," Mae says.

"He's in ICU," Jack says. "Broken bones, and a lot of bumps and bruises, but he'll be okay."

"Stella?" Mae says. Her throat aches, and it makes her voice scratchy. "Where's Stella?"

"She's right here," Jack says. He rests his hand on something, and Mae lifts her head to see him scratching Stella's ear. The dog is curled at the foot of the bed, her heavy head resting on Mae's shins. Mae lets her head fall back on the pillow, sighing with relief.

"She led us to you," Jack says. "To both of you."

"Did you find it?" Mae asks.

"You found Brady," Jack says. "You and Stella."

"No," Mae says. "That…that *thing*. Did you find that thing?"

She's almost glad that she doesn't have a name for it, because that would make this all too real. Mae can still feel its talons around her. She can feel it crushing her ribs, and she can see it's looming form in the tree. She can see the black feathers, so harsh against the snow.

"What are you talking about?" Jack asks.

Mae looks at him. His brow is creased with the utmost concern. His free hand rests on the wall above her head, hovering near the red call button. Mae closes her eyes, and Jack sighs.

"You're tired," he says. "Get some rest."

"Sure," Mae murmurs. "Right," she says. "Tired."

Lex Vranick
About the Author

Lex Vranick is a poet and fiction author who has been writing since she could hold a crayon. She holds a Bachelor of Arts from Excelsior College and is a Juris Doctor candidate at Florida State University College of Law. She is a twelve-time participant and eleven-time winner of National Novel Writing Month. Her poems have been published by Cagibi, Kissing Dynamite, Soft Cartel, and others. Lex was born and raised on Long Island, but currently resides in Tallahassee, Florida with an abundance of houseplants and her four-legged roommate, Ozzy.

Twitter: @lexvranick
Instagram: @lexvranick
Facebook: Lex Vranick
Website: www.lexvranick.com

DATING IN MURDERVILLE
V. A. VAZQUEZ

"Holy shit," Darby said, as her '93 Geo Prizm rolled up the dirt pathway in front of the cabin, pebbles spitting out from underneath rubber tires. She grabbed the photograph out of her jacket pocket and held it up next to the windshield. Other than the crime scene tape that had been strung across the glossy 5x7, the two cabins were a perfect match. The online travel agency she'd contracted with had done their due diligence.

Double-checking her reflection in the rearview mirror, she pulled out her Canon S120 and positioned herself in the center of the frame. "Guys," she said, clicking the record button. "You are not going to believe this cabin." She flipped the camera around, so that her viewers could see the rental property. The building had probably started out as one of those Tiny House kits that came with everything flat-packed and ready for assembly: knotted-oak planks hammered together with a corrugated tin-house roof and a shower bag rigged up to a pole out front. She stepped out of the car, panning the camera across the clearing. "We are all alone in the wilderness out here."

A cheeky grin at the lens: "All alone, *for now.*"

She kept the camera gripped in her left hand while she fiddled with the latch on the door. Inside was a cast-iron stove, but without any wood chopped and stacked to the side. She probably should have known this was going to be more of a DIY weekend than she was used to. An industrial cabinet with a stainless steel countertop and pump-sink had been shoved against the wall, a sturdy ladder had been screwed into the loft-bed, and a few battery-powered LED lanterns hung from hooks. Since the cabin was off the grid there was no electricity available, and no phone service or wi-fi either.

She wandered around the cabin, shooting more B-roll footage than she'd need: close-ups of tarnished copper pots, a ceramic carafe filled with mismatched utensils, an acoustic guitar missing three strings. Always better to have too much than too little; she'd found herself shit outta luck more than a few times during editing since starting her YouTube channel. Darby finally tucked her suitcases away in a corner where their plastic shells wouldn't ruin the rustic 'canopy and stars' atmosphere.

A knock on the door resounded.

She turned to look at him through the glass: tall and broad, with skin the color of sweet, curdled milk. He had copper-brown hair that twisted into beach waves, and stubble scrubbed across his jawline. His ears were poorly proportioned, sticking out from the sides of his face like the floppy handles on a plastic bag. "Hiya," he said, the left corner of his mouth tugging up in a smile. "You must be Darby?"

"Stand still for just a sec," she said, unlocking her cell phone and pulling up the police sketch. She held the phone next to his face, comparing the two of them. It had taken weeks of browsing online dating sites to find a close enough match, but it had been worth it. When the sun went down, in the shadows of the LED lanterns, he would be a carbon-copy of the FBI's facial composite.

"Good enough?" he asked, shifting to the side, so that she could see his profile better.

"More than good enough."

She unlatched the door and opened it, leaning against the frame.

"I'm —"

She cut him off. "Finn."

He quirked an eyebrow.

"No, I'm —"

"You're Finn." She glanced back into the cabin, specifically at the loft-bed. "If you're staying here this weekend, you're Finn. I don't have room for anyone else."

His smile widened, a flash of off-white teeth.

"I'm Finn then."

She pushed the door open half-an-inch wider.

"Come on in."

He walked into the cabin and tossed his backpack, an Osprey Aether, faded and ripped from thru-hiking, into a corner. He smelled like the sticky tree-sap that oozes out of conifers. "Nice place you've got here. Airbnb?"

"Travel agency."

"Didn't think people still used those."

"Only for the YouTube channel," she said, pulling her tripod out of its carrying case and setting it up in the center of the cabin. She screwed the Canon S120 onto the quick-release plate. "We try to get as close to the actual crime scenes as we can. This cabin is almost identical to the one where Rachel Moore was strangled."

"You're the first person who's ever messaged me on Tinder to say that I look like a police sketch," he said, slumping down onto the bottom rung of the ladder. "Is that usually how you pick up guys for your show?"

"I'll pin a mugshot on my bulletin board and then swipe-left until I find someone who could pass. That's how we cashed in on the Ted Bundy thirst-train as soon as it pulled into the station. Swiped-right on some dude from Cedar Falls, Iowa who looked like his identical twin. I was on the next flight out; our YouTube video dropped the same weekend as the Zac Efron film. 1.2 million views."

"There are that many women interested in banging serial killers?"

"Everyone loves a bad boy." Darby shoved her hands deep into her pockets. "Look, I know it's a bit weird —"

"A bit?"

"But there's a market out there. All of our videos get demonetized right after they're posted, but we have a Patreon that brings in enough to pay our bills."

"How long have you been doing this?"

"What? *Dating in Murderville?*"

"Yeah."

"About three years. The AV Club called us *The Bachelorette meets My Favorite Murder.*"

"Any of these guys ever get a second date?"

"Let's not get ahead of ourselves." Darby centered her Tinder match in the frame and pressed record. "Mind if I ask a few questions before we get started?"

"Shoot." He paused for a moment before adding: "Or stab. Or strangle. Whatever you want."

"We're keeping that in the final edit. What do you know about the Blue Mountain Strangler?"

"Never heard of him until you messaged me on Tinder."

"But you must have looked him up afterwards, right?"

"Sure. Strangled seven women in vacation cabins across the East Coast. Sent a bunch of letters to the police and signed them Finn. They still haven't caught him, right?"

"Right. This will actually be *Dating in Murderville's* first date that's still an open investigation. Does that make it smuttier?"

"What? That the guy's still out there somewhere?"

"Yeah."

"I think it's a bit creepy."

"Maybe. We'll see how many hits we get. How do you feel about playing Finn this weekend?"

"Um . . ." He scrunched up his nose, like he'd squished

his hiking boots into some bear-shit. "I'm really excited to be here at Blue Mountain Lake, and I'm looking forward to getting to know you better."

"Darby."

"What?"

"Say 'Darby.' Not 'you.' It's for the viewers."

"Oh." He threaded his fingers through his rust-colored hair, trying to fix it for the camera. "I'm really excited to be at Blue Mountain Lake this weekend, and I'm looking forward to getting to know Darby better."

"Cute. They'll love you," she said, stepping out from behind the tripod.

"So what exactly do you need me to do?"

"We're going to role-play some scenarios."

"I've got some rope in my pack, if you want —"

She swallowed hard. His hands were rough; she imagined them wrapped around her throat, his thumbprint pressed into her windpipe, his fingertips leaving bruises underneath her ponytail.

"You like hiking, right?" she asked, gesturing towards the discarded pack.

"Triple Crowner. Just finished the Continental Divide last year."

"Great. I want you to go for a hike."

"That's it?"

"Go for a hike and then come back to the cabin. Don't let me know you're here. Just stand in the woods and watch me."

"Watch you?"

She walked over to the door and pointed towards the tree-line. "Stand right behind one of those trees and watch me. You can take photos if you want to; you should take photos. Record audio notes saying what you want to do to me."

"What are you going to do?"

"Same things Rachel Moore probably did. Journal. Cook. Chop some wood maybe."

"Chop some wood."

Finn looked uncomfortable. She couldn't have him skittering off like a spooked squirrel, out into the trees and down the road to the I-87. So she back-tracked: "I like it when guys watch, okay?"

Not a lie, but Darby tended to keep business and pleasure separate. The *Dating in Murderville* weekend getaways always looked way hotter in post-production than they did while filming. Finn didn't need to know that though.

"Okay, I'm game," he said, getting back up to his feet. He dug a water bottle out of his pack, along with a Garmin GPS device. His hiking boots had dirt that had lodged into the treads; he left behind pebbles and grit as he walked his way back towards the door. "Photos. Audio. Anything else?"

"That's it."

He unlatched the door, pushed it open.

"Finn."

He looked back, even though it wasn't his name.

"Don't hold back. In the audio."

He grinned, nodded once, and took off into the woods.

Darby turned back towards the camera. After fiddling around with the lighting and re-positioning her chair more times than she could count, she pressed record: "On this week's *Dating in Murderville* . . . Rachel Moore rented a cabin in the Adirondack Mountains for a little R&R, some time away from the rise-and-grind of Wall Street. But when the Blue Mountain Strangler showed up on her doorstep, her weekend getaway was cut shorter than her breath. This serial killer is still being pursued by the FBI, and by thirsty bitches like us who've seen the police sketch. We've tracked down a dead-ringer for this bae-on-the-run, and we're ready to try out some erotic asphyxiation with the Blue Mountain Strangler. Choke me, murder daddy."

She paused for a moment. Too much? Whatever, they could always fix it in post-production.

"If you like looking at crime scene photos, but don't want to end up on an FBI watchlist, check out NordVPN. Keep your data private, so that no one finds out what kind of kinky stuff you're into. Go to NordVPN.com/murderville to get three months for free."

Switching the camera off, she glanced towards the door. She'd told him to go on a hike beforehand; he wasn't already standing out there, was he? She went over to the Osprey Aether that was still heaped in the corner. There was a keychain hooked to one of the side-zips: a yellow metal tag stamped with a map of California. She tried to pick the backpack up, but Finn's gear had the weight of a cement brick. She ended up hauling it over to the industrial cabinet and shoving it into one of the drawers. Out of sight, out of mind.

She unzipped her suitcase. She'd found one of the leaked crime scene photos on WebSleuths and had gone thrift-shopping for the perfect dupe of Rachel Moore's final outfit. It was all high-end hiking gear that she wouldn't have been caught dead wearing otherwise; she'd list the items in her online shop after this video dropped. She could probably make bank if she offered to not wash the garments before shipping them. There were some sickos watching her channel.

After zipping the Patagonia fleece sweater all the way up, Darby grabbed the tripod and headed outside. What would Rachel Moore have done on a normal day? Cook dinner. Take a shower. There was a splitting maul stuck in the stump by the doorway. That was the first order of business: chop some wood. She put one boot on the stump to help keep her balance and pulled hard on the handle. The maul dislodged, sending her a few steps backwards. She looked towards the tree-line again. Had he seen that?

She pressed record on the camera. "If you've ever wondered if Darby O'Connor knows how to handle wood —" She picked up a log and placed it on the stump, checking for pre-existing cracks at the edges. Gripping the maul in her hands, she lifted it overhead and brought it down hard onto the log. It shattered in half. She picked a chunk up and held it in front of the camera. "Chop-chop, motherfuckers."

She repeated the process, bringing the maul down

hard each time.

She closed her eyes.

She thought she heard something rustling in the maple trees.

Darby continued with her day: stoking a fire in the stove, pumping water into the soup pot, boiling spaghetti for dinner. Every now and then she'd look out the door at the tree-line, trying to place Finn in the picture. Was he crouched behind one of the shrubs? Had he scrambled up a trunk? Was he perched in one of the branches far above the ground?

She'd chopped wood. She'd cooked dinner. The only thing left on her to-do list was to take a shower. "Enough with the foreplay," she said to the camera. "Let's get naked with a maniac."

Out in the clearing she took the shower bag down from the pole, bringing it back into the cabin. She wondered if Finn had seen her, if he knew what she was about to do; she wondered if he was chomping at the bit for some *Dating in Murderville* action. Pumping water into the bag, and grabbing her towel, she headed back outside. She strung the bag up onto the pole and turned towards the tree-line.

Was anyone even out there? She hadn't seen him all day. Either he was really good at hiding, or he'd already gotten sick of her bullshit and had gone home. How would she explain that to her viewers? *We had the Blue Mountain Strangler episode all ready to go, guys, but then the serial killer bailed on me . . .*

She tugged off the fleece, tossing it onto the ground. As she grabbed the hem of her T-shirt, she was surprised by the warmth pulsing between her thighs. He wasn't her usual type — with the beaded-hemp necklace dangling just above his collarbones and the weapons-grade cannabis she'd smelled in his back pocket — but something about being stalked in the wilderness was revving her engine.

Her jeans followed, leaving her in a mismatched sports bra and panties. She unknotted her bleached-blonde hair from the ponytail holder. Was he taking photos of this? Was he zooming in on all her best parts? *Should've made him sign an NDA*, Darby thought, *unhooking her sports bra and flinging it to the side. I'll probably end up on PornHub. Amateur Hiking Babe Showers in the Woods for Peeping Tom XXX.*

She pulled down her panties and stepped out of those as well.

Fuck it. As long as he links back to the YouTube channel . . .

She pulled the shower head out, and a light spray of water drizzled down onto her scalp. She ran her fingertips through her hair, scrubbing her palms over her face. This wasn't her first time being stalked by someone from OKCupid or Bumble. They'd hover outside of greasy-spoon diners, conspicuously visible behind the dashboards of their beige Toyotas and far too nervous to pass as legitimate serial killers. Afterwards they'd show her some of the pics they'd taken: blurry candids of her eating an omelette, face half-covered by the aluminum window frame. The covert two-second snap of someone ashamed to be behind the camera.

A real serial killer wouldn't be ashamed. He'd take his time, letting the lens follow the trickle of water droplets down her torso as she showered in the woods. He'd make love to her through the shutter. And after he was done, after he'd walked away from her lifeless body, he'd keep those photos saved on an external hard-drive where he could worship them.

Again, that warmth. Like someone had poured liquid candle-wax into her groin and let the heat simmer there.

She pushed the shower head back in and toweled off. A loud crack echoed through the clearing, coming from behind the cabin. Wrapping the towel around her chest, she hurried around back. There wasn't anyone there. She scanned the tree-line, even checked the dirt for footprints. Nothing.

"Creepy shit going down in the woods," she said to the camera, putting on her clothes and heading back into the cabin. "Just the way we like it here at *Dating in Murderville.*"

Everything was as she left it, except for one thing. Lying on the cabin's hardwood floor . . .

A cell phone.

Not hers; it must have been Finn's. It was unlocked. Sitting down in the desk chair, she clicked on the camera button and scrolled through the photo roll. Sweat dribbling down the back of her neck as she chopped wood. Smudge of tomato sauce at the corner of her lips as she taste-tested their dinner.

Enough photos of her in the shower to piece together a flip-book.

The first ones were better than she'd expected. He'd made her look like a real influencer: all of her flaws smoothed away by Facetune, the colors of the wilderness saturated through the Lo-Fi filter. She'd ask Finn to send her some of these later; maybe she'd post them on the Instagram account, get her followers hyped for the upcoming episode.

But as she kept swiping through the photos, she realized that the camera was sneaking closer, inch-by-inch. By the time she reached the last one, Finn was almost close enough to touch her, to reach out and brush his knuckles against the damp flesh at the back of her throat. How had he managed to take that photo without her noticing? She liked to think that, after three seasons of *Dating in Murderville,* she was an expert at knowing when someone was watching her, at being able to tell where that threatening gaze was coming from. But she hadn't spotted him once among the maple trees.

It was unsettling.

And it turned her on.

She closed the app and opened up the audio recordings. She clicked on the first track.

"I'm watching you from the woods. That sounds weird. Does that sound weird? I don't want to come across as a creeper here. But I guess that's what you asked for, so . . . I'm watching you from the woods. You're really pretty.

Like even prettier than you looked on YouTube —"

She pressed pause and moved onto the next track. She didn't want to listen to him wax poetic about how pretty she was. That was too high school for her. *Do you like me? Check YES or NO.*

Second track: no words this time. Just the pounding beat of his breath against the mic. She could feel the heavy wet heat on her cheek, seeping through the speaker. The track played on and on. She pressed pause.

Third track: a voice.

Not Finn's: a woman's. Shouting. Crying. Begging. And then, there were no more words — just the rattling clutch of her throat, trying to expel sound but unable to. And throughout everything, Finn's breath. Never breaking its steady rhythm, not even when the woman finally went silent.

The track ended.

"Holy shit," she grinned, clicking the play button again and trying to figure out which sound effects library he'd downloaded his tracks from. Who would have thought that beach-bum Finn would be so committed to his character? The woman's sobs echoed through the cabin, vibrating in the woodwork and the screws. Just like her Hitachi Magic Wand.

Shoving the cell phone into her back pocket, she unlatched the front door and took a few steps into the clearing. "I'm not recording right now. I just wanted to say that you're fucking amazing. Way better than any of the other guys we've recruited for this show. That audio track?

The strangle-wank one? Unbelievable."

She waited for Finn to respond, to call out Thanks! from deep in the woods, but there was nothing. *He's probably some kind of method actor from Los Angeles. That would explain the California keychain.*

"Let's call it quits for five minutes, and talk about how we want to approach the next scenario. I was thinking that you could break into the cabin, maybe chase me around for a few minutes . . ."

Silence.

A palm warbler chirped overhead, its trill sending a ripple of goosebumps down her spine.

"Are you out there?"

When had it gotten so dark? Even if he was out there he blended right into the shadows cast by the maple branches, all of them trembling weakly like the thin bones in her ankles, her wrists, her throat.

"If you don't say something, I'm going to pack it in for the night. You're creeping me out a little, which . . . good for you, but not really what *Dating in Murderville* is about."

Silence.

"Hey, asshole!" she called out as loudly as she could. The palm warblers shot up from between the branches causing them to shudder in the darkness. "If you don't get out here right now, I'm calling the cops —" Her breath stuck thick in her throat. How are you going to do that?, she asked herself. *You're off the grid. There's no cell phone service out here.*

As if on cue she heard a ping from the cell phone. She checked the bars in the upper-left corner of the screen: no cell service, but one unopened message was waiting in the inbox.

A photo of her.

Taken a few seconds ago.

With a line of text overlaid on top:

Are you scared, Darby?

Sprinting back into the cabin she grabbed her jacket and rooted around for her car keys, but they weren't in either pocket. She had put them in there when she'd arrived; she was sure that she had. *This is why you don't set up dates on Tinder,* she thought to herself, staring out the glass-plate door. She was so preoccupied with the maple trees that she didn't even notice the shadow leaning against the wall in the corner: solid and sturdy and *real.*

His elbow hooked around her throat, tugging her backwards into the cabin. Her boots kicked out as she was hauled off the ground. She tried desperately to nail him in the kneecap, to gain any traction at all, but she was left flailing in midair. She brought her fingers up to grip at the inside of his elbow, sinking her nails in and carving out bloody troughs there.

His breath heaved, thick and suffocating, against her face.

He tossed her onto the floor, the back of her skull knocking against the hardwood, and straddled her. His hand wrapped around her throat, crushing her windpipe like a plastic straw from a stainless steel dispenser. She looked up into his eyes, but there was no trace of the man she'd recruited from Tinder, the one who'd tried to get a second date before the first one had even started.

She gasped out his name — or the name she'd given him when he walked through the door — but the skin between his thumb and index finger was too tight, pressed down against her larynx. She let out a guttural rattle like a busted engine in a used-car lot. His fingers eased up, giving her space to use her voice.

She tilted her head to the side . . .

And saw the red light blinking on her camera.

She could have laughed. *This asshole.* He wasn't some kind of serial killer lurking in the woods; he was just trying to get footage for the YouTube channel. So she leaned forward and gasped out the word that was resting, sore and swollen, on her tongue:

"Harder."

"What?"

"You heard me, *Finn.*"

And before she knew what was happening his lips slammed up against hers, so hard she could feel her teeth clatter around in their sockets. She hiked up his T-shirt, scoring deep lines into his back with her fingernails. "Do your worst," she said, reaching down the front of his hiking trousers and cupping his groin.

"You couldn't handle my worst." His voice sounded deeper than when he'd arrived, more ragged. Like he'd smoked an entire pack of cigarettes back behind the treeline, leaving the filters for the park rangers to clean up in the morning.

"Try me," she said, bucking her hips upwards. His breath stayed steady, even as hers hitched and sputtered. He grabbed her by the throat again, cutting off her airway, as he rutted against her. She felt the muscles in-between her thighs clenching up, as her desperate swallows pushed outward against his thick palm. And then her entire body seized, all of that warmth oozing out of her core, and she crumbled beneath him.

"What the —" She would never have been able to tell from his voice that there was an erection that could bust through wooden planks tucked in the front of his boxer-briefs. "Did you just *come?*"

"Sure did."

He laughed. She liked the sound of it more than she'd ever admit.

"Okay," he said, wiping his palms against his thighs. "We can work with that."

...

By the time she woke up the following morning Finn was already gone. There'd been a round two, and then a round three, and then she'd lost count. She stumbled down the ladder to check her Canon S120. Every movement reminded her of what they'd done the night before, the memories replaying like a scratchy VHS tape: the twinge of her shoulders from when he'd pinned her wrists to the mattress, the ache of her scalp from when he'd wrapped his fist around her ponytail and tugged, the throb of her . . .

He'd at least had the decency to leave the camera on the tripod instead of snatching the footage for his own personal spank-bank. She checked her reflection in the glass-plate door. There were bruises all over her throat from where he'd strangled her again and again and again.

Best *Dating in Murderville* episode ever.

She started packing her suitcases, ready to head back out onto the I-87, when she heard a knock on the door. "Hey, I thought you'd left —"

But Finn wasn't standing at the door.

A police officer was.

"Excuse me," he said, a tight smile locked onto his lips. "I was wondering if I could ask you a few questions."

"Yes?" She unlatched the door and leaned against the frame.

"Have you seen . . . Ma'am, are you alright?"

He'd noticed the bruises on her throat.

"Just a little recreational bondage. What can I do for you, officer?"

He looked like a deer caught running across the highway at rush hour, but he managed to pull a photograph out of his pocket and unfold it. "Have you seen this man anywhere around here?"

It was a photograph of Finn. The Tinder match from California.

"Sure. He was spending the weekend at the cabin with me."

"When's the last time you saw him?"

"We fell asleep together, after —" She motioned to the bruises on her throat, hoping that he'd get the idea without the gritty details. "He must have left before I woke up this morning."

"And what time did you fall asleep?"

"Maybe four o'clock last night?"

"Ma'am, you'd better *come down to the station.*"

"Why?"

She took half of a step back into the cabin. The words come down to the station shoved a hook through the lining of her gut, tugged hard on the muscle there.

"This man was strangled in the woods yesterday afternoon."

The gut-hook tugged harder, ripping into the muscle fibers; she felt some acidic bile from her stomach ooze out into her abdominal cavity.

"That's impossible. He was right here, I swear —"

"Are you here on vacation?"

"Yes, I was just packing up —"

"Why don't you grab your suitcases, and we'll give you a lift to the station? We just want to understand what happened."

With every second that passed, more fluid ounces of acid dribbled out of her stomach, sloshing up towards the water-line of her throat.

"Sure."

She watched while the officer wandered back over to his car, a broad yellow line with the words *STATE TROOPER* brushed across the doors. When he was far enough away, she grabbed her camera off the tripod and opened to the last recorded file. She pressed play.

Finn. Sitting on the ladder, looking into the camera. She must have been asleep when he filmed this; the shadows from the LED lanterns cut deeply into his cheekbones, making his face look more angular, more handsome, than she'd remembered.

"Hey Darby," he said, grinning rakishly at the camera. He had a dimple carved into his left cheek that she hadn't noticed before. "Heard a rumor that you might be out here this weekend. I'm a longtime watcher of Dating in Murderville and wanted to make sure that this episode was special. Thought that the real-deal might catch a few more hits than one of your usual substitutes. Seriously, Darby —"

He held up the beaded-hemp necklace, the one she'd seen Not-Finn wearing yesterday afternoon.

"Where did you find this guy? eHarmony? Was his profile pic him completing a triathlon? Or cuddling a sedated tiger at an African wildlife sanctuary?"

It had been the second one.

"You deserve better."

He leaned in towards the camera.

"I've heard that none of these guys get a second date. At least that's what the Ted Bundy lookalike in Cedar Falls told me before I snapped his neck. But who knows? Maybe I'll be lucky enough to get a repeat performance. I don't usually do the whole relationship thing; I'm a no-strings-attached kind of guy. Well . . ." He pulled a nylon rope out of his back pocket. "Some strings attached. But I think that you and I could make a real go of it. What do you think?"

She tried to ignore the way the bruises on her throat throbbed as he stared into the lens.

"You're my kind of girl, Darby, and I think that I'm your kind of guy."

She watched while he stepped forward and flipped off the camera.

The officer pounded on the glass-plate door.

"Everything alright in there?"

"Yeah, sure." She pulled a USB drive out of her suit-case and quickly uploaded the footage. The local police would confiscate her camera for evidence. But this footage — this was millions of hits on YouTube. This was a contract with Viral Nation for professional representation. This was a book deal with HarperCollins, her own NPR podcast, a Lifetime Original Movie starring Leighton Meester as the distraught YouTube influencer stumbling through the woods as she was pursued by the Blue Mountain Strangler.

And, if she happened to drop hints on *Dating in Murderville* about where she'd be filming next . . .

Who could blame a girl for wanting a second date?

V. A. Vazquez
About the Author

V. A. Vazquez comes from New York City where she has previously worked as a theatre producer, an arts educator, and a ghostwriter for famous fashion editors (which you wouldn't be able to tell from looking in her closet). She writes urban fantasy and specializes in stories that involve women (or men or non-binary folks) romancing monsters, preferably the slimy Lovecraftian kind. She currently lives in Scotland with her husband and their wee doggo.

www.vavazquez.com
www.facebook.com/vavazquezauthor

KING OF THE FOREST
AMBER M. SIMPSON

The white Subaru bumped along the rutted dirt road as it ascended the forested mountain toward the cabin. Jostled about, Katie gripped the edges of her seat—teeth clenched, dark hair swinging in her face. Her head ached from the long, difficult climb up the mountain, and the densely-packed trees that crowded the narrow road seemed to suffocate the very air from her lungs. She scratched at the bandages wrapped around her wrists.

"Almost there, honey," Will said, covering Katie's wrist with one hand to stop her from scratching. "I'm sorry for the rough ride. No one ever really came up here except Uncle Tobin, and my family once or twice in the summers growing up, so this road is definitely not the best. Maybe soon we can invest in a nice, smooth blacktop. We've got the rest of forever." He smiled in that crooked, dimpled way that Katie used to find irresistible when they'd first started dating. Now she just frowned, turning her head away to gaze through the window at the passing blur of seemingly endless trees.

We've got the rest of forever. Yes, Will's uncle Tobin had made sure of that, disappearing six months ago and leaving his remote mountain home in his inheritance to his only nephew. Thankfully they weren't going to live in it full-time, but use it as a summer vacation home. It was an idea that still didn't appeal much to Katie—this summer, in particular.

She wasn't dumb. She knew the reason behind Will's enthusiasm for spending the summer in his uncle's old isolated cabin was for her benefit alone. She knew he thought that, by getting her away from everything, it might calm her mind; bring her peace or some such bullshit. But what he didn't understand was that, no matter where he took her, the darkness inside her went too.

Katie looked ahead through the windshield just as a large deer sprang out from between the trees, darting directly in front of the car. "Will!" she screamed, and Will hit the brakes—but not quick enough. They struck the deer head-on, flying hard against their seatbelts.

"Jesus Christ!" Will cried, breathing hard, shifting the car into park. "You all right?" Katie, staring with wide eyes at the bright red smear of blood across the hood of the car, nodded minutely. Will unfastened his seatbelt and got out to check on the deer, and the damage, while she let her head rest against the seat and closed her eyes. She didn't want to be here—she never should have come.

Count backwards from 100. That's what the behavioral therapist had told her. *When things get too crazy, just count.* The car had become stifling, and Katie rolled down the window to hang her head out, the numbers gliding through her brain. As a gentle wind caressed branches and leaves, a low moan seemed to float on the air, picking up in pitch and intensity, becoming the wailing cry of a hungry newborn.

"Katie!" Will was back in the car, grabbing hold of her. She'd scratched through the bandages at each wrist, fresh blood trickling down her arms. She hadn't even noticed. As Will worked to stop the flow of blood the deer suddenly hopped up from in front of the car, scampering off into the woods nonchalantly. Will's mouth fell open. "I swear that thing was stone-cold dead just a minute ago."

Katie's insides squeezed with a deep sense of dread.

When they pulled up to the cabin a short while later Katie was reluctant to get out of the car, but she didn't have a choice as Will all but dragged her out, then ushered her inside to clean up her wounds.

"What were you thinking?" Will asked, re-bandaging her wrists in the small, cramped bathroom. "Why do you keep scratching at these? Do they hurt?" Yes, they hurt. Everything hurt, but nothing more so than her heart. It should have stopped beating long ago, along with her still-born son's.

Katie looked into her husband's handsome face, but he couldn't seem to look her in the eye. Just as well. The look of pity she found in his eyes, more often than not, only made her want to claw them out.

"This place creeps me out," she admitted, going with

the safer of two truths. "I don't like it here."

"You just need to get used to it," Will said. "I used to love coming out here as a kid. All that nature and fresh air." He finished with her wrists and finally met her eyes. "Why don't we go take a look around before it gets dark? I can show you the places I liked to play as a kid. Maybe if you get acquainted with the forest, you'll make friends with it." He smiled that dimpled grin, but Katie only sighed and looked away. She didn't have the strength to argue.

Following Will's lead through the forest a half hour later, Katie resisted the urge to scratch at her wrists. Her anxiety was through the roof, her head darting toward every sound. More than once she caught the dark, beady eyes of a forest creature peering out at her from between the trees, making her skin goosepimple. She felt as if she were on display, the entire forest her audience. The heavy weight she carried with her everywhere was crushing her full force, squeezing her insides and making it difficult to breathe.

Will scampered boyishly ahead of her, excitedly pointing out different areas he'd played as a kid. Katie nodded her head at the appropriate times, her hands clenched into balls at her sides. Entering a small clearing—its only inhabitant a gnarled old oak, half-black with rot—Katie froze in her tracks.

"Oh, wow," Will said, walking around the base of the tree, gazing up into its withered branches. "This tree used to be like the king of the forest! We used to climb up and swing around like monkeys." He chuckled, shaking his head. "It never looked this bad though," he added. "It was always so full of life. Now it looks about dead." He gazed at it a few more moments, then shrugged his shoulders and walked on. But Katie couldn't move. Something about the old oak tree terrified her to the core, yet she felt her legs moving her toward it against her will.

The closer her body came to the tree the quieter the forest around her grew. Standing inches in front of it she became hyper-focused on every detail, studying its every ridge and furrow. She pushed her palms to the rough bark, and though it looked half-dead she could feel a light quiver—a vibration of life.

"Ow!" she hissed in pain as a splinter stabbed through the soft padding of her thumb. Blood welled, the bit of wood buried deep in her skin. Sucking the blood from her finger she walked slowly around the base of the tree—and noticed something strange. A few inches above her head something white protruded from the bark, glinting in the sun. Reaching up Katie gripped and pulled, the object breaking off easily in her hand. While staring at it, turning it between her fingers, disbelief flooded her senses.

She was holding a human tooth.

With a startled cry she dropped the tooth, jumping back and wiping her hand against her shorts. She tripped and fell backwards over an exposed root, her wrists stinging with pain as she used her hands to catch herself. A sharp wind rattled the tree's brittle branches, the sound once again like a crying child's, and Katie looked back up.

A horrified scream ripped out of her throat as a single

blue eye winked at her through the bark.

"Honey!" Will was on her in seconds, pulling her from the ground in a frenzy of concern. "Are you okay? What happened?"

"There's an eye in the tree," she cried, "and it winked at me!" Will's eyebrows furrowed as he looked from Katie to the tree. "I swear to you, Will, there was!" she insisted, clutching at his arms. "I saw something white poking out, so I—I grabbed it and…and it was a tooth, Will! A human tooth! But I dropped it and…I fell and then…the eye—it…it winked!" She was close to hyperventilating, a panic attack swelling in her chest.

Will's eyebrows remained furrowed as he walked closer to the tree and examined it. Even in her panic and fear-fueled state, she knew he was only humoring her.

"Look for the tooth," she urged. "I dropped it right where you're standing."

Will crouched down to look and Katie closed her eyes to stop the world from spinning. 100… 99… 98… She heard a crunching of twigs behind her and she whirled around, heart thumping violently in her chest. It was the deer they'd struck earlier with the car, staring at her from between two trees. Dark blood matted its fur.

"Will, look!" She turned her head to Will as she spoke, and when she looked back, the deer was gone.

"Honey." Will's voice was low but firm, and once again, she saw the pity in his eyes she'd come to loathe. "I think we should go back to the house and rest a bit, maybe take a little nap. You've been through a lot lately, and I'm sure you're exhausted."

Katie shook her head. "No, I—"

"Come on." He wrapped his arm around her, steering her out of the clearing. "A nap is all you need."

Katie jerked out from under his arm and marched back to the cabin herself, hot tears burning her cheeks. He didn't believe her; of course he didn't. He'd pulled her from a tub of her own blood—had plunked her in a facility for the mentally disturbed. Once a crazy, always a crazy. Losing a child had been hard on him too, but Katie had lost herself along with the baby, and she wasn't sure she'd ever recover.

Back at the cabin she refused to speak to him, but allowed him to tuck her into bed. He'd been right about one thing: she was absolutely exhausted.

"I'll be in to join you in a few minutes," Will said, smoothing her hair. "I'm just going to call Mom first and let her know we made it here safe. You know how she worries."

Katie turned a cheek to his lips as they came down for a kiss.

She listened as Will made his call in the other room, speaking in hushed, fervent tones to the person on the other line—her doctor, no doubt. Of course he'd call him. She could only imagine what Will was saying about her.

What to do about poor, mental Katie?

Burying her head in the pillow, Katie counted down from 100. She tried not to think about the eye in the tree, or the deer that should have been dead—certainly not about the baby's cry she'd seemed to hear twice already. After about the fifteenth round of counting she could feel the sleep medication taking effect. She clung to the dark abyss of sleep just as she'd clung to it the night she'd tried to take her own life.

A pity she hadn't stayed there.

…

Will woke from a disconnected dream, his head heavy and foggy. There'd been blood in his dream—dark, thick and oozing—but he wasn't sure whose it was. He reached a hand toward Katie in the dark, but the bed was empty; the sheets on her side were cool. Breaking out in a cold sweat he stumbled out of bed, calling Katie's name.

A quick search of the house confirmed his suspicion that she wasn't inside, and after grabbing a flashlight he ran out to the forest. "Katie!" he cried as he rushed through the dark trees, his breath coming in short, ragged pants.

He searched the forest for what felt like hours, calling his wife's name over and over, drenched in sweat. A crunching of twigs grabbed his attention—a large deer was watching him. Its eyes glowed in the beam of the flashlight, dried blood staining its hide. Will knew it was the deer he'd hit in the Subaru earlier, and the hairs on the back of his neck stood on end.

After a few moments the deer walked away, turning its head back to Will several times as if it wanted him to follow. With no better ideas Will followed the deer, wondering if he was dreaming. He was surprised to be led

directly to the clearing he and Katie had visited that evening. The deer stood and watched as he shone his flashlight
on the withered oak, his breath catching in his throat at the
sight of Katie, who was stark naked on her knees before it.
Her back was to him, but he could see the jerk of her right
arm as if she were hitting or pulling at something.

With shaking hands he touched her bare shoulder,
shining the light down on her. He nearly passed out. In
Katie's right hand she gripped a sharp length of tree root,
slicing it over and over again through her left wrist. Blood
covered the front of her and spattered to the ground, wa-
tering the old oak.

"It needs our blood," Katie whispered, her eyes soft
and cloudy as if still in a dream.

"*You* need the hospital." Will pulled her up and away
from the tree, the sounds of the forest seeming to grow
louder, the wind picking up and whipping through the trees
as if hissing at them.

"You've made it angry," Katie said in a strange, sing-
song voice, swaying on her feet. Tearing his shirt off Will
wrapped it around her gushing wrist, and he began to lead
her from the clearing. But the deer stood in front of them,
blocking their way.

"Get outta here!" Will screamed at the deer, flailing
his arm at it. "Go on, go!" But the deer remained motionless, staring them down. Will heard the rush of feathers
behind him, and he turned to see a large owl swooping
out of the gnarled branches of the tree. Flying straight into
Will's face its sharp talons clawed at his skin, hot blood

oozing into his eyes. Crying out Will let go of Katie and dropped the flashlight, flapping his arms at the bird as he tried to smack it away.

When the owl finally took off Will wiped his eyes and looked for Katie. He let out a low, garbled moan when he saw her back at the tree, now busy slicing the other wrist. Close to fainting Will ran towards her—and stopped when the ground beneath Katie shook, tree roots erupting from the earth, undulating back and forth like quivering tentacles.

Frozen in horror, Will could do nothing but watch as the roots wound around Katie's nude body and pulled her down into the earth at the base of the tree, swallowing her whole. Will's knees buckled and he dropped on them, the shock and disbelief at what he was seeing stealing the air from his lungs. He should have believed her, what she'd seen, but now it was too late.

Hot tears stung the cuts on his cheeks as one more root burst from the ground and slithered toward him, snakelike. It crept up his torso and chest to curl around his neck. Will had time for one final, shaky breath before the root squeezed, crushing his windpipe. His last thought before it snapped his neck was: *So that's where Uncle Tobin went.* The root jerked him forward, pulling his lifeless body across the ground to disappear beneath the tree.

...

The forest was alive with a cacophony of sound. The sun shone brightly over the treetops, bathing everything in a rich, golden glow. And at the center of it all stood the magnificent oak—tall and proud; once again revived—its deep green leaves swaying in the breeze, the king of the forest once more.

Amber M. Simpson
About the Author

Amber M. Simpson is a dark fiction writer from Northern Kentucky with a penchant for horror and fantasy. Her work has been featured in multiple anthologies, as well as online. She assists with editing for Fantasia Divinity Magazine & Publishing, where she has gotten to work with many talented authors from all over the world.

While she loves to create dark worlds and diverse characters, her greatest creations of all are her sons, Maxamus and Liam, who keep her feet on the ground even while her head is in the clouds.

https://www.ambermsimpson.com

https://www.facebook.com/authorambermsimpson/

https://twitter.com/Amber_M_Simpson

https://www.amazon.com/author/ambermsimpson

https://www.bookbub.com/profile/amber-m-simpson

https://www.goodreads.com/ambermsimpson

THAT VIEW FROM THE M62
C.E. HUNTER

Thursday the 17th
November 2016

"Can we do it then? Can we just go?" whispered Jay, eagerly awaiting his brother's response.

"I don't know, mate. I mean, it's pretty damn scary there. You sure you're up for it?"

"Lew, it's my birthday today, alright?! I'm old enough to not be scared anymore. Let's just go, c'mon...."

"Listen though, the first time you started hearing the stories though you wouldn't sleep for a week. We're not going if you're just going to bottle it up and then cry again."

"Shuddup Lew! I'll just go on my own," Jay seethed as he stomped towards his bedroom door.

"Fine, fine. I'll take you, but we gotta wait until Mum's gone to bed. You know the rules about going there at night. Just stay quiet until then, and grab your flashlight and coat so that you're ready."

The boys spent the next two hours sitting peacefully in their respective rooms, both watching the clock tick by second by second. Every movement of the hands passing the numbers fed the anticipation young Jay was feeling to finally go to Rathton Reservoir, which was known to the locals as Wrathton Reservoir. The boy's Mother had forbidden them from going a long time ago, for fear of their safety. The reservoir was a large body of water, wrapped in dense woodland and narrow footpaths, situated just a short walk away from where the boys lived.

Rumours had circulated for years about the haunted nature of the walking trail that surrounded it, and over those years many people had gone missing. It was feared that they had been consumed by the cold, unforgiving depths of the water. The entire reservoir harnessed an eerie stillness over it, a hush that could not be explained by the few locals that lived just a stone's throw away.

Lewis has always boasted to his younger brother about how he once strolled around the paths at night, unfazed and full of swagger. He would scare Jay as he recalled tales of the spectre that followed him around, the one that attempted to lure him into the water. Lewis, being the brave champion he claimed to be, was apparently not tempted at all by the intrigue. He would tell Jay how he stuck his middle finger up, then waltzed away instead and returned home unscathed. Jay, always dubious of his brother's claims, remained excitable nonetheless.

In the eighteen years since Lewis' birth, nine people had gone missing when supposedly visiting the reservoir. The nearby motorway curves around the area, the view breathtaking enough to draw many visitors to admire the scenery. The roar of traffic from the main roads is defended by the wooded landscape, shielding the village from the rest of the world. Locals urge adventure-happy travellers to not wander the footpaths after dark, as this is when the reservoir allegedly comes to life.

"Stick to the main paths."

"Walk in the daylight."

"Never approach the water."

These were just some of the standard cautions that the locals would force upon travelers. Some fright-happy youngsters would often attempt to approach the walkways at night, but their own fear would normally stop them better than any warnings did.

The sound of the disturbed water carried on the wind, threading through the leaf-canvased passageways like an omen-clad invitation to stray from the paths. It gently whistled through the branches, drawing unwitting walkers to investigate further. More often than not only stories returned from the shores of the reservoir, telling of disappearances, apparitions and horrors that leave the locals with respectful fear.

For Lewis and for Jay, however, their inquisitive naivety could not keep them from disobeying their mother's orders and investigating for themselves. As the sound of her footsteps heading up the stairs became louder, Jay's smile widened.

"Goodnight boys," their Mother shouted through the bedroom doors.

"Night Mum, see you in the morning," the boys replied, almost in unison.

Jay got up, grabbed his coat and zipped it up tight. He then removed his flashlight from his bedside drawer and clicked it on, ensuring that the batteries still worked. All was in order. He sat down on the end of his bed, thrilled at the thoughts of adventure that awaited him.

"I can't believe tonight's the night."

...

The next hour passed by unforgivingly slow, as if fate was attempting to prolong the wait. Lewis crept out of his room and peered over towards his mother's closed door, then he carefully made his way over to Jay's bedroom. He lightly opened the door to find his brother sitting on the edge of his bed, flashlight in hand, coat zipped up and his face brimming with nervous excitement.

"C'mon then bud, let's do this," Lewis said.

As discreetly as they could the boys left their house, proceeding up the rough roads towards the reservoir; guided only by the flashlight and the sound of the water gently lapping up amongst the banks in the distance. As they progress an ear-piercing screech, like metal scraping against metal, fills the air. The brothers stop and turn, looking toward one another.

"It's not too late to turn back, mate," Lewis said to

Jay, anticipating that fear would be ruling his thoughts.

"Not tonight Lew, I need to do this. I don't care how scared I get, I'm going."

A defiant Jay marched on towards the footpath entrance. His warm breath vaporised in the cold night as he drew in larger, and deeper, breaths to calm his nerves. The quiet that surrounded the area was so acute that even the slightest noise echoed around them. As they approached the footpaths surrounding the water Jay stopped, gripping tightly onto his flashlight. Bitter air snatched at their exposed skin, and the fog that hovered over the water brushed against the stones and gravel under their shoes. A gentle breeze brought with it the stench of pond water, mold and a discomforting aura of evil.

Lewis slowly raised his flashlight, revealing the metal sign at the entrance.

'Welcome to Rathton Reservoir'

A 'W' is strategically carved into the metal to show the word as 'Wrathton'. Lewis pointed the light towards Jay, and through his blinded squint he could see the nervous look in his eyes.

"C'mon mate, I can see you're scared. Let's just go home," said Lewis.

"No Lew, I want to do this. Please?"

Lewis sighed heavily and pointed the flashlight back towards the path. A hesitation in his own steps weighed his foot down, but he continued to lead the way forward.

"Come on then, before I change my mind…" relented Lewis.

Jay hadn't picked up on his brother's own trepidation, as he was focusing all he could on portraying a confident and unmoved demeanour.

The public footpaths that circled Rathton were narrow, forcing walkers to almost step in single file. An abundance of leaves and branches would normally teem with wildlife, but nothing except the wind disturbed the woodlands that enveloped the dirt paths. Lewis and Jay cautiously continued forward, staying as close together as they possibly could.

They'd only been trekking for a matter of minutes when, ahead of them, Lewis could see the path begin to curve around and descend lower towards the water's edge. The elder brother slowed his pace, watching as the thick mist crept and clawed closer to their ankles. Pushing a low-hanging branch out of his way, he abruptly halted. His hand, unsteady, shook the flashlight from left to right as he focused on a mysterious figure lurking among the trees. Jay's fingers clutched painfully into Lewis' arm as he pulled himself close to his brother and protector.

"Lew…Did you see that?!"

"Yes mate, I saw it. I think we've seen enough, don't you?"

The boys started to retreat, inch by inch, stepping as gingerly and quietly as their bodies would allow. Lewis fixed his flashlight on the area where he thought he could see something, and he wouldn't take the beam, or his eyes, away from it. The figure they were focusing on twitched at the sound of a twig snapping under Jay's boot, confirming to Lewis that it was not just a figment of his imagination.

"Run!" shouted Lewis, who turned and dragged Jay with him. The boys glanced back towards the direction they came from, and began to frantically sprint towards safety.

"What was that?" a panting Jay bellowed as he dashed forward.

"I don't know, just fucking move!"

"It's following us Lew!" Jay screamed as he looked back.

"Stop looking. Just run!"

The path once again began to descend towards the water, as though they had somehow doubled back on themselves. The seemingly-circular path they were travelling morphed with the darkness, becoming a maze of mayhem with no apparent exit in sight. With Jay now out in front, and an adrenaline of terror coursing through their veins, all they could do was persist.

"Just keep fucking running. Run!" Lewis screamed to his brother.

Faint, incoherent murmurs and moans blistered past their ears as they raced towards hopeful salvation. Through the erratic light cast by the shifting flashlights ghoulish, silhouetted arms reached out from the ground and the mist. They stretched and clawed at the air, hoping to clutch one of the boys in their crooked fingers. Talon-like nails scratched at anything they can reach, scrabbling for their prey.

The boys reached another curve in the path, continuing round it before skidding to a complete stop. Lewis threw his arm around Jay, keeping him from proceeding any further. In the blink of an eye the woodland cleared, and they stood directly at the edge of the reservoir. Frozen, petrified, they attempted to catch their breath and assess what was going on. A small, pebbled beach lay before them, along with a vast body of water as black as the night sky.

"Oh, shit," Jay uttered through his gasping breath, "Did this happen before?"

"I'm sorry Jay, I lied. I've never been here before, but we have to get out of here."

Heaving, and terrified, the brothers stood looking over the star-lit reservoir, watching the water gently caress the night. Jay turned around to look at his brother, the flashlights shining towards the ground and reflecting just enough so that they could see each other's faces.

"I don't care," replied Jay, "I just want to get home. Are they still following us?"

"I can't see anything," Lewis said, pointing the flashlight back towards the woods behind them.

As Lewis turned back around his brother was no longer by his side. He looked up to see Jay, at the mercy of the mist from the banks, as it wrapped itself around his legs and pulled him towards the water. The melee ended as quickly as it began, and from out of the white cloud the ghoulish arms stretched out once more to grab hold of Jay. The razor-sharp nails pierced into his clothes and his skin, incapacitating him. A large arm reached upwards and covered Jay's mouth, muffling his attempts to scream. Lewis could do nothing but stand and watch, his dread anchoring him to the spot as tears streamed down his face.

His lip trembled as he watched his younger brother get swallowed up by the black wrath of the water. Lewis whimpered as he tried to speak, all his extremities trembling as the desperate fingertips of Jay were the last part of him to submerge beneath the surface. As the water settled Lewis' rigid body fell limp, and he collapsed to the floor. His heart was broken, and his will dispelled. His eyes locked on the spot where he witnessed Jay succumb to the entity of the reservoir.

...

Date Unknown

The muffled echoes of terrified screams woke Lewis up with a shock. Sweaty and breathless, he climbed up from his bed to compose himself and erase another night of restless dreams from his mind. Swiping the bottle from the floor, containing what was left of his whiskey, he slugged it down. Lewis stared vacantly into the nothingness that surrounded him, the stale odour of dried up vomit, rotten food and shame engulfing the once-warm family home he still lived in.

Sheltered, hidden, lost and forgotten, Lewis was a shadow of the man he once was. From the stained and tattered mattress situated in the corner of the room, to the grease laden worktops in the kitchen, there was little here which resembled the loving environment Lewis had grown up in. Long, heavy curtains forbade the light from coming in, and the fireplace held nothing but charcoal and crisp wood. All that remained of that life was the photograph hanging beside the front door. A splintered frame with a cracked glass pane houses a photo of Lewis, Jay and their mother out for a family bike ride. The photo hangs crooked, as the wall beside it is caved in with a fist-sized crater. Yes, this is the house he knows, but this is not his home.

Lewis walked across his room. staring at his reflection in a dirt-covered mirror. The face looking back at him was not quite his own. A frailty cowered in his eyes, his withering and neglected body hunched and thin so that it could no longer support the weight he carried in his heart. Yet, on this day, Lewis was defiant. He was determined, and ready, to do what needed to be done.

He was finally ready to go back and face the presence at the reservoir.

In the painful days since the loss of his brother all he could do was watch the remnants of his life decay and crumble around him. On this night things were different. Lewis angrily lashed out at the mirror in front of him, tearing it from the wall. He clambered down the stairs and grabbed a coat, before kicking the door open and aggressively making his way towards Rathton.

Outside, the small village he had remained in was deserted. Embers, ash and dust had replaced the people Lewis used to spend his days with, and he gritted his teeth as he ventured towards the walkways. Autumn colours scorched the sky as nightfall loomed over the reservoir, where Lewis would be poised and ready to confront whatever may face him. He stopped himself at the entrance, tilting his head to the side, while removing a flick-knife from his pocket. Climbing up to the sign Lewis took the knife and carved a "W" next to the word Rathton. The harsh blare of the blade scoring through the metal drowned out all other sounds. Lewis then climbed down, and walked forward.

He entered the walkways with an arrogance and assurance in his step that he was going to achieve something with this endeavour. Thoughts raced through his head about what he may discover, but that mystery did not cause hesitation as it did before. He was determined to uncover the truth that he had feared for so long.

Lewis stopped as he cast his eyes over a familiar sight, the path where it began to curve around and descend lower towards the water's edge. He walked forwards, placing his hand on the very branch he had on that night. He slowly pushed it out of the way, seeing no figure among the shadows as he had before. Even with the last glimmers of daylight he was unable to make out anything but trees and foliage. Lewis stepped from the path into the woodland, pressing forward into the arms of the trees. Looking up he watched the night cast darkness over the reservoir, rolling over the tops of the trees like a shroud of black cotton enveloping the world. His vision could now only stretch as far as his arms could reach, leaving Lewis only his wits to rely on.

Suddenly, he realized that he was not alone. While turning to make sense of his surroundings he noticed the definitive sight of flashlights coming down the paths. Unafraid, Lewis crept forward to gain a better vantage point. Through the tree line he spotted two people walking up the gravel towards where he stood. Who were these people? Lewis stood completely still, attempting to camouflage himself amongst the shadows. The flashlights leading their way scanned across where he was, revealing the large trunks of the trees that shielded him. The two people were clearly cautious, and afraid. Lewis was reminded of the paralyzing fear he felt all those nights ago, and found himself rooted to the spot.

Unexpectedly, the snapping of a thick twig under the boot of one of the unsuspecting investigators startled him. Lewis twitched from behind the tree, and he could tell the flashlight beams had caught him. From the distance he heard the haunting sound of a terrified scream.

"Run!"

Confused, startled and scared, Lewis gave chase without further thought. He instinctively followed the vague figures in front of him, the light from their flashlights beaming through the branches as they capriciously led the way. The mass of undergrowth beneath his feet disabled him from keeping up with the fleeing pair, and he stumbled clumsily as he tried to make his way to the path.

Lewis eventually reached the path, but he had lost sight of the flashlights. The sound of the water was all that guided him through the pitch-black night now. Steadily, but with renewed determination, he moved towards the reservoir. The calming sound of the water grew louder as the trees began to clear, and the outcry of a disheartened shout resonated over the reservoir.

"NO! JAY!"

As he stepped out of the tree line and onto the stone-filled reservoir edge Lewis' jaw dropped, his eyes widening further than they ever had before. He tried to bleat out an attempt at communication, but his voice betrayed him and left him silent. All pigment left his skin, leaving nothing but a pale and ghostly vessel, once again unable to act. Screaming, laying on the ground in front of him, was a man. A man who appeared heartbroken, and bereft of will. His sobs chilled Lewis' blood, rendering Lewis motion-less. Clawing at the stones beneath him the man tossed handful after handful into the water, bellowing as loud as he could.

"Why? Why? Damn it, Jay! Bring him back..."

The cries were so familiar to Lewis, and he found himself once again reliving his own horrific nightmare at the will of the water. It wasn't long before the mist snaked its way back towards the helpless man. Lewis watched as the man raised to his feet, positioning himself for a fight. His hands clenched into fists, ready to beat anything that came his way. Saliva dripped to the ground from his gap-ing mouth as he heaved, a ruthless sense of violence and aggression coursing through him from the anguish in his heart. As the fog lapped at his feet the man's angry stance softened, and he breathed a sigh of relief as a comforting voice whispered from the cloud that was slowly consum-ing him.

"Lew, it's okay, I'm here. Come in, come with me."

"Jay?!" the man replied. He was perplexed, but consoled.

No sooner than he let his guard down did the ghoul's arms return, and they begin to drag him down to his demise. His struggles were met by further grasps at his body, halting him from finding a way to be free. With the water at waist-height the man ceased his struggle, and gave himself over to the black chasm taking him. The last thing the man saw, just before he went under, was himself.

The two locked eyes, a cold and scarring stare joining them in that moment. The man realized now what Lewis had known since reaching the water; he was watching his own death. As the Lewis in the water was being pulled down he began to shriek, a blood-curdling cry of dread which was silenced by the hands of the entity protruding from the mist. As he watched himself submerge into the water Lewis stood still, then he fell unconscious. He hit the ground with an abrupt thud, the screams still booming through the night as they gradually increased in volume and frequency.

With a groan of shock Lewis once again awoke in his bed, breathless and panicked. Beads of sweat trickled from his forehead, down to the exposed floorboards beneath his feet as he scanned his surroundings. The hollow shell of a house he used to call home was once again where he found himself, his ever-lasting nightmare on repeat.

...

Friday 17th November 2017

A log fire burns brightly in the warmth of a loving household. Sitting on the chair beside it is a mother, weeping as she clutches a wooden framed photograph tight against her heart. A hand-knitted blanket covers her shoulders, but it can do nothing to protect her from the shiver of loneliness she now feels in the house. She stands, walking towards the front door, and she neatly hangs the photo back where she had removed it from. In the picture a devoted and loving mother sat proudly with her two sons, enjoying the summer bike ride they had taken that day. Gently wiping the tear from her cheek she turns to head up the stairs, proceeding slowly. Her grieving heart weighs heavy this day, aging her body and not allowing for any haste.

As she halts at the bedroom door of her eldest son she wraps the blanket snug to her shoulders to protect from the cold. She reaches towards the door handle, but does not immediately open it. First she pauses, taking a breath of nervous expectancy before turning the knob and stepping inside.

Before her is the perfectly preserved bedroom of her eldest son. She has kept everything where he had left it, from the unmade bed in the corner to the mirror on the wall. It's exactly the way he left it.

"Why do I still feel you here?" she mutters to herself as she stands in the doorway, surveying the room.

She gasps as the mirror upon the wall zips from the hook, crashing to the floor in a flash. A disturbing gust of air passes her by, travelling out of the bedroom and down the stairs, causing her to shudder and wither on the floor.

"You're restless today, Lewis," she sobs aloud to the apparent nothingness, "But I'm here son…I'm here."

C.E. HUNTER
ABOUT THE AUTHOR

C.E. Hunter is a writer from the grey shores of Grimsby in the UK. He lives with his fiancee, their three children and their two cats, Trevor and Lucifer.

He predominantly writes tales of horror and crime, often with intriguing plot twists and complex protagonists. Death, murder, pain, and hopelessness are common themes in his work. Happy endings are not his forte.

You can keep up to date and connect with him via twitter, @MrCEHunter.

THE WARNING COLOR
GALINA TREFIL

Every year the amanita muscarias sprung up out of the ground on Tabitha's 20-acre redwood forest property. Unhindered, their white stocks and broad, toadstool tops fattened beautifully. They eventually weighed several pounds, rather than ounces, as they did in many other places throughout Albion. The reason for their impressive size here was simple: Tabitha's family refused to pick them. Hers was a drug-free home, whose people wanted nothing to do with these red mushrooms speckled with white warts. The fungi were known for bringing on hallucinations, and worse, to those who swallowed them. "If even the deer won't touch it, we sure as heck shouldn't," Tabitha's mom always said.

If only Mom were here right now; she'd know what to do.

Tabitha had only walked a short distance from her house, just far enough to pick huckleberries for a pie. She'd never intended to actually go into the woods because, after all, this was bear season. Actual attacks were rare, and they were made rarer still by locals refusing to push their luck by exposing themselves to the predators. Or, as some would argue was even more important, exposing the bears to any human unpleasantness. Yet today had produced something far worse than the easily spooked, furry giants.

Tabitha stood frozen, her gaze anxiously moving from one strange man's face to the other. Their hair was unkempt and unclean, much like their tattered, stinking clothes. They weren't good-natured hippies, like so many around here were. In their eyes lay a threatening undercurrent, which made their trespassing only worse. Standing where the amanitas grew they didn't say anything at first, not even when they realized that they'd been caught harvesting the wild drug. One just tightened his grip on the chunky mass of fungus in his hand, turning apprehensively to his partner for instructions.

Finally, the more weather-beaten of the two intruders spoke, "Hey, kid. How you doing? Your mom and dad home?"

Tabitha knit her eyebrows. They weren't, and as such she wasn't going to answer that question. She was a true teenager of the Emerald Triangle after all, and was very aware that people coming up out of the woods was never a good thing. To the contrary there was only the question of how bad the outcome would be. In this corner of the world everyone knew that, by trespassing, one was taking their life into their own hands. "Never trust an addict," Mom always warned. "You don't know how far they'll deviate from their own humanity just to get one more high. The only thing scarier is a dealer, because you never know what they'll do in order to keep their business going."

"You guys are lucky," the fourteen-year-old girl finally asserted. "My dog hasn't heard you yet. And he gets pretty…defensive." She watched them bristle at the thinly-veiled threat. The two men looked over her shoulder in the direction of Tabitha's distant, A-Frame house. "Look, I don't know what direction you guys came from, but you better be careful to go back that way as soon as possible. My dog…when he gets worked up, he's really hard to control. I mean, if he even sees a deer cross our front yard he takes after it like he's Cujo."

One of the men shifted in his shoes, visibly frightened and eager to flee. But the other only scanned Tabitha's gaze and then ran her lanky body over for any physical signs of dishonesty. "Cujo, huh?" He finally inquired, relaxing his shoulders in a way that made Tabitha uneasy. "Yeah, that was a good movie. My friend's kid was one of the extras when they were shooting in Mendocino. Got paid pretty good money too." He stooped to pick up another amanita, tossing it into a paper grocery bag that had been brought specifically for this looting. "I like dogs, even the bad ones. And I'm pretty good at speaking their language. Don't worry. I bet, if your dog comes over here, we'll get on just fine."

The second trespasser, mimicking the one who was clearly the leader, fell into line and resumed the illicit mushroom-thieving. His face was still clearly nervous, but the flower plucking continued.

Tabitha swallowed, not knowing what to do. She didn't like dogs and, despite their popularity in the area due to the very problem that was just now happening, her family didn't own one either. She had a cat — a nice, cuddly, fluffy kitty, who was probably asleep inside the safety and security of the house. Oh, to be inside that house now... with the doors locked and a phone in hand.

"I think I've seen you before, kid," the leader mused, cocking his head to the side. "Down at the Albion store. You like to drink blue sodas, right?" She shivered slightly. "Yeah," he nodded. "You buy a blue soda, or a Koala Springs, and then raid the ten cent candy bins up in the front of the store."

"Lots of people drink sodas and eat candy. The store wouldn't sell them otherwise."

He smirked like a snake at her increasing unease. "I've got a talent, you know," he informed her, scanning the ground for another mushroom. "Some people call it a 'photographic memory.' Basically I get to remember all sorts of random, mundane stuff about totally random, mundane people, even if we've never spoken to each other before. Most of the stuff is just garbage, really. But, every once in a while, I wind up in a situation, like now, where knowing a little something extra is actually kind of cool."

"I don't know," Tabitha insisted. "All kids eat candy. I'm not exactly unusual."

"Maybe not, but I also remember other things from down at the store...Like, your parents aren't the types to spare a dollar for a guy down on his luck, are they? Yeah, they both dress like they're easy-going folks...Your mom wears all those 'Earth First' and 'Save the Whales' t-shirts. But, when you get down to it, they're a couple of stingy, snotty bastards, aren't they?"

Tabitha frowned. Putting her fear to the side and staring at him intently for a moment, she realized that, much like he asserted, they had seen each other before. In fact, most people in Albion village knew who this guy was, even if most of them took pains to not know him by name or directly speak with him. If trying not to be too critical of him one could say that he was a street urchin, with a tendency to panhandle. Sometimes he sat by the front door of the grocery store with a cardboard sign that claimed he was a veteran. "Don't buy it," Dad, who actually was a Vietnam vet, always said. "That jerk's never served our country a day in his life. Just look at the tears on his face. That tells you everything you need to know."

The tears...Ah, yes. There were three of them, tattooed under his eye with cheap ink. No, she didn't know what that meant. Dad had never explained it, saying she was too young to hear and he shouldn't have even brought it up. The tattooed man looked up at her with an overly-inquisitive scowl, her temporary silence betraying the fact that she was weighing her words carefully.

"I don't know what you're talking about," she finally stated. "Mom and Dad give to charity all the time. They're always fighting to protect the environment." And that's where they were right now — at yet another meeting where outraged hippies were raging about how they needed to save the forest, and all inside it. Tabitha dragged herself away from her resentment of that fact, concentrating on the problem at hand. "And, frankly," she declared, "if I'd ever seen you before, I think that I'd remember it."

"You don't like us taking your mushrooms very much, do you? I guess we are sort've poaching your crop."

"Actually, I don't give a damn about the mushrooms."

"No?"

"Nope. None of us here do, that's why they're so big."

"You guys weren't planning to sell them?"

"My parents both have good jobs. We don't need to sell magic mushrooms," she snorted, instantly regretting the snarkiness in her tone. The tattooed man's eyes narrowed in her direction and, taking a few steps back, she tried to casually shrug. "Go ahead and take them. Just get out of here."

She took about ten more steps away when he loudly mused. "I tell you, back when I was your age these could never have gotten so big around me. You know what their nickname is, right?" Tabitha turned back, but didn't answer. He grinned broadly. "These are 'Santa's mushrooms', kid. They're called that because—"

"Because they're red and white, yeah. That's not hard to figure out."

"No…They're called that because they're so much damn fun. How is it that a girl as old as you hasn't even tried one before?"

"Because red is a big, fat sign from nature that reads

'stay away', and I'm a very literate person," she quipped.

He laughed, moving towards her. "Come on," he urged. "Don't you want to see what made Alice fall into Wonderland?"

"Not really."

"What a square. I bet you've never had a drink, or a cigarette either."

"Liver failure and lung cancer? No thank you!"

"Man, girl, you're uptight. It's too bad. Somebody as young as you are should learn to loosen up, experiment…"

"Hey, if you want the stuff, you go get it. I'm going to go back inside my house now. But, if you guys aren't out of here in ten minutes — "

"You'll what? I think that we both know your parents aren't here, or you'd have shrieked for them already. So, what will you do? Call the cops?" He glared, continuing to advance. "What would be the point of that? Way out here, in the woods, it'd take them an hour to get here."

Tabitha swallowed. "Yeah, you're right. I think that I'd call the fire department instead. They're only a couple of miles down, and I bet they'd get here pretty damn fast."

"They would," he nodded, reaching into his patchy jacket for a cigarette. He lit it up and offered her a drag, snickering when she refused. "Why don't you whistle for that dog of yours?" He inquired, blowing the smoke in her face. "I sure would have by now if I were you. That is… if you have a dog. Then again, I think that we both know that you don't. Really, this whole place isn't very secure at all, is it? Pretty damn stupid of your parents if you ask me, especially when they've got a young girl to take care of."

She backed away a bit more, keeping her eyes on him with increasing caution. "Hey," he sighed. "Don't get the wrong idea here. I don't want to hurt you. You're just a kid — annoying, and a bad liar, but a kid. The rotten thing though is I know that, no matter what you say, you do recognize me." He took another drag, eyebrows knitting pensively. "What do you think that I should do right now in this uncomfortable situation? You see, I really don't want to go back to prison, especially not so soon. I somehow doubt that my parole officer would appreciate finding out what I'm doing here — menacing a minor, trespassing, harvesting. There's a lot of possible outcomes, I suppose, but none of them are good for me."

He paused, taking a drag of the cigarette.

"When I left, I owed a lot of guys in the Big House money…If I go back there then, sooner or later, it's pretty likely that I'll wind up housed with one of them again. That might very well get me killed. So you see, to a degree, this is a life-and-death scenario for me. What can I do to be sure you won't snitch on me, kid? Hmmm? If you were just a couple of years younger, I'd spit out some elaborate, horrible threat and call it good enough. But at your age… nope, I don't think that'll work."

Tabitha shifted from one foot to the other, unease digging deeper into her spine.

"Look, I told you: just take the damn mushrooms and go away. That's all that you have to do, and it's not like anyone would even notice. My parents don't go checking where they grow, not like if they were a bunch of carrots or cabbages from our garden or something. I mean, if I hadn't actually seen you guys stealing them it never would have even occurred to me that humans had done it at all. I'd have thought that some really stupid animal ate the am- anitas instead, and that it was probably out in the bushes dying."

"Yeah, but you did catch us. And there's the rub," he sighed, tossing his cigarette to the ground and stomping on it. "Now, I'm going to have to do something that I really don't want to, and I don't think that you're going to like it very much either."

Tabitha sucked in her breath…and then bolted. He took off after her, yelling for his companion to help him catch her. "Get back here!" She could hear the ex-con roar- ing at her. "We're not going to hurt you! You just need to eat some mushrooms. That's all!"

She tried to make it to her house but he beat her to it, standing in the doorway with his arms outstretched to grab her. She took off around the house, crashing at top speed through a wall of rhododendron bushing and then disap- pearing into the redwood trees. She was a fast runner and, what's more, she knew her way around this forest in a way that they didn't. But how long could she possibly run for?

Deeper and deeper into the woods she fled; deeper than, under normal circumstances, she would ever dare. And then, hearing the two men only about twenty feet away, she hid behind a great, massive tree trunk. "Hey, kid, this is all really unnecessary," the tear-speckled man yelled. "We are going to get you, we are going to give you some amanita and you are going to forget all about seeing us at all. In the long run, girl, it's going to be good for you. Hell, you'll have a good time, I promise. You'll like it, it's fun…Why do you think we're up here to get them in the first place?"

"Let's just go," his companion hissed. "I didn't come up here to assault no teenage girl. I don't need them kind of charges, man."

"What? You think that, after her seeing us, we're getting out of this any other way?" The leader growled quietly. "We drug her, or we kill her. Those are our two options, and I'd much rather go with the former."

"Why are you being so extreme?"

"Because I've got tattoos on my face, jackass!" The leader spat, shoving him aggressively in the shoulder. "You think that she'd forget to mention that when she talks to the local pigs?"

"That's on your head because you were dumb enough to get them!"

"Dumb? Dumb…you say?" The tattooed man gripped his companion by the head, suddenly pulling the man's face down hard into his upraised knee. "I earned those tattoos! I killed for them! Three tears for three corpses, you goddamn dirtbag. I put work in and protected my people, bitch, and that's a lot more than your squealing ass has ever done when you've been behind bars! Now, we've got a job to do. We've got to catch that little girl. We'll do just like I said: send her to Wonderland, so she'll be too off her rocker to know what happened. And, even if she does remember us, her parents will be so pissed about her being high that they won't believe her."

"It's a stupid plan!" The wounded man spat, wiping at his now generously-bleeding nose. "Like most of your plans are goddamn stupid! We should get out of here before things get worse..."

Louder and louder they bickered. Tabitha began to wonder if she had a shot at sneaking even further away from them, maybe even making her way to a neighbor's house. She took a few successful steps and then, predictably, a stick snapped under her shoe. They turned towards the sound, instantly bolting after her.

For a moment Tabitha thought she might escape the forest, but then a hand shoved her forward, sending her crashing into the ground. "No!" She repeatedly screamed, unsuccessfully trying to scramble up before the tattooed man succeeded in pinning her.

"I'll hold her down!" He yelled. "You shove the stuff in her mouth!"

"No," she shrieked. "Don't! It's not just a drug, you morons! Too much of it can kill you. That's why it's the bad color! It's to warn anyone with sense to stay away..."

"Hey, brat, don't worry. It's not like we don't know how to do drugs properly," he laughed wholeheartedly. "Just relax, and enjoy the ride."

"No..."

Grabbing a single mushroom from his accomplice, the tattooed man bent over her face, bringing it closer and closer to her pursed, unyielding lips. As he pinched her nose shut to force her reluctant mouth open he continued laughing, until something made him suddenly go quiet. He froze, as did his partner. Tabitha's eyes followed the direction where both men were staring, and she swallowed hard. What she saw was infinitely more terrifying than being forced to swallow a piece of amanita. From out of the thicket a big-eyed, brown-furred bear cub approached, woofing curiously at the strange, bipedal creatures which his protective mother had never allowed him near before.

The tattooed man's accomplice, after a dazed pause, fled. In response the startled bear cub let out a cry, and everything after happened fast. Something huge came crashing out from the undergrowth, and as it roared the man with the tear tattoo was wrenched off of Tabitha by a muscled, mountain of power that was operating upon sheer maternal instinct. The man fought; the mother bear fought harder. She had nearly four hundred pounds of rage behind every move she made, giving her a distinct advantage.

Tabitha wanted to run, but she knew that was no use. She lay on her stomach, her quivering hands clutching the back of her neck. She prayed as her assailant's blood flew onto the trees, onto the leaves, onto Tabitha herself. His screams echoed in her ears as his fluids pooled between her clenched fingers.

From the ground Tabitha watched as the bright, white warts on a single amanita were painted with gore. To be undone by fungus, Tabitha thought grimly, was horrid. To die for fungus, to die for someone else's fungus, was the worst reason for death! Then again, he wasn't really dying for that, was he? No…He was dying for trying to hurt a kid. This was Mother Nature herself, at her finest, getting a brutal job done. This guy would mess with no human, or animal, again!

After a few minutes the tattooed man suddenly stopped screaming. The silence that ensued was worse, and in a way much louder than his wet, gurgling screams had been. Squeezing her eyes shut tightly Tabitha fought the urge to cry out herself, and she held perfectly still as the mother bear's hot breath thundering across the skin of her blood-spattered arms.

The baby bear was whimpering but, thank God, wasn't close by. From the various snorts, squeals, and grunts moving further and further away Tabitha could tell that they were retreating. She still didn't move for a full half an hour after that. When she finally, ever so slightly, raised her head, the first thing that she saw made her clasp her hand to her mouth. There, lying on the ground a foot away, was meat. It was a clump of detached, human meat with a single bone sticking up out of the oozing mess.

Tabitha looked away, clutching her still-shaking hand over her lips, unable to stomach the sight of what the bear had done. With extreme caution she slowly pushed herself to her feet, peering around in all directions. Seeing no wild animals, or the other man, she fled through the forest back in the direction of the house. All but catapulting herself inside she let out a long, anguished shrieked, bringing forward her mother who had returned from the environmental meeting.

"Tabitha!?" She gasped, rushing up and clutching her daughter. "What happened to you? What's going on?"

The whole story came tumbling out, during which her mother's eyes grew colder and colder. "Alright," she finally murmured, hugging her daughter tightly. "You're alright, and it's going to be alright. You're going to go take a shower, and put on some clean clothes. I'll fix you something to eat. It's going to be okay."

"But, Mom, the guy out in the woods — "

"Yes, yes, he's dead. There's no point in worrying about him anymore, is there?"

"But…"

"Tabitha, sweetheart." Mom's voice was now very firm; commanding even. "That bear was a God-send. It did you a favor. You know how often this kind of thing happens? Well, never! You were luckier than other girls — a thousand times luckier."

"I don't feel lucky," Tabitha protested, wiping at some of the dried blood on her neck.

"Well, you are…That man was going to hurt you, but instead he got exactly what he deserved. Once you were drugged, God only knows what he was really planning on doing to you. I'll tell you this much: that mother bear didn't do anything that I wouldn't have. To Hell with that junkie filth!"

"What do you mean?"

"If the forest wants him, the forest can have him. We aren't obligated to do anything. And why should we?"

"But…"

"He was a trespasser; an intruder with ill intention. If we alert the authorities, do you know what will happen?"

"No."

"They'll hunt that mother bear down and kill her, probably kill the baby too. All that she was doing was protecting her cub, and I don't blame her for that. I certainly don't think that she should die for it, do you?"

"No."

"She only hurt the bad man. He bloody-well deserved it, so let him rot! I'm sure that he'll be doing more good feeding the creatures out there, than he ever did in life. No one's going to miss him…"

Tabitha swallowed down a lump of anxiety and, as the months progressed, swallowed down the truth of what had happened as well. Most likely one of her parents eventually did say something though, because rumors sprang up in Albion about a fortuitous bear encountering the now-missing drug fiend with the tears.

What had been the man's name? No one was really sure. No one, even the tattooed man's own companion, really felt like pursuing the matter too much either. After all, in the mind of most people bear attacks were exceedingly rare. If anything bears were accused of a plethora of maulings and deaths, many of which had never even taken place. These beautiful, powerful creatures needed protection and defense against such horrible, false claims…and, for as long as there were people in Albion like Tabitha's activist parents, defense was exactly what the bears would get.

Sometimes Tabitha would find herself thinking about the tattooed man, laying out there in pieces in the woods. He had been willing to do almost anything in order to avoid being identified. Could anyone identify him now when, after so long, the tattoos had long-since been eaten away? Not likely, she thought, fingering the bear-shaped pendant which she now continually wore around her throat.

Was this the fate that he'd deserved? She didn't know, but with time she also discovered that she ultimately didn't care.

"It's one thing to say that you love the Earth," one of the leaders at her parents' activist meetings said. "It's an entirely different thing to actually prove it; to be willing to go that extra mile and suffer for your beliefs. The day will come when we all have to endure hardship in the name of our values…."

Well, at least I know that I can do that, Tabitha thought, letting out a cold, morbid laugh.

GALINA TREFIL
ABOUT THE AUTHOR

Galina Trefil is a novelist specializing in women's, minority, and disabled rights. Her favorite genres are horror, thriller, and historical fiction. Her short stories and articles have appeared in Neurology Now, UnBound Emagazine, The Guardian, Tikkun, Romea.CZ, Jewcy, Jewrotica, Telegram Magazine, Ink Drift Magazine, The Dissident Voice, Open Road Review, and the anthologies "Flock: The Journey," "First Love," "Sea of Secrets," "Coffins and Dragons," "Organic Ink volume One," "Winds of Despair," "Waters of Destruction," "Curses & Cauldrons," "Unravel," "Hate," "Love," "Oceans," "Twenty Twenty," "Forgotten Ones," "Suspense Unimagined," "Mythica," "Dark Valentine Holiday Horror Collection," and "Scary Snippets Valentine Edition."

www.facebook.com/Rabbi-Galina-Trefil-535886443115467/
https://galinatrefil.wordpress.com/

ATCHAFALAYA
A. S. MACKENZIE

The cicadas were buzzing so loud, and so incessantly, that the sound was a near-constant drone that bore into his head. Maybe that's what the deer flies were after, he thought, because all they seemed to want to do was bite him there. Working together, he bet, one bug helping the other.

This area of the Atchafalaya was even more inhospitable than most, and that's saying something for a bottomland, hardwood swamp that covers over 15,000 acres. There's a lot of non-hospitable land in this basin, but this piece edged out in front of the pack.

He sat so still in his spot that you'd think he was one of the cypress tree knees he sat between. The constant pattern of deer flies landing and departing on his face, neck, and hands did nothing to incite any movement. His breathing remained slow, steady, and controlled.

He was a sight to behold. He knew this, but out here it didn't really matter. There wasn't anyone around for miles to tell him he smelled awful and looked worse. The mud he covered himself in, literally covered, was the primordial slop from under the water not far behind him. Multiple millennia of decomposing vegetation gave the mud great properties to help keep him cool, and it prevented *most* bugs from attacking him. However, it smelled like millennia-old vegetation decomposing on him.

The mud covered his head, faces, neck, arms, and hands. The rest of him was covered in his ghillie suit, his own special design that was meant to mimic the surrounding swamp as well as it could. The many shades of green and brown covered the various, tattered strips of cloth stuck around him in a skewed pattern. There were a couple of small branches that held some Spanish moss sticking out from his back, and there were palmetto fronds sticking out from the side of his right leg.

His left leg was smooth and brown, a near-perfect replica of the cypress knee directly beside him. The suit had a hood he had loosely flopped over his head, but it didn't cover his ears or face. He knew he was cloaked well enough in mud to not be seen, not that there was another person around for miles to see him. He constantly reminded himself of this as he sat on a small mound of moss and dirt, which seemed perfect for his task.

His legs were positioned in front of him, knees up and relaxed. Between his legs sat a tripod, which held the CZ-USA's 550 American Safari Centerfire Rifle, loaded with .458 Lott rounds. The man who sold it to him last year asked if he was going to hunt elephants, because that was about the most ethical thing you could do with that caliber round.

He had laughed then, explaining it was mostly for show to one-up his shooting buddies at the base.

He didn't laugh now.

The rifle was equipped with a Leupold 3-15x56mm scope, which allowed for 15x magnification and an exceptionally wide field of view. The FireDot reticule and the low light compensation meant that his target would be easily viewable in the dim, low-light of the swamp.

His hands were controlled, holding the rifle lightly. His elbows were propped on his knees, and his cheek hovered above the stock. He didn't rest his cheek on it because he didn't want to waiver his view and smear his mud; the latter being the more important to him since any weakness in the mud barrier meant instant deer fly attraction.

His spot was three feet from the water's edge, which was in front of him. Though, to be fair, he wondered if it could even be called water at this point. The green slick of algae on top, and the sweet tea color of the liquid underneath, meant that this little stagnant area wasn't exactly 'fresh water'.

The cicada drone didn't waiver, nor did the buzz of the deer flies. The scene around him was unchanging. Still trees. Still water. Buzzing deer flies. Eventually a noise broke through the din of cicadas and deer flies. A single, loud crack - the sound of old wood snapping in half. It came from an area about 300 yards away from him, towards his 2 o'clock.

There wasn't a follow up sound.

He thought he might have imagined it at first, fighting against the rising adrenaline in his system. The noise had startled him, and he was using every trick he'd ever been taught to remain motionless.

Breath in for a three-count.

Hold for a three-count.

Breath out for a three-count.

Hold for a -

Cra-crack!

His breath held for a little longer than three counts. That noise came from the same direction as before, but now was closer to 200 yards away. He glanced down to the algae, not moving his head. Still as a carpet. The originator of the noise wasn't close enough to make the algae undulate with a wave, yet.

Eyes back to his scope. Through the magnification he saw a palmetto plant shake in the distance. He watched as a couple of King Rails tried to fly out of their home inside the fronds, likely to avoid whatever was causing the disturbance. He witnessed one bird escape, but the other was snatched out of the air by a very large hand. From his position he could hear the plaintive, terrified chirps of the bird, then the subsequent silence.

He slowly panned his rifle to the right just a few degrees, seeing if his prey lined up in his scope. He knew this was the one, the thing that took out their boat. That took his friends. That took his brothers.

Looking down the scope, he waited to see it.

An arm poked out from behind a giant cypress. Even from here he could see that the thing had to be six feet long. Covered in thick, long…fur?…he guessed, the arm had all manner of leaves and moss stuck to it. The body, legs, and head came next, all covered in fur. All covered in leaves and moss.

The thing stood eleven to twelve feet tall, and had to top the scales at five to six hundred pounds. It wasn't exactly humanoid in shape, but more ape-like. The legs were shorter than the arms, which were used as locomotion much like apes. It walked with a stepped sort of gait, leading with its arms as its knuckles formed a foot of sorts. That was where the similarity to apes ended.

The head, if you could call it that, was easily a quarter of the thing's overall height. The forehead and crown came to a small, blunt point. The eyes were deep-set under heavy brows, which had a different fur than the rest of it did. These were thinner, more numerous, and seemed to drape in front of the eyes. No, he thought, not drape; they swayed. It was a system to keep the flies away from its eyes. The nose was mostly non-existent, just two large orifices below the eyes and above the mouth.

The mouth - that's where any semblance of similarities took a different direction. The thing held its mouth open due to the two exceedingly large, exceedingly sharp tusks that erupted from the lower jaw like reverse walrus tusks. The jaw was large; there didn't appear to be any cheeks, much like a dog, just some jowls. The remainder of the lower jaw, and most of the upper jaw, showed several receding layers of teeth, curved back and sharp like a shark's. The upper jaw revealed two smaller, but equally sharp, tusks of its own. Those, when the creature closed its mouth, sat between the lower tusks.

Along the side of the head were three small, fin-like protrusions. There were three on each side, about the size of a bass dorsal spine. They flexed, swayed, and twitched independently in multiple directions.

His breathing technique resumed, and he felt his heart slow. He could see proof of his slowing pulse in the lessening of small jumps his scope made, though it made the thing in front of him seem to jump slightly with every bump of his heart.

He wasn't worried about calculating windage here for his shot, since there was no wind to speak of. The air was incredibly still and stale. The only effect he needed to worry about was the heat, but he didn't think that would be too much of a factor at this distance. While the spots of land between himself and the thing down-range were very warm, the algae coated water between was cooler. He didn't think the presence of heated, rising air would throw off the shot more than a few millimeters.

A grunt that he felt in his chest rippled across the swamp towards him. The thing stood still, staring at an old log that must have fallen ten years ago. It was black, moss-covered, and had large, shelf-like mushrooms growing from it. From his vantage point he could see that the log was hollow, and it was turned towards the water where the top of it had plunged in like an oversized straw. A big, gross straw.

Another grunt. He watched through the scope as the small fins on the side of the head twitched, maybe even a little quicker than before. Then, they stopped. It stopped. Nothing moved on the thing as it just stood there, staring at the log.

He nearly jumped when the creature's arm shot forward and grabbed something. He cursed to himself, his breathing and heart rate even faster than before. He worked to calm himself and maintain his position, trying to maintain his appearance as nothing more than a small lump on some land in a swamp.

Looking through the scope he watched as the thing lifted its arm, revealing his new prize. It was a cotton-mouth, from the look of the pattern. It must have been an older one, because it was huge, but now quite dead. Or at least it was on the way to death. The head was in the monster's hand, and the reptile looked to be in the midst of death throws, its body contorting into twitching s-curves before hanging limply. The snake was easily four-and-a-half feet, or even five; the body was as fat as his fist, too, and unmoving - just a long, dangling carcass of a former snake.

He watched, slightly stunned, forgetting his breathing technique as the thing lifted the dead snake up and dropped it into its gigantic mouth like it was eating a string of spaghetti.

Like a worm about to be put on a hook.

Like how Doyle would hold the worm up and say 'thank you' to it in that false, pious voice he used when he was trying to show how much better he was than everyone. He wasn't, he just liked to sound that way.

He liked to, past tense.

An unwelcome memory poured into his head: They had been sitting on the small bass boat. Doyle was in the bow seat, Ed in the driver seat, himself at the stern. They were all laughing at Doyle and his stupid jokes, and for a moment the scene felt so real. He could even smell the air and see the condensation dripping off of Ed's beer bottle, and he remembered how the sun felt coming in through spots in the tree cover. There was no breeze, but the cicadas were quiet enough. Almost like they wanted them to have that fun. Almost like they didn't want to interrupt anything because they knew what was coming.

They didn't.

They didn't know about the hand that would reach out of the swamp water and grab Doyle by his head. Didn't know about the roar that would fill our ears and heads to the point they nearly burst. Didn't know about the blood we would see; would be covered with. Doyle was gone.

They didn't know.

Ed tried to get the boat going, tried to turn the key on his brand-new boat and get them away. He knew Ed never saw the arm lash out again and grab him around the bicep, and he did know that Ed saw the mouth.

That giant mouth.

The long tusks.

He knew Ed saw those.

Blinking away the welling tears, he refocused on the scope.

The view was empty, save for the scene of the swamp.

His heart stopped and sank.

Days and days he had spent out here, waiting for the thing, waiting for the chance to take it out. To vindicate his friends. His brothers. To show the authorities that they hadn't just 'gotten drunk and had an accident'. That he didn't black out and dream the whole thing. He needed to show them, and now the thing was gone.

Keeping his focus, trying to remember all that he learned in the Army, he willed himself to reign in the panic. To reign in the fear. To reign in the sorrow.

He panned the rifle slowly to the right, then to the left. He spotted the thing, nearly sighing with relief. He kept that in. Part of him congratulated himself for keeping quiet and still, and at the same time chided himself for needing to. He watched as it lumbered through some more palmetto thickets, looking, he assumed, for more to eat.

He felt another low grunt.

Doing everything he could to keep calm and focused, he waited for the thing to lash out and grab its next meal.

He waited.

Another grunt, but this one was a little different. It went high at the end, like a question. He started to wonder if these things had some sort of primitive reasoning, some sort of thought process beyond hunting for food.

He wanted to rebuke himself for giving this thing more intelligence than he figured possible, but he couldn't shake the idea. Sure, it was large and violent, but could it also be capable of learning? Could this thing that killed his friends be some sort of advanced, hidden species stuck here in the primordial swamp? He told himself those were questions for another day, for someone else. His mission was clear and concise. He was here to kill it, and he was determined to make that the reality in his world.

It remained as motionless as he was.

This dragged on an indeterminate amount of time, never giving him the opportunity for a clear shot through the foliage. Finally it moved slowly backwards, from the way it had already come. Its head seemed to be scanning the ground on the little island which, since it was surrounded by water, only had so much at which to look. Soon the creature seemed to find what it wanted, using both hands to reach for it. With what looked like effort, especially for something so huge, it lifted up a large stone. Bits of moss and dirt fell away from it, as though it had been plucked from the ground. It was slightly rounded and very brown, but there was some lighter color underneath.

It was probably a big piece of granite, or something from when the swamp and the surrounding land wasn't yet primordial. It was from when stone like that was all around, and the first invertebrates were still swimming in their single-cell bodies, he thought. The thing stood, holding its new prize at about chest height. The muscles in its arms were flexed from the weight, but it held the rock still.

Squaring its body towards him it brought the stone against its chest, flexed, and launched the rock through the air with a loud grunt.

Right towards him.

He pulled his eyes from the scope and watched the stone fly through the air, knocking aside small branches that would have stood no chance of changing the trajectory of the missile. When he was in the Army he had been a Ranger, so he held a hefty knowledge of arcs and parabolas, as well as trajectories of thrown or launched objects. He did a quick mental guess, figuring that the stone should land about forty feet in front of him. A thrown distance of over 550 feet was incredible.

He watched as the stone made contact with the algae-covered water. Heard the 'floomp' noise it made as it crashed in, the brown water splashing up through the new escape hole in the algae and then splashing back down. The ripples in the algae carried themselves all the way to the edge in front of him.

If he had felt like it was appropriate to the event, he would have applauded. He kind of wished he could have recorded a throw like that.

He closed his eyes and cursed himself for the thousandth time. The camera. In his haste to get all the gear and provisions he needed for his hunt, he forgot to grab a camera. He had wanted to show everyone what it was that he took down; he wanted them to see the power the thing had, but in his desire to see justice met he forgot the thing that would have helped him immensely. He had reminded himself of this many, many times over the past couple days.

As he refocused himself he realized he had just watched a creature throw a stone that had to weigh at least two hundred pounds over 550 feet. His blood turned cold; that was more power than he had assumed the monster possessed. Watching the thing he could see that it wasn't even breathing heavy. Its arms were back down on the ground, positioned to help it stand as it looked.

At him.

The air caught in his throat.

No, he thought, No way. *There's no way it could have known I'm here from that distance. It couldn't have.*

It stared, hard.

The image through the scope started to dance a little. He realized his hands were shaking, that most of him was shaking. This thing was staring directly at him, no question.

Calm the Hell down, he yelled internally. *You've got a big ass gun, and that thing's a long way from reaching me with those hands and tusks.*

The gun. Yes, of course, the gun. He worked to resume his careful breathing, trying to slow the wobble of the scope. Going through his mental checklist, he quickly accounted for wind (none), distance (200 yards), and elevation (flat).

The thing remained locked in a stare across the water at him. If there was awareness of the gun aimed at it then the thing either wasn't afraid, or wasn't concerned with what it could do.

Regaining nearly all of his composure, he lined the reticle up with the thing's brow. He knew that these rounds, developed by an elephant hunter, would have no problem reaching the brain through the bone.

Breath in, 1…2…3…

Hold, 1…2…3…

His finger left its spot on the trigger guard, resting lightly on the trigger.

Breath out, 1…

He worked slowly to squeeze the trigger, not pull, so that by the time he ended his exhale it would fire the round.

Fire the round and kill the monster.

Kill this thing that killed his brothers.

His concentration was so great in that moment, his mind so narrowly focused down that scope, that the world could engulf itself in flames around him and he wouldn't know it.

The world didn't engulf in flames.

It fell, however, in shadow.

A big shadow…with tusks.

He never made it to three.

The thing across the swamp watched with the same hard stare it had started with, watched the man it knew was there all along. Watched until there wasn't anything left to watch.

The thing turned its large form away and resumed its hunt for food.

A.S. MacKenzie
About the Author

A.S. MacKenzie is an Atlanta based author who loves all things thriller, sci-fi, horror, comics, and fantasy. His work includes shorts, novellas, and an upcoming novel, along with a several ongoing serial stories through his monthly newsletter. You can find him most days on Twitter (@a_s_mackenzie) going on and on about comics, movies, music, books, and so much more. Also, he is on Instagram (@a.s.mackenzie) where he shows off his love of cooking, travel, and other bits of randomness. He lives with his wife and a weirdo of a dog. (he/him)

Head to www.asmackenzie.com for some free short stories and how to sign up for the newsletter and the exclusive serial stories.

There are currently three short form eBooks for free download through Prolific Works

https://www.prolificworks.com/author/asmackenzie
Twitter: https://twitter.com/a_s_mackenzie
Instagram: https://www.instagram.com/a.s.mackenzie/
Other Instagram: https://www.instagram.com/oneposthor-
rorstory/

Spots

Ariana Ferrante

Someone was screaming.

Maria looked up from her garden, dropping her tools into the ditch she'd been digging for seed pods. She scrambled to her feet, eyes quickly landing on the source of the frantic, pained wails.

It was a young man, tattered clothes stuck to his skin with sweat. The bottom half of his dress pants were torn off at the knees, revealing red spots coating his bare legs. He wasn't wearing any shoes, and as he lifted his legs in long strides Maria saw the broken, bloodied blisters on the bottoms of his feet, open and raw and staining each patch of verdant grass he stepped on.

He raised his arms - his upper appendages just as covered in red lumps as his legs - in a panic, waving them back and forth as he emerged from the forest that bumped up against Maria's backyard. He kept screaming, never ceasing except to catch his breath. If he was trying to say something coherent Maria didn't catch it between his end-less stream of exasperated, gravely shrieks.

"Sir!" she cried, stepping out into his path. "Sir, please tell me what's g..."

He crashed into her, the union of their bodies tearing the wind from her lungs and throwing her to the earth. Instinctively she clung to him, fingers coming away wet as they dug easily into the bump-riddled arms of the panicked man.

"Oh, Jesus..." she gasped, releasing him immediately. In her panic Maria couldn't even think of screaming, couldn't think of processing what might be on her hands. All she could think of was dealing with whatever was wrong with this person on top of her.

"I can't go back," he gasped, eyes wide and pupils the size of pinpricks. He pushed himself off her, rising to his feet and staggering backwards. "Can't go back, can't go back."

"Sir," Maria prompted, rolling onto her stomach and pushing herself to her knees. "Sir, please breathe and tell me what's wrong. Where can't you go back?" *If I can just get him to breathe*, she thought, fixing her gaze on the hysterical figure, *maybe he'll calm down and I can call an ambulance.*

"The woods..." he panted, eyes glazed over in a pan-icked fog, "...the people in the woods, the circle, I stepped in the circle. The circle, the goddamn circle."

"What circle?" Maria asked, finally standing.

"The circle - the mushroom circle," he continued,

starting to pace back and forth. "I stepped in it, and they came for me - made me dance, made me dance for days, for weeks. Couldn't stop dancing, couldn't eat. No sleep, no drinking."

He groaned, eyes rolling back in his skull as he finished his latest string of syllables. The bumps on his arms, rosy red and bigger than I remembered, started squirming beneath the surface of his flesh. "Oh God," he moaned, his entire body starting to tremble. "Oh God, they're coming. I'm coming back, they're taking me back!"

Maria opened her mouth to say something, lifted her hands to do something, *anything,* but whatever was happening to him was far faster.

He collapsed to the grass-covered earth, his body spasming and contorting like a snake. He grabbed at his tattered clothes, tearing them to pieces and littering the ground with rags. He tore at his bump-riddled flesh, clawing and clawing until his skin gave way, red from the lumps mingling with the crimson slickness of blood.

The lumps prodded the inside of his flesh again, surging with growth and breaking the skin. Maria could finally see that the red lumps were the heads of spotted mushrooms, lifting further into view as his frantic spasming grew weaker and lesser. The stench was unbearable. It was rotten and gag-inducing, like meat left baking in the sun as it boiled in bloody juices until it was thoroughly cooked. The skin flaked away like papier-mâché, peeling back to reveal more growing fungus trapped beneath the muscle and sinew.

At last the man stopped moving, body still dotted with mushrooms as new growths sprouted all over. In his panic he'd curled himself inward, like he was trying to disappear into nothing. One of his wide, glazed eyes burst from its socket, another mushroom cap filling the space it once occupied.

And then, all at once, his body - or what was left of it - began to melt away.

The remaining skin dissolved like wet tissue paper, leaving behind only organs and bones that were quickly vanishing too. They regressed into piles of sludgy human viscera, which the ground consumed like a sponge would water. Within moments the only thing that remained of the man from the forest was a circle of red mushrooms, and the discarded, blood-soaked rags that used to be his clothing.

Maria's legs gave out beneath her, sending her trembling frame to the dirt. She wrapped her arms around herself, eyes still fixed on the circle of red-capped fungi that the young man once occupied. She stared and kept staring, watching, waiting. She waited for some sort of sign, for the dream to melt away like the man's flesh had, to reveal itself to be nothing more than a trick on her senses. A horrible, *horrible* trick.

But nothing changed. The screaming was gone, the man was gone, *his whole body was gone.* All that was left were those mushrooms, those awful mushrooms that burst from his flesh like candy from a piñata.

Maria finally forced herself to stand, to do something other than stare. She inhaled, mouth agape as she filled her lungs with the first breath of air she'd taken in what felt like an eternity. She wondered if she had breathed at all during the entire ordeal. She wondered if she should have, or if that would have made it even worse.

She winced, a sudden pain shooting up the length of her left arm. Maria clutched her red-stained fingers with her right hand, only to pull away in horrific realization. Slowly she looked down, raising her arm into view and starting to scream.

It was covered in bulging, squirming red spots.

ARIANA FERRANTE
ABOUT THE AUTHOR

Ariana Ferrante is a 22-year-old college student, playwright, and speculative fiction author. Her main interests include reading and writing fantasy and horror of all kinds, featuring heroes big and small getting into all sorts of trouble. She has been published by Enchanted Conversation Magazine, Soteira Press, and Nocturnal Sirens, among others. On the playwriting side, her works have been featured in the Kennedy Center American College Theater Festival, and nominated for national awards. She currently lives in Florida, but travels often, both for college and leisure- when there's not a pandemic in place. You may find her on Twitter at @ariana_ferrante

SURVIVAL IN THE WOODS
MCKENZIE RICHARDSON

He hadn't wanted to go into the forest in the first place. It was an idiotic dare he never should have accepted, but when you're young your pride is all that matters.

It had been three days since he'd first gone in. While he hated to admit it, even to himself, he was hopelessly lost. His ration of protein bars and water bottles had been depleted more quickly than he'd expected. Who would have thought he'd be in here this long?

The woods just off the paved road weren't very big, and they were bordered on each side by fields of corn and sweet potatoes. It was just a patch of uncontrolled forest in the midst of precise lines of crops, and if you just walked in a straight line in any one direction you should find your way out eventually. Yet, somehow, he was always getting turned around.

Desperation was creeping in when, in the darkness, something caught his eye. He rubbed his face, trying to clear his blurry vision as he strained to make sure what he was seeing was real. When he opened his eyes the light still burned brightly through a break in the trees. It glowed like a beacon, calling him to safety.

Without hesitating a moment longer he pushed his way through the brush toward the luminosity.

As he approached he was able to take in the full power of the blue-tinged, circular glow. It blazed above him on some unseen structure, and as he extended his hand up toward the light he was surprised to find that the surface was slightly sticky.

When he pulled his hand back it felt damp with residue. Bringing it to his face he sniffed, noting that it smelled sugary. Perhaps some sort of juice or nectar? Tentatively he put a finger to his tongue, and he was relieved to taste sweetness. He licked the rest from his palm, then reached up for more; he was barely able to control himself.

By that point he was half-starved, and the relief of the discovery of something edible overwhelmed him. Up until then he had only encountered sticks and leaves in the forest, and he wasn't very good at determining what was safe to eat. Once he had eaten his fill he curled up next to the glowing comfort, and with his stomach fuller than it had been he slept soundly through the night.

When the sunlight peeked through the leaves the next morning he cracked open his eyes. In the daylight that filtered down to the forest floor he examined his surroundings, and the thing he'd slept next to was now visible. It was some sort of plant, a giant, oblong oddity that grew from a thick stalk. It towered over him, immense and smooth. It was so heavy that some of it rested firmly on the ground, the stalk unable to support the vegetation's full weight.

The plant was so tall that he could just barely reach the top, and that was if he stood up straight with his arm fully extended. The circular rim he had seen glowing the night before revealed a hole in the middle of the plant, but it was too high up to see inside. It was a bit like a gourd with a carved-out top, the red and pale-green coloring standing out against the darker shades of the forest.

There were streaks along the rim, perfect traces made by his fingers from his frenzied feast the night before. He was thankful for the plant for giving him the energy to carry on, and after a quick breakfast of more nectar he set off in another attempt to find his way out of the endless woods. The trip was easier in the daytime, and it was even more manageable now that he had eaten. He expertly maneuvered over and around the prevalent obstacles; the fallen branches, the jutting rocks, the not-so-inviting thorn bushes. Despite eating, by midmorning his energy level had sagged. He searched for food, for some sort of berries or even another one of those strange, gourd-like plants, but all he found were bitter leaves that numbed his tongue. After a few mouthfuls he thought better of eating more.

His pace slowed as hunger set in, and his movements became less nimble. He stumbled over branches, lost all sense of direction and his confidence of escape began to dwindle. Dusk came quicker than he'd anticipated, the trees overhead darkening as shadows crept in. His stomach raged against its emptiness, tightening uncomfortably.

He nearly cried in relief when he saw a glow in the fading light. A familiar, pale-blue radiance beamed through the trees, and it didn't take long to realize what it was. He had found another one of those plants, but as he got closer he saw that this wasn't quite true. It wasn't another one, it was the same one. The tell-tale trails his fingers had left that morning seemed to form mouths, the streaks laughing at his foolishness.

He had wasted the day going around in circles, and he had nothing to show for it. He was merely back where he'd begun.

Landing with a huff at the base of the plant, he put his face in his hands and pinched his lips tight. The feeling of hopelessness plagued his mind, and he was frustrated at his own failings. After a moment he began to feast on the nectar once again, since there was no point in wasting the opportunity to eat. He'd need the energy the next day if he ever wanted to get out of here.

As he settled down to sleep that night a thought infiltrated his mind. It felt foreign, as if not quite his own. He thought that, just maybe, he could stay. At least here, with the plant, he had food. He could survive on the nectar; he could stay right here and be safe.

He slept deeply, heavily, peacefully, soothed by that promise.

Despite his thoughts the previous night, when the sun rose he set out once more with new resolve. He would find his way out of this damned forest, getting out once and for all. After this he never wanted to see another tree again. He trekked on, keeping his pace steady so as not to push himself too fast. As he'd learned the day before rushing quickly only drained his energy, making him more prone to mistakes.

He must have walked for miles, climbing over decaying trees and weaving through countless branches. At midday he stopped to rest. He could feel himself wilting, like a drooping flower, but he needed to push on. After a short break to stretch his sore legs he continued, a second wind fueled by determination assisting him along.

A rumble overhead indicated that it would rain soon, and he prayed for the precipitation. His mouth was dry, his lips cracked and his tongue like a hard, useless stone. Soon the sky burst with lightning and thunder, but the storm passed too quickly. Much of the rainwater had settled high in the leaves overhead, far out of reach. He kept his eyes open for a puddle, a drop on a leaf, or even a patch of damp earth. At this point any moisture would be welcome, but there was nothing.

The sun dipped down in the sky, soon disappearing behind the endless ceiling of trees. It grew dark, and he couldn't keep his feet moving much longer. As he searched for a place to rest for the night a familiar glow caught his eye. A hand seemed to grab at his shriveled stomach when he again saw the plant, and he didn't have to step closer to know that it was the same one as before. He had done it again. All of that work walking in circles, just to find his way back at the start.

He wanted to cry, but there wasn't enough moisture in his body to bring forth tears. Instead he began to eat the remaining nectar, what little he could reach.

Too soon the stickiness around the rim went dry. On the tips of his toes he circled the plant a few times, running his fingers along it in search of any residue of sweetness, but there was none left. He curled up in the soil at the base and tried to sleep, but his stomach wasn't quite satisfied.

He slept intermittently, fitfully tossing and turning, every prod of a stick feeling sharp enough to tear his skin from his bones. Partway through the night the lightness in his stomach couldn't be ignored. He hadn't eaten enough. He needed more. Thinking back on the storm the previous day, a hopeful thought struck him. Perhaps water had collected inside the massive plant, its hollow, gourd-like structure acting as a cup. Perhaps he could climb up and get a drink.

The night was still dark, but once his eyes adjusted a bit he was able to see the base of the plant beneath the glowing rim. A sense of optimism filled his chest when he felt a loose vine hanging down on one side. He pulled on it, testing it, then threw his whole weight onto it.

Satisfied that it could hold him he began to climb up the vine, his slowly-deteriorating muscles complaining all the way.

When he reached the top he swung his leg over the rim. Straddling the side he was thankful for the thick walls, which could support his weight as he looked down into the base. Beyond the blue glow it was dark, but the scent of sweetness was much stronger up here. There was probably more nectar than what he could have gotten from the ground, but all his mind could think about was a cool drink of water to sooth his rasping throat.

He leaned over, gripping the edge of the plant with one hand as the other reached down into the darkness. He stretched his fingertips as far as they would go, straining to find the bottom. He tried to convince his bones to grow just a little bit longer, but it was no use; he couldn't reach.

He hauled himself back up, not even knowing if all of this was worth it, if there was even anything inside. He rested his head on the plant's rim, clinging to the top as his nose took in the overwhelming sweetness. As he lay there his fuzzy brain wrapped around an idea. He fumbled in the pocket of his jeans, pulling out a quarter.

Once more he leaned out over the opening, extending his hand to let the quarter fall.

Holding his breath he waited in the silence, then nearly screamed with joy when the sound of the definitive splash reached his ears. There was liquid at the bottom, he just had to figure out how to get to it. He yanked on the vine he had used to climb up. At first it resisted, probably tangled on something at the other end, but after quite a struggle it released its hold and he was able to reel it up.

When he felt the loose end in his hands he threw it down into the plant, a light ripple resonating at the bottom. After testing it again he slowly lowered himself down.

It was warmer in here, almost comfortingly so, and

the sugary smell of the nectar made his head feel heavy. It was enough to make him want to release his grip on the vine, to give in to the aroma that seemed to infiltrate each of his pores. But he had to stay focused. He just needed to get a drink; things would be easier when he was hydrated.

As he went down, deeper into the plant, he reached out intermittently to see if he was close enough to the water yet. Finally, as his muscles cramped and his head swam in protest, he felt a dampness seeping through his shoe.

He thrust his hand downward, longing for the liquid that had collected at the bottom.

When his fingers touched the wetness, however, they began to burn.

Fiery tingles of pain rushed through his hand, shooting up his arm and into his torso. He let out a shriek when the pain finally registered in his sluggish brain. In the shock of the unexpected sensation he let go of the vine, the only thing keeping him hovering over the acidic liquid.

He fell deeper inside, tumbling in uncontrollably. He scrambled for a hold on the vine, but it was no use. With a horrible splash his whole body was swallowed up by the burning liquid. It felt like being plunged into a vat of alcohol, that was then set aflame. His hands flung out at the curved sides of the plant. He tried to climb up its walls, to do anything to get out of the pool, but they were too slippery to grasp. His thrashing merely sent sheets of the caustic substance in all directions, allowing it to rivet down his face in heavy drops. He closed his eyes, but his eyelids were useless against the burn.

He grabbed for the vine, but the end that had touched the liquid had begun to deteriorate. It came off in pieces in his hands, sizzling audibly. He lunged upward, reaching for the vine at a higher point where it hadn't been burned away. Kicking his legs out he felt the vine in his hand, relief cooling the pain for a split second. But in the next moment his skin began peeling off of his palms, the muscles and tendons slipping against bone.

Unable to hold on he fell back once more. Fluid rushed into his mouth, searing and blistering as it slid down, eating him from the inside.

It eroded the lining of his throat until he couldn't even scream, just exhale desperate gasps of breath that came out in raspy whispers. He was never getting out of there. He would never find a way out of the forest, out of this plant. His skin continued to melt, and his body sunk to the bottom of the cup-like base, the liquid bubbling and gurgling all around.

After a moment the screaming and splashing that had disrupted the quiet of the night died down, and all was silent once again. A cool breeze tickled the leaves in the trees, making them shiver. And, in the silence, the pitcher plant digested its latest catch, giving it the energy to survive a little longer in the untamed woods.

MCKENZIE RICHARDSON
ABOUT THE AUTHOR

McKenzie Richardson lives in Milwaukee, WI. A life-long explorer of imagined worlds on the written page, over the last few years she has been finding homes for her own creations. Most recently, her stories and poetry have been featured in anthologies through Iron Faerie Publishing, Black Hare Press, and Dragon Soul Press. In addition, she has published a poetry collaboration with Casey Renee Kiser, 433 Lighted Way, and her middle-grade fantasy novel, Heartstrings, is available on Amazon.

McKenzie loves all things books and is currently working towards a master's degree in Library and Information Sciences. When not writing, she can usually be found in her book hoard, reading or just looking at her shelves longingly. For more on her writing, follow her on:

Facebook: https://m.facebook.com/mckenzielrichardson/
Instagram: https://www.instagram.com/mckenzielrichard-son/
Blog: http://www.craft-cycle.com

BETWEEN THE TREES
DUSTIN WALKER

I notice the dark clouds just as I'm parking the car. They hover in the distance, hanging over the ocean like a swirling mist of dirt and ash.

"I dunno, kiddo, it's going to rain pretty quick here," I say, glancing at my daughter, Paige, in the backseat. She clutches a bright-pink Fisher Price camera, the same color as her fingernails.

"Really, Dad?" Paige tilts her head sideways. "We're islanders, we don't let the rain stop us. That's what pussy mainlanders do."

"Hey, *language!*"

"But that's what you say!"

"That doesn't mean you can say it."

I turn away so she doesn't see me grin at having my own words thrown back at me. I peer up at the clouds again, which don't seem to be moving that fast. Since this is probably going to be our last getaway together for God knows how long, I sure don't want the afternoon to be a disappointment.

"Okay, twenty minutes. We boot it down the trail, snap a few shots of the cliffs and then we boot it back. Deal?"

"Deal!" She opens the door and hops out.

Our car is the only one in the parking lot, which isn't surprising in this weather. Grey autumn skies frame the gnarled arbutus trees and towering cedars, bathing them in a pale, monochrome light. The wind is starting to pick up now too.

I zip up Paige's cherry-red jacket.

"Let's do this!" she cries, pumping her fist into the air.

I laugh. Sure, easy for her to say. Even though I don't think there's a damn thing wrong with getting a bit wet and muddy, her mom sees things differently. I caught Hell a few weekends back when she got a cold after we were stuck in a storm. After that Paige was conveniently 'napping' every time I tried to call her that week, and from then on I didn't want to give Deborah another excuse to keep her from me.

It takes us maybe ten minutes to walk through the woods to the coastline. Tourists often picnic at Oceanside Park because it has that rugged, West Coast feel to it, even though it's just on the edge of town. Fingers of barnacled rock stretch out toward rolling cliffs that have been worn smooth by the elements, and cedar logs bob and shift on the surrounding grey-stone beach as the surf surges in and out.

The dark clouds have crept closer to shore, but not

by much. We have time. "Okay, get snappin'. We're not sticking around for long."

Her camera clicks and whirs as she points it at a log, a twisted arbutus tree, a lonely patch of grass sprouting between the rocks — just about everything except the cliffs themselves.

A loud crunch snatches my attention.

I turn around. At first I don't see anything, only the thick grove of cedars we just walked through, but then I get a glimpse of him. A boy — can't be more than ten — in a black hoodie watches us from between the trees. The kid just stares, his hands unmoving by his side.

I think maybe he wandered off the trail or something, so I wave to him and call out, "Hey there! You okay?"

He doesn't move, just keeps staring.

I wonder where he came from. I guess he could have walked here, but the nearest house has to be at least a few miles away. More importantly, why the Hell is he just watching me like that?

A couple drops of rain snap against my shoulder, and I realize everything has turned a shade darker. I look up and the charcoal clouds are almost on us, like heavy, black tar spewing from the sky.

"Okay, kiddo, we gotta…"

She's nowhere near me.

I spot her running toward the mammoth boulders and cliffs that straddle the coast. Her bright red jacket stands out like a fresh wound against the grey rock, and my heart quickens.

"Paige, get back here!" I yell, but she just turns and waves at me. Then she takes a few more photos before carefully climbing down the other side of the boulder.

"Paige, no!" I sprint for the rocks, running as hard as I can. Just as I reach the top of the cliff my left ankle rolls, popping against a patch of uneven stone. My foot explodes in white-hot pain and I hit the ground. I grit my teeth, hauling myself back up. Fortunately it takes me just a few more hobbling steps to make it to the top.

I scan the rocks and beach, then the churning surf below. Nothing.

"Paige!" I scream. "Where are you?"

I don't even feel my ankle anymore, everything from my rib cage down going numb.

She must be playing near the water somewhere.

I stumble down the other side of the ridge, onto a flat shelf blotched with moss. Again I peer over the edge, frantically scanning the shoreline. My breathing quickens, and every sensory detail becomes razor-sharp. It's almost overwhelming: the salty reek of the ocean, the pounding surf, the rapid tapping of rain against my jacket.

My ears strain to pick up any sign of Paige — a giggle, or even a cry for help muffled against the surf, but there's only the steady crashing of waves on stone.

"Paige!" I scream again, so loud my voice cracks and turns raspy. "Paige!"

I grip the side of my head and dig my fingernails into the scalp. *This can't be happening. Where the fuck is she?*

Movement at the edge of the forest catches my attention, and it's the boy in the black hoodie again. He stands just at the tree line, but this time he isn't staring at me. His gaze is pointed at a tide pool only a few feet from the surf's reach.

I don't know how I had missed it. Floating in the shallow water is Paige's bright-pink camera.

My stomach twists so tight it turns my legs to rubber. I grip the rock wall with one hand to steady myself, watching it bobbing in that ink-black pool. Then I'm off again, stumbling down the path as I ignore the grinding pain that ripples through my foot.

But I'm moving too fast. My sprained ankle slams against a rock, agony detonates and I pitch forward. My knee hits the ground first, then everything is a swirl of dark skies, tall trees and grey stone.

Then it all goes black for a moment.

A crack of thunder rips through my skull and I open my eyes, only to have them flooded with crashing rain. I blink away the water, trying to focus. My thoughts are murky and scattered as waves of pain radiate from the back of my head. I can just make out a silhouette of someone standing over me.

Is it her? Did she hear me fall?

The figure kneels down beside me and then leans in closer. Only then can I make out who it is, and my heart sinks. The boy from the woods looks down at me with this cold, blank expression, like a department store mannequin.

I manage to push out the words: "Wh…where is she?" It's little more than a whisper.

He doesn't react, doesn't even blink.

And then he's gone.

Maybe I slipped back into unconsciousness for a few moments, but it was like he just vanished into thin air. Here one second, gone the next.

I manage to drag myself up along the rock wall until I'm standing. Wobbly, but standing.

The trees at the edge of the forest are blurry and I stare hard, trying to focus. It takes a minute or two. My legs also feel more solid as I come back to full consciousness, but my head is still pounding. I yell, "Paige! Where are you?"

Only wind and waves answer me. It dawns on me then that the downpour has stopped.

I start walking toward the forest, figuring she might have hid there to get out of the weather. After just a few steps I spot her red coat among the trees. She presses her way out of a patch of cedars cloaked with vines. Clumsy, slowly, and then she stops to look at me. Even from a hundred yards away I can see how wide her eyes are.

"Paige!" I yell and half-jog, half-limp toward her.

She screams. A piercing sound that sinks deep inside me. Once I'm closer I can see her hair is slick against her head, and she's soaked. I search her body for wounds, for broken bones or blood, but there's nothing. She seems physically unharmed, yet she's still screaming. A steady, unbroken wail that sounds almost mechanical.

I take her into my arms, squeezing her tight and telling her everything is okay, but the screaming doesn't stop. As I hold her my ears buzz and pop from the decibel of her voice.

I keep telling her she's safe and everything is fine, but it's like she can't hear me; it's like she's in her own world. Only after several minutes of me hugging her, rocking her and kissing her tear-streaked face do her cries gradually devolve into sobbing.

I slip off my coat and wrap her in it. She's shivering. Before I can pick her up and carry her back to the car she pulls away from me, pointing at the cluster of cedar trees she ran out from.

"There." Her voice is empty. Distant.

"What do you mean? What's there?"

"The boy." And she starts crying again. I take her back into my arms and stare at the forest, at the dark spaces between the trees.

"Shhhhh, you're safe now. Everything is fine."

It's a lie, of course. That hollow look in her eyes tells me things are anything but alright. That creepy little fucker said something to her, or did something to her.

"What happened? What did he do?"

She doesn't answer. Her chest rises and falls against mine in heaving sobs.

The clouds seem to be leaving. Ash-colored light pushes away the darkness, but the shadows set deep in the forest remain. I have a feeling that the kid is still in there.

Part of me wants to charge into the woods and find that little son-of-a-bitch, but I have a wet, cold daughter to think of first.

I carry her back to the path and into the woods, the

same way we came in. The added weight puts even more pressure on my ankle, and I grit my teeth against the pain. In ten minutes we'll be back at the car, then I can get her dry. Paige drapes her arms around my neck and presses her head against my shoulder. She's still shivering, but her crying has stopped.

"It'll all be over soon. Don't you worry," I tell her.

Halfway down the path a flicker of movement catches my eye. I stop and stare into the forest, past a particularly thick cluster of cedars crossed by a fallen tree. I can't see him, but I know he's there.

Little fucker is following us.

There's a thin side-trail that twists around the trees and into the brush. I tell myself to keep going, to just head to the car and get her dry, but there's a smoldering rage inside me. The more I think about what that little shit might have done to my daughter the more I want to find him.

I decide to take just a few steps down the side-trail, to see if I can spot him somewhere. Maybe catch a glimpse of his hideout, so I could tell the cops where to look.

I don't know if I got twisted around, or what happened, but all of a sudden I'm fifty feet into the woods. We're surrounded by limp ferns dotted with black spots, and a carpet of deep-green moss that creeps over rocks and up the fungus-speckled trunks of trees. Twisted branches scratch at our faces.

My heart is slamming against my chest again. I worry that my head is all messed up from the fall, because I sure as Hell don't remember trudging this deep into the forest.

I wouldn't have gone this far with Paige, not in this condition.

I turn to go back toward the main path when I get the feeling we're being watched. It feels like there's a person hiding high in the trees, eyeing our every step, so I look up.

The scene hits me hard.

For a moment I can't breathe. The boy in the black hoodie hangs from a tree limb about a dozen feet off the ground. His empty eye sockets, set in putrid-white tissue, look down at us as his body twists in the breeze.

"Jesus." I whisper.

My limbs go numb and weak, and I notice my grip on Paige is loosening.

I hold her tighter, my gaze still glued to those hollow eyes and the thick rope squeezing the kid's neck.

And in that moment everything goes quiet. All I can hear is Paige breathing, slow and deep.

"Daddy." She says quietly. "We need to go."

"Okay, kiddo." I turn and start walking. "We're going — "

"We need to go, NOW!" She kicks me hard at the top of the knee, and she starts clawing at my face.

I let go of her and she runs into the brush, screaming once again. I chase after her, moss-draped branches tearing at my cheeks as I stumble and trip over stones and logs. My ankle is on fire and my head is throbbing, but I'm able to gain some ground on her. She's just a few feet ahead of me when we burst out of the trees and into the parking lot.

She collapses onto the gravel, sobbing.

I pick her up and try to brush the tears from her eyes. She fights me at first, but then throws her arms around my neck and squeezes.

"Shhhhhhh, it's okay. It's okay."

I stare back at the forest, hating myself for ever wandering into it.

...

Paige is quiet as I wrap her in a blanket. I keep telling her she's safe and everything is alright now, but she barely acknowledges me.

Her skin is cold, and she's still shivering as badly as before. I start the car, blasting the heat and cradle her in my arms. Then I rock her back and forth, watching the dark clouds fade into the horizon. They unravel and dissolve, like tissue paper in hot water.

Paige's breathing is slow and laced with heavy sighs, her head resting against my chest. I'm not sure if she's sleeping, but she's not sobbing anymore which, I guess, is a good sign. A reason to worry a little less, maybe.

Yet I do still worry, of course. I can't stop picturing that boy in the woods with his empty eye sockets, like tiny black funnels, looking down at us. Or the blank expression on his face as he looked down at me as I lay semi-conscious on the rocks.

But it can't be the same kid. It just wouldn't make sense.

My brain really must be scrambled from hitting my head. It still hurts like Hell too, and the pain reminds me that my judgement probably isn't at its best right now. I need to call 911. Get Paige checked out by a paramedic, and report the body to police, but I can't remember where I put my damn phone.

I pop open the middle console and feel around the cup holders, doing my best not to disturb Paige in the process. She shifts her weight, and I feel something hard press against my stomach. There's something in her jacket pocket. I reach inside and find her pink camera. It's covered in a skim of dark-green slime from the tide pool, but otherwise seems intact. She must have picked it up sometime after I fell, then took it into the woods.

I set it on the dash and keep rummaging for my phone under the seat, then in the door compartments. I try to think of where else I might have put it, but I'm having trouble concentrating.

My eyes keep drifting back over to the camera.

The thing has a presence about it. It's a weird sort of magnetism that tugs at my attention, pulling my focus away from everything else.

I grab the camera, turn the thing on and hit 'Play'. Then I start swiping through the images she took.

The log.

The twisted arbutus tree.

The lonely patch of grass sprouting between the rocks.

And then a picture of me.

I'm laying at the base of the cliff, just a few feet from the ocean.

For a second I'm horrified to think that Paige would

snap a picture of me while I'm unconscious like that, but then I take a closer look at my face. I realize that my eyes are vacant, and my head doesn't look like how a head is supposed to look. The surrounding rocks are speckled with blood.

I throw the camera against the windshield. It bounces off the glass, landing on the passenger seat.

"What the fuck!?" Everything seems to spin a little. I can taste the saliva thickening in my mouth as my adrenaline spikes. "What the Hell is happening?"

Paige murmurs in her sleep. I stroke her hair and squeeze her tight, breathing in the apple scent of her shampoo — anything to prove to myself that this is all still real, that I'm not dreaming or in a coma or something equally terrifying.

I glance over at the camera. Other than a small crack running down the side it seems fine. I need a second look at that photo. Maybe the head injury is just messing with my mind.

I gently reposition Paige, stretching over her and picking it up again. When I hit play the picture is the same. I'm still laying there at the base of the cliff, unquestionably dead.

The camera says there's one more image left to view, one more picture that was taken after I fell. I'm about to swipe over to see the final image, but my finger stops just above the screen and hovers there.

Something deep inside me says that I don't want to see this photo.

That I should *never* see this photo.

So I put the camera down again, and I kiss my daughter on the forehead.

It doesn't really matter. Paige and I are together, and the dark clouds are gone.

DUSTIN WALKER
ABOUT THE AUTHOR

Dustin Walker is a former journalist, a current marketer and a perpetual writer of dark fiction. Gritty, psychological horror is his jam. His work has previously appeared in places like Dark Moon Digest, Silver Blade Magazine on the NoSleep Podcast. He lives on Vancouver Island, Canada, with his wife and daughter.

HALLOWED GROUND
A.G. HILTON

The Servant, like his forebears, truly believed in God; believed in His power, in His almighty voice. He knew that God spoke and worked most clearly through His creation, that in the pastures and hills and forests of this very farmland the true God was far closer than any stuffy church.

He stretched his hands in the morning air, sensing that the last chill of winter had melted away. Spring waxed in the air, a time for new life, for new growth, a time for the Good Work.

Blessed be the Harvest. Praise be to Him.

...

Brie watched the countryside rush by in a flurry of greens and browns, and she couldn't help thinking that she would rather be back home for this two week hiatus. But one look at her husband, William, quieted the thought. She knew he felt trapped in his job, and although he wouldn't admit it he felt trapped in the city. She'd agreed to taking this two week vacation, to going to some backwater area in the Carolina hills, because she knew he had to get out; he had to recharge. The trip was already doing him good, judging by the slight smile on his face as he navigated the winding back roads.

"Are we almost there?" came the hundredth unison inquiry from Thomas and Milly in the back seat.

Brie turned to the children, trying to keep an even-keeled response and said, "Soon. Why don't you two enjoy this beautiful view? I know, let's play I Spy again."

A collective groan came from the back seat. "But there's been nothing but stupid trees the whole time we've been driving," Thomas whined.

Will cut in, "Hey, you complain about those trees now, but wait until you're up climbing around in them! And, if I remember correctly, this place has a tire swing. Let me tell you, Grampa had one on the old farm and there's nothing like a tire swing ride. Now we're almost there, so just think how fun that will be."

The children considered this, and for the time being ceased their inquiries. Brie slipped a hand stealthily over the center console and gave Will's thigh a grateful squeeze, which broadened his grin further.

After twenty more minutes of driving along through pine-wooded foothills, the land opened before them. Immediately Brie recognized the scene from the Air BnB's webpage, although it was much livelier now. Where the initial image pictured a cottage bordered by the tall, harvest-ready stalks of corn that filled the adjoining field, the scene now burst with the vibrancy of spring as new shoots of corn struggled brightly through the soil. Behind the cottage could be glimpsed the highest boughs of the old oak, where the tire swing was purported to be. Beyond that the forest rose in a solid wall. Cool, dark, and impenetrable, the cloud-dappled blue sky hanging in bright contrast above.

Will pulled the car into the gravel driveway, triggering excited shouts from the kids, and Brie spotted an old Chevy in the drive. An old man sat expectantly in the open truck bed, throwing them a wave as they approached.

"Who's that, Honey? Is this the right place?" asked Brie.

Will shrugged. "We'll find out, I guess." He brought the car to a stop and got out. "Afternoon," he called to the man.

The old man rose and ambled toward him, smiling in a pleasant, sleepy way. "Reckon you must be Mr. Braddon," he drawled. "James Sutter at your service. I own the place."

"Good to meet you in the flesh. Is everything alright?"

"Oh, everything's just fine. I don't mean to intrude, but I thought I might welcome you to the place. Gotta say I'm rather proud of the way I got it spruced up."

"Oh, well, we appreciate it. Beautiful place you got here! Reminds me of my grandfather's farm." Will looked to the vibrant corn shoots. "Your corn sure is doing well for so early in the season."

"Real good soil around here. My family's always worked hard to keep it that way."

Brie came forward with the children, trying to catch Will's eye. At last he took the hint and turned to them. "Oh, Mr. Sutter, I'd like you to meet my wife, Brie. These are our kids, Thomas and Milly."

Sutter smiled and nodded. "Howdy there." He stood for a moment, looking them over with admiration. "I think you're all going to like the place, and it'll like ya'll just fine too. Plenty of beautiful sights to see, especially," he hooked a thumb over his shoulder toward the tree line, "out yonder over the creek."

"We can't wait to take it all in."

Sutter gave another nod of approval. "Well, let me get on out of your hair. Don't want to be a bother. Key's in the lockbox like we discussed, and my place is around the bend if'n you should need anything."

The old man got back in the truck, disappearing down the road in a puff of dust.

Will put an arm around Brie's waist. "Well, the natives seem friendly enough." He turned to the kids. "Now, who wants to go check on that tire swing?"

They were off with a cheer, Will hot on their heels.

"Hey, be careful!" Brie called after them.

Will turned and gave her a childish grin, shrugging before following the kids around the house. Brie had to admit that the place was beautiful, more vibrant than other rural locales she had seen, yet she couldn't shake a feeling of vulnerability that came over her as she saw the small cottage dwarfed by the row of pines. They looked like they might lean over and snatch up the house if they wanted. She shook her head at the thought, chiding herself for thinking like some caricature of a city dweller who was too afraid to let her kids get out in the fresh air.

Will and the kids played long into the dusky evening. Brie joined in, surprising herself by taking off her shoes to walk with them through the cool creek that ran along the property's wooded border. Will taught the kids to look for crawdads and salamanders, and she could sense her husband's nostalgia. It was strangely infectious.

Later, after the kids had gone to bed, Brie found Will at the sink, absently washing dishes and gazing out the window toward the forest. She came up behind him and rested her head between his shoulder blades. "Have you found the miracle for the middle aged man?"

"Hmm?"

"You were like a puppy out there today."

He chuckled. "I may be paying for it tomorrow; my lower back already feels a little stiff. Pretty different from sitting at my desk all day."

"Yeah, but I can tell you love it."

"Honestly, it makes me feel young again, alive. And this place…I don't know, it's just great with the woods and everything. When I was little I loved exploring the woods and playing pretend."

She leaned closer to his ear. "You know, the kids are asleep. Maybe we can play some pretend of our own."

He turned to face her coy smile, and as she led him

away from the sink she realized that she was enjoying the trip much more than she had expected.

...

In the darkness The Servant prostrated himself beneath the yawning sky above the pines, in deference to that which had brought the Incarnation to his forebears. Again, God had provided the ram in the thicket. All would be provided for.

He threw his head back and howled into the void, unleashing those sacred words spoken to him from the Hallowed Place.

Praise be to Him.

...

They spent the next two days traveling to the surrounding towns. Brie could tell that Will wasn't thrilled to be spending time in boutiques, ice cream shops, and visitor's centers, but he had promised her as much and kept quiet. Truthfully, she enjoyed being away from those looming pines no matter how ridiculous the notion was. When she lay down at night some part of her brain couldn't help but think about how present the forest was, how silent and brooding over them it felt.

But, whatever she was feeling, Will clearly didn't sense it. Each evening, when they came back exhausted from their treks, the kids dragged themselves to their beds. Then Will would always insist on taking a walk. He had asked her to come once, but she'd refused. She'd felt childish when he had asked why, and all she could say was that she was too tired.

Brie woke on the third day feeling sleepiness weigh on her like a leaden jacket. She didn't feel that she had slept poorly like the prior nights — the sounds of the insects in the woods had lulled her to sleep almost immediately — but somehow it seemed she had been sleeping too deeply. Strange dream fragments clung to her mind like spider-webs, images of trees in torch light, branches reaching like skeletal fingers. Once or twice she had stirred, and she seemed to remember that the bed was empty beside her. As she looked over now she realized that Will had apparently gotten up early.

"Where's Daddy?" she asked as she found the kids already up and slurping at bowls of cereal.

Thomas shrugged, scooping a spoonful of milk. "He said he needed to take a walk."

"I see." Brie rubbed at her temples, wondering what could drive Sleepy Head Will Braddon to take an early morning stroll. Sometimes the call for breakfast wasn't enticement enough, but the thought was fleeting. God, she was so tired.

"Morning, Beautiful." Will entered with a flurry, a thin sheen of perspiration on his forehead. "It's great out there!" He went to the coffee pot, pouring her a cup and offering it to her.

"Thanks. I feel like I need to hibernate, but you look like you slept well."

"I guess so. Had some wild dreams last night, but I

feel great. Wonder if it's the mountain air?" he asked with a grin.

"Beats me, but I want whatever you're having. Where were you this morning?"

"I just took a walk."

"Where at?"

"Out in the woods."

Those words, *The Woods,* stirred something in her mind. She thought of the way the trees seemed to lean toward the house, and she suppressed the urge to shiver.

"Daddy?" Will looked across the table to where Milly stirred her remaining cereal absently. "Can we play in the woods today?"

"Sure, Pumpkin. And let me tell you, there are some neat spots out there. Special places."

"I thought you wanted to see some waterfalls?" Brie cut in. "We were planning on hiking some trails at that park, remember?"

"Yeah! Waterfalls!" Thomas shouted and splashed in his cereal.

Brie thought she caught the ghost of some odd expression cross her husband's face. Was it irritation, some veiled anger? But then it was gone, and he smiled as he had all morning. "I had forgotten. Don't you worry Mill, we'll have time to go exploring later. I promise."

Milly seemed cheered by this, but Brie couldn't shake that image of the leaning trees from her mind. *God,* she thought, *I'm a city slicker if there ever was one.* Though she couldn't explain why, she didn't want her kids going beyond those trees again.

The rest of the day was wonderful. Once they were away from the cottage Will seemed to lose some of the frantic energy he'd been harboring. In total they took in two beautiful waterfalls, as well as a lovely lunch and dinner in the adjoining town. It was dusk when they returned to the cottage, the kids rejoicing and leaping quickly from the car.

"Can we go exploring now, Daddy?" Milly asked.

"It's getting dark, Kiddo," Brie responded.

Milly kept her eyes on her father. Will said, "We could take a little walk before it gets dark." Brie shot her husband a look which, under other circumstances, would have been more than adequate to convey her feelings on the matter, but Will shrugged it off. "You don't have to come if you don't want to."

"It just doesn't seem like a good idea. Not very safe."

Will walked to her. "It's perfectly safe. I used to do this stuff all the time as a kid, and sometimes we'd even go out with flashlights and dare each other to go deeper. It can't hurt to take a little walk."

"Fine," she said, hating that she was giving in so easily. "But just for a bit, and I'll come too."

Milly let out a cheer, cutting across the yard toward the creek with Thomas on her heels. Will and Brie scrambled to follow, Brie calling for them to wait up. Soon the family had crossed the gurgling stream and penetrated the forbidding row of pines. Once beyond the barrier they seemed to enter another world entirely

The forest floor lay beneath a carpet of fallen pine needles. Because of how close the pines grew together the sunlight was stifled, making the space dim and the air stuffy. Yet the absence of much shrubbery meant the walking was easy, and their line of sight extended deep into the rows of flaking tree trunks.

Thomas turned to his sister suddenly. "Tag, you're it!" he yelled, sprinting ahead.

Milly followed him, and soon the two became small figures down the pined avenue, diminishing faster than they ought to. The sun was still far from set, so they had plenty of time to dally, yet the sight gave Brie anxiety. The kids seemed so impossibly far away. She called, "Hey, not so far you two!"

Will took off after them, and Brie felt the forest press closer. She bolted after him, gripped by a sudden, claustrophobic panic. Above them the pine boughs choked off all of the day's remaining light. Her feet squished down, no longer on pine needles but on a strange, soft loam that sucked greedily at her shoes. She was about to call out again when the dimness of the forest gave way, and she nearly crashed into the kids who stood between two large trees that leaned together to create a tunnel of limbs.

Brie grabbed a hold of each child and shook them, "You need to listen! You can't go running off like that. What if you got lost?"

"Sorry, Mommy," said Milly with a shrug. "We just wanted to play in the Special Place."

Movement caught her eye, and she looked beyond

her daughter to see Will deeper in the trees. He looked indistinct, like he had become merely a shadow. She shivered. Looking back the way they had come she saw warm shafts of fading light falling on the blanket of pine needles between tall, healthy trees. Looking forward everything changed: the trees became smooth, black things devoid of bark. The ground was a soft, almost-swampy mess. The boughs created an oppressive canopy, and a mist swirled from deeper among the trunks. Without a word Will began to walk toward the coiling fog.

"Will, where are you going!?"

"Just looking," he said in a soft voice.

Keeping a grip on the children she took one step after him, then stopped when the hairs stood up on her arms and the back of her neck. A warm sensation washed over her lower belly, proceeding down as if the air around her were charged with some fierce, base, primal energy. All at once she felt that she needed to plunge madly into the trees, deeper and deeper, pulling the children along with her, needing to pull the children with her. But, a heartbeat later, when she examined the thought it horrified her with how alien it felt, as if it had not been hers at all.

"Will!"

He twitched, as if receiving a blow to the face. When he turned he looked bewildered and confused, his eyes darting between the strange trunks surrounding them.

"We need to go back," she said weakly.

"A bit further?" his voice was small, his tone distracted.

"We're going back now."

Will stared at her for a moment, eyes clouded with something that Brie couldn't place, something that she had never recognized in him before. At her words it seemed to clear, and finally he nodded. She turned without waiting for him, hurrying the children back the way they had come until they had crossed the creek that lined the border of the forest. By now the sun had almost set. Dinner, or what little they ate that could be called dinner, was consumed quickly and quietly.

Brie sent the kids straight to bed with a firm reprimand, but Will was reticent regarding the incident. They lay side-by-side in the upstairs bedroom, and Brie kept playing the scene over and over in her mind. She couldn't shake the image of the look that had been in Will's eyes, and the thought that perhaps it hadn't been Will looking out at her.

She let the thought die. She still felt silly thinking such ridiculous things, but she wouldn't deny any longer that this place, with its deep forests and hidden hollows, made her feel small and weak. The forest was old, far older than the massive skyscrapers, and it was vaster than she cared to consider. Suddenly she didn't care for how beautiful it looked on the surface, and she didn't care that the place was somehow letting Will recapture his childhood.

Something is wrong with those woods, she thought. *Maybe it's making something wrong with Will too.* Maybe she could convince him to leave early, offer to get them another place somewhere in town to finish the trip.

She listened to Will's breathing in the dark, a part of her trying to determine if the sound was somehow different, while a cold breath from the forest drove the fog from between the trees toward the lonely cottage.

…

The time had come. In the Hallowed Place the elements were prepared, and the Servant worked under His gaze to ensure that all would be proper. As he had for nights now The Servant began the litany and, in his mind, a second voice, more powerful, added to his own.

The Divine Presence swirled around him like a mist as the call went forth to bring all things together.

Praise be to Him.

…

Sleep suffocated her. It drove her down to darkened depths, where she may have otherwise been perfectly willing to submit and let herself be still under its smothering influence. Yet something was wrong. She didn't know what, but a panic rose in her chest that caused her heart to thud wildly. Something was wrong, and she needed to get up now. With great effort Brie felt herself rising from the murk like a waterlogged corpse, free of whatever had been holding it to the lake bottom.

Thrashing in the bed, she reached over to Will's side, but felt nothing. Where could he be? The clock on the nightstand read 2:45 AM. Darkness reigned. Go back to sleep, a voice whispered in her mind. *Rest, and know that all is well.*

But all was not well. She knew this as surely as she knew her children's voices when they called out in a crowd.

The children.

She didn't know why, but at the thought of Thomas and Milly all her panic converged into a fine, maternal point: she had to check the children. Despite the grogginess that tugged at her Brie stumbled through the dark cottage, heedless of the unseen things she bumped into. When she arrived at the small room Thomas and Milly had claimed as their own the spell of sleepiness shattered.

The door was open; the children were gone.

Her panic became a frantic flurry of thought as she called their names and flew through the cottage. She realized a chill hung in the air, and saw that the back door was open to allow mist to intrude. It settled upon the carpet in dewy drops, and the fog lay thick and all-enveloping beyond the door. Even so she could see three shapes walking, hand-in-hand, as they crossed the stream and vanished through the trees.

"Thomas! Milly! Will!"

The three figures disappeared into the darkness of the forest, as if they had never been there. Brie launched through the door, the night air speckling her arms and bare calves with goose flesh, but she barely noticed. Her bare feet tingled as they crossed the cold, pricking grass, and they went numb as she splashed across the creek.

The world beyond the pines may as well have been a cave. It lay there, dark and yawning as if in wait for her. She wanted to call out again, but their names died in her throat, choked off by the fear that something else may be listening. The very trees around her leaned close, whether to grab her or eavesdrop she wasn't sure. Then the clouds broke, and shafts of bright moonlight trickled between the branches in silvery beams.

She pressed on.

She couldn't see the three figures, but she knew they couldn't be far ahead. Her mind could focus on nothing but the children, of bringing them back. As she pressed deeper into this wooded realm and neared the first of the strangely maligned and ancient trees, as the soft earth began sucking at her bare toes, she felt a crushing will press against her own. It came wrapped in that primal sensation of aggression and lust which had struck her at this threshold earlier, but now it was fierce and directed at her. It hated. Hate, ancient and powerful, seemed to drip like sap from the trees about her.

This place didn't want her. The thought seemed insane, and yet she knew it to simply be true. She knew now that her initial misgivings had been justified. The place didn't want her and her stench of city living. It wanted Will, it wanted the children.

A cry tore from the darkness. Long and wailing, it carried like an alien song through the forest. The trees swayed about her, though there wasn't a breeze. The all-enveloping mist abated momentarily, allowing Brie a glimpse of a fire and three silhouettes against the flames.

Finally finding her voice, Brie screamed the children's names as she came closer. One of the smaller figures seemed to turn its head as she approached, and she recognized Milly's voice at once, "Mommy?"

Her little girl's voice sounded dreamy, drugged almost, and Brie's panic came back full-force. The forest around her screamed in frothing hatred as she set foot into the open space where the fire burned. It was a deep, wide hollow from which the surrounding trees seemed to retreat to form a tight encirclement, like an army at siege. The bonfire burned brightly, and she could finally make out the distinct image of her family standing hand-in-hand before the blaze. From around the fire came a fourth figure, lanky and stripped to the waist. After a moment she recognized the old man who rented the cottage, James Sutter.

Sutter held a knife aloft in her direction. "Begone, this is a Holy Place! This is Holy Work."

Heedless of the blade, she ran to her husband. "Will! What are you doing?"

He turned slowly, and when his eyes met hers she realized that she couldn't see Will at all. Those eyes held only contempt, the contempt of the forest made flesh. A coldness filled her guts, and she stumbled away from the thing that had once been her husband. Her eyes darted to the children; they too looked at her with alien hatred.

"Why did you come, Mommy?" Milly asked. "He doesn't want you here."

She looked at the three of them in bewilderment, then lunged forward. "You're coming back with me!"

A deep sound resonated through the hollow, stopping her cold. It was the groaning of bark under great stress, the grinding of earthen plates far below the mountains. It was the moan of the wind between the trees, and she became aware of a massive shape looming beyond the fire. It rose alone, twisting into the air like an old, impossibly huge oak tree. Mouth agape, she watched as things that looked like branches twisted and writhed. All around them the forest responded with a great rustling of its own, which roared into the deepest and most archaic parts of her brain.

She screamed; her mind swallowed beneath a force of will, ancient beyond reckoning, as the dark thing rooted beyond the flames twisted more violently. A deep bellowing rang through her bowels, and the man called Sutter fell to his knees as a split like a bloody wound opened in the thing's center. An eye, crimson and impossibly large, gazed at her across the flames with a disdain that dissolved all thoughts to one maddening chorus: Blessed be the Harvest.

Praise be to *Him.*

A.G. HILTON
ABOUT THE AUTHOR

A.G. Hilton is a new voice in the world of horror fiction who made his debut in 2019 when his short story "Good Boy" featured in the Tales From the Old Black Ambulance anthology. Hailing from Winston-Salem, NC, he grew up on a steady diet of horror and fantasy films, all the while fostering a love for the fiction of King, Matheson, and Lovecraft. He studied creative writing at Gardner-Webb University and began seriously penning stories of his own while living in the countryside of Shelby, NC. His work seeks to infuse the madness of Cosmic Horror into the dark corners of rural life. He now lives in Belmont, NC where he enjoys long discussions on writing and photography with his fiancé. When not conjuring monstrous stories, he fills his daylight hours as a technical writer. You can keep up with his work on twitter @nightsidetales.

THE VALLEY OF THE SHADOWS
CHRIS HEWITT

Logging season was almost over. The first rains had turned the narrow, dirt tracks to thick mud, which threatened to shut down the brother's operation. Within a fortnight the valley would be unreachable, and the season had already been a disaster; everything that could go wrong had. They'd wasted weeks repairing aging equipment, and that was *before* two of the crew walked off the job leaving them shorthanded. It didn't help that their permit restricted their activities to the east side of the valley, rendering everything west of the meandering stream off limits.

That portion of the area was the ancestral lands of the Blackfoot, not that they'd ever seen any of the tribe up here. Out of luck and out of time, the desperate brothers eyed the untouched western slope, their only chance to meet their quota.

"It's superstitious bullshit," said Ryan.

"Even so, I'm still not so sure," Dave replied.

"What was it the old man used to say? 'You make your own luck'."

"Yea, usually after he'd got drunk and lost at the craps table."

Dave had never forgiven their father for losing the family business. The brothers had bought it back, but only by running up some serious debts; Debts they were still working off. Another bad season and it wouldn't just be their equipment that got repossessed.

"We've mouths to feed," said Ryan, taking a swig from his pewter hip flask, the only thing their father had left them. "I'll get Charlie up here with the dozer, get that stream moved tonight."

"Okay," said Dave. It didn't sit well with him, but for once his brother was right, it was their last chance. Moving the stream was unlikely to fool anyone, but it would make their work easier and it might just help drain the treacherous valley basin. "Let the guys know we'll need to put a shift in tomorrow. I want off this mountain before the weekend."

Ryan tucked the flask into his jacket and set off down the mountain, barking orders into his radio. Dave leaned against a large boulder and took in the spectacular sunset, visible now thanks to the receding rain front. It was little consolation for another day wasted. Far below he could see the lights of the town blinking on, and he waited for one in particular. Three long flashes of their porch light signaled his daughter's nightly ritual for him, acting as a reminder of why he was up there.

...

Sunrise brought the promise of blue skies, even though it remained bitterly cold. Charlie had brewed up a pot of coffee on the campfire, and Dave filled a large mug. "One day I'll find out what your secret is."

"I told you, a spoon full of grease," joked Charlie.

"It's keeping me regular," added Travis, raising his steaming mug.

Charlie laughed. "You're still full of shit though?"

Travis winked. They went way back, since Travis had worked for her father back in the day. Charlie was a gifted mechanic, and it was only her skill with a spanner that kept the brothers budget operation up and running. Travis was an old school lumberjack, and everyone called him Chief as a nod to his experience and ancestry. Between them the two veterans had more years of experience than the rest of the crew combined.

"Where's Ryan?" asked Dave.

"Down at the stream bed," replied Charlie. It had only taken them an hour to divert the stream the previous night, which was easy work with the right tools.

"He's started early," added Travis. Dave got the implication.

When he caught up with Ryan, he was gossiping with Jacob. The big greenhorn was an honest worker, but he was easily led. He sheepishly handed Ryan back his flask.

"How's it looking?" said Dave.

"We should have done this years ago," said Ryan, giving Jacob a nod to get started. "Just need to clear the worst of this brush, then it's all money."

Dave snatched the flask, pouring a good slug of liquor into his coffee. "We don't need any fuck-ups today."

Ryan scowled and looked away.

"Get this done and you'll be able to get that new pick-up," said Dave, holding out the flask. Ryan reached to take it. Dave wouldn't let go, not until his brother looked him in the eye. Not until they had an understanding. It took a good few seconds before Ryan capitulated.

"Good, let's get on it," said Dave, releasing the flask.

...

The crew spent the morning moving their gear from the top of the eastern ridge down to the valley basin, the stream nothing more than a ditch now. It had taken them another hour to cut a muddy path through the overgrown brush to reach their prize, and as they'd hoped the ancient maple was far more valuable than anything they'd logged this season. Ryan was already celebrating, knocking back the last of his liquor.

"Boss!" yelled Jacob, pointing at the first of the trees they planned to fell.

Ryan scrambled over and found Jacob, slack jawed, peering up at the mammoth maple. All along its trunk intricate, carved symbols wound their way from its base, reaching high up into the foliage. Ryan ran his hand over the strangely scarred bark. "What the Hell is this?"

Jacob nodded into the forest. "Seems like a lot of 'em got those markings."

Ryan feared for the quality of the timber. "So what, we got some graffiti joker! This ain't a fucking art gallery. Take an etching if you give a shit."

It was no skin off of Jacob's nose; a tree was a tree. The sound of the chainsaw was music to Ryan's ears as he headed back to camp for a refill. He'd only got a few yards when the chainsaw spluttered, then died.

"She's just cut out," hollered Jacob, trying to restart the chainsaw.

Ryan ripped the radio from his belt, he yelled. "Charlie!"

"You don't need to shout," said Charlie, appearing behind him. Travis, as always, was behind her, another chainsaw slung over his shoulder. Charlie clambered through the mud and branches to examine the broken equipment, while Ryan turned his attention to Travis. "I ain't paying you to stand around!"

Travis gave a half-hearted salute, spitting a wad of tobacco at Ryan's feet before sauntering over to the tree. He saw the markings and rubbed his thick beard. "You know this is bad luck, right?"

"Looks like good luck to me!" Ryan retorted.

Travis looked over at Charlie and rolled his eyes.

"I didn't take you for the superstitious type, Chief," Ryan mocked.

Travis rolled the tobacco around his mouth before breaking the tension. "On your head be it, Boss!" he said, sarcastically. He spat another brown bullet as he fired up his chainsaw, all the while staring at Ryan threateningly. Travis made swift progress. The chainsaw cut through the trunk like butter, and was almost halfway through the thick trunk when, with a screech of steel, it tore itself from Travis' grip, sending him sprawling.

Ryan snapped. Sprinting over, he wrenched the chainsaw from the tree. After several failed attempts to restart it he threw the useless machine across the forest floor in a fit of incandescent rage, almost hitting Charlie. "What the fuck is it you people do around here!?"

Dave arrived on the scene just in time to prevent Travis from knocking Ryan on his ass. He seized his brother by the collar, pinning him hard against the tree. With his struggling brother in one arm he twisted around, gesturing to the crew. "Guys, take a break. Go grab some lunch."

"Fucking bullshit!" spat Ryan, squirming to escape. Charlie was speechless. She snatched up her tools and stormed off, Travis and Jacob chased after her.

"I'll sort this out," Dave shouted after them. If they lost Charlie they could kiss goodbye to the business. He waited until the crew were out of earshot before releasing his brother. "We're done, you hear me? We're through! If you want to follow in his footsteps I'm not going to stop you." He took the flask and threw it across the clearing before heading off after the crew, adamant that it was the last time he'd be fixing his brother's mess.

Ryan slumped down against the tree, wiping the back of his shaking hand across his dry, cracked lips. He didn't need his brother. He didn't need anyone; he'd show them all.

...

It was blisteringly hot in the afternoon sun. The crew was back in camp, and Charlie had been throwing equipment around since she returned. Dave had hoped she might have calmed down, that maybe Travis had talked to her, but if he had he'd failed.

"I've had enough, he's out of control," said Charlie, her back to Dave.

"Two more days, that's all I'm asking. You've seen what we've got here, it's good," Dave begged.

"What you've got is a dangerous, alcoholic prick for a brother," Charlie spat, throwing tools into a holdall. She snatched the last spanner, her back ridged.

"You're right," said Dave, putting a hand on her shoulder. "Please Charlie, you know what I've got on the line here. Help me."

Charlie dropped the spanner, leaning against the table. She liked Dave, and she knew his family well. She was aware who the real victims would be if the brother's business failed, and she didn't like the thought of a kid suffering. Two days. She could do that, right? She turned to face him. "I should - "

The sight of Ryan marching through the camp brandishing an axe stopped her mid-sentence. She gestured, drawing Dave's attention.

"Oh, God!" he groaned, dashing off after his axe-wielding, crazy-ass brother. Jacob and Travis followed. Charlie turned back to her workbench with a sigh, picking up the last spanner and throwing it into the bag.

...

The tall trees cast long shadows, dark fingers that stretched out towards the camp. They turned the valley into a barcode of light and dark stripes, blinding Dave as he ran after his brother. He finally caught up with him at the foot of the ancient maple tree, stopping to catch his breath. He knew better than to get between a maniac and their axe.

"That's gonna take him a while," said Jacob, catching up.

Crazed, dehydrated and drunk, Ryan chopped at the tree, a season of frustration and anger flowing through him. As he swung the axe back one last time there was a thunderous crack. Dave and Jacob instinctively ducked, hands over their ringing ears.

The next time they looked up it was into a sky full of birds taking flight, and further down the valley a herd of deer made their escape. The sound was still reverberating when Dave spotted his brother's body in the tree's shadow, twenty feet from the trunk. He feared the worst, until Ryan jerked himself upright with a start.

"Was that lightning?" asked Jacob.

Dave stared up at the cloudless sky. "I don't think so."

Ryan dragged himself to his feet and dusted himself off, and for a moment the brothers exchanged confused looks before a change in the tree line demanded Dave's attention. A low rumbling and creaking confirmed his worst fears. "Timber!"

Ryan saw the danger and started running. He needed only a few yards to escape the toppling tree, but he could see the tree's shadow becoming darker as he ran. He was almost clear when his outstretched hands touched something solid, something that barred him from reaching the light.

What had started as a low rumble now sounded like a freight train. Dave saw terror in his brother's eyes, watched his pathetic, pathetic attempt at escape. Before he looked away he saw Ryan's hands reaching up, a futile attempt to stop the unstoppable. The blast of debris billowed out from the ground-shaking impact, throwing Dave to the floor.

He didn't see the tree's shadow scatter like cockroaches across the valley.

…

"You okay, Dave?" said Travis.

He was shell-shocked. Dave's world moved in slow motion, and he watched numbly as Jacob reached the fallen trunk. After a moment Jacob's shaking hands removed his baseball cap, and that was when Dave knew his brother was dead.

"What happened, where's Ryan?" yelled Travis.

"It fell," said Dave, his face a mask of confusion.

"He...he got stuck."

Travis looked at Jacob, a solemn shake of his head confirmed Dave's story. "Jesus!"

"He couldn't - " Dave's mouth continued to open and close, but no more words came forth.

"It's alright, son," said Travis, wrapping an arm around him. "Let's get you back to camp." He gestured for Jacob to follow.

They made it to the ditch, but when Travis looked back for Jacob he saw him standing in the shadow of another tree, eyes wide and fists flailing. Jacob looked to be screaming, but the valley remained eerily quiet. Travis turned to head back, to give him a moment to grieve, but Dave grabbed his arm. "Wait!"

The two men stood transfixed at the sight of the big lumberjack relentlessly throwing himself into an invisible barrier. It was as baffling as it was disturbing, and Dave had a sickening sense of deja vu.

Jacob abruptly stopped his gymnastics, staring back towards the forest as if he'd heard something. Dave followed his gaze. All across the valley a subtle ripple spread through the shadows as a myriad of skittering shades crept from their hiding holes, slinking back into the forbidden forest. They reappeared as a dark wave, funneled into a single shadow.

Rushing to his stricken friend Travis thrust out his arm without thinking, and Jacob seized it like a drowning man. Travis pulled with all his might, but even with Dave's help they couldn't free Jacob or Travis' arm. The dark wave rolled towards them, gaining speed.

Terror turned to abject horror when the wave broke over Jacob's boots. He began to sink, his twisted features pushing hard against the shadow's edge. Inch by inch the shades devoured him, and Dave was thankful he couldn't hear Jacob's screams. Jacob tried to hang on, his fingernails tearing into Travis' arm, threatening to pull them both to their deaths. His bloody grip only slipped when his eyes turned to lifeless, black orbs.

They watched as Jacob's corpse disappeared, dragged away by the ebbing, dark tide. They watched, frozen in fear, as the wave dispersed into skittering motes that scattered into the shadow of the woods.

...

Travis leaned back, exhausted, his arm still stuck within the shadow. A handful of greedy shades remained, eagerly fighting for the drops of blood dripping from his arm. "I can't believe the stories were real."

Dave sat with his head between his legs. "What are you talking about?"

"My grandfather used to tell this bullshit ghost story about the shades, how they were evil spirits that lived in the shadows. Used to scare shit of me and my brother."

"Are you shitting me," said Dave, shaking his head. "You think it's ghosts?"

"No. I don't know. It's just…"

"What?"

"The story went that the ancient tribes imprisoned

all the shades in sacred trees, trees that they marked so everyone knew to leave them alone."

Dave laughed. "You think we just busted a bunch of bogeymen out of a prison tree?"

Travis twisted and turned, trying to free his arm. "Fuck, I don't know! Have you got another explanation? Because right now I'm all fucking ears."

Dave picked up a stone, flinging it at the feeding shades. There was no reaction, so he picked up a branch and proceeded to stab at the swirling devils. Nothing seemed to affect the formless fiends, and they didn't seem to be of this world. "I don't know. All I do know is they killed Ryan and Jacob and they don't look done. We need to get the hell out of here."

Travis gestured to his arm. "In case you haven't noticed I ain't going anywhere."

"There's gotta be a way."

"Yeah, there is."

It took Dave a moment to realize what Travis was thinking. "There's got to be another way!"

"The sun's setting Dave, it's taking my arm!"

Dave leapt to his feet. The shadow had already crept past Travis' elbow, and they were running out of time. Dave doubted he'd get to the camp in time, but maybe he didn't need to. "Where's Charlie?"

"She was at the camp!"

Dave scrabbled for his radio and stabbed the talk button. "Charlie! Charlie! Come in."

Static.

"Please Charlie, pickup!"

Static.

"Give it to me," said Travis. "Charlie, pick the fucking radio up! We're in trouble down here."

"You can tell that bastard I'm done!"

"Shut up and listen," screamed Travis. "We need an axe down here now, or I'm a dead man."

"Not fucking funny!"

"Charlie, listen," said Travis. There was real fear in his voice. "There's something in the shadows. Stay away from the shadows. Do you hear me? It's not a joke. Jacob and Ryan are dead."

Static.

"Charlie?"

Static

"Charlie!"

"I'm on my way!"

Travis threw the radio back at Dave, breathing a sigh of relief.

It seemed like an eternity before they could make out the sound of Charlie gunning the dozer down the mountain. She'd heeded his warning and kept to the sun-lit part of the valley. Travis was trying to put a brave face on things, even with the shadow now engulfing half of his bicep. He was struggling to keep the rest of his body clear, fearful that he'd lose another limb, or worse. At least his arm had stopped bleeding, the unhappy shades slinking off to hide. "Yeah, that's right, piss off bastards! You're not getting me, not today."

Charlie arrived in a cloud of thick, black smoke. Hopping from the dozer she picked her way over to the stricken duo, throwing the axe into Dave's fumbling hands. "What the Hell are you doing?"

"My arm's stuck."

Charlie looked at the two men as if they were mad. She grabbed Travis' shoulder, tugging hard. She was determined to put an end to their nonsense.

"Don't," yelled Travis, but it was too late. He lost his balance, the toe of his boot slipping. Dave wrestled Charlie to the floor, keeping her back from the barrier. There was already movement along the tree line. Pointing, Dave screamed at her. "Look!"

Charlie stared in disbelief as the shades swarmed, her hand clasping her mouth. It wasn't a joke. The familiar handful of eager shades were already crawling towards Travis' boot as the dark wave flowed from the forest.

"Do it!" Travis begged. "Chop my foot!"

Dave was struggling to find an angle where he could get a clean strike without slipping and becoming trapped himself. He raised the axe up high, closing his eyes.

"Wait!" barked Charlie. "I've got an idea. It's the shadows, right?"

Both men nodded, but she was already running. She shouted back. "We'll use the dozer!"

Travis's arm was lost to the setting sun, and he felt the shades nipping at his steel-toed boot. He saw their countless hungry brethren, only yards away now. With a roar and a plume of black smoke the dozer burst into life.

Charlie swung the machine around, pointing it towards her target. She jammed the kill switch and gas pedal before leaping from the dozer.

Travis let out an agonized scream as the wave of shadows flowed over his boot. Within seconds the shoe and his toes had vanished, the shades licking at the exposed flesh of his foot. In their feeding frenzy the shades climbed up the shadow's edge, inching towards Travis' arm.

"Get ready, we're going to have to run," said Charlie.

Travis laughed maniacally through gritted teeth. "Try and catch me, you asshole shades!"

They watched the dozer's progress towards the tree, plowing through the indifferent darkness.

"Ready!?" barked Charlie as the dozer smashed into the tree.

There was an almighty crash, and shuddering groan, but against all odds the tree bent. Not by much, but it was enough to shorten its shadow and drag back the wave of ravenous shades. Travis fell free, Dave and Charlie each taking an arm. They were slipping and sliding, the ground a mixture of mud and blood, as they tried to drag Travis away. The more they struggled the less progress they made, their feet bogged down in the thick sludge. Travis was staring back at the dozer when he saw it topple. "Oh Christ, *pull!*"

There was no time to react. With a wheezing groan the dozer tumbled, and with its weight removed the tree sprung back upright.

"Move," screamed Dave, pushing Charlie away and

jumping aside as the shadow engulfed Travis. Behind it the dark wave followed, crashing down on Travis' legs and torso. Blood and tobacco exploded from his mouth as he gasped his last breath, and when Charlie dared to look she vomited. The sight of her half-eaten, lifelong friend was too much.

...

The sun was setting fast, the long shadows stretching halfway across the valley. What remained of Travis' corpse gurgled as the shades continued to devour the contents of his chest.

"Charlie! Get up, we need to go," Dave urged.

"I killed him," Charlie sobbed.

"Bullshit, they killed him and we're next. Get up!"

Charlie didn't move.

"Charlie! If we stay here, we're dead!"

Dave clambered over and pulled her to her feet, and they staggered towards the camp. as they approached the ditch the hairs on his neck bristled, and he froze. He wasn't sure why, but instinct told him something was dreadfully wrong. With the sun now low in the sky the ditch cast its own shadow, and from where he stood it was as if the stream flowed with water again. He reached for Charlie's hand but she'd slipped ahead, the shadow of her head merging with that of the ditch.

The shades didn't hesitate. Dave watched in frozen horror as Charlie clutched her face, stumbling backwards. When she twisted towards him he found himself looking at an unfamiliar face. Her eyes and nose were gone, her high cheek bones exposed. Her once pleasant smile was replaced by a broad, lipless grin. The shades flocked to her shadow, flaying her alive as she twisted and screeched in agony. Little more than a skeleton fell into the ditch, visible briefly before it disappeared into the turbulent shadows.

Dave dropped to his knees, as much out of despair as to ensure he didn't suffer the same fate. He scanned the ditch, watching the shades slink away as they headed up the valley. His jaw dropped as they flowed from the ditch back into the forest, using the tallest tree's shadow as a bridge.

There was no way out. He was trapped in a rapid-ly disappearing oasis of light. Behind him Travis' head spl0shed into the mud, the shoulders that had supported it completely devoured by the relentless monstrosities.

Defeated, Dave slipped down into the mud. His thoughts turned to his family. He fished into his pocket and pulled out his wallet, running a trembling finger over the faded photo. The thought that he might not see his wife and daughter again turned his sorrow to white-hot anger. With fists clenched tight he pummeled the mud, his anger roaring from his lungs.

As if to answer his cries the forest roared back, a soul-destroying sound that shook the valley. Dave dragged himself back to his feet one last time, standing defiantly and ready to face whatever fresh Hell the forest had in store. If he was going out it would be on his feet, fighting.

As if to test his resolve something monstrous moved

within the forest, uprooting trees in its wake. It seemed as if the forest was alive, a single organism that howled. Slowly, inexorably, the water-logged forest began to slide down the mountain. Dave gasped at the sheer scale of the landslide, half the valley racing away. With it went the web of shadows.

Light turned to dark, and Dave found himself trapped within the cold shadows as the shades rushed towards him. He felt them slide over his boot, felt them tear into his flesh. He screamed out in pain, but his voice was lost in silence. He closed his eyes tightly, hoping that it would be a quick death.

Light flickered across his eyelids, and he opened his eyes to streaming daylight. In the distance he saw the shades unwillingly being dragged away with the receding forest shadows. The process repeated, plunging Dave in and out of shadows. All the while the vicious shades fought against gravity, flowing with increasing speed around every obstacle to reach their prey. With all avenues exhausted, all shadows gone, they disappeared with the rumbling forest far below.

Dave could not believe his luck. He was alive, basking in a spectacular sunset where trees once were. The shadows that remained seemed empty, normal, and he looked to the heavens to thank whatever gods had spared him. The distant rumbling seemed a world away as he watched the first bright star twinkling in the twilight. It was beautiful, and it reminded him of his…his heart stopped.

He fell to his knees, and through tearing eyes peered

down the valley to the town far below. The streetlights were already on, and here and there he saw the townsfolk turning on the lights in their homes. A tear fell from his cheek as one particular light flashed on and off. He held his breath. It flashed again, before one by one all the lights flickered out. There would be no third flash, no screams, no salvation.

His greed had killed them all.

Dave was alone. The sun had set, and an unnatural silence had descended over the icy valley in the wake of the landslide. Sinking down into the mud he stared up at the countless stars, praying that the shades would take him in the night.

He could not face another sunrise.

CHRIS HEWITT
ABOUT THE AUTHOR

Chris lives in the beautiful garden of England and in the odd moments that he's not walking the dog, he pursues his passion for writing fiction. Chris' background is in software development, which is another way of saying he's well-versed in writing horror, fantasy and science-fiction. Keep an eye out for several short stories being published throughout 2020.

Twitter: @i_mused_blog
Blog: http://mused.blog/
Amazon: http://mused.blog/author

THE BEAST IN THE BLACK ISLE
DANIEL PURCELL

His parents were fighting again. They did not see him wander off from the car park, nor see their child slip into the forest that filled the heart of the Black Isle in Scotland. It swallowed him up imperceptibly, as though he was never there. The young boy was upset, and had just wanted to get away from the screaming that reverberated about the naked trees. It followed him as he crested a hill, though it ceased by the time he stumbled down the stone steps that led to where the spring water collected in a stone trough.

Before the boy reached the trough – locally known as the Clootie Well – he marveled at the peculiar sight of every tree in the vicinity having rags of clothing, old and new, hanging off their branches. It was like entering a bat cave, though with larger, more colorful inhabitants. The Clootie Well at the bottom of the stream was dilapidated, shrouded in overzealous vines and unkempt shrubbery. The oak tree beside the well almost stooped over it, perhaps trying to nurture it within the comfort of the shadows cast by the clothes overhead. Lurking in the shade the well was scarcely perceptible, and maybe it was intended to stay that way, forgotten and untouched.

It was a bright afternoon, though the area was cast in fluttering shadows from the odd, hanging garments. The young child trotted about the recesses of the forest, paying no heed to the portents. Or maybe he did, and chose to ignore how strange it was for so much clothing to be in the woods. The darkness enveloped him as he reached the vines, where he ineffectually tugged at them until his hands squelched in the mud that slicked the edges. He reached the stones of the Clootie Well: the water within was clear, and he saw dirty coins lying at the bottom. The putrid stench of the sludgy earth around it hit him as a breeze blew through the forest, and he scrunched up his nose in disgust.

He wiped his soiled hands hastily on his dungarees. "Ack," he moaned, trying to clean his hands. He consequently further muddied his clothes; his mum and dad would not be impressed. The boy huffed, disheartened at what had seemed like a splendid adventure to begin with. An idea twinkled then in the back of his mind, like a star in the firmament. He fished in the front pouch of his dungarees, pulling out a tarnished, two-pence coin and flicking it upwards into the well. It splashed into the water with a *plop* sound.

He waited.

What for, he did not know.

"Ack," he said again, more petulant this time, as he glared at the well.

Then the water shimmered, the liquid beginning to discolor. Something big moved – no, *galloped* - behind him amongst the dangling rags. The boy turned and saw a silhouette, one that stood still among the strange clothing. After a heartbeat the ungainly, detestable, six-limbed creature sidled forward.

Closer.

As it drew closer its silhouette grew larger, to the point where the boy had to tilt his head up to see it.

Then it tore through the clothes, reaching for the child. It merely managed to rip at the front of his dungarees, the boy scrambling backwards in the nick of time. Then he let out a shrill little scream as he fell from the edge. He landed in the mud, shuffling backward out of the shadows and away from the thing.

The beast was part horse and part human, a horrid jumble of limbs and hooves jutting out at disconcerting angles. The two beings were fused together into one nightmare-inducing creature; a rider who could never dismount from the beast it was permanently attached to. The thing was skinless, its body raw and livid. The horse mouth whinnied, eyes blazing scarlet as it trotted and jittered about the well. Then it grew further in stature, contorting this way and that as its naked, sinewy muscles writhed like snakes.

"I am the Nuckelavee," the human head stated, looming above the boy, its voice like a nest of insects whirring.

"You have wandered where you do not belong, and have awakened dark magicks. I am glad that you did though, as the others before you had. It has been too long since I had prey."

The boy looked about the forest, at the ragged, old clothes tied to the branches. *At the others.*

Then the Nuckelavee roared, the jaw of the horse gaping inexorably wide, like a cave. The too-long arms stretched towards the boy, but he managed to scurry out of the way just in time. The thing was so close that he could smell the putrid flesh of the beast, the creature coming within inches of his face.

He got to his feet and ran, screaming for help, but the only answer he received was the braying of the beast. He could not hear mum or his dad, and was not even sure which direction he had come from.

The child hurtled down the forest, scarcely able to stay upright as the Nuckelavee closed in on him, clawing and chomping at his feet. Then one of the boy's shoes fell off, tumbling away as he crashed to the ground. He looked up ahead and saw that there was an old, wooden bridge over a stream. He did not remember crossing it, but maybe it would lead to a house.

"You will belong to the forest, young one," the Nuckelavee whirred, the human part of it stretching and drawing closer to the boy's face as it taunted him, "Then there will only be suffering, darkness and perpetuity for you."

"You aren't real," the boy whimpered. He added,

more to himself than for the creature, "Only Daddy can scare me, not monsters."

The Nuckelavee sneered. "So many monsters lurk in this world, and in the other. You will learn this, soon enough."

The world suddenly seemed to darken, and then several drops of rain splashed down upon them. The Nuckelavee gave an ear-splitting hiss, its hooves beating the earth manically. Water. It did not like water.

The boy took a chance, scuttling towards the bridge without warning. The Nuckelavee followed – though doing so spasmodically, each drop of rain causing it tremendous pain. The boy felt the ground tremble with the beast's discord, but he managed to dart across the stream.

The Nuckelavee was in too much agony, and too distracted, to notice where the boy had led him. The old bridge collapsed under the great weight of the thrashing beast, and even as it fell the monster tried to follow the child. It let out a jarring screech as it plummeted into the stream, the muscle and organs sizzling as it thrashed about. Then it began shrinking, its body decaying rapidly.

The boy clambered across the bridge quickly, and just when he thought he had made it to the other side a lanky, broiling arm darted out of the water. With a burst of effort he threw himself across the last few planks, scooting backwards from the bridge until he was pressed up against a tree. He cowered there for what felt like hours, covering his face and trying not to weep.

By the time he realized he was not alone it was already

too late. Strong fingers gripped his arm, wrenching it away from his face. This was much worse than any monster, he thought. It was his father, and the man was not very happy.

As the boy was dragged back to their vehicle the water in the Clootie Well gave a single ripple, then it was still and glassy once more.

DANIEL PURCELL
ABOUT THE AUTHOR

Daniel Purcell lives with his girlfriend in Glasgow, Scotland. He studied English at the University of Liverpool -- where he was born -- and has travelled extensively around the world, living in America for six months along the way. When he's not travelling or procrastinating, he mainly enjoys writing and reading speculative fiction. He has upcoming short-fiction being or already published with Farther Stars Than These, three Black Hare Press anthologies (Oceans, Ancients, and Lockdown Sci-Fi #4), 101 Words, a Rogue Planet Press anthology ('Unexpected Turbulence,' in the Halloween 2020 edition), Eerie River Publishing ('The Beast in the Black Isle' in It Calls From The Forest Volume 2), Iron Faerie Publishing (FAERIE, HEXED, FOUR HORSEMEN: FAMINE and PLAGUE Anthologies), Unity Volume 1: A Magical Realism Anthology, Tritely Challenged Volume 2, and AntipodeanSF (November.)

NATTMARA
RACHEL OSEIDA

Finding the sword had been easy; it was getting the teeth that made Kess' stomach churn. At sunset he had ventured out to the graveyard with a shovel and began to dig. More than the digging, or the bodies, it was after that, when he had to reach into their mouths and search for teeth worthy enough to bring back to her, that made him nauseated.

The moon was almost directly above his head, and Kess knew he was going to have to hurry up if he was going to make it back to her in time. All he could think of was the sight of Mara's face when he returned. He cracked open the stiff jaw of the eighth body, a girl who looked no more than ten, to find the last tooth. *Maybe younger,* he thought. The corpse had been buried long enough that it was getting hard to tell.

What was left of the maggot-eaten eyes seemed to stare at him as his fingers scavenged around in its rotten mouth.

Images of his sister rattled around in his head. He thought of Kaelie's bright blue eyes, the color of the summer sky. He could hear her soft voice, melodic as a calm river. Her small body, so much like the one he was currently staring at, was wasting away. He thought of her sick at home, her golden skin gone gray, her forehead burning when he left.

What would she think of this? Would she even still be there when he got back? Kaelie needed him, and what was he doing? Grave robbing for a girl he'd just met?

He shook his head. He couldn't think like that. *This is for Mara*, he thought.

He yanked on the corpse's canine tooth, digging it out from the festering gums. His mind seemed to scream at his obliging hands, encouraging him to run the other way. He was repulsed, yet he continued to pull until the last tooth released.

He dropped the white, pearly thing into the small sack with the rest of the teeth. His heart ached to see Mara smile again. Just the thought of her smile made him feel warm, like having the sun kiss his skin. He crawled out of the grave, staring at the mess that surrounded him. *It's for her,* he reminded himself.

His hands were caked in dirt, and whatever was underneath his fingernails. He sighed. *She better be worth it.*

...

Mara could feel the boy's soul as surely as he could

hear her screams. They racked through her body as the wisps of his soul crept along the forest floor. Her onyx nails dug into the dirt, the icy wind ripping through the trees. He was so close to the edge of the forest, far closer than anyone had come in years, and if it weren't for the barrier then she would have sucked the life right out of him.

Her limbs began to twitch as he edged nearer. He was close enough that she could see him through the tangled oak, and she screeched as the taste of him swam through the air. He was all young flesh, rich blood and everything else delicious. He smelled of desperation, of hope and slightly of stupidity, but she knew he couldn't be perfect.

She dragged her ragged body through the barren earth, stopping just before the barrier. Concealed by the last of the trees she watched him as he kicked at the invisible wall.

He was clearly not from the town; none of them would dare to get this close to the barrier. Or, more specifically, this close to her. They had not caged the forest for fear of the knotted trees or rotten earth, but for fear of what she could do. The fear that when they looked upon her they could not see the demonic wraith, but only a vision of beauty.

She stood, her legs trembling as she stepped out into the clearing. It took a second before his eyes landed on her, but when they did they did not let go.

"Hello," she said, hoping her voice didn't sound as hoarse to him as it truly was.

"Uh…" he stuttered.

She rolled her eyes before plastering the best smile she could muster over her face.

"Hello," she repeated.

"Hi…" he said, stepping closer so that he was right in front of her. His eyes flicked over her sham of a body. "What are… I mean, you are… well, you're…"

"Gorgeous," she finished quickly.

"Well, yes, but, uh, I was going to, uh, ask what you're...doing here?"

"That won't be of any importance soon enough," she said, catching his gaze before he had even a second to react. His eyes were molten gold, so bright she wondered if her vision would have sunspots when she looked away.

Love me. She let the command ripple through his mind. *You're going to do exactly as I say.* The commands took a second longer to sink in then she was used to, but as they did she watched his eyes glazed over. She broke her stare as he shook his head slightly, a smile settling over his features. He radiated joy; it was wretched.

"What's your name?" he asked.

"Mara," she hissed.

Unfazed by her change in tone he continued, "Well, beautiful Mara, is there anything you need?"

Her body was shaking, her throat begging for even a sliver of his soul.

"You are going to find an iron sword," she said.

He nodded along with her shaking words.

"And you will bring it to me with six teeth. Six per-

fect teeth."

"Of course, my love."

"And you will bring them to me by midnight."

He paused, his head still nodding before saying, "Then I will see you tonight."

He turned to leave, and just before she had time to step back into the trees his head turned back to look at her. His eyes narrowed as he asked, "What do you need them for?"

She cocked her head, scanning him for a second before responding, "Because I am finally going to get out." Then she retreated back into her prison, leaving him to his task.

…

The moon hung directly over Mara's head as she watched her errand-runner come into view. The moonlight glinted off his golden hair, making him shine in the dark. She did her best not to scowl as he smiled lazily at the sight of her. Any repugnant stare she had on her face quickly faded away at the sight of what was strapped to his back.

It was a large sword, not that the size mattered for what she intended to use it for, but it must have been up to his waist in height.

Out of his worn coat pocket he pulled out a small burlap pouch. When he was close enough he opened it, pouring the contents into his hand. She stared at the six small, white teeth, and her blood began to pulse in her veins. The spirits from each of the teeth mixed with his, their scent wafting through the air. Her starving body twitched excitedly.

His voice broke through her hunger. "Is it all to your satisfaction?"

He unslung the sword from his back, tossing it towards Mara.

"Don't - " The word fumbled off of her lips. Before she could finish it hit the barrier, repelling back towards him.

"Move!" she screamed as he jumped out of the way. He was quick, but not quick enough. The blade sliced his thigh, releasing a cry from his throat. The thick scent of blood filled the air as he closed his hands around the wound. She was practically seizing as she watched the blood flow from the gash, the deep, crimson beads seeped through the gaps in his fingers. He screamed again, and she could feel the death laced with his soul. *He can't die*, she thought, *not when I'm so close!*

He crawled towards her, using one hand to pull himself through the grass while keeping the other firmly placed on his leg that was dragging uselessly behind him.

"Look at me," she commanded.

His head swayed from side to side before he leaned it against the barrier. Her blood pounded in her ears.

"Look at me!" she screamed.

He lifted his head, letting it slump back at an impossible angle. His face was so ashen that it might as well have been white, his sun-like warmth replaced by the cold of the silver moon that hung overhead.

"Look at me," she pleaded. "Please, just look at me."

His misted eyes drifted across her face.

"Look. At. Me." She said it slowly, letting him register each word before uttering the next. She watched, her body shaking, as his eyes zoomed in and out until finally settling on her. He began to focus, and for a brief moment she caught his gaze before her body crumbled to the ground. Another scream escaped her lips, and he echoed her cry.

…

Kess' eyes were still on her as she fell, feral shrieks escaping her throat. Blood was pouring from his thigh, his leg was pounding, his head was spinning, his vision was closing in, and all he could do was look at her. His mind screamed for him to turn away, to run to town and go back to Kaelie, but how could he when she was there?

She shook. No, she convulsed. Each of her limbs seemed to pull her in a different direction. Her hands were clasped together so tight that her nails dug into her palms, and he swore he could see blood dripping down her wrists.

His ears began to ring as black spots coated his vision. He fumbled along his leg, which was slick with blood, and the warmth from the gash left the rest of him feeling like ice. The wind was whipping around him, causing goosebumps to trail over his skin. He didn't have to be a healer to know that he was losing far too much blood. It was seeping out of him with every heartbeat. He shrugged off his jacket, peeling his shirt off so he could wind it around his leg.

Kess tied it as tight as he could. Mara had calmed down slightly, her thrashing reducing to a tremor. Her eyes flicked up and locked on his, the bright gold of her iris' seeming to have darkened to a deep amber. Her words echoed in his head, even though her mouth didn't move an inch. *Stay calm, you are going to do exactly as I stay.* She paused before saying the last sentence with more force. *You aren't going to die.*

Funny, Kess thought, *because it sure feels like I am.*

It felt wrong for him to dwell on his pain when his sister was writhing in her own back home. He wanted to go back to her, but his body remained rooted firmly in place. He looked at Mara. Her face, ever so lovely, was a mask of pain.

"Where are the teeth," she choked out. Each time she took a breath she seemed to cringe.

He swept his hand across the grass until coming across the scattered pile from when he had dropped them. He counted each one, making sure that he had all six before looking back at Mara.

She nodded at the sight of them. They were the best teeth he could have found, cavity-free and almost unblemished.

The clouds overhead grew darker, distant claps of thunder echoing across the clearing.

"Eat them," she said. Her voice was a command, and his body could not help but oblige.

He shoved them in his mouth, cracking the teeth under his own. They tasted of rust and dirt as he ground them down enough to swallow. He could feel her eyes on him, watching him feverishly. His eyes, on the other hand, were watching as the blood seeped through the shirt he had tied around his leg. Too fast, he thought. His head was evidence of that, as it hadn't stopped spinning from the moment the sword had hit him. When he lifted his head to look at her black clouds swept over his vision.

"Focus on me, focus on my face. Don't let it win." Her voice was like the soft, warm glow of morning light. It cut through the ringing in his ears just enough for him to focus on her next words.

"I need you to pick up the sword and drive it straight into the barrier."

Kess shook his head. He slumped back against the invisible wall, weakly pounding his hand against it. His leg was on fire.

He had burned himself before, but that pain had been nothing like this. This felt as if the sun's fire was burning through his veins. He focused on her body that was shaking again, her limbs jerking out in any and all directions. It looked as if she was fighting with her own body, fighting to maintain control over her appendages.

Her fist pounded manically on the wall between them, sending vibrations through his head. His world shook, and he could have sworn that the trees were knotting together.

"Do it now, " she cried. The wind whipped her hair, which appeared almost gray in the moonlight. In fact, her entire body looked gray. Her once-warm skin was now the color of the lifeless corpses he had dug up earlier.

Then his body was moving before he even realized what was happening. His hands had found the sword, and he hefted up the metallic monstrosity so that it was pointed at the barrier. It was much heavier than his lifeless arms should have been able to hold, but with everything Kess had left he slammed it through the barrier. Kess watched as it sent cracks of light all across its walls, and he slumped back against the ground to watch it crumble in front of him.

But most of all he watched her. He watched as she shook against the ground. He watched as she stared, eyes wide, at what he had done. He watched as what was left of her warmth faded, leaving a gray, hollow wraith in her place. And he watched as her ravenous body launched towards him.

…

She broke through the shattered barrier and slammed herself onto him. He was thrashing beneath her like a fish, and she clutched his neck hard enough to dig her talon-like nails into his skin. His skin was ice, his face so bloodless that he might as well have been six feet under. Her heart rate matched his, rapid and desperate as it hammered against her ribs. She pressed her cold lips to his, and there were so many tastes flowing through her that Mara almost forgot there was only one soul she was consuming.

There were notes of love, which tasted of rich, sweet blood. There were overwhelming hints of pain and sorrow, which most closely resembled a juicy piece of raw meat.

The death lingering inside him could only be described as tasting like dirt, which she did her best to ignore.

She had forgotten how good souls could taste.

Her limbs had stopped trashing, and she could feel his essence filling up the empty cavity inside of her. The place where, if she had a soul of her own, it would have been. Her heartbeat was steady now against his, which had grown so faint that she could barely hear it at all.

She pulled away, letting Kess' soul settle inside her. It was such a unique sensation to feel almost full, especially after so long, that nothing else could compare. Her body was calm for the first time since the barrier went up, and a brief smile swept across her lips before vanishing the next second. Her eyes widened, and she clutched her chest as she frantically searched for a wound that wasn't there. There was a deep warm pain spreading through her limbs, a rush of emotions swimming through her that weren't hers.

Betrayal, pain, longing, sadness. Tears lined her eyes, and she blinked them away.

Images flashed through her head of the boy dying before her; he was caring for a small, golden-haired girl. Her smile was so bright that it was impossible not to love her. Mara watched as he chased her across a large, grassy meadow. Laughter erupted when he caught the child, and he spun her around in the air. Mara saw the girl, a little older now, running into his arms. She could feel what he did, could feel the love and warmth that the girl radiated wherever she went. The image flipped one last time.

This memory was cold, and the girl had gray-tinged skin. Although she still smiled when she saw Kess it was not the same. Her eyes were no longer the sky-blue of a warm, summer stream, but the dark, cold navy of a winter ocean.

Mara shook her head. She had seen people's memories before, but never like that. These took over her mind, transporting her to that moment inside of just the sensation of being inside his head. Her eyes lined with fresh tears that she didn't know she was capable of shedding, the remnants as his emotions welling up inside her. They ran through her body, forcing sobs from her throat.

When the hunger persisted she didn't resist. He was still this time as she pulled the last of his soul out of him, and she sobbed wildly as his emotions filled her up. *Stop*, she screamed at them uselessly. *Please, make it stop.* More of his memories washed over her, and she tightened her grip around him. She was lost in a forest of emotions with no way out.

She broke the connection once more, pushing herself off of his lifeless body. Rain began to fall from the dark clouds that hung overhead, building until the water was pouring down in sheets. He shivered, barely conscious on the ground. She stared at the grass, not daring to look at him. Not that it mattered. She knew tears streamed down his cheeks just as certainly as they flowed down her own. Her body ached to steal whatever was left of the soul inside of him. She scolded herself; how could she cause him more pain, now that she knew how he felt?

Pain.

There was so much pain, it lashed through her veins making her blood pound. She gripped the sides of her face while planting her head into the sopping, wet earth. She rocked there, letting her tears fall onto the ground. Her face was hot, and her blood felt as if it was boiling in her veins. There was so much heat that she was sure if she wanted to she could have breathed out flames. The temperature built inside of her until there was nothing left to do except open her mouth and scream.

...

His eyes were closed when her ear-shattering shrieks returned. He had fallen against the ground, glad that one of his ears was spared from the awful sound. He pried one eye open just enough to see her grasp at handfuls of grass. Her body shook, but it was not seizing as he had seen before. She shook now, but only because her sobs sent tremors through her core.

Kess couldn't remember when the rain had started, but he was soaked now. He looked over to see her body completely still, as if the rain had drowned her. He had never seen her this motionless, and even the constant up and down of her chest from breathing was gone.

This must be death, he thought. My eyes have just stopped on this one image. But how could that be, if he could still feel the cold rain pouring down on him? The wind was still whipping through the trees, sending a chill across his drenched body.

Darkness began to creep back over his eyes, and the white noise in his ears grew until it was all he could hear. Just before the world went dark he could have sworn he saw Mara rise, then dart back into the trees.

THE CALM

JAMES DORR

It was on a bright summer's day, in the Year of Our Lord 1755, that they came to the village. They had mustered out of Massachusetts, under the flag of Governor-General William Shirley to fight the French, and the wind had pursued them. It had followed them from the well-kept farms and ordered towns that they had grown up in, west and then north as their detachment, commanded by Captain Laurence Pindar, broke off from the main body.

It chased them up through the Berkshires and into Vermont, a mixed troop of British regular army and raw colonials. It whistled after them through Brattleboro and Newfane and Windham. As they marched up, first to the West River valley and from there to the Battenkill, it trailed them. They held the hope of meeting then with the Mettawee and Otter Rivers, either of which could bring them to Lake Champlain, as they entered into the sow-backed ridges and valleys of the east slope of the Taconic Mountains.

Of all the troops one named Philip Latham knew the wind best. He was from the western part of Massachusetts, and had been elected corporal of his town's militia. *Le vent de la mort*, as the French trappers called it, had come down to the lands of the English settlers.

The wind that presages death.

This was a Huron Indian superstition, or so Latham had been told, and it had been brought east from the Great Lakes. The idea that a wind, at least one which persisted so indefinitely, could only bring ill fate was shared by the Iroquois tribes as well. Especially a wind as this, one that, even as they pressed into the mountains, still rustled the treetops. It lay in wait for them to swirl their hats off whenever they broke into the infrequent clearings, those patches of grass where they rested while the officers grazed their horses.

Latham kept this lore to himself, of course -- no sense in spooking the others, as enough men were already lost to desertion. Most men in his group were away from home for the first time, and it showed. The lot of them felt uneasy about their own shadows, much less the brooding, patch-shadowed peaks they caught glimpses of from time to time as they hacked their way through tangles of honeysuckle and wild grape.

They were surrounded by wind and forest, and they had to push ever upward until, at last, they came out on a ridge-top and saw the village.

The captain halted them. "Lieutenant Barnstone," he called, "bring the maps up." Still well outside the village proper the men looked down from the ridge, noting the empty town square with its well in the center. While the officers were conversing they saw the town's rough-granite church standing squat on the far side, with signs in its churchyard of recent activity. They looked for any vestiges of life, yet they saw no movement. The houses on the square's three other sides were all barred and shuttered tight.

Shuttered against what? Latham wondered. Perhaps a coming storm? Beyond the small town stood a half-mile high mountain, the peak lost in darkened, fog-like clouds that hugged its cragged sides. They did not spread out in the sky as most clouds did, but huddled close to the mountain's bare-rocked surface. As for the wind that would bring a storm to them -- Latham realized now that, for the first time, the wind appeared to be dying down.

He looked toward the other men, then to the captain and his lieutenant as the officers called him over with the other non-coms. "This village should not be here," the lieutenant began. "At least it is not on any of our maps, which gives us a problem. Not knowing what this village is, we have no way of knowing which side its inhabitants support. Whether they would welcome us with open arms, or -- "

"Or whether they would shoot us, if they had the chance to," the captain said for him. "We may as well be blunt. We have lost men every mile of the way once we entered these mountains, and between the hard march and the unfamiliar surroundings the men need resting, a chance for cooked rations. I propose that we take a risk and make camp in the town here, but not all go in at first. I want some of you men to take the horses -- we passed a small meadow not a mile back -- and the wagons with them. See that they're hobbled there, then be ready to join back with us the instant there's any sign of trouble…"

And so the captain's orders continued, detailing some of the men as pickets to remain on the ridge-top, at least until given orders to come down. Others, including Latham, were to precede the main body of soldiers into the village, and then they were to spread out into open areas. They had been instructed to guard the dirt paths between the houses, the church and the churchyard in case of an attack. Latham, in point of fact, was to take his group and scour the churchyard for any townspeople who might be hiding there, and if he found anyone he was to bring them to the square where Captain Pindar would set up the main camp.

And the wind, meanwhile, slackened further. This allowed other sounds to come, such as the murmuring within the houses as the first troops passed slowly between them. The men, their bayonets fixed on their muskets, were alert and ready for hostility. The murmers were soon drowned out by the sounds of drums, and the scouts passed through to the square without incident. The doors and the windows remained shut tight as the main regiment descended. They entered the town in battle order; carefully, warily, until they too reached the village's center.

"You, the people of the village," the captain then

shouted. "You see we are here, and that we will not harm you. We ask you to come out, to send someone out to us. We wish to buy provisions from you, and to use your well to fill our canteens with. To camp here peaceably only for one night, and then to be on our way."

This time several of the doors opened. Latham watched from the churchyard, where he and his small group had been inspecting what seemed to be signs of a recent funeral that was interrupted mid-way. Men from the houses came out to the square, but never strayed too far from their own front doors. They were short, bent men, as if Aboriginal or other native blood was mixed in their veins. Some of them shouted, but not in English. Some seemed to speak French, while others spoke in a tongue that sounded like that of the Oneida tribespeople, yet not entirely that either. Latham listened, hearing a snatch now and then of words or phrases that he recognized.

"*Gardez!*" a few called, their broken French allowing Latham to understand them. "*Gardez-vous de la fin du vent! Gardez son éxtremité!*"

And Latham, at least, realized what they were saying. *The wind that presages death -- beware its ending!*

But Captain Pindar shouted over them: "*Damme, is there no one here who speaks English!?*"

Then there was silence, a moment of quiet as the villagers retreated softly back into their houses. They closed the doors quietly behind them, and even the wind sank down to a sigh before dying off to a whisper.

Next to Latham, practically in his ear, a quiet voice

murmured, "I speak English."

Latham jumped back, nearly tripping over a shovel -- another sign of the ceremony that had, for some reason, been abandoned. Before him a man stood, robed as a village priest.

"I - I am Corporal Latham," he stammered. Then, regaining his wits, he bowed hurriedly. "Begging your pardon, sir, but I was startled. I did not hear you come up behind me, even in the sudden silence following our captain's shout."

"My pardon, then, *Caporal*," the priest answered, turning and leading him to the square where the captain waited. "I am Charles Devinette, *curé* of the church where I came out a side door. Here in our village we have become used to moving with little sound, staying inside when our work does not call us out. 'Out of sight, out of mind,' as say the English, yes?"

"Uh, yes," Latham answered. "This is our commander, Captain Pindar. Who, as you may have heard, wishes to let your villagers know that we only wish to camp here for the night. We wish to rest and reprovision ourselves."

The priest nodded, then shook hands with the captain. "My children," he stated, "the flock of my village, wish you no harm either. With your permission I will call them out again, but only for the briefest moment. I will explain to them that you must be sheltered, even as they are sheltered themselves, and that they must each take one or two of you with them into their houses. To let you wait with them..."

The captain shook his head. "Damme!" he said. "You mean what you wish is to separate us -- to get us in small groups where you can kill us? Your language is French, at least what I can make of it, though some of you are Indians by the look of you, I would imagine. Likely most of you, even if you live in white men's houses." The captain smiled then, a bitter, tight-lipped smile. "Probably massacred, those that built them, eh?"

"*Capitaine, non!*" the priest protested. "We massacre no one. We are on neither side! As for our bodies, our language, our ways, we are, all of us, only what life makes us to be, yes? Here in these mountains there are *êtres* -- *things* -- much older than the French or the English. Older than even the Iroquois. They are things that are even more silent than we are, things that strike when the wind dies!"

The wind was indeed silent as the priest suddenly turned, bolting back into the churchyard. Latham followed on the priest's heels at his captain's hasty orders. He ran as quickly as he could, but the priest was faster; they dodged gravestones, jumping over the long, narrow, wicker basket used to carry the newly deceased. Latham deduced that the funeral must have been interrupted when the wind showed signs of stopping its constant hum. They dodged the shovel that Latham had almost tripped over before, and then the priest disappeared through a stout, oaken door in the church's stone side, locking it with a firm click! behind him.

Latham stood, transfixed, as the air became completely stagnant. The leaves of the trees outside the town ceased their constant rustling, and every iota of motion was stilled. Even the murmurs inside were halted -- until a sudden scream rent the air! It came from beyond the village, from the meadow where horses had been taken. Shouts from the men who had been posted with them broke the stillness, followed quickly by the captain's barked orders to form up in ranks. He wanted a defensive square with riflemen inside, and bayonets outside.

Latham turned, running to join them. As he did he spotted something odd over the church roof. The fog from the mountain beyond the village was streaming downward, tendrils already having reached the plateaued grass where the horses had been tied. He galloped on, dashing through the cluttered churchyard when, with a sharp jolt, he felt the earth drop away beneath him.

He landed in darkness. The newly dug grave, with its corpse already in it, had been left unfilled when the gravediggers had hastily dropped their shovels to flee the impending calm. He tried to climb out of it, scrambling up its crumbling side, but his foot was caught in the winding cloth of the corpse's shroud. Latham attempted to extricate it, but he just became more and more entangled.

Overhead the air became heavy and hot with mois-ture, darkening as the fog rolled in behind him. He tried to scream, but no sound would come out. He longed to give some warning, even if he could not join the others. They would be faced outward in their defensive formation to stave off whatever it was that ignored those inside the houses -- out of sight, out of mind, as the curé had said.

The fog would ooze on, steadily winding through the pathways between the houses until it converged on the square. While, in the square itself, behind the men, was another threat -- he tried to scream again, but the words would not come out.

He tried to warn them that, in the square's center, he had seen more danger. Out of the well, where they had been planning just minutes before to refill their canteens, another something was rising. It had appeared haze-like, slowly forming in misted tendrils into some dim shape. It was something long-forgotten, covered in hints of scales and half-rotted tentacles, of bone and horn-like beak, as if of some race of ancient sea creature had been long-trapped beneath the ground. It feared the wind only, as the slightest breeze could tear its fragile form apart and scatter its substance into atoms.

That was why, when that which it feared became still...when all that moved were things filled with blood's sweetness...it hunted.

Latham's scream would not come! He felt a copper tang fill his mouth as he trapped himself even more firmly within the shroud's vise-like embrace, a burst of pain cannoning through his mouth. He fell on the corpse, rolling under it as, in new darkness, he heard the echoes of more screams.

Then silence.

And then, once again, the wind blew. It brought with it the murmur of voices, and soon the villagers fished him out of the unfilled grave. As the French trappers used to

say: Wind portended death for some when it stopped blowing, and for others there was no grave til another end took
them.

...

But now, for Philip Latham, there was neither. The
villagers took him in, an unwitting orphan, and saw to his
hurts. They fed him and clothed him. He became one of
them, working side-by-side with them in the fields. They
found a wife for him; helped him to establish a family.
And always, now, he fled indoors with them when the
wind began to slack in its blowing. He lived like this until
a time came, scarcely twenty years later, when another war
spread to the mountains.

This war, however, was not with the British. This
regular army had raw colonials fighting side by side, and
rather was a struggle against them.

Except in the village, where sides still did not matter.

The priest was long dead by then, unfortunately,
and none could speak English. A detachment of New
Hampshire volunteers, under Captain Nathaniel Flambard,
arrived at a time when the wind was once again beginning
to die down. As for the villagers, even their French had become unintelligible by then to anyone but themselves. And
so, this time, they could give no warning. Even when the
new captain screamed as he stood in the village square, the
well behind him and his troops arrayed with him in loose
formation, they could say nothing. The captain looked for
someone, anyone, who could speak English, but found

naught.

"We wish not to harm you," he shouted. "We wish only for provisions. To fill our canteens here, to rest for the night and then to be on our way."

Some who remembered the last time soldiers arrived brought Latham out to the square. He stood a moment, remembering when he too was a soldier. He attempted to give them some word or some sign, to make the captain understand that his men were in danger, but he scurried back inside when the other villagers did.

Just before the wind stopped completely one of the other officers turned to his captain.

"What do you make of it, Nate?" he asked.

The captain shrugged. "The whole village is mad, and stupid, from what I can gather. That man, the one who stood here, seemed the worst of them all. Harmless enough now, I assume, but something must have happened years back that gave him quite the fright. Did you see the inside of his mouth when he tried to talk?"

The soldier nodded. "That blackened stump? Aye, sir. I wonder if we shall ever know what happened, what could have frightened a man so much that he would bite his own tongue off."

JAMES DORR
ABOUT THE AUTHOR

James Dorr's latest book is a novel-in-stories from Elder Signs Press, TOMBS: A CHRONICLE OF LATTER-DAY TIMES OF EARTH. An Indiana (USA) writer and poet working mostly in dark fantasy/horror with forays into science fiction and mystery, his THE TEARS OF ISIS was a 2013 Bram Stoker Award® finalist for Superior Achievement in a Fiction Collection, while other books include STRANGE MISTRESSES: TALES OF WONDER AND ROMANCE, DARKER LOVES: TALES OF MYSTERY AND REGRET, and his all-poetry VAMPS (A RETROSPECTIVE). Dorr is an active member of SFWA and HWA, and has in earlier times been a technical writer, an editor on a regional magazine, a full time non-fiction freelancer, and a semi-professional musician. He currently harbors a Goth cat named Triana.

Moonshadow Monster
Gina Easton

"I think we're lost," Eric said.

Alex shifted her gaze from the road to briefly glance at her son. He sat in the passenger seat beside her, anxiously staring at the unfamiliar countryside around them.

Dusk was quickly deepening into night. Damn it, Alex thought angrily. They should have been there an hour ago. She tried to figure out where they went wrong, which exit sign they could have missed, but the answer eluded her. Strange, though; she prided herself on being a confident driver, always good with directions, and with Eric watching the road like a hawk it was unusual for them both to have missed the turn-off.

Still, here they were, driving through completely unfamiliar territory with the shadow of night hovering over them. The green road sign, illuminated in the flashing of the car's headlights, told her that the nearest town was fifteen miles away. Mike would have a good laugh when he found out just how far afield they had strayed.

Suddenly the car lurched and heaved, listing heavily to the right side. Alex could hear something crunching under the wheels, and an unmistakable pop as air burst from the rear tire.

"What's that, Mom?" Eric asked, the anxious expression deepening on his face.

Alex rolled her eyes, cursing inwardly. "Flat tire," she said tersely. Signals flashing she pulled over to the side of the road, grabbing the flashlight from the glove compartment. She got out of the car and hurried to inspect the damage. Just as she'd thought: The right, rear tire had a gaping puncture, air continuing to leak from it as it slowly flattened to pancake status.

"Great!" Alex sighed in exasperation. "Just what we need." As if their luck hadn't been bad enough already, now they were stranded in some God-forsaken area with the night breathing over their shoulder. She grabbed her cell phone from her purse, sighing at the screen contemptuously. Of course she would find out, just when she thought things couldn't get any worse, that there was no service available.

The passenger door slammed, and Eric joined her at the rear of the car.

Alex smiled at him wanly. "Well, Sport, you feel like flexing those muscles of yours? How about helping me change the tire? There should be a spare in the trunk." *I hope to God Mike remembered to put the spare tire in,* she prayed. *Shit. I should've checked before we left the house.*

Eric didn't answer her. He was staring at the flat tire, at what was caught underneath it.

"Mom?" He asked in a shaky voice. "What's that?"

Alex looked to where her son pointed, fighting to suppress a shudder. There was some sort of animal, or, more precisely, the remains of an animal, pinned beneath the tire.

She took the flashlight and moved closer to inspect it. The animal was impossible to identify, so ripped and mangled was the body. Peering down at it Alex realized that it was really just a loose amalgam of skin and bones. Everything else, such as the muscle, fat tissue, and viscera, was gone, as though the contents had been sucked out of the frail body by a vacuum. It was one of the sharp, spindly bones that had punctured the tire.

Alex straightened up, turning away in revulsion. "I don't know what happened to that animal, but it was already dead when we hit it. At least I don't have that on my conscience."

Eric was staring strangely at the corpse. "It's weird, isn't?" he said hollowly. "It's like something just turned it inside-out, then ripped everything apart." He turned to his mother, his pale face illuminated in the soft moonlight. "But you know the weirdest thing of all, Mom? There isn't any blood. Not one drop."

Several minutes later Alex was rooting through the trunk of the car, searching for a newspaper or cloth, *anything*, to wipe away the grisly remains from the tire. She didn't mind the aggravation of changing a tire out in the middle of nowhere, but she wasn't about to contaminate herself with any disease-infested, dead animal leftovers.

Eric stood silently by, glancing nervously over his shoulder from time to time. Alex looked up from her search, impatiently brushing stray strands of her dark-blonde, shoulder-length hair from her eyes.

"Eric," she said in exasperation, "I could use a little help here."

He started, looking at his mother guiltily. "Sorry, Mom. But do you think it's such a good idea to change the tire ourselves? Maybe we could go for help."

Alex gazed at him incredulously. "Go for help?" she repeated. "You saw that sign, right? The nearest town is fifteen miles away. What're we supposed to do, walk there? In case you didn't notice," she added sarcastically, "it's dark."

"I know, Mom." Eric shivered, despite the warmth of the summer's night air. "But I just don't think we should stay here."

Alex examined her son more closely, noting how young and vulnerable he appeared right now. Normally eleven year-old Eric was quite mature, some might even say precocious, but now, with his goosebumpy arms crossed over his thin chest, he resembled a much younger version of himself. A frightened version.

"Eric, what's wrong?" Alex asked, concern creeping into her voice. She knew that Eric was an extremely sensitive child, and she thought that the sight of the mutilated animal had upset him more than he cared to admit. She came around the side of the car and put both her arms around him in a reassuring hug.

"It's hard to explain," he whispered, his breath cold against her cheek. "It's just a feeling I have. A creepy feeling, like we're not safe out here, like whatever killed that animal might still be around."

Alex felt a chill slide down her spine as some of her son's fear transferred itself to her. She'd been so busy worrying about the flat tire that she hadn't stopped to consider the implications of the dead animal, but Eric was right. Something had killed that animal in a vicious, savage fashion, and she didn't particularly want to find out what had done it.

That would be a fitting end to an exasperating, awful day, she thought. To be attacked by some maddened creature, a bear most likely, would be just peachy. She straightened up, surveying the country-side. *I must take charge,* she thought, as she felt her son's trembling beneath her hands. *I have to show him that we're in no danger.*

Suddenly her eyes lighted on a single dwelling in the distance, off to her left. A small farmhouse sat at the top of a gentle hill, a weak light glowing from its windows. *Definitely within walking distance.*

"There," she pointed, relief flooding her. "We can go over to that house and ask for help. At the very least they'll have a phone, and maybe we can call a repair service tonight. Even give your dad a call and tell him all about our adventure."

Eric looked doubtfully at the farmhouse, but his expression brightened a little.

"Will we have to go through those woods?" he asked, a tremor lacing his tone.

Alex cast a glance towards the trees. "I'm afraid so, Sport. It's the only way to get there, but it's not such a big deal," she replied reassuringly. "The woods aren't too dense, and at least we'll have enough light." She looked at the sky with its smattering of stars. "It's a full moon tonight."

They set off at a brisk pace through the trees, Alex holding the flashlight. She was ready to flick it on, just in case, but the moonlight was sufficient to guide them. The woods were eerily silent as they moved through them, no bird songs or animal cries penetrated the dark layer of night. Eric trotted beside her, clasping her hand tightly as his head swivelled from left to right, alert for any alarming noise or movement.

"This is the kind of night they love," he whispered.

"Who?" Alex asked curiously.

"The monsters, creatures. Whatever you want to call them."

Alex stole a glance at her son to see if he was joking, but his small face, with the sprinkling of freckles across his nose, was pinched and pale. His hazel eyes were wide with fear.

"Eric! I always thought you had an overactive imagination, but this takes the cake! You see what comes of watching too many horror movies?" She tried to humour him out of his fear. "I suppose you expect to see Jason in his hockey mask come leaping out of the trees at any moment?"

"No, Mom," Eric replied, tight-lipped.

It wasn't Jason, Freddy or any of the other larger-than-life celluloid villains that he feared; nor was it the plastic, special-effects psychos with their maniacal, leering grins. It was something much older, something primitive and feral and cunning beyond belief that he dreaded. There was something driven only by a deep thirst, a bloodlust and an insatiable hunger for human flesh, hovering in the peripherals of his mind.

He stumbled over an errant tree root and cried out loudly, his hoarse voice ringing out in the deathly still night. Beside him Alex jumped, then shook his hand furiously. "Jesus, Eric will you calm down? The last thing we need is for one of us to sprain an ankle because you're spooked!"

Eric looked contrite, but miserable. "I'm sorry, Mom," he whispered. "Now it'll know where we are. It'll track us down."

Alex rolled her eyes. "What are you talking about, Eric? There's nothing following us."

"The werewolf," Eric said.

Alex laughed shortly. "*Werewolf?* Eric, honey, come on. Even with your imagination you can't actually believe in werewolves."

"That animal --- " Eric began.

"Was killed by a bear," Alex said firmly. "I'm sure

there are bears in these woods from time to time, but they rarely attack people." At least to God, I hope they don't, she thought. "Anyway, that bear is probably miles away from here by now."

Eric looked skeptically at his mother. There was a slight crackling noise behind them. "Did you hear that?" he asked sharply.

"Probably just a couple of twigs falling."

Another noise, closer this time, was followed by panting and snuffling.

"Mom!" Eric exclaimed, panic rising in his voice.

The snuffling turned into a rhythmic growling.

"Run!" Eric screamed, pulling at his mother's hand. Without thinking Alex found herself in a desperate flight through the woods, careening helter-skelter as brambles and branches tore at her face. Behind them came the sound of something crashing through the woods in pursuit, something large.

Alex had only one coherent thought in her mind: **Get Eric to safety.**

After what seemed like ages they arrived at the farmhouse, both of them pounding furiously on the front door. After a heart-stopping moment it opened, light spilling forth as they stumbled inside. A tall man, dressed in dungarees and cradling a shotgun, stared calmly at them.

"Oh!" Alex gasped, trying to get her breath. Looking at the gun she wondered if they'd traded a bad situation for an even worse one. Eric slammed the door shut and stood beside his mother, both of them staring warily back at the man.

He gazed at them for another moment, sizing them up, before lowering the gun. "Would you mind slipping the bolt on the door, boy?" he asked casually. "No telling what might come bustin' in this time of night."

Alex had regained some of her composure and was smoothing down her tangled hair. She noticed that her blouse had numerous little rips and snags from where the brambles had torn the fabric, and the two of them were a bit of a mess.

"We're awfully sorry for barging in on you like this," she tried to explain, "but our car broke down, so we headed for your place through the woods. My son has an overactive imagination, and…well, he thought that… something was chasing us," she finished weakly, a tight laugh escaping her.

The man, who looked to be in his mid-sixties, continued to evaluate them, his expression stoic. "Would you folks like to sit down?"

"Uh…yes, thank you," Alex replied uncertainly, taking the proffered seat by the empty fireplace. "I'm Alex Conway, and this is my son Eric. We were on our way to visit some relatives, distant cousins actually, on my husband's side --- "

"You say your car broke down?" the man interrupted.

"Yes. A flat tire."

The man nodded. "Name's Meredith," he said.

"Well, pleased to meet you, Mr. Meredith. I don't want to put you to any unnecessary trouble, so if I could just use your phone to call a garage --- "

"Can't," Meredith said curtly.

"You don't have a phone?" Alex asked incredulously.

"Of course I have a phone, but it won't do you no good tonight. The nearest service station is Fred's, and he closes at six pm. It's now," he looked at his watch, "going on nine-thirty."

Alex stared at him in dismay. "Isn't there any other repair shop around?"

Meredith shook his head. "This isn't like the city, you know. Small towns like this, we close early. People like to go to bed early, get up early."

"Well, can I use your phone anyway? I'd like to call my husband."

"It's in the kitchen, to your left." The man was watching Eric, who was gazing anxiously out through the curtains of the front window.

"See anythin', boy?"

Eric turned around and shook his head.

"But you saw somethin' in the woods?"

"Not exactly," Eric replied hesitatingly. "But I heard it. My mom did too, only she pretended it was twigs falling."

"Ah. What do *you* think it was?" The man's eyes bore into him with their intensity. Eric looked straight into that gaze, and held it. "A werewolf."

Meredith's eyes flickered slightly, but he didn't flinch or show any other sign of surprise.

Just then Alex re-entered the room. "Damn," she said.

"No answer. I forgot tonight is the night your father plays soccer, and he'll probably be out for a while with his buddies."

"You from the city?" Meredith inquired.

"Yes," Alex responded.

"It'd take you a couple hours at least to drive back there, but you don't even have a car. You might as well stay the night, I've plenty of room."

Alex gazed around the sparsely-furnished living room, shivering involuntarily. "That's very nice of you, Mr. Meredith." She glanced in her son's direction. Eric had relaxed slightly in the last few minutes. No way was she going to get him to go through those woods again, even if she could persuade Meredith to help her change the tire. However, she sensed that if she made that request she would be turned down flatly. Besides, she'd been driving for ages; her neck and shoulders ached, and she was perturbed by the events of this frustrating day. She didn't relish the thought of a long drive back to the city tonight, having to explain everything to Mike...who would just find the whole escapade very amusing.

Yet she didn't feel at ease with this strange, taciturn man. Under ordinary circumstances she would never agree to stay the night at a stranger's house. *But,* she reminded herself, *these aren't ordinary circumstances.*

"You folks hungry?" Meredith asked.

Eric and Alex nodded. It seemed like ages since they'd last eaten.

"Just let me fasten them shutters, then I'll fix you up

something." Meredith spared a cursory glance out the front window before he carefully fastened the shutters.

Alex watched as he prepared them a simple meal, content to stand off to the side after he declined her offer of assistance.

"Do you live here alone? Or is there a Mrs. Meredith?"

The man paused briefly for a moment, laying down the knife he was using to slice bread for their sandwiches. "Once upon a time," he replied. "I'm a widower now."

"Oh," Alex said, her eyes downcast. "I'm sorry."

They ate in silence, Eric gulping most of his first sandwich in a few bites before reaching for another. When they had finished Meredith sat back in his chair, and stretching his legs out he lit a pipe. He blew smoke lazily for a few minutes before saying, "Your son says you were chased by a werewolf tonight."

Alex laughed uncomfortably, slightly embarrassed as she glanced at her son. "Yeah, I know." She shrugged her shoulders. "Kids, right?" She tried to steer the subject away from Eric's 'monsters'. "Do you have any children, Mr. Meredith?"

"I had a son." He paused, blowing more smoke rings. "He's gone, too."

Alex winced. Twice now, in the space of just a few minutes, she had succeeded in reminding the old man of the two greatest losses of his life. *No more personal questions*, she chided herself.

Meredith fixed his flinty gaze upon her, grey eyes unreadable. "Werewolf killed him."

Eric gasped. He turned pale, instantly beginning to tremble.

Alex gawked at the man. "Mr. Meredith!" she exclaimed indignantly "I hardly think that's a thing to joke about. I don't approve of you frightening my son like that, nor making fun of his imagination."

"It's God's own truth," Meredith replied matter-of-factly. "And as for being frightened, well it makes perfect sense for your son to be frightened. And if you had a little more sense, lady, you'd be scared too. Especially seeing as how you had a near miss with that thing out there tonight."

"You see Mom, I told you! It was a werewolf!" Eric cried.

Alex jumped to her feet, furious. "Listen, mister," she said. "I don't know what twisted game you're playing, but if you get off on scaring little boys then we'll just leave right now, night or no night." She grabbed her purse. "Come on, Eric. Let's go!"

"Mom, no! We can't go out there!" Eric screamed, a look of terror on his face. "The werewolf will get us!"

Alex lost all patience. "For God's sake, Eric! How many times do I have to say it? There are no such things as --- "

A piercing howl cut through the night.

Alex froze, feeling her blood slow to an icy trickle in her veins. She had never heard a noise quite like it in her life. It was an ululation of power, of triumph and hunger. Yet it was somehow sorrowful, as if the great creature were trying to shake off a nagging hurt that gnawed away at its core. Eric crouched on the sofa, shoulders hunched as though shielding himself against the eerie sound. It issued again, louder and even more chilling.

Meredith sat in his rocking-chair, never missing a beat. He cocked an eyebrow at Alex, as if to say *I told you so.*

She lifted a shaky hand to her head, smoothing back a lock of hair that hung down over her face. She cleared her throat.

"So what, you have wolves in these woods," she stated, striving for a normal, calm tone. Meredith's craggy face never changed expression from its wooden neutrality. "Not wolves, one creature only. Every living thing in those woods stays far away from it. Everything that's still alive, that is."

"And you honestly expect me to believe that there's a *werewolf* lurking in the forest?" Alex's short laugh sounded hollow.

"Lady, I really don't care what in Hell you believe. It's not my business to convince you one way or another, but you're the ones who barged into my home uninvited, and you asked me those questions. And you were chased by something out there tonight."

"It was just a feral dog, or maybe a bear," Alex said stubbornly.

Meredith spread his hands, smoke billowing as he gestured with the pipe. "Fine, but I advise you not to go out there again tonight. Especially not tonight. The moon's full, you know."

Silence descended among the three of them, eerily contrasting with the spine-tingling howl of a moment before. Eric seemed to have recovered slightly from his fear, now that he understood exactly what kind of danger they faced. He looked intently at Meredith and pointed.

"I hope you got silver bullets in that gun, mister."

For the first time since they'd met Meredith smiled, a grin that threatened to crack his leathery skin.

"The finest sterling in the county, boy," he replied.

"Have you ever shot a werewolf before?" Eric asked curiously.

Alex sighed and shook her head, sitting down once more. Plainly the old man was off his rocker. She supposed it wouldn't do any harm to humour him in his delusion; she couldn't very well argue with him all night. She only hoped he didn't scare Eric any more than he already had.

"Shot at him once. Missed, though," Meredith responded.

"Did you get a good look at him?" Eric's tone was eager as he forgot his fear in the excitement of the moment.

"Sure I did. It was a night similar to this, when the moon was full. The night that monster got my boy, Jack." A frown, that might have been of pain, furrowed the man's brow.

"I'll never forget that creature as long as I live," he continued. "It was tall, almost seven foot, and covered all over with dark, bristly fur. It walked upright, like a man, with a sort of loping gait. It weren't no man though."

Meredith's eyes, glittering with intensity at the memory, looked almost silver-coloured in the glow from the lamp on the table. "I caught one glimpse of its face, but one glimpse was enough to give me nightmares for a long time after. If it had ever once been a man, there were no traces of humanity left. It had the expression of a mad creature who'd looked into the very flames of Hell and *liked* what it saw. Its eyes glowed red, as though it had absorbed those Hellish fires."

He paused for a moment, taking a drag of the pipe before he carried on.

"And it was *hungry*. A gleam of lust still shone from its eyes, even though its snout and most of the thing's body was dripping with blood and gore. My son's blood. It wanted more. And you knew that, however much it got, however much it killed, it would never be enough to satisfy that terrible hunger for human flesh and thirst for human blood. It ripped Jack apart, then flung him aside like he was no more than a broken rag-doll. I had the presence of mind to grab my shotgun before it could charge at me, but I guess the shock must've warped my aim and I clean missed the thing. Managed to scare it off, though, send it lurching back to the woods for cover."

Alex shivered, wrapping her arms tightly around herself. Despite the craziness of the story Meredith sounded so convincing. Could he really have made up something so horrific on the spot? Maybe he had been so grief-stricken over his son's death that his mind had invented this grisly delusion, and now nothing could shake him from this mad belief. Most likely his son had been killed by a bear, or maybe a coyote.

"For more than a year I been waiting for that thing to attack again. So far it's made do killin' off other animals, livestock, pets, whatever it can get. The Millbournes down the road lost their two mastiffs to that werewolf. I tried goin' after it a few times, but it's too damn cunning. Knows how to hide itself real good. It's been bidin' its time, but it's out tonight. Knows you're here, likely followed your scent right to my door. I got a feelin' tonight's the night. It won't be able to resist the new blood scent, especially when there's sweet child's blood to be got."

There was an appalled silence. Alex was becoming increasingly nervous, and she was surprised that Eric hadn't totally freaked out yet. She was rapidly approaching that point herself. *I have to remain calm*, she admonished herself. *The crazier Meredith gets the more rational I have to remain.*

Eric watched the old man intently. To Alex's amazement he seemed less frightened now than when they'd arrived at the crazy old coot's house.

"Hasn't anybody else tried to kill it?" he questioned.

Meredith snorted pipe smoke through his nose. "Some folk refuse to believe it exists. They prefer to make up stories about how their livestock get killed, stories about how so many animals around here are found dead --- all tore up and mangled. The ones who do believe are too scared to do anything but stay locked up in their houses after dark, particularly on a full moon night. They got their shotguns seated across their laps, listenin' for the slightest noise. It wasn't their son who got killed before their very eyes."

Alex wished she could find some way to shift the conversation, and she wished she was anywhere but there. She hated being stuck out in the middle of nowhere with her son and a delusional man, one with a shotgun who was talking about killing some dangerous, rabid animal that was lurking in the nearby woods. This 'werewolf' topic was disturbing and unhealthy for an eleven year-old boy, but both Eric and Meredith were fascinated by it and showed no inclination to discuss anything else. She didn't like the feverish look in Eric's eyes, and she had to admit that she was alarmed by the obsessive glint in the old man's eyes. What if he took it upon himself to go werewolf hunting in the middle of the night, shotgun blasting in the dark-drenched forest?

She stood up. "I'm going to try to call Mike again," she announced. "Maybe if I tell him exactly where we are he could borrow a car and come pick us up."

"Shh! Quiet!" Meredith's harsh whisper stopped her in her tracks. "I heard something. Outside."

They froze, six ears listening intently.

"Boy," Meredith said softly, motioning to Eric, "move slowly over here, towards me. I want you far away from that window, just in case."

Eric glanced over his shoulder at the shuttered window, then gingerly crept on tip-toe to the old man's side

"I didn't hear anything," protested Alex, her voice also low. Meredith waved her to silence as he got to his feet, swiftly and silently reaching for the shotgun.

All three of them stood in frozen tableau, the only sound their uneven breathing. The minutes dragged by, agonizing in their slowness. Alex watched her son as he stood in the shadow of the big man. Instinctively he'd gone to stand by Meredith, rather than his mother. She felt a fleeting sense of hurt, but she forced herself to ignore it.

Eric was pale, poised like a hare ready to take flight at the slightest danger. She was conscious of her nails digging into the palms of her tightly-clenched fists, and she didn't know how much longer she could stand this. Any second now she'd have to start singing, dancing, screaming, anything to break the spell.

Then an ear-splitting crack came from the kitchen, accompanied by the sound of glass shattering.

Meredith moved so fast he was like a blur before Alex's eyes.

"Stay here," he snapped as he raced towards the kitchen.

"Mom!" Eric screamed, running to Alex's side.

"Come on," Alex urged, grabbing her son's hand and heading for the kitchen. The thought of staying behind in this room was unbearable; she had to see what was happening.

In the kitchen they found the window shutter torn nearly out of its frame, one corner left dangling awkwardly. Bits of splintered wood and broken glass lay scattered over the countertops and floor. The back door was ripped from its hinges, exposing the deep, encroaching shadows of night.

There was no sign of Meredith, but from somewhere close by came the sounds of a fierce struggle. From the noises carried back to them on the preternaturally still air it sounded like a very large animal indeed. Angry snarls and growls tore through the air like bullets, then there was the sharp retort of the shotgun.

"Oh my God," Alex murmured, frantically searching the room for some place to take cover.

Another gun blast assaulted their ears, followed by a third. Then came a high-pitched scream of agony, whether animal or human it was impossible to tell. A shiver of fear bolted down Alex's spine. She grabbed Eric and pushed him behind her, then lunged forward to grab a hefty knife from the rack on the counter. As she turned back to face the gaping entrance a large shadow loomed in the doorway.

The scream froze in Alex's throat as she saw Meredith stumble through the entry.

His face was ash-pale, but triumphant as he raised the still-smoking shotgun in a kind of salute.

"Got him!" he gasped, staggering towards a chair. He collapsed into the seat, Alex helping to ease him down.

Eric dashed over to the old man. "Did you really kill him?" He asked, wide-eyed.

Meredith nodded wearily. "I did, boy. He was a tough old son-of-a-bitch, took two shots full in the gut before the third one finally blew his head off." His tone was one of deep satisfaction.

Eric whistled in admiration. "Awesome! Can I go out

and see?"

"Eric!" Alex said sharply. "You'll do no such thing." Her attention returned to the old man, and for the first time she noticed the bloodstains that seeped through the left shoulder of his shirt.

"You've been injured," she said in alarm.

Meredith briefly surveyed himself. "Guess I have," he responded matter-of-factly.

"We should get you to a doctor. We don't know how serious that wound might be, and at the very least you'll probably need a rabies shot. Do you have an emergency number out here, or is it better if we just take your car to the nearest hospital?"

He didn't respond, so Alex busied herself gathering clean cloths and warm water as she tried to organize a plan. "Where's your disinfectant?"

"Don't have any," Meredith finally snapped as he gingerly removed his shirt to inspect the damage.

"No disinfectant? Well, that's ridiculous. Everyone should have at least a rudimentary first-aid kit," Alex chided. "Especially you, living so far from any major centre."

Meredith just glared at her as she brought the water and cloths over to the table.

"Wow!" Eric exclaimed as he got a good look at the deep claw marks that had gouged through Meredith's shoulder. "Those are something wicked!"

"They're definitely nasty," Alex agreed, her hands shaking slightly as she dabbed warm water onto the lacerations. "You're going to need stitches."

Meredith winced, gritting his teeth as the warm, soapy water penetrated his torn skin.

"Look! Your hand's bleeding too," Eric pointed out.

They all looked at his left hand, where several large tooth-marks showed just above the wrist.

"Oh, damn," Alex said. "Now you really will need those rabies shots. We should get to the hospital as quickly as possible, since a bite like that really needs medical attention." She stopped as she saw the intense look exchanged between Meredith and her son.

"What is it?" she asked, puzzled.

"Nothin', Mrs. Conway. Nothin' for you to worry about," Meredith replied softly. He gently took the cloth from her hands and finished cleaning the lacerations to his shoulder, then he tore a strip off and bound it round his injured hand, quick and neat as can be.

"Served as a medic in the army," he offered to Alex's quizzical expression.

"You know, I been thinkin'," he continued. "You two should just take my truck and drive to the nearest town for the rest of the night. It's only fifteen miles away, and they got a pretty good motel. It's probably a lot more comfortable than what I got to offer, and it's goin' to be kind of busy around here for the next while. I gotta get the sheriff out here to take a look at that thing I killed. There's gonna be a lot of questions, and you folks won't get any sleep at all if you stay here."

"Well…"Alex said hesitantly, though secretly relieved at not having to spend the remainder of the night in this creepy farmhouse, "If you don't mind lending us your truck we could drop you off at the hospital."

"No need," Meredith responded. "The sheriff can do that. Like I said, he's gonna want some answers. He's gonna have to see this thing with his own eyes to believe it. At least he'll finally realize that folks around here have been tellin' the truth about that creature in the woods."

Alex sighed. "You still say it's a werewolf?"

Meredith's steely gaze never wavered. "I'd show you where it's layin' out there, but you'll have to excuse me if I say I'm feelin' kind of weak right about now."

Alex held up her hand. "That's all right, Mr. Meredith. I wouldn't dream of traipsing through these woods in the dead of night, let alone dragging you back out there. Those wounds are proof enough that something pretty savage attacked you. I only hope there aren't any more of them out there," she finished with a shudder.

The old man smiled grimly. "I promise you there won't be."

...

Meredith handed Alex the ignition keys as she climbed into the truck, "Sure you know how to drive this thing?" he asked.

Alex smiled. "Yes, Mr. Meredith. We city girls can do some things, you know. As a matter of fact, I learned to drive a truck before I drove a car. My dad had a truck similar to this one, and he taught me how to drive. Tomorrow we'll be back with your truck, and we'll bring a repairman from that garage in town you mentioned."

Meredith smiled wanly as he reached across to shake Eric's hand solemnly. "Well, boy, was this your first encounter with a monster?"

"Yes," Eric answered.

"It won't be your last, I'll wager. People like you and me, those who believe in monsters, we always come up against 'em from time to time. Don't forget to be on the look-out."

"Yes sir, "Eric replied somberly.

Both mother and son watched as the old man walked back to his house, closing the door behind him.

"God, what a strange character," Alex remarked as she pulled out of the driveway. "I wonder how he's going to explain that dead animal to the sheriff?"

"He won't have to," Eric said. Alex glanced over, surprised at his grim tone. She was even more startled to see tears trickling down his cheek.

"Honey, what's wrong?" she asked, her foot lightly touching the brake pedal.

Eric turned to her, an anguished expression on his face. "Oh, Mom! Don't you know why he wanted us to leave?"

Alex looked confused, shaking her head slightly, "What do you mean? He thought it'd be better for us if we stayed in town, and under the circumstances I can understand why."

Eric shook his head despairingly. "No, Mom. That's not the reason at all. You don't get it, do you? He was bitten by a werewolf. Don't you know what that means?"

"N…no. Wait, what?" An alarm sounded faintly at the back of her mind.

"It means that he's gonna turn into a werewolf. The victim of a werewolf bite, if they survive, always turns into a werewolf."

"That's ridiculous! You can't…He can't believe that's true."

"Of course he believes it, Mom. That's why he's gonna do the only thing he can to stop it: He's gonna kill himself with a silver bullet."

"Oh my God!" Alex cried, bringing the truck to a full stop. She jumped out of the cab and started the climb up the driveway. *That crazy, deluded old fool.* She had to get to him, had to stay with him until the sheriff arrived. Hopefully she could take the sheriff aside and explain Meredith's peculiar delusion.

As she neared the house a single shotgun blast rang out in the night.

Alex stumbled in her tracks. "No, no. Oh my God," she whispered.

She heard soft footsteps, then Eric's cold hand was in hers. Her arm encircled his shoulders as she hugged him to her. Alex watched the tears run unchecked down his small face, and she was dimly aware of a burning sensation behind her own eyes.

"He had to do it, Mom," Eric whispered brokenly. "I would've done the same thing."

Wordlessly, heart clenching in sorrow and fear, she

pulled her son even closer, wishing she could somehow shove him back inside her womb where he would be protected and safe forever. As the tears fell steadily from her eyes she looked up at the house, wearily wondering how she was going to explain all this to the sheriff.

GINA EASTON
ABOUT THE AUTHOR

Gina Easton is a writer who, after working for many years as a registered nurse, has finally decided to pursue her long-time goal of becoming an author. She has had several short-stories accepted for publication in horror anthologies and magazines.

She also has two horror /dark fantasy novels due for release in 2020.

PROPAGATE
CAMERON ULAM

Someone outside was tugging on the zipper of the tent—it rattled in protest, creeping down from the top in staccato bursts. The young boys inside—none of whom wished to reveal his terror to the others—watched wide-eyed and silent as the jagged entrance parted. No other sound came from outside, except the quiet whispers of the wind. The zipper suddenly jammed on some invisible barrier, and shadowy hands reached in, gripping and stretching the sides of the slit until it was wide open. There was audible grunting as something leaned its head in through the dark, flapping entrance.

"Gotcha!" Martin Stoker's face flashed to life within the gaping entryway; with the help of a plastic flashlight positioned under his chin, he achieved a perfect, spooky angle that caught the shadows just right.

Martin watched with a chuckle as half of the boys within flattened themselves to the back wall of the flimsy tent; two in the back grabbed one another, erupting into a chorus of harmonized shrieks. Martin's son Jasper, on the other hand, sat straight up, glaring at his father as he reached for his own cheap flashlight; the boy clicked it on, flicking it upwards to shoot a beam directly into the eyes of his father. Martin laughed, throwing up an arm to guard his eyes, "Hey, hey, alright, I give," he said, sticking his hands up in surrender.

"You promised, Dad" Jasper whispered, his shining, wet eyes peeking from their corners at his friends; the boy's hands were clutched into tight fists.

Martin deflated—he had promised. It had only been a few months since Jasper had joined the Boy Scout ranks, but his son had taken the commitment seriously from day one. Jasper had always been a creative child; there had once been a time when Jasper had proudly plastered the family fridge to capacity with his own drawings and paintings. Things had been different ever since his son's first day of middle school—Jasper had begun the slow descent into the murky puddle of tweenhood. Painting and drawing were replaced by all things rustic: camping fires, survival techniques, you name it. Martin had been hesitant—the Scouts was by no means a perfect organization—but, regardless, he had signed Jasper up the week his son had first begged him to join.

Martin smiled humbly, "You're right pal, and I'm sorry. I'll leave you guys be." He tossed them the flashlight, "Just in case yours short-circuits." With a wink Martin turned to begin the short, but steep, trek up the hill to the house. He turned to look back once at the glowing tent, but found his gaze extending beyond the yard, focusing instead on the dark woods surrounding their home. Wind whirled through the trees with a low sigh, and Martin stood staring at the shifting, black pines, their synchronized movement mesmerizing him.

He shook his head, freeing his gaze, and thought to himself that the forest was a comparatively safer place than the city—no murderers on the loose, no pedophiles wandering dark streets corners—the boys were safe out here. He turned, his boots squishing into the soft earth, making quite smacking sounds as he plodded back up the hill to the house. The swaying trees whispering secrets behind his back.

The boys sat, huddled in a tight circle, each taking his own turn to spout off a spooky campfire tale he'd picked up from last year's trip to summer camp. Holding flashlights to light their pale faces story after spooky story filled the tent, the flimsy walls shivering quietly around them.

One of Jasper's closest friends, Richie, snatched the flashlight from another boy's hands after the story had come to a bum ending. He held the flashlight in proper position under his chin, narrowing his eyes and tilting his head down at a menacing angle, "And now, a story to chill your BONES!" he boomed, furrowing his brow and twisting his mouth into a maniacal grin. "This is a local legend, folks, so cover your ears if you'd like to sleep tonight!"

Jasper snorted at his friend, "Oh, this should be good," he said. That past school year Richie's voice had deepened seemingly overnight into a low, manly rasp, and in turn his arrogance had deepened with it. Everyone at school seemed to love and appreciate his friend's new found confidence and charisma—Jasper, on the other hand, despised it.

Richie sneered at Jasper, "We'll see who pisses themselves first, man," Richie laughed, "my dollar's on you." He pointed his flashlight at Jasper's crotch. The boys in the huddle burst into a frenzy of laughter; Jasper reddened, reaching over to swat the flashlight from his friend's hand, but Richie pulled it from his reach. "Eh eh eh," he said, smiling, his eyes mean-spirited as he wiggled the light tauntingly.

Jasper groaned, "Get on with it then," he said, sitting back on his sleeping bag with a thump and a slightly busted ego.

Richie cast the light back onto his face, "Pardon the interruption folks, we were experiencing some technical difficulties. We are now back to the usual programming." There were hushed snickers from two of the other boys, and Jasper winced as Richie continued. "The chilling tale I have for you tonight is one that has been passed down in this town for generations. For years, the people of Windhoek have whispered tales of others that live among us. According to legend..."

"Your Grandma tell you this one at bedtime?" one of the boys jeered, sending the circle into another fit of giggles.

Richie smiled and went on, "Actually, yes," he shot

the boy who had mentioned his beloved Gam Gam a look, "the story goes that there are creatures who live in the darkest corners of Windhoek forest, and others that walk as imposters among us." He moved the flashlight closer to his mouth, the light bouncing off his teeth with an eerie glow.

"They've earned the name 'Yippers' from the sound they call out into the dark while searching for their next victim. Some think they're aliens, others call them demons. My Gam Gam says they were originally called something by Native American tribes that translates to "Glass Men." It was said that, if you found yourself looking into the eyes of a Glass Man, you would see the creature in human form—a trick of the eye that it uses to gain your trust. The creature would then attempt to take a piece of you—and no, I don't mean a lock of your hair or a fingernail clipping— what it truly desired was a hand, a foot, an ear…anything fleshy. It could use that stolen limb to mirror you…to mold itself into your form: flesh and blood, memories and all."

Richie paused to inhale deeply, "There was a very rich, well-known businessman that went missing back in the 70's. Gone for over two weeks, and a search party scoured these very woods for any sign of him. Three long weeks later someone found him out here—wandering naked in the forest, his foot stitched mysteriously around the ankle. He didn't remember anything surrounding his disappearance, and it was said he simply smiled and laughed while recounting the array of gaps in his memory, attributing the situation to a hearty drinking binge. Years later he went on to become the senator of Pennsylvania for a record-breaking stretch; the man was loved and adored by all—however, those who had known him prior to his disappearance swore something had changed about him. My Gam Gam dated the Senator back in high school. Twenty-some years later, she saw him speak at one of his political rallies. She told me there had been something about him that evening that made her uneasy...yes, the crowd had applauded and called out to him in adoration, but my Gam Gam said his eyes had flickered too much, like an old film reel...and his smile had stretched what seemed to be an inch too wide."

Richie took that moment to flash all his teeth, pulling at one of the corners of his grin with a sharply hooked finger.

"My Gam Gam says anyone from this town who ever got rich and famous, or who became some sort of millionaire, got a piece of them snatched up by one of those monsters somewhere along the way...a slice to their body, here," he slashed a hooked finger theatrically across his ankle, "or maybe here," he held up his middle finger to the group and sawed an imaginary blade over it. The boys in the group cackled; Jasper sat enamored. This was the first time he had heard of these 'glass men'. He leaned forward, shushing the others, his ears pricked and ready for the end of the tale.

Richie lowered his flashlight and clicked it off, pitching the tent back into darkness. Jasper huffed, turning his light on, "That's it? Seriously?" he jeered, "Do you even know what they look like?"

Richie's eyes flickered at the challenge, then relaxed and focused on his friend. He smiled. "No more than you do, pal," he said, "they could look like my Gam Gam for all I know." Richie's expression livened with mischievous inspiration, and in one swoop he passed his gaze over each of the boys in the circle. "Say, fellas," he said, "how do you feel about a late-night hunting trip? Let's find out if the legends are as true as they say!"

The boys glanced at one other from the sides of their eyes, Jasper included; the wind still whined through the trees, and it was getting colder. Each of the boys began to internally weigh the pros and cons of his warm, cozy sleeping bag against some unplanned, not to mention like-ly fruitless, late night trek into the dark forest.

Jasper fumbled for an excuse, "Sounds like a great way to get ourselves lost the day before the merit badge ceremony," he said, hating himself for every word. He was hoping, more than anything, to get his friends off the idea—he didn't like those woods. Ever since he was little he'd had nightmares about those pines gobbling him up.

He had seen a television show once where people talked about their own irrational fears—sometimes of scary things like snakes, other times of dumb things like pickles—but Jasper wasn't afraid of the woods in other places, just the specific set of trees which sat behind his home like rows of dark, swaying giants.

Richie's eyes sparkled. "Let's have a good, old-fash-ioned vote then," he said, sitting up straight to look over the group, "Whoever's too chicken to go, raise your hand."

The group sat still, ogling him and gaping like fish, unsure of what to do; no one raised a finger.

"Alright, then it's settled," Richie said, flashing a Jack-O-lantern grin, "That was easy, eh?" He hopped up onto his heels, grabbing his dirty boots. He began thumbing at the tangled laces, and one by one the others grabbed at their own shoes, pulling them on begrudgingly.

A small current of fear shot up Jasper's spine—base to stem—but he ignored it, instead fumbling for his own boots in the dark tent, "This better be quick, Richie, my dad could walk down to check on us any minute," he said.

"No worries man," Richie replied, nodding, "we'll be back before you know it. It'll be fun—you'll see—and dude," he jabbed Jasper in the ribs with a sharp elbow, "you'll thank me later when everyone at school is talking about what a wild night we had out at Jasper Stoker's place." Richie winked, flashing his charismatic grin; Jasper grimaced, unable to match the enthusiasm in his friend's wide smile.

It was around 3 A.M., and dew clung to the tall blades of glass which swatted their ankles as they trudged deeper into the forest. The darkness hung thickly around them, cut only by the narrow streams of light cast forward into the darkness by plastic flashlights. Everyone held a flashlight, except for one unfortunate soul—Tim Whelby, who had forgotten to plug a fresh D cell in the morning before attending the camp-out. He walked in defeat alongside his friends, watching bright streams of light crisscross and reflect dully off the prickling needles of the trees surrounding them.

Jasper held his flashlight with a firm grip, walking with numb feet and shivering uncontrollably—it felt as though the temperature had suddenly plummeted to below-freezing, which was impossible...it was only September.

He had just finished berating himself for not wearing wool socks when a discernible, but muffled, click echoed from somewhere off in the distance; each of the boys stopped, legs rigid—their ears all pricked. Silence hung around them, the wind licking at the flaps of their thin jackets. A second clicking resounded from their left, this time so substantially close that Jasper glanced down at his mud-speckled boots, thinking that he must have stepped on a dry branch. The floor held nothing but a bed of dusty pine needles.

The orbs of the other flashlights hung lazily in Jasper's peripheral vision, but without warning they suddenly clicked off, one by one.

Confused, he looked up from his shoes and the pine-littered ground; he saw Ritchie smacking a flashlight from the hands of his friend Paul, who looked dumbly down as Richie snatched the thing up from the ground and thumbed it off with a soft click.

It was dark now, and Jasper couldn't see anything beyond the dingy ray of his own light, which wobbled in his shaking hand; what was going on? It was now pitch-black, aside from the small circle of illumination cast by his own light. He pointed the beam towards the spot he had remembered Paul standing—the light fell on nothing but a cloud of dust and barren forest ground. Jasper gulped, "What the Hell is going on? Richie?" His voice was shaking. He folded his left hand over the trembling wrist of the hand which held the flashlight…an attempt to steady the tremoring stream of light cast before him—it jittered like an old film reel.

The forest around him was quiet, except for the whirl of air passing through the trees. Jasper's hand began to shake more violently as adrenaline leaked into his bloodstream. He felt his dinner rise to his throat, and he quickly gulped it back down—his hand was vibrating now, and he felt the plastic handle slide from his grasp and clatter to the ground. He cursed. The light beam sputtered as the flashlight bounced chaotically, allowing Jasper to catch partial sight of two boys kneeling on the forest floor. On its final bounce the cheap flashlight clicked off, and darkness again drew its curtain.

Jasper yelled out to his friends, both arms stretched out in search of any of them. He staggered forward blindly, his hands grasping at the air, when his shin hit something—a knee? He reached down, relieved when his fingers touched the warm shoulder of one of his friends.

"Dude, are you okay?" he gasped, but silence echoed back at him, "Say something!" he yelled, smacking the boy's shoulder, but there was no response. Falling to the ground pine needles slid between his fingers, and he raked them across the loose soil in search of his flashlight; dust billowed around his desperate hand—he coughed violently, then let out a sigh of relief as his hand closed around the cold, plastic handle.

Crouched on the ground Jasper heard a low click at his back; he swiveled, flashlight teetering as he sank his thumb into the soft rubber button—click—the beam illuminated the frightful scene before him.

Tim Welby lay splayed out on the forest floor, blood trickling from his left ear in a thin stream; Richie was hunched over him, his right hand gripping a bone-handled pocket knife. Richie was rowing his arm repetitively, and Jasper felt his consciousness begin to slip when he realized what was happening. His friend was sawing through the flesh of the unconscious boy's ankle with feverish desperation; blood spurted up the front of his Richie's windbreaker as he tore relentlessly with his blade, appearing to attempt a full 360 degree filet around the ankle as he twisted the loosened foot this way and that.

A ray from Jasper's flashlight landed on Richie's face, and his head snapped up to the source; Richie's hand continued to saw without interruption as he smiled wide, his half-crazed eyes darting in their sockets. His friend's skin was white—clammy like death—and his forehead was speckled with sweat. Richie's eyes were lively as he held a hooked finger out to Jasper, slicing it theatrically through the frozen air. Without touching his mouth Richie's smile began to stretch to his cheeks, then out to the side of his ears, rows of impossible teeth gleaming in Jasper's spotlight. A screeching, unnatural laugh—the sound of rusted car parts whining in an old engine—erupted from the back of Richie's throat. Jasper felt a rock of dread clatter to the pit of his stomach, fear binding him where he stood.

The laughter stopped abruptly at that moment, and Richie's massive jaw suddenly unhinged like a snake's, falling to his chest with a soft thump to display the endless rows of pearly canines within. Jasper's eyes did not blink—could not blink– as he watched his murderous friend stagger towards him, light illuminating a nightmarish face as the distance closed between them.

Without warning Richie halted, planting his feet in a wide, awkward stance. He began to wave at Jasper, his hand flopping lazily on its wrist; Jasper could now see soft, yellow stitch marks etched into it, botched transplant work that no self-respecting physician would have ever laid claim to. Jasper looked up into the thing's eyes, his mind screaming as he searched for any lingering sign of Richie left alive within this horrid façade—within this nightmarish parody of his best friend.

The creature glared at Jasper, still waving the false hand like a gruesome flag; however, as Jasper's eye's adjusted to the dim lighting he saw that the monster was not looking at him. It appeared to be gazing over him, into the blackness of the trees. The thing he'd once called Richie raised a milky finger—one that was not its own—to point, its eyes locked somewhere far beyond the spot where Jasper stood.

The glass man parted Richie's lips, sneering in amusement. "Mother's here," it grumbled, voice cracking and eyes flickering with white static as the pointing finger jittered.

A *click* loud enough to shatter his consciousness pierced Jasper's right eardrum, and a thin, frail hand slid in cold comfort over his shoulder. He looked down—eyes straining—and saw the withered hand of an ancient woman gripping his collarbone with decrepitly arthritic fingers. The thick, yellow nails pressed inward and sank into his skin, and he felt warm blood begin to crisscross in rivers down his chest as consciousness fled from him, deserting him in this place of darkness and deception—the place his nightmares had always lived.

...

Martin Stocker woke to the sounds of soft tapping; he rolled over, half asleep to throw his arm over his wife... *just the wind.* He lay there, lids too heavy and mind too foggy to process the mystery noise, let alone investigate it. He felt himself doze off when a heavy rapping on the storm door ripped him from sleep and back to reality. A disturbing feeling of vertigo overcame him, cold, unexplainable dread shooting through his body like ice as he squinted at the clock's glowing orange numbers. 4:00 A.M.

Shivering, he threw the blankets back from his feet and looked over to see that his wife was still fast asleep, her jaw opened as wispy little snores escaped her open mouth. *How can she sleep through that?* He jumped up, planting two feet on the frigid floor. He knew that, if he didn't get up quickly, he was likely to fall back into the plush covers which called out to him. The hall door was open and he slid through it, his bare feet squeaking on uneven floorboards with each step through the darkness. He reached the staircase and felt with his toes for the first step down.

A metallic rapping sound erupted once again from the floor below him; Martin cursed under his breath, glancing back over his shoulder with half-adjusted eyes to see if it had woken his wife—nothing. Turning back to the stairs, with both hands gripping the rail, he descended the dark, uneven staircase of his home like a teetering toddler as the pounding echoed from below.

He reached the ground floor and, all at once, realized that the person at the door could be Jasper. He sighed with relief, silently mocking his own sleepy stupidity as he flipped on the light to the family room.

A yellow glow filled the room, illuminating the back door, and Martin could make out the brown curls of his son's hair through the foggy glass—*Jesus, when had it gotten so cold?* Geometric crystals of ice were beginning to spread over the glass, and they continued to grow as Martin watched in fascination. *The boys must be freezing out there*, Martin thought to himself. The image of six, young Boy Scouts sitting in the E.R., blackened with frostbite, suddenly invaded Martin's thoughts.

He rushed forward, snapping open the lock with a twist and throwing open the heavy door. Martin reached down for the latch on the storm door, and he glanced up to see his son—as if burned, he drew his hand back to his chest reflexively, his breath catching with a sharp inhale.

The boy stood only a few steps outside the door; he was peering through the glass and smiling, but his teeth—too many teeth—were showing through a mouth set much too wide, saliva pooling down his blood-speckled chin. He was waving happily at his father, but the shoddy stitching around his wrist was already beginning to loosen. The small, unstable hand flopped lazily on and off its setting.

The boy's jaw dropped suddenly to his chest, revealing a gaping throat and impossible rows of teeth—Martin screamed as the small, stitched hand suddenly shattered through the thin glass, clamping around his gasping throat. He looked at his son, the whites of his eyes gleaming as he struggled within the boy's inhuman grasp. Jasper held his father, lifting him into the air with an arm that was now much too long; Martin's feet dangled freely, and his vision began to fizzle to black as he heard his son whisper from below—a rusty voice that was not his child's.

"Daddy, where's Mommy?" it growled, squeezing into the flesh of Martin's neck. The eyes flickered with white noise that Martin could now see, and hear—*taste*.

The conscious world left him; his hanging feet went limp, toes drooping lifelessly towards the floor.

The creature suddenly tossed Martin's body to the side of the room; it collided with one of the walls, and there was a *pop* as Martin's neck cracked from the force. His body crumpled to the floor, folding over itself like an old rag doll.

The thing grimaced at the man's lifeless body, taking a staggering, unnatural step towards the dark staircase. Its foot jittered—freeze-framed for a moment—then skipped ahead like damaged film.

It ascended the creaking stairs, white noise bubbling from its tiny throat as it called out for its mother.

CAMERON ULAM
ABOUT THE AUTHOR

Cameron Ulam is a Speech-Language Pathologist residing in a southern suburb of Cleveland, Ohio. An alumna of Kent State University, she received a master's degree in Speech-Language Pathology in 2015 and currently works with children on the autism spectrum to support the development of communication skills. Cameron writes primarily within the genres of horror and speculative fiction; her stories have appeared in audio format on multiple podcasts, including the "Creepy" and "Scare You to Sleep" podcasts. She also has published work in other horror anthologies, including the Midnight in the Pentagram anthology by Silver Shamrock Publishing. Cameron is currently working on a few short, speculative fiction pieces, as well as her first full-length horror novel, which she is looking to complete by the winter of 2020.

Cameron is an avid lover of cats, watercolors, podcasts, and all things terrifying; you can often find her hoarding vintage horror novels from the shelves of her local thrift shop. Find out more about Cameron's latest publications on Instagram/Twitter @ Ulam_Writes or check out her website, Cameronulam.com.

Spirit of the Forest
Ville Meriläinen

O tto Vennamo woke up to a throbbing leg and a splitting headache, and light seared his cracking lids
when he tried to move. His limbs were bound in place, and
any attempt to get up made him lose balance and hit his
head on the frozen trunk of a tree. Icy shrubs stung his face
as the impact made him keel over.

Through the haze in his mind he heard Russian cursing from close by. When a rough hand grabbed him by
the collar, setting him upright, Otto tried to open his eyes
again. Recollection came to him with the sight of a wounded Red Army soldier sitting by a campfire, and another, the
one who'd picked Otto up, circling the fire to sit beside his
comrade. Both were young, around the same age as Otto's
nineteen years.

The Russians had tied him up, but let him keep his
gloves and hat. They'd made a fire out in the open, sug-
gesting they weren't worried of being found. Either that,
or they cared less about being found than they did about

the cold.

This, in turn, suggested they were lost. Otto's unit had ambushed a tank and splintered the escorting enemy squad, but what came after he couldn't remember. One of the Russian soldiers had been shot in the leg. Otto's own was bandaged as well, over the trousers and without a splint, but he appreciated the effort nonetheless. He couldn't remember who'd done that either.

The healthy Russian searched his rucksack and came to Otto with a glass bottle. Otto leaned over for a sip, but spat it out when it burned his mouth. The Russians exchanged a few words in surprised tones, and Otto recognised the taste. He wasn't being poisoned, he'd been offered a gesture of peace.

"*Sorry,*" Otto said, one of the few Russian words he knew. The soldier squatted to his eye level, grinned and spoke. Otto only shrugged, but then nodded at the bottle. The second mouthful of strong vodka didn't taste any better, but it dulled his aches and soothed the cold creeping into his bound limbs.

The Russians held another brief conversation, then the wounded man asked Otto something. He shook his head, and the Russian tried again: "English? You speak?"

"Yes," Otto said. "What happened to you?"

"You did, bastard," he said, though with a small laugh. He pointed a finger back at Otto. "But I got your comrade. He's down in the bog now, a knife in his back."

Otto cringed, but tried to keep his flaring temper from showing. His brother and cousin had been with him during the assault, and the thought of sharing a fire with the killer of either made the twine dig into his wrists as his fists clenched.

The other soldier noticed Otto's anger. He cleared his throat, waving his hand. "Ah, Piotr is only boasting. It was a mercy killing. He slipped on a ridge, fell onto rocks and broke his back. You would have done the same." He brought the vodka to Otto's lips, grinning when the draught made Otto cough. "I borrowed your matches to start a fire; I hope you don't mind. My own went missing in the chase, but I'm not complaining when the most important thing survived."

"Lost our way as well," Piotr said. "Maybe you can help us find our way back?"

Otto swallowed the alcohol and grunted. He was a city lad, unfamiliar with the northern wilderness, but there was no question of what would happen if the Russians found that out.

"Listen, friend," the other soldier said. He swallowed some of his vodka, then pressed a hand to his chest. "My name is Alexei. What is yours?"

"Otto," he said. "Otto Vennamo."

Alexei nodded. "Otto Vennamo," he repeated, stretching the surname so that Otto had trouble recognising it as his own. "I know what you're thinking. You take us anywhere, best thing that happens to you is you become a prisoner. Worst, you go down with a bullet in the back of the head. But, listen, it doesn't have to be like that."

"We went past a dried river crossing, our tank and

us," Piotr said, inching closer across the melting snow. "If you can bring us there, we depart each our own way. Our sergeant doesn't need to know we caught you. Our thanks for your help."

Otto tried to scan his surroundings, but everything beyond the campfire's reach was under the shroud of a Finnish winter night. "Not much of a choice, is there," he said, "but I can't say where we are in the middle of the night. How far did you run?"

"Far," Alexei said. "I carried you from where we fell, until we couldn't hear the shouts chasing us anymore. By then we didn't know where we were. We rounded a bog, for what it's worth, and from the open went on to deeper woods for shelter."

"There were rocks in the bog," Piotr helped. "Huge ones, boulders."

"Can you find the way back there?" Otto asked. "I think I can get us to the crossroads from there."

The Russians shared a glance, and Alexei said, "I think so. It hasn't snowed all night, so we should find our footprints in the morning."

Otto nodded. The same bog was circled with red in every map he'd seen. He wasn't one for superstitions, but after every local soldier he'd shared a tent with tried to spook him with the same stories some of it had stuck deep enough to make him glance at the shadows now.

They said that, in the ancient days before Christianity, pagans had buried their dead by those rocks and held rituals there, until the souls of the dead merged together into a powerful spirit and made it sacred ground. When Christians came, and slaughtered the pagans, the spirit awakened and killed all those who spilled the blood of its kin. At this part of the story every storyteller had leaned closer to Otto, the whites of their eyes wide, and continued in a whisper that the war had brought the monster, *hiisi*, back to protect its home.

"I think I can help you," Otto said. He didn't bother asking how he'd know he could trust them to free him afterwards. He could not.

For what it was worth, Alexei gave him a blanket for the night and moved him closer to the fire. Otto fought against sleep for as long as he could, but after Piotr started snoring the sound lulled him off as well.

Otto awoke to Alexei shaking him by the shoulder and speaking in rapid tones. "Wake up!" he said, switching to English. "What the Hell is this? What happened here?"

Otto pushed himself up with an elbow. Groggily, he eyed over the snow around the campsite. It had been disturbed, but he saw nothing worth alarm about it. "Snow's fallen off the branches. What else?"

Alexei spat more words Otto recognised, all of them curses. "*This*, idiot!" he snapped, pulling Otto to stand up. His feet were still tied together and the lad teetered, nearly falling.

Then his legs lost feeling, and he did collapse into a sitting position. The dents weren't from falling snow, but from clawed feet. They were too long and narrow to be a bear's paws, and too large to be a wolf's. A trail of blood led away from the camp, towards where, Otto decided amidst numb thoughts, the field of the *hiisi* lay.

"*What the Hell is this?*" Alexei demanded, shaking Otto harder. "Did your people do this? Where is Piotr?"

Otto swallowed hard as he studied the camp. Piotr was gone, but his backpack was untouched.

"Please," Otto said, voice trembling. "You have to cut me loose."

"Idiot!" Alexei snapped. He let go, and Otto fell on his side. The Russian walked a few steps outwards along the trail, breath rolling in small clouds before him, then shouted, "Piotr! Piotr, my friend, are you there?"

"Stop shouting," Otto hissed, but then realised the *hiisi* already knew where they were. He groaned and sat up, trying to get another look at the prints. On second thought they looked more like bear tracks, if a little deformed. He thought he should've felt foolish for thinking otherwise, but in the back of his mind remained a feeling of uncanniness.

Alexei had whipped himself into a frenzy, and returned to Otto with the glare of borderline panic in his eyes. He pointed at the print, and again asked, "What *is* this?"

"Bear tracks," Otto said, in an effort to convince himself as well.

Alexei's tone made it clear that his string of unfamiliar Russian words were more curses. "In my cold country, we have more bears than people as neighbours. I know tracks when I see them, and this wasn't made by one." He grabbed the tuft of hair peeking out from under his hat. "I didn't sleep long. I couldn't have. I had to keep watch, and I only closed my eyes for a minute. Then he was gone."

Alexei was right, of course. It was beyond unlikely a bear had snuck into their camp and dragged Piotr off, not without waking either of them up. But, was it any likelier that a wrathful spirit had done so? Otto tried looking around, but though the woods were sparse here, and the sky clear, it was still too dark to see far this early in the morning.

"Alexei," Otto said. "Please cut my bonds. We're in danger. I need to be able to run."

"Run from what?" Alexei shouted, waving a hand over the tracks. "The fucking Leshy?"

"I don't know that word," Otto said, "but I'm guessing we might be talking about a similar creature."

Colour drained from Alexei's face. "Creature?" he said slowly. "I swear I'll cut your throat if this is a plot, or a trick."

"If I had freed myself for long enough to do something to Piotr, I would've fled," Otto said. He held out his bound wrists. "Cut me free, now. Hurry."

Alexei hesitated, until a howling from the deep woods resounded. It was a cry like a human voice straining itself to sound lupine. He wheeled towards the sound, and in the grey gloom of the morning they saw an enormous shape stalking between the trees.

Alexei faced Otto. The Russian soldier had none of his past evening's joviality left in him; he was a frightened boy now, much the same as Otto himself was when the Finns had first attacked his unit.

Alexei gave the shadows one more fearful glance, then dug his hand into the belt pouch beneath his coat and brought out his knife. He sawed through the lengths of rope tied around Otto's limbs, sliding the knife back in his pocket and slapping Otto on the shoulder.

The *hiisi's* howling became a rasping scream, and they ran.

For no more than twenty paces, before Otto realised Alexei was not with him. Against his instincts, he stopped for a look behind and found the Russian sprinting after him, stuffing the bottle of vodka into his other pocket and waving for him to go with his free hand. His face was stricken with fear, and so was Otto's once he saw the massive shape darting between the trees.

It did not run as men did, nor beasts; it seemed to slip from shadow to shadow, moving with terrifying speed in the shade of pines. He would not escape it with a leg so bruised, but what else could he do? So they ran, Alexei first after him, then in front, and eventually leaving Otto further and further behind. He could see the *hiisi* now, a seething giant of mist with an empty eye socket fuming with smoke. It ran hunched over, making no sound as its feet flew in a blur over the drifts.

"Don't you have a gun?" he shouted towards Alexei.

"Lost it in the fall," he replied. The field opened ahead, but Otto was already lagging and the pain in his leg was getting worse. Shooting at a vengeful spirit was unlikely to do any good, but it was better than trying to fight back with his fists when it caught up. Alexi had halted in the clearing, exhausted, and Otto stopped alongside him.

Alexei had fished out the bottle of vodka, sipping deeply from it. A thought sparked in Otto's head, and with a burst of vigour he yanked the crusted bandages off his leg. He made the Russian shriek when he grabbed the bottle. "Oy! You could've asked!" Alexei snapped, crying out again, his voice indignant, when he saw Otto stopping to stuff the bandages into the bottle.

As Otto lit a match the *hiisi* dove out from the shadows with a tearing sound. A wave of rotten stench washed against them, the ground trembling from the massive weight as the creature gave up its spectral hunt, emerging wholly into the world of the living.

The gauze caught flame, and Otto threw the bottle. It broke against a rock by the *hiisi*, splashing burning vodka onto the nearby lichen, as well as the fur coating the thing's feet.

The men dashed from the woods towards the frozen bog that Alexei had mentioned, leaving the startled monstrosity behind. It was the very place Otto had thought about last night, the place they shouldn't go. The ritual stones stood on the southern side, towards where the trail of blood they'd unwittingly followed led.

Trees crashed from the giant's frenzy, and over the sound of cracking wood rose a wail that made Otto's marrow quiver. "Someone must hear that," Alexei said. "Someone will come looking! Someone with weapons."

"The *hiisi* sings our deaths. No one hears it but us," Otto said, recounting the stories. "We need to get somewhere it can't find us, and fast."

Alexei stopped running, heaving deep breaths as he leaned against his knees. "And where is that? Where do we hide from…from a monster?"

"First, we need to gain more distance," Otto said. He grabbed Alexei by the shoulder, but continued at a pace less brisk. "I can't smell rot anymore, so it's gone back to the spirit world. Gives us a chance."

"The spirit world…what in the Hell is that thing?"

"A creature who protects holy ground from intruders. I've heard a lot of stories about it, and we just need to hope the ones about how to escape it are true."

As they jogged towards the rocks, their pace painfully slow, Otto cast a glance over his shoulder. The *hiisi* stood at the edge of the forest, reverted to a grey, amorphous shape. In the light of early dawn he saw it clearly for the first time. The sight of the abomination of moss, flesh, and fur still made him feel as though he was trapped in a nightmare.

Alexei stopped, shaking his head in increasingly wider arcs until he said, "Why is it after you? I see why it would take Piotr away, but…"

He trailed off, and Otto said, "It's a pagan spirit, and I'm Lutheran. We're both enemies to it."

They watched it lurch towards them, then Otto gritted his teeth and resumed jogging. Alexei caught up once he noticed his companion pulling ahead. "Why did it stop following us?"

"Fire forces it back into the spirit world, but the only way to make it lose track of us for good is to hide inside a place built by human hands for a full night."

"Okay," Alexei mumbled, still in disbelief about the creature following them. His enchantment broke when he noticed the distance Otto had gained along the trail of blood, and called after him, "Are you planning to hide amidst the rocks?"

"I think it took Piotr's body there. If we find its nest, we must take something from there."

The *hiisi*'s movements had become uncertain, and it followed them across the bog in a zig-zag pattern. The men couldn't resist looking at it now and again, if only to temper their resolve against the chill of the morning slinking into their muscles. Its keening resounded over the crunch of ice and snow under their feet, causing tremors to run up their spines. The giant wandered blindly, yet seemed drawn towards them as if an invisible tether guided it back whenever it began to veer too far.

The men found Piotr's corpse in the shade of the tallest stone. Were it not for the tatters of clothing matching Alexei's there would've been no way to recognise the mass of meat and ground bone as ever having been a human being. The sight made Alexei curl over, and Otto had to fight against the convulsions in his own gut from the sounds of his companion retching. Otto kept his gaze fixed on the ground, purposefully avoiding the soldier's remains as he crossed into the centre of the circle of stones. He sifted the snow until he found two apple-sized halves of a black, glass orb buried there.

When he returned to Alexei the Russian sat on the ground, staring vacantly out at the approaching giant. He brushed his nose with the back of his glove, sniffed and said, "I smell rot again."

"We have a shot at getting away now," Otto said, presenting the fragments. "We can force it back into the world of the living with these."

Alexei rotated his head to the shards, slowly, as though the mere act of turning took a tremendous amount of concentration. "Why would we want to do that?"

"We probably don't, but holding the pieces has the added boon of hiding us from it until the dark."

"How'd you know to look for them?"

"It's supposed to leave one of its eyes behind when it hunts, so that people in need of protection can summon it if it's away from the sanctuary." Otto gave him a wry smile. "I thought the soldiers from around these parts were trying to scare a city boy with their stories, but it turns out everything they'd said has been true so far."

Alexei observed the halves and, just as slowly, returned his gaze to Piotr' corpse. He gagged, but managed to get to his feet. "What do we do now?"

"Keep going. As long as the sun is up the power in the shards ensures it won't see us because it's blind inside my pocket. It can't smell us over its own stench, and it can't hear us because of its crying."

"And what happens once the sun sets?"

Otto said nothing, but the way he glanced at Piotr was enough.

...

The men kept a pace as brisk as they could muster, until the *hiisi*'s cries grew distant and eventually faded. Without food or water the December day sapped their strength as fast as it ate away the light, and Otto's hurt leg began to slow them down even more as the terrain turned hilly.

That far in the north daylight was a brief guest, and it would take at least another two hours before they made it to the crossing of which the Russians had spoken. From there it was still a good walk to either camp, and they only had forty-five minutes of daylight at best.

When the strained howls arose from afar—perhaps the creature was still in its den—Alexei nudged Otto's shoulder and pointed upwards. Silhouetted against the red sky was a woodsman's hut on the hillside, and it was a welcomed sight indeed.

"Will that do for cover?"

"It should!" Otto exclaimed, wrapping his hand over the shard in his pocket. The wailing was drawing nearer, and they hurried up the last stretch to the house. The cottage was old, untended and apparently abandoned. The glass of the windows had shattered, and the shutters drooped on their hinges. The door was unlocked, but they pounded on it anyway. When no one came to answer the men stepped in.

Inside the cottage they found a bunk bed, a table and a rusted stove. On the table was an oil lamp, but not much else. Through the window beside the bed Otto saw a woodshed, and a chopping block that still had an axe stuck in it.

"I'll see if there's wood," he said. "Might be there's nothing to eat, but at least we can boil snow on the stove to drink."

"And have a fire prepared if this is where your story falls apart," Alexei muttered.

Otto nodded, stepping outside as he scouted their surroundings for the *hiisi*. The wailing had become lower-pitched, the menacing tones showing it was still hunting, but he couldn't see it yet. He hurried over to the woodshed, breaking the lock with the axe and gathering up an armful of dry wood.

As soon as he turned around he dropped the logs. Against the wall, just below the window he'd looked out a moment ago, lay the flayed body of the presumed resident. Beside him, half buried in snow, was a torch that had never been lit.

"Alexei," Otto said, repeated louder until the Russian appeared in the window. He waited for Otto to speak, then followed his gaze to the body before letting out a groan. Neither spoke for a whole minute, then Alexei said, "I found torches under the bed. They're handmade, the good kind." He swallowed hard. "I think our fellow here knew more about the creature than you do."

Otto nodded slowly, still staring at the body, then brushed his nose. Cold clogged his nostrils, but even through dripping snot he could smell the foetor wafting from the woods. As calmly as he could he gathered another armful of snowless logs and returned inside to fill the stove. Alexei sat on the bench by the table, watching him work as he fiddled with a torch.

"We can blind it with these, then keep going," Alexei suggested. A shiver ran through him when the *hiisi* howled, and he jumped up to close the latches of the shutters. "Better than sitting and waiting. We can't be too far from the camps anymore, right?"

"Too far is exactly where we are," Otto said. He strained his arms to close the last shutters, and saw the massive shape of the *hiisi* coming up the hill in the last rays of the sun. It was still blurry, and still sticking to the shadows. It slid away behind a pine when he tried to focus on it, like a floater in his eye.

Alexei leaned forward, pressing his fists against his brow. "What do we do then? Are we safe here, or not?"

Otto yanked the shutters to set them properly on the hinges, then turned around. In the bright glow from the oil lamp and stove the hut could've been cosy, had it not been for the approaching monstrosity. He noticed a crucifix on the wall, and a small bronze plaque inscribed with lyrics from a children's hymn underneath it, beseeching the company of a guardian angel at the ends of the earth.

"I don't know," Otto muttered.

Alexei grunted, then got up and pulled out a chest from under the bed. He set beside the bundle of torches, removing the container of kerosene for the lamp.

"If it comes in," he said, "what if we trapped it, then set the hut on fire? It's not as though the resident needs it, and the trees are cleared far enough not to catch fire."

In his tone was a grim seriousness that chilled Otto. "I suppose," Otto said, after a moment of consideration, "we should start spreading the kerosene."

Once the red, dying streaks of daylight vanished completely from between the shutters the *hiisi*'s stench overwhelmed the hut. Its movements carried a soft, swishing sound outside, as though it didn't walk; rather it swept its feet over the snow drifts. It rattled the shutters with its nails, and the men sat still, holding their breaths with torches in hand. They were poised, and ready to toss them into the lit stove.

The *hiisi* pressed upon the door, and they saw the reflection of their torches in the black sheen of its nails when the door finally creaked open. There had been a plank to bar it with but they'd left it outside, hoping that the old stories had one more truth to it.

The *hiisi* came in, heralded by a rank cloud. It had to enter in a crouch, yet it still loomed over the men. It stared them down, then screamed as it took a step forward. Alexei thrust his burning torch at the creature while Otto threw open the shutters behind them. The *hiisi* shrieked, swiping at Alexei—it managed to knock the torch from his hand, successfully igniting the kerosene.

Otto jumped out the window, Alexei following right behind. The Finn landed on his hurt leg and stumbled, while the Russian darted past him, leaving him on the ground. The *hiisi* screamed as fire bloomed inside the house, then came the sound of an enormous inhalation as it went into hiding.

Alexei slammed the door shut, jamming the plank between the door and the baluster of the porch with a thud. As Otto forced himself to his feet he retrieved the pieces of the *hiisi*'s eye in his pocket, pressing them swiftly together.

Inside the *hiisi* tore itself out of the grey cloud with a scream of surprise. Otto threw the now-fleshy eye into the fire, then sealed the latches. He'd barely taken a step back when the *hiisi* knocked the shutters loose. It swung towards him with its trunk-like arm, but it was too big to fit out the window.

Alexei came around the corner, cringing when he noticed the burning creature, but he continued in a determined stride towards where they'd carried more torches. After lighting one he dodged the *hiisi*'s feeble attempts to strike him, until he managed to light the thing's long beard of hanging moss on fire.

"I guess it doesn't consider Christian hands human enough," Otto said. The *hiisi* gave a final shriek, furry face aflame, and its arm fell limp against the side of the burning house.

"No one will ever believe this," Alexei mumbled, "but I avenged Piotr. That's what matters most." He brushed his face. "We grew close as brothers, out there on the battlefield. I owed him this."

Otto nodded. He'd forgotten about his unknown, fallen comrade during the day, but now the dread of learning his own brother might be lost returned to him. They turned away from the dead spirit and waded into the night, leaving the house to glow beyond the hills.

"Tell me, Otto, where did you learn to speak English so well?" Alexei asked. His tone sought levity, but from the look on his face Otto thought he was trying to change the subject for his own sake. "For enemies, we've gone through quite the adventure together. None of it would've been possible without a common language, I think."

"I'm half American," Otto said. "My parents met when my dad visited family in New York, so I spent most of my childhood there."

Alexei chuckled at that, with a weary shake of his head. The torch's fire made his features look far older than his age. "Twice the enemy, then. I learned from a defector, a scientist who worked with my father and lived with us. I never asked how Piotr learned it. I wish I had." He chuckled again, though there was a forced twang to it. "The vodka was his, you know. He always had a bottle of the good stuff stashed somewhere."

Alexei stopped. Otto faced him, but turned away and towards the stars shining past the firs when he found the Russian choking back tears. "So stupid of me," Alexei said, groaning as he wiped his eyes with the back of his glove. "We should've both died in the attack anyway. You came out of nowhere."

Unsure of what to say to that, Otto kept quiet.

After a moment Alexei kept walking. "And yet you saved my life, the day after you tried to take it."

"I could say the same to you."

Alexei was quiet until they made it to level ground. "Yes, I suppose that's true," he said at last. "But I didn't think of you as a person, even when I was carrying you on my back. You were an enemy who was useful." He made a hesitant sound, then said, "We were going to kill you once you took us where we needed to go." Otto shrugged, having figured as much, and Alexei added, "I'm not going to do that now. I swear on my mother's life."

"No," Otto said. "I won't either."

"I understand if you don't trust me, and I won't blame you if you attack me when I turn my back."

"I trust you, and if I recognize you on the battlefield I'll aim a little too far to the left."

Alexei laughed at that, and after a moment he gently patted Otto's shoulder.

They'd almost used up the torches when they came to the dried crossing the Russians had spoken of. They lit the last two there, shook hands, and parted ways. Otto was shuddering with cold, starving, exhausted and thirsty when he reached the carcass of the Russian tank. The Finnish fortifications weren't far anymore. His leg ached from the strain it had been put through, and he stopped there to sit on shrubs and let it rest for a time.

It was in the twilight state, that dusky time between dreaming and awakening, when he heard the howling. Otto rose, his hurt leg stiff, and he shivered involuntarily. He thought he'd only closed his eyes for a moment, but his torch lay dead beside him and the dark was lifting. If he hadn't woken up then he might've frozen to death; a tragedy, as he was so close to being rescued.

He listened intently, blinking sleep from his eyes, but the sound didn't repeat. He rose to his feet, realizing he'd been holding his breath, and exhaled deeply before sucking in gulps of cold air. Otto carried on towards the camp, and had nearly reached it when an eerie feeling of being watched settled over him. On the path, far back in the grey gloom of the morning, a blurry shape moved amidst the pines.

VILLE MERILÄINEN
ABOUT THE AUTHOR

Ville Meriläinen is an award-winning Finnish author. His short fiction has appeared in various venues online and in print, including Pseudopod, Cast of Wonders, and Intergalactic Medicine Show. Find his novels Ghost Notes and Spider Mafia at https://amzn.com/e/B00KC7KJ9S and reprints of his short fiction at https://curiousfictions.com/authors/111-ville-merilainen.

WHEN CALLED
DAVID KENNEY

I do not like people named Frank, and I do not trust anyone with that name. A strange prejudice, perhaps, but we
all live by many irrational rules, rules that treat luck and
happenstance as revealed truths. Some people hate all dogs
because one dog once bit them. Is that rational? Perhaps it
is a safe bias, but hardly a rational one. I know someone
who refuses to eat fish because he claims not to like the
taste, and yet I can hardly believe that he has sampled even
a fraction of a percentage of the edible species.

There are fewer Franks in the world than there are
fish. However, I believe his aversion, like mine, is much
more sensible than it first appears. Whether you explain it
mystically or biologically, the sense of control and purpose
that the rule imposes on a chaotic world is a healthy one.
Perhaps avoiding fish prevented the food poisoning that
threatened a life-changing chance encounter with the love
of his life. Or, maybe when tasting fish for the first time,

his body just sensed mercury.

When Frank called that day, I knew I had made a mistake. I felt a shiver through my insides as soon as I heard his voice; a hard sensation to describe.

Imagine your world is a field of mushrooms. You have received many warnings against tasting any except for the most identifiable kinds, since the most malicious varieties of that organism disguise themselves as the most delectable. The death cap mushroom, for example, is often mistaken for its innocuous cousins, but once you've invited the death cap into your body its conduct is extravagantly hideous.

The feeling I had that day, when Frank called me, was that of the arrogant man who ate the wrong mushroom. It was that of a man at the first spasm of his innards, before panic or the real pain sets in, at that instant where the only thing on his mind is the warning he was provided with, the simple rule he decided not to follow. It was the feeling of great loss from a little act.

The sting came suddenly and unexpectedly, as all disasters come, cutting short and making meaningless the pleasant time that preceded it.

"Mr. Cross? This is Frank, Frank Dwyer." The face came before my eyes as I heard the voice, a face that seemed to carry more years than it actually held, brittle and fissured like a ripe apple in an early frost.

"Oh, hello Mr. Dwyer."

"Please, call me Frank."

I was mumbling, "No, that's fine I'd rather…" when

he interrupted me and continued, "I'm just checking in to make sure everything is fine with the house."

"You really don't need to…" but he cut me off again.

"Stuff comes up in an old house like that. It's just been playing on my mind so, like I said, I just wanted to make sure that you're settling in all right and nothing has come up." He was nervous, which made me nervous. I had awakened something awful by having dealings with this man. What horrible thing was he going to tell me about his former house?

I knew it had been a bad idea to give him my phone number, but at that point I had already trespassed so far that it seemed only a little thing. I never saved his, which is why he got the jump on me with this call.

In my own defense I had already set my heart on the place by the time I knew the owner's name. At first the estate agent only mentioned a Mr. Dwyer, and the look on my face seemed to truly frighten her on my second visit when she let the owner's first name slip.

The house was what I had wanted for so long: it was out in the woods, no neighbors, a beautiful, rustic split level. It was large too, and cheap for the size of the place and plot. Here I now was though, alone in my beautiful home with that death cap feeling spreading through my guts.

"No, everything is just fine, thank you." The last thing I needed was for this nosy idiot to get a bout of nostalgia, to make a suggestion to come over for barbeques, or to start making unannounced visits.

"Well good, good. Like I said, it's been on my mind,

and there was just a little thing I wanted to call you up and mention…" There was a silence for about five seconds, and I thought I was going to throw up.

Then he continued, "The thing is, um, there is just a funny thing that happens out in the yard at night." He kept pausing. Why did he keep pausing? It was like he was waiting for me to say something, but I didn't want to say anything to him. I wanted this noxious human being to be gone again, back with the other Franks, far out of my life. Whatever structural problems or pest infestation he was going to tell me about was fine. I could deal with that, I could pay the price and move on.

Every moment I was feeling sicker and sicker. I thought about simply terminating the call, but hanging up would be like closing your eyes at night when your closet door was slowly opening.

Finally he started talking again. "Yeah, so, the thing is: at night, there's this weird, sort of, trick of the light or optical illusion or something like that happening out back by the woods."

Just tell me what you need to tell me, you rotten, disgusting man!

Then he laughed. I couldn't believe he was laughing. It was a nervous sort of laugh, but to me it sounded like derision. "I'll just say it - when you look into the woods at night, it looks like there's a person out there."

"There's someone out in the yard?"

"No, no, no, Mr. Cross, no one's out there; that's what I'm saying, but you shouldn't go out there."

"I shouldn't go out there?"

"Right. It's just a trick of the light, so don't worry about it."

...

Frank was the janitor that worked at my school when I was a child. He was a weird guy. As a kid, you sense things like that: weird people. Calm, analytic words could be used to describe him - frustrated, lonely, bitter, secretive - but they would fail to convey the reasons we tried to avoid him, what we sensed about him. It is funny how children can sense when something is wrong. They spend their lives aimlessly seeking attention, but often recoil when confronted with a certain type of consideration.

Anyway, in the back of the house there is a spacious deck that sticks out from the second story, and I began to sit out there every night. At first, I would watch movies on my laptop, but having to constantly pause the show to listen became disconcerting since any rustle or chatter would set me on edge. The vibrating light and teeming sounds from the computer seemed incongruous, almost offensive, to the primitive surroundings.

The laptop became intolerable. The wind and creaking boughs always grew louder whenever I tried to focus on the screen, competing for my attention. Soon I found myself just sitting and staring. I felt like a sailor staring from the prow out into the sea, seeing the still, fixed yard and the darkness beyond that held many things. It was not always quiet though. The cachinnations of coyotes were new to me and, as you can imagine, quite unsettling. The discordant, almost pained yelps would come closer, then move farther away, then come closer again before suddenly stopping all together.

Seeing animal eyes upset me greatly. Though the main arc from the under-deck light faded some twenty or thirty feet from the woods, it could still be seen reflecting in the eyes of animals close to the penumbra of pure blackness. Shapes on the edge of the forest were distinct enough, and that is where I often concentrated all my scrutinizing efforts.

You can imagine my alarm when two new dots of light appeared one night.

At first, I was not sure if I actually saw them. I stared for such a long time, and they sat so anchored in one place that I thought that it must be a reflection from a wet or metallic surface. And then they blinked. They started to move, disappearing momentarily and reappearing closer to the ground. As the eyes encroached near enough to the light I could see it was no more than a small animal, a raccoon or opossum.

Strangely enough, it was in those moments of relief that I suddenly became most afraid, as though my lack of concern was a danger in itself. It was in these quiet moments that my hands would start shaking. My mind would start playing tricks on me, and I would imagine that, right there, where I had just been looking, in that place, that patch of darkness, something still lingered. I would imagine that now stood a man in the darkness, a figure staring at me with eyes that did not reflect light, and I would sit there as if in a trance. I stared at one spot where I could see nothing, nothing but the nebulous outline of scrub and thicket, but I had the feeling that something was there, a deep feeling of wrongness and menace, like something was staring back at me and waiting.

People always sound craziest when they say they are not crazy, so I will skip that statement. You are thinking that I am less than sane, and I know it. But, you must try to understand. Even the most cynical person, a person who professes to see no greater intent in the events of his life, still takes notice of uncanny coincidences. I would be crazy not to act on the information provided to me in that phone call. If the previous owner of your house called to tell you never to dig out in the garden, what would you do? What you think is strange is my fixation on Frank. In your life Franks may not be something to fear, and I am sure there are plenty of Franks out there that are very nice. Life may have taught you to fear spiders or snakes, or someone hiding in your house, but my life has taught me to be extra careful when dealing with Franks.

On the second week after the call, on a rainy night that compelled me to keep my vigil indoors, I sat on a chair just inside the sliding glass door. I was staring out into a delicate mist that segregated the normally-banded world of form and shadow beyond the light's reach, and that was when I finally saw him.

...

I was worried, when I moved in, that the house would be too large. Before moving here, I had only ever lived in apartments, and my concern was about the many rooms of the house. Something about being alone in a house full of rooms that should be empty worries me. I consider it a less rational fear than my abhorrence of Franks, but the mind will wander when you live alone, and even silly things can seem quite serious. At this stage, I was not worried about anything in the house, as whatever it was that concerned me was undoubtedly out in the woods still.

I have friends. We get together, sometimes. I wouldn't say that I really like any of them. I would say that they are all pretty good people, if not all that enjoyable to be around, and three of them came to my house one night.

For a week I had observed the thing outside. After seeing it, or him (strangely enough I prefer to think of it as a him), for the first time, he became quite distinct on the subsequent nights. Right around when the moon came out the figure became visible. He never moved; he was always quite still, and at first I did doubt my senses. The strange call from Mr. Dwyer, the sleep deprivation or the long hours spent staring into darkness could have simply taken their toll. I believe firmly in the body's ability to adapt in mysterious, unmeasurable ways when under unsustainable strain, and perhaps my mind knew that I needed to see something, so it saw.

Perhaps this was a stump that I had seen many times before, one that was taken up and molded by my perception into what I believed must be there. It is not so strange a thought. The system of internal impulses that conducts our reasoning faculties are just as complex as, and even more enigmatic than, the network that governs our optic senses. Even so, I know that many people believe in total nonsense. Optical illusions are common. Is it strange to think that we could bring such an illusion into existence by sheer willpower? But no, he was there. He became clearer every night. He would stand there, still as a tree, but not a tree.

I am sure of that now.

My three friends were in awe of my new home, though upset to find that I did not own a television. We played a board game, on the deck of course. While they complained about the impracticality of playing outside on such a cold night, I carried out a table, chairs, and lamp. It took me a while to find an extension cord, which angered them further. Like I said, they are not particularly pleasant people. The uncongenial mood they set with their protests did not lessen as the night progressed, and before the second hour of game-play was up all three started to make excuses for leaving.

The whole night I had not looked towards the yard, hoping that one of them would notice something independently. Surrounded by spectators the whole thing seemed like an exposition, a great unveiling, and I felt like I was about to introduce them to some strange, exotic pet. Just before they took their leave I halted them. "Wait! I have something to show you."

Ushering them to the railing, I urged them to look out across the lawn.

One of them made a comment on how nice the yard looked, and another joked about my poor upkeep of the lawn. I said something hurtful to them, then, for breaking the solemnity of my revelation. Insulting my guests in this way was inappropriate, but understandable, given the circumstances.

I told them to look. They quieted quickly.

It was ridiculous though, as there was nothing in the woods. The four of us stood there for fifteen minutes, searching for him, for Frank (so I had begun to call him, for it was indeed a Frank waiting for me out there.) Fifteen minutes was nothing to me, but I was suddenly acutely aware of what a long time it must have been for them. I was about to make my apologies when a stubborn cloud finally yielded up the harvest moon, and there he was, still blacker than shadow and more conspicuous than ever.

"There you are! I see you!" I howled in exultation, and they all jumped. "You see! There he is. Frank! Frank, we can see you!" I pointed a finger across the lawn, looking to my companions, but they were not looking at Frank; they were only looking at me.

"Damn it!" I said, "Look out there. Look at him!" They just stared at me, like infants trying to figure out an adult's commands. Like I said, they have good hearts, but not much else.

They did not comprehend the situation, but I am a reasonable person and could understand why they were anxious. I raised my hands in a placating manner, one that signaled that I was calm and in control. They just needed a bit of assurance, and then I could get the confirmation I needed.

"Alright, settle down. I just got excited. I should have explained beforehand." At this point I managed to conceal my elation at the prospect of sharing this experience with other people. After the long wait I now knew Frank was out there, and once I could get these bozos to look out and become my witnesses, we could all go out together and confront Frank.

Motioning with my hands and slowly turning my head from them towards the direction they needed to look in, I continued, "I just need you to see something out in there…" but I stopped short, because Frank had started to move.

For the first time Frank was moving. Not much, but he was moving. Slowly he rose, like a cobra emerging from a charmer's basket, his shoulders oscillating back and forth, back and forth. His head was tilting against each sway, like a perverse dance, and with each bizarre rotation his arms heaved out and rolled back to an escalating, jarring rhythm of wind and creaking boughs that seemed for a time to grow deafening as the whole forest broke out in an unharnessed cacophony of night noises. Back and forth, back and forth, to the screeching and howling of animals. Frank swayed against the wind, then with the wind, flourishing his movements as they grew wilder the more I stared.

I had spoken to him. I had called out his name. He

knew that I knew, and now he was reveling in my ac-
knowledgement. My friends were gone; they had left at
some point, but I could not leave Frank. Now that I called
him he was waiting for me to leave, waiting for me to stop
watching, waiting for me to abandon my post and forsake
my defenses. Every time I blinked he seemed to grow
more animated when my sight returned. He wanted me to
close my eyes; I could sense it. He turned now and swayed
and undulated, stepping from side-to-side in an effusion of
cankerous delight. An hour before dawn my eyes closed
for a moment before I could shake myself awake, and he
was gone.

I collapsed on the wooden planks in exhaustion.

…

A week had passed and the seriousness of the situation
had escalated nightly, so I decided to go on the offensive.

The Frank who previously owned my house lived in
a retirement community, a small enclave of well-kept little
bungalows around a man-made pond. The whole com-
pound was called Cedar Ridge, despite the fact that it was
located in a valley that did not contain any cedar trees –
probably because people associate them with graveyards.
It surprised me that he had moved to a retirement complex.
As I have said, he merely seemed like a middle-aged man
who just looked old.

His car was out front, and I put my hand on the hood
to see if it was warm. I had wanted to get here early enough
to catch him returning from his night activities, but I did

not trust leaving the porch to enter my house until well after sunup.

Coming here was a big risk.

I was not afraid of this man, at least not while the sun was out.

He looked tired and haggard, more so than I remembered, and he was very surprised to see me. I told him that I just had a few questions about the house, and that no, I did not want to come in for a cup of coffee.

I mentioned the 'illusion' out in the woods, asking if he thought it was a bear or some other dangerous animal that I should be worried about. He shivered and pulled his robe close around his neck, blaming his distraction on the cold weather and early hour to avoid my questions. Normally I pride myself on my ability to read people's reactions. However, with the wind blowing into his face and his fidgeting to keep warm, it was nearly impossible to interpret his pained expressions. I decided to do what I had promised myself I would not.

Our ancestors, back before recorded history, would have had to come together when people started disappearing from the village. The men would gather their spears and go out into the wild to find the cave of whatever was killing them off. A bear's home might seem like the worst place to confront the beast, yet the bear is not at ease; he panics, turning to fight when he wishes to flee, and backing up when he wishes to move forward. His uncertainty overwhelms his senses, making his actions confined and more predictable.

With only the option to back further in or try to charge out, he loses the normal cunning unpredictability that makes animals so dangerous. As long as you have a plan for both the furious charge and the mock retreat, then you have a good chance of overcoming the brute. I was on the hunt now, and had my spear. Three days before I had been to a pawn shop, and now I had my weapon tucked into the back of my pants. I was ready.

We sat down at the small table in the kitchen, and I refused a drink. Before he could sully the conversation with pleasantries, I began.

"You think this is funny, Frank? You think that you can mess with me and get away with it? Do you?" He mimed confusion, raising his hands and puckering up his face, but it won't work with me. "I learned long ago to not try to figure out why people do the things they do, so I don't care what kind of game you're playing. I don't care how much you miss the house. I don't care how much you like hiding in the woods and looking at people through windows, you sick pervert. I'm not here to help you deal with your problems. I'm here to let you know that I'm done messing around."

I had rehearsed these lines more than a hundred times, probably more than a thousand, while standing out on the porch through the long nights and on the car ride over, but I still got worked up saying them. I almost took out the gun to show him that I was not joking around, but it looked like my threats were having their proper effect when he broke down and started weeping.

This was it. This was my moment.

"I don't feel bad for you. You crossed a line last night. Scared the shit out of me when you smashed the light. That's right. And do you think I didn't hear you come in through the door below me? Bet you didn't think I heard that. I heard you. I heard you walking around too. I didn't come down, but I will next time. Next time, I'm coming down and I'm going to sort you out. I've put up with this for way too long. It's gonna stop, and it's gonna stop now."

There was more I wanted to say, but he looked horrified. Strange, that seeing true horror in someone else's eyes is so disconcerting, even if you are the one who is causing it. Though I had worked myself into quite a frenzy, now standing and looking down on him, his look still stopped me cold. As I said, I am very good at reading people, but as understandable as his fear was, it still unnerved me. I wanted pure confusion or pure contrition, but this was neither.

This was something else.

Then a fit took him, and he shuddered uncontrollably, hiding his face in his hands. Pity began to seduce me, so I cautiously eased off on my attack for a moment. The reprieve must have been what he was waiting for, because just as my resolve hardened and I had begun speaking again he sprang up. Before I could finish my first word, he knocked me back into my chair, shouting – *NOOOOO!!*

He had me by the collar with his tightly-coiled fists, spittle spraying in my face as he continued in a frenzy.

"You're a liar! It's not real! It was never real! You're

a liar! You're a liar! You're a liar!" He struck me then, but reacted as if he himself had been struck. Staggering back his crazed eyes glazed over, and what was a face filled with hate and malignancy turned into one of stupefaction. I was too stunned to move to help as he reeled and collapsed on the floor, quickly rebounding only to crumple again like a wounded deer frantically trying to stand and flee on a broken leg. Finally he reached the sofa in the adjoining room and crawled up onto it, murmuring furiously under his breath.

The neighbors must have heard the shouting, and I expected any moment to hear a knock at the door. I could see Frank in the other room. He was sitting now, rocking back and forth, utterly distracted, wringing his hands and jabbering to himself. I suddenly realized that I was breathing too hard. My heart was no longer thumping but lurching irregularly, so I closed my eyes and put all my concentration into regaining control of my organs.

When I opened my eyes he was staring at the floor in defeat. I was desperate to be in control again, so I stood up. Though I meant to sound threatening, my voice came out like a frightened child's. "Why have you been waiting in the woods outside my house?"

The old man began a chuckle that quickly turned into a gulping sobs.

"Oh, no, no, no. I was not a good husband, but I never deserved this," looking up at me he must have seen the confusion in my eyes, because he began to confess, though seemingly more to the walls and ceiling than to me.

"I should have been there. I shouldn't have stayed out night after night and left her alone. All those nights, all those years, it was my fault. When she started to accuse me of being out in the woods, I just laughed at her. From the start she was so sure that it was me. The thought of a burglar or stalker never seemed to enter her mind, and the more she suspected me, the more I wanted to be away. Then I came home one night and found her out on that porch calling out into the darkness. She'd gone insane. I was standing right next to her, but she thought I was out in the woods. She kept pointing, calling and shouting. She was so angry at me and at whatever she saw out in the woods, and it was that night that I'd finally realized how much she'd changed. But I couldn't hold back any longer."

Frank paused, and I took a moment to interject.

"What did she call it?"

"What?"

"What did she call it, the thing outside?"

"Well, she thought it was me. She called it Frank."

I could not move and sat as if in a trance for the rest of his story.

"I tried to help her. She was wasting away, and refused to leave. She wouldn't see a doctor, even when I brought one to the house. It was unbearable. Then she thought it was in the house. She said she called me so I came in, and then she'd accuse me of making noises in the other rooms while we were both sitting together or lying in bed. She was terrified of it, but she would turn to me and threaten to go and confront it. She would say it like she was threatening me, like I didn't want her to go check the house. I couldn't take it. I just couldn't take it anymore. I stayed in for weeks with her, never went out at night. I knew that she needed me there, but I couldn't take it anymore, so one afternoon I just left. I stayed away for two days. I don't know, maybe I thought that if she became frightened enough while I was away, she would agree to leave with me or at least get help."

He paused for a while, his eyes wandering vacantly around the room until his head turned my way and he fixed them on me. "Look around this room, Mr. Cross. Go ahead, look around the whole house, if you want. You won't find one memory. Not a picture or postcard, no relics at all, not one memento of my old life." I looked around, noting the bare walls and new furniture. He continued, still staring at me. "Why? Why does it look like I have no past? It's because I can't remember her without seeing the look on her face when I found her. I came home after those two days and found her, and now I spend every day and every night trying not to remember that face. I thought she was crazy. She had to be crazy."

He began to cry again, mumbling things that did not make any sense. I almost fell for it. Bravo, Frank, bravo. This was the real illusion, this was just an old wily bear that knew not to panic. Of course it was. How else could he have gotten this far? I laughed.

It is strange how quickly the faculties can return, even after a great shock to the system. I felt then the euphoria of regained control. You see, evil people - Franks - realize that there are two emotions that normal people cannot control: fear and pity. When you mix the two in the right way the victim becomes not only confused, but also paralyzed. Then the monster offers hope where there is none, comfort where there is none and humanity where there is none. The dupe cannot help but believe and follow, because it seems the only way to regain control.

Sorry, Frank, it's not going to work on me.

I took out my gun. "You see this, Frank? This is for you the next time you come near my house. I'm not just going to watch anymore. If you come for me, I'm coming for you."

He shook his head furiously, "No, no, don't confront it. That's what my wife did. Get out of that house!"

"Shut up!" I yelled, "You're not scaring me out of the house, Frank! I'm not gonna run from you, Frank! You just try coming back. You just try coming back, Frank. I'll be waiting." and I was going to say more, but instead I just ran out of the house, got in my car, and drove home.

...

There is no need to go out on the porch anymore, as he is no longer in the woods. I have never been good with resolutions. I promise myself that I will never do this or that again, but I always do. Likewise, I often tell myself that I am definitely going to do something, but put it off indefinitely. And I have put off the Frank business for a few days now. There is always a reason.

I write this during the day because there are never any

problems during the day. Frank only stalks around at night, and despite my confrontation with him at Cedar Ridge, he has been in the house. He has been in here since that first night when he broke the lamp, when he entered through the door below the porch.

At first he always lurked in other rooms, moving things and shuffling around. Before dark I would turn on all the lights in the house, only to hear, one by one, the bulbs smash in rooms down the halls or up the stairs. Investigating would mean going into a darkened room, which is just what Frank wants so that he can shuffle up behind me in the dark, lay his hands on my shoulders or around my neck, and pull me into the shadows. I stay where I am. Sometimes I feel him in the room with me, in the shadows, staring at me from a closet or a corner. He will roll something out, a button that he has torn from a shirt or some bauble he has found in a box.

He wants me to get up, to walk over to investigate, to turn my back to the room so that he can get at the other lights while I am not looking. I fell for this only once. Luckily it was a room with several lamps, so I was safe. My own drowsiness has become the real danger. I wonder if he has put something into my drinks, or released some sort of sluggish vapor into the air. I enter into an almost mesmerized state, but always manage to keep my eyes open. When this happens I know he is near, and hoping that I will close my eyes.

I was unusually tired around 5 o'clock and thought I would sleep for an hour before the sun set. This was yesterday, and the mistake I made was going into my bed. People only make foolish decisions during the day. Setting the alarm on my phone and checking that the volume was at its height, I lay down on my side on the bed.

When I awoke the room was in total darkness, save for the blue moonlight that lit up the far side of the room. I became fully awake at once but did not move. I knew that would be the end, for Frank was there. He was in the bed, under the covers, lying beside me. All night I lay awake, my face to the wall, with Frank behind me on the bed, slowly running his fingers through the hair on the back of my head. Up and down, up and down, hour after hour, up and down. The hard bones of his fingers would sometimes turn to stroke a lock of hair between them, and when the hand would slide down to my neck the pulpy flesh between knuckle and joint would tickle me with its hairs, but I stayed still.

All night I did not move. He knew I was awake. I could not control my breathing, and every now and again he would make little sounds, a low chortling resonation or a quick, clicking jabber. He laid still too. His weight on the bed caused me to lean into him slightly, and I could feel his fleshy body with my shoulders, rump and feet. I did not move; hour after hour, I did not move.

For one moment only I considered jumping out of the bed and running for the door. He seemed to sense this thought, quickening the pace of his sickening murmurs and running his hands through my hair more vigorously. All night. He was there all night. Then, in the hour before dawn as the black of night began to wash with lighter colors of day, he rolled away and was gone with two quick pats on my head,

It is strange. Away from the house I am not afraid. It is hard to know which state of mind is sincere, and which is simply a trick of the light. In the afternoon I went to a motel, resolving never to set foot in the house again. Overtaken by the calm of the day I thought that my rules had saved me. It was simple. Frank was in the house, so I should not be in the house. I like rules. Rules are simple, and this whole thing happened because I broke a rule. But then I remembered what had happened when I had confronted Frank, the fear and panic on his face, the cowering and contrition. I remembered the command I had over him.

My room at the motel is paid for, but I will not sleep there tonight. I do not know what has made me come back. I suppose, for one thing, it is because this is my house, not Frank's. I knew that my resolve was due in large part to the daylight, that is why my first act was to walk to the end of the lawn and throw my keys as far as I could into the woods. I have visited every fixture in the house, put in a new bulb, and then smashed it. I get to decide when lights are broken here. I get to decide where I live and where I sleep, not Frank. I get to decide when I see Frank. The sun is setting now, and I am going back into that bedroom with my gun, but not to sleep. I will face the wall and wait.

When he creeps in, when he lowers himself into that bed and begins his chuckles and caresses, I'm going to turn around and finish Frank.

DAVID KENNEY
ABOUT THE AUTHOR

Born and raised in Minnesota, David Kenney has spent the past five years teaching rhetoric and composition at a university in Wisconsin while completing his PhD in nineteenth-century literature. In between, he spent several years abroad, working as a bartender and accounting clerk in Ireland, where he enjoyed the "mighty craic" of Galway and Dublin. Heavily influenced by Victorian ghost stories, David's own tales attempt to recapture the time before the lightbulb, when dark corners of the world still had to be explored with only a small flame. Stories from his "Lost Archivist" series have been recently published by Rogue Planet Press in Lovecraftiana: the Magazine of Eldritch Horror.

The Heralding

Ian Ableson

"Like, a lot of birds?" Harrison asked.

"Fuck, no, kid, not a lot of birds," crackled his car speaker. "You think I don't know what a lot of fucking birds sounds like? And it ain't bugs either. I'm telling you, this is something I've never heard before, and I've lived around here for near sixty years now. This is something weird as *shit*, and I'm telling you we gotta check it out."

"Right," said Harrison with a sigh. He ran his fingers through his hair and checked his watch. Almost six. If he were heading home right now he'd be stuck in rush hour, but out here he'd seen hardly any cars for twenty minutes. Corn, sure, but no cars. "And why don't you just go look at it yourself?"

"Cuz the sound's coming from the state's land, and if I wanted to get to it I'd have to cross old Winnie's property, and old Winnie hates me. No way she'd ever give me permission. I might have done a lot of things, but I ain't trespassing on old Winnie's land, even if it's only fifty feet of her property between me and the state forest. I owe her dead husband that much at least, and he's been in the ground five years now. Fuck, kid, didn't your sister fill you in on all of this?"

Harrison thought back to the text he'd gotten from his sister. As far as he could recall, it said something like *Got a call from old Jerry, something weird at the cabin. Go check it out? Call him on the way up.* He stifled another sigh. "She was a little vague. What's it sound like?"

"Sounds like someone fell asleep on the low end of a church organ is what it sounds like," said Jerry. "Never heard anything like it. My guess is that it's some weird-ass new equipment from the developers that are tearing up old Rigby's land. You hear that Aspen Airs bought the old Rigby farm? Already done plowing shit, so they're probably gonna make it into another fuckin' strip mall or something. Wouldn't put it past those idiots to store their equipment on state land where they think nobody's looking just so they don't have to keep towing it back and forth from the city. I'm not gonna be able to be at your place till eight or so, but then we'll nip right on over there and check it out."

Harrison considered the clock again. It was about another hour or so to the family cabin, and to walk the trail across the twenty acres or so of forest to the state land would take half an hour at least, maybe more in the fading light that eight o'clock would bring. Harrison had to admit that Jerry was still relatively spry for his age, but the wiry, white-haired, bespectacled man's body had started to fail him in the past couple of years, and his presence would slow their progress even more. If Harrison wanted to have even a chance at getting to get back to town and sleep in his own bed, rather than crashing at the cabin, there was no way he was going to be able to wait around for his dad's old drinking buddy.

"Sounds good, Jerry," Harrison lied. "I'll see you in a bit."

"Alright, see ya soon kid."

Harrison hung up his phone, sighing deeply. He had absolutely zero desire to be driving to the family cabin on a Tuesday night with work in the morning, but he supposed it was a part of his newfound responsibilities. When his father died last year he, his brother Aaron, and his sister Kerry inherited the cabin. Harrison had become the cabin's caretaker without volunteering, since Kerry lived in Florida and Aaron's job as a global marketing executive took him all over the world. Harrison, despite being the youngest, was the obvious choice to keep an eye on the small cabin and the twenty or so acres of land that it sat on until they decided what to do with it. The cabin's fate was a heated debate in itself, of course. Aaron desperately wanted to keep the cabin, Kerry desperately wanted to sell it and the land it was on, and Harrison hovered somewhere in the middle, so as of yet no decision had been made.

Harrison was truly torn as to what his eventual vote regarding the cabin would be. On the one hand the extra money would be nice, but on the other hand his job as a mid-level software developer for a mid-level company provided him with all he needed for his fairly modest lifestyle. And, on top of that, it was hard for him to imagine selling the cabin that had been such a major part of their childhood to some stranger. Every year, for the first eighteen years of his life, Harrison had spent some greater or lesser part of his summer up north at that cabin with his family. They had explored the forest, hiked the trails and had once tried talking to the birds who nested by the cabin when they were little.

Even old Jerry, pain in the ass that he might be now, was a huge part of Harrison's childhood. When Jerry's hair was less white, and his gait less shuffling, he'd spent many a summer morning teaching Harrison how to shoot a bow. Jerry had been a patient, if stern, teacher, and Harrison didn't want to lose the place he loved.

As the vibrations from loose stones in the driveway rattled his car, Harrison couldn't help but smile a little at the sight of the little cabin sitting quietly in the woods, just the way it always had. He rolled down the window and let the sweet, herbal scent of the pines fill his nostrils. The chirping trill of a toad sounded somewhere in the distance, probably from one of the many small pools that dotted the forest. Harrison breathed in slowly and released it, allowing the cool air to course through his veins and reinvigorate him. His irritation at his sister and old Jerry faded as the tension in his body seeped away. He'd been so caught up in his work lately; maybe a night at the cabin, away from the city, wasn't such a bad idea after all.

He parked outside the shed, a small, slapdash structure about fifty feet or so from the cabin itself. Harrison had only glanced in the shed since his father passed away; at some point they would need to go in there and sort through the piles of rusted tools and old paint cans from projects long past, but so far the opportunity had yet to arise. Even with his father dead and gone, and Harrison himself in his early thirties, somehow going in the shed without permission still felt like a violation of his old man's personal space.

The shed was much closer to the trailhead than the cabin itself, so Harrison locked his car and started down the path towards the state land. Deep down he knew how ridiculous it was to lock the car on his family property, when no other humans were around for miles, but Harrison was enough of a city boy that he couldn't even fathom leaving it unlocked anywhere, no matter the circumstances.

Dappled evening sunlight speckled the trail as Harrison walked deeper into the forest. He walked quickly and with purpose, and with hardly any attention paid to his route; the trails themselves were so solidly cemented in his memory that he knew he would be able to picture them till the day he died. The old fence that marked the boundary between his family's property and the state land had long since rusted and fallen into the soil, but he vaguely knew where it had once been. By the time he reached the boundary his mind had been soothed by the peace of the evening forest, and it had wandered on to other things to the point that he'd nearly forgotten that he was supposed to be listening to something.

Then, to his mild astonishment, Harrison heard the sound.

It was very similar to what Jerry had described; some sort of odd, low-pitched hum. It was louder than he'd expected though, more like the bassline at a rock concert than a gentle note from a church organ. It definitely didn't sound natural—not unless there was a humpback whale hiding in the trees—but it also didn't sound like any artificial machinery Harrison had ever known either.

Holy shit, the old man was right; there was something bizarre going on in these woods. Snapped out of his peaceful trance by the realization, Harrison covered one ear and spun around. He listened intently, trying to determine the general direction of the sound's source. He set off to the east, away from the trail, towards where he thought the sound might be coming from. After a few minutes he was rewarded by a sharp increase in volume; it felt as though his very bones were reverberating with the sound. Wincing in discomfort Harrison covered both ears with his hands, continuing his search.

After a five minute hike Harrison was scowling in confusion. He'd had no luck finding the source of the sound, and every time he thought he was approaching the loudest point it started getting quieter again. It was as though the sound was coming not from one distinct point, but from a circle of land a few hundred feet in diameter. Working off of that theory, Harrison walked back to what he thought would be the approximate center of the circle and stood still. In a moment of inspiration he knelt down, ignoring the smears of mud coating his jeans, and pressed his ear to the dirt.

Nothing.

So whatever it was, it wasn't underground. Then where was it coming from? There was nothing else there, except for more forest. Harrison sat on the ground, stumped. Maybe he should just go back to the shed and wait for Jerry. The old man lived much closer to the land than Harrison did; he might have a better idea about the identity of this mystery sound. Maybe there was some species of rare bass cicada or something? Besides, if Harrison stayed out here much longer he was liable to get hearing damage.

Without warning the sound stopped.

Harrison looked around, but nothing appeared to have changed. He stood, intending to do a walk around his imaginary circle again; a final check before he doubled back to the shed. The moment he stood to leave a vine wrapped around his foot. Harrison stared. Where had that come from? He made to leave, but his foot was thoroughly ensnared. With a sigh, he knelt down to free himself.

That was when a second vine wrapped around his left hand, and a third wrapped around his right hand. A final vine, thicker than the rest, wrapped around his torso, constricting him like a snake. Before Harrison had a chance to respond the vines began to pull him, wrapping him up and pressing his body down against the dirt. More vines, and now shrubs and grasses as well, started to creep over his body, forcing him into the mud.

As he was swallowed by the vegetation, Harrison screamed.

...

Harrison faded back into consciousness in complete darkness. His head pounded with such ferocity that it made him nauseous, and his first few seconds back in the world of the living were spent concentrating on forcing the warm sensation of vomit back down into his throat.

He quickly became aware of a few surprising revelations regarding his current situation: he was lying down on a flat, smooth surface, he was tied tightly in place with little movement available to his arms or legs, and his wrists were throbbing nearly as much as his head was. There was a small pressure against his back as well, but it caused no more sensation than what might be caused by an errant pebble situated between his body and the surface he was tied to.

For the first few moments Harrison focused only on what his senses could tell him. The darkness was full; he could see nothing. He heard nothing; there was no sound. He tasted blood; it was possible his nose had been bleeding, or maybe tongue. He ignored his sense of touch, for all he felt was pain. But the smell...

He knew that smell. It was a mixture of dust, mold, old chemicals, wood shavings, and dirt. The combination should be utterly revolting, but to Harrison it was buried as deeply into his brain as his own name. In a fraction of an instant he knew where he was. He was back on his property, roughly tied to his father's long, wooden workbench in the shed.

"Shit," he muttered quietly. The word escaped from Harrison in a fraction of an instant, and he immediately knew that it was a mistake. There was a sound, like the rustling of leaves, perhaps ten feet away from him. Harrison desperately tried to picture the shed's current condition in his mind and pinpoint the sound. By his estimation the sound came from the direction of the ancient, rusting metal shelving unit that held old cans of varnish and paint. The rustling sound crept closer, except it wasn't just rustling anymore; it had gained a slithering quality to it as well, the sound a wet sack of soil might make as it was dragged across the floor.

The sound stopped, and a rush of air warmed Harrison's cheek. His nostrils filled with the smell of freshly turned earth. A few clumps of something gritty fell onto Harrison's face, one slipping into his mouth. It was the taste of dirt, mixed with the blood that was already in his mouth.

There was a strange rattling sound. It could have been a laugh, perhaps, or it could have been a guttural growl. A new sensation now, this one of cold, rusted metal, pressed hard against his cheek.

"You are here, yes! You are the structure-builder, yes? Not the first, but progeny of the first, yes yes. This is your structure. Do not struggle, we have bound you with old steel from the forest. Barbed wire fences, yes, placed by men many years ago. Could bind you with reeds and vines and thorns, yes, but old steel is stronger. Much old steel in the forest."

That rattling laugh again erupted, spraying chunks of dirt over Harrison's face. He choked on one of the clumps and coughed harshly, trying to eject the soil from his mouth without vomiting as well. His head now throbbed in a combination of fear and pain, but in his muddled state of mind he spat out the first questions that popped into his brain. "Why…why the fuck am I here? Who are you?"

The presence above Harrison shifted slightly, as though to move away. "A question, yes. You came here because of the Heralding, yes?"

"The Heralding? What the Hell is a Heralding?"

"The sound from the trees."

"Yeah, sure, Jerry called and told me that there was a weird noise coming from the state land. Was that you?"

"The Heralding was not for you." The presence loomed over him, and rusted metal brushed briefly against his neck. It rubbed gently back and forth against his unshaven whiskers in a slow, methodical rhythm, almost like a very slow shave.

"The Heralding was for me. Forest can't fight, no, not against axes and saws and earth-moving machines. But me, I can fight. Forests don't like to herald, no no no. Don't like the blood that we bring. Very slow to retaliate, a forest is, but the forests are getting wise, yes. They know that they need us now. The trees that you heard were calling because the forest was in pain, yes. Pain and fear, yes, that's what leads to a Heralding. The trees need help against the structure-builders, like you."

Slimy tendrils of something, maybe pond weeds or wet leaves, brushed against Harrison's cheek. The metal on his throat pushed down a little harder.

"What? No!" Harrison's voice broke. He coughed violently again, and noticed that the pressure on his throat lessened a little when he did so. Maybe he had a moment to talk. "I'm not hurting the forest. I don't even live here most of the year, I just come visit!" And besides," he added, "The trees that were calling aren't even on my land! That's state land over there!"

"Your land, state's land, conservancy's land, the forest doesn't care for this," the thing growled at him. "Small distance from here, perhaps three hundred trees away, there was a wound done to the forest. Many trees cut. Grass destroyed, flowers destroyed, nests destroyed, soil removed and replaced with stone. It is not the first time this was done to the forest, not by far, but the forest knows that it will not be the last, and so the forest Heralded. It was wise to do this. I have not been above ground in many years, many many years, but now that I am here…" The metal maintained pressure on Harrison's neck, but now the slimy tendrils of the thing crept over his neck as well, cold and damp and horrible. "I see that the forest was very wise to do this."

The Rigby Farm. Gerry told him the developer had already finished clearcutting. Harrison had never really considered the Rigbys' land to be part of the same forest as his, but he supposed if you looked at an aerial map and only considered the trees…

"I didn't do that!" he squeaked. "That was the developer from Aspen Airs! Don't even know who he is! I can find the bastard's name if you let me go!"

"No proof you have of your claims. You are a structure-builder, the forest knows this. The wound done to the forest will be repaid unto you." The tendrils lay across the full length of Harrison's throat now, but the metal withdrew.

"This old steel is strong. Stronger than flesh and blood and bone, yes. You can die with this, yes, but it is not right. Too fast, too easy, and not a proper punishment for a wound to the forest. There is a plant beneath you, grown through this table with my help. Japanese Knotweed, it is called by humans. It was brought to this land by your ancestors, many years ago. A problem for the structure-builders now, it is, and many of your kind try to kill it when they find it, but it is a tough plant. Very tough. It grows through stone, through human-altered wood, through anything. Grows through your structures, makes them crumble. Normally grows slow, yes, but I will make it grow fast. It is an appropriate weapon, a good way for you to die."

The earthy breath filled Harrison's nostrils again, and the presence loomed mere inches from his face, its voice dropping into a satisfied whisper. "You will crumble too, when it grows through you."

The subtle pressure in Harrison's back, the one he'd

assumed to be a pebble, moved slightly, just enough for him to feel it. It began to push against his back, gently at first, then in earnest. He arched his back on the table, but this gave him only the slightest reprieve before the eager plant pressed against his back again.

"Fuck!" he screamed in panic. The creature was no longer above him, but he knew it was still in the room. The knotweed hurt now, bruising his skin, searching for a weak point. Harrison strained unsuccessfully against his restraints, the barbed wire slicing deeply into his wrists. The pain was dizzying, but through that pain came an idea, a last idea, that presented itself to him. "This wire! The old steel! Where did you get it? What part of the forest?"

The creature made an unconcerned noise, but it responded. "I found the old steel between the two small ponds where the frogs and tadpoles thrive, and the rows of white pines. There is more, much more, but I needed only this."

"That's the northern boundary of my property! The barbed wire was put in to mark the fence fucking ages ago! I can't do anything on the other side of it, by human law. The developer owns the Rigby land now where the trees were and he's cutting them down to make a fucking strip mall or something. Please, I promise, I couldn't have destroyed - " Harrison's words melted into screams as he felt the knotweed pierce through his shirt and puncture his skin, entering his body in the lower back just to the right of his spine. The pain was excruciating, but even worse was the sensation of movement in the wound as the plant searched for a weak point to continue to grow.

The creature did not respond at first, and the only sound in the cabin was Harrison's screams. When it eventually spoke again, it sounded thoughtful. "What is a developer?" it asked in a calm voice, nearly drowned out by Harrison's screams as the knotweed expanded in his flesh.

Then there was movement, and a sound at the far end of the cabin. The door opened, light flooding into the shed. There was a flurry of movement to Harrison's right, but through the mask of pain he never got a clear glimpse of the creature—only a flurry of leaves, dirt, some twigs or branches, and something wet dragging across the floor—before it vanished beneath the table and sank into the hole that the knotweed had made.

"Harrison? You in here, Kid?" came a concerned voice. Muddily, Harrison made out Jerry's silhouette against the sunlight that now filled the cabin. "What...why are you tied to the table? Holy shit, is this a sex thing? Fuck, Kid, I didn't mean to interrupt! I just heard yelling... Jesus Christ, you're bleeding! Is that barbed wire? Kid, we need to get you —" But Harrison, suddenly colder than he'd ever been in his life, lost consciousness. He didn't hear anything else.

...

Harrison spent three days in the hospital before returning to the cabin. Jerry had managed to cut through the barbed wire using a pair of bolt cutters he found in the tool shed and, in a surprising show of strength, dragged the much larger and younger man out to his car and rushed him to the hospital.

Although he'd lost a fair amount of blood on the workshop table, and in Jerry's car, the wound hadn't struck anything vital. Harrison had stabilized quickly. He'd spoken to Kerry and Aaron over the phone once and Jerry twice since the incident, but he hadn't been able to bring himself to tell any of them about the creature, even after a few probing questions from Jerry about whether he'd made it to the source of the sound. He did, however, thank the man profusely for taking him to the hospital, and he even managed to get Jerry to accept payment to get the car reupholstered, despite the old man's protests.

Harrison knew how it would sound if he tried to tell anyone about the creature, and he also knew that he didn't want his siblings trying to send him to therapy. He didn't want to catch glimpses of furtive discussions about his mental state among the hospital staff, and most of all he didn't want to think about the events preceding his injury. Each time he let his thoughts drift back to the shed his nose filled with the smell of earth, his breathing quickened, and every rational thought in his brain was crowded out by dark thoughts and an overwhelming sense of panic.

When Jerry dropped him off back at the cabin after his three days were up, he kept his eyes glued to his feet. The moment Jerry's car was out of sight he made a break for his car at a dead run, determined not to look up for fear of catching a glimpse of the horrible shed. He clicked his key fob as he ran, almost crying in relief when the head-lights flashed in response. He wrenched the door open with fumbling hands, then promptly tripped in his haste to get into the car and drive far, far away.

Harrison sprawled unceremoniously in the dirt, landing hard on his shoulder. He snatched at the open car door, intending to use its weight to haul himself back to his feet, but he froze in place the moment he saw the front driver's side tire.

A plant, perhaps thigh-high, had grown straight through the tire, now flat and useless. Harrison scurried around the car on his hands and knees, not even bothering to rise to his feet, panic lodged deep in his throat as he confirmed that all four tires were in the same state.

Harrison whimpered quietly, putting his head in his hands. There was no doubt in his mind that this strange, bamboo-like plant was Japanese Knotweed.

He'd only had his head in his hands a few moments before he smelled earth, then he felt the warm caress of breath against the back of his neck. He thought about running, but then he thought about how much greenery there was between him and the main road. How many trees, how much soil, how any holes, and he saw little point in it. Harrison screwed his eyes shut tighter and waited.

The horrible voice, the one that had filled Harrison's nightmares for three days, spoke. "Give me a name."

"What?" Harrison whimpered. A small weight, hardly heavier than a mouse, rested on his shoulder. A single drop of water trickled down his shirt.

"Developer. The one you mentioned. The forest thinks you're talking true. Give. Me. A. Name."

Harrison unscrewed his eyes, waiting a moment for them to focus. His throat stuck, choking out his reply. He felt the horrible slimy feeling, tendrils cold and clammy, on the back of his neck.

"Do it," whispered Harrison's nightmare.

With trembling hands, Harrison fumbled his phone out of his pocket and googled Aspen Airs LLC.

Ian Ableson

About the Author

Ian is an ecologist by training and a writer by choice. He writes a variety of genres, but the horror and mystery stories seem to be the ones that get published most often. He spends his days working for a local land conservancy as a stewardship manager, which involves a lot of time spent standing ankle-deep in marshes while scowling at a clipboard. As such, many of his stories feature some sort of environmental influence. They say to write what you know, after all. He's been published in a variety of anthologies and magazines (again, mostly mysteries and horror). He lives and writes in Southeast Michigan.

MOTHS TO A FLAME
O. SANDER

I thought I saw her last night. Kate stood in the shadows of the trees that edge up to our property, barely picked out by the moonlight. She was hard to make out, almost not there, but I thought she was. It's funny how the mind can play tricks. She's been missing for two months, but this is the first time I thought I saw her, so maybe something deep inside me still hopes.

Who could blame me? I was caught from the moment I first saw Kate perform. She spun fire poi and danced in a costume of shining metal scales. The costume moved with her, describing her body in shimmering flame-light. She became fire herself in it, as she spun the balls of flame on their chains, otherworldly and unforgettable. She burned in my memory after that performance.

The Kate I saw dancing is hard to reconcile with the one from last night. That was a creature of fire, movement, and a joy that was almost palpable as she swayed and spun

her poi. This Kate under the trees was all sad motionless-
ness, silent moon-silver, and shadow; a wraith, a specter,
only barely there. Rationally I know it has to be a trick
of the dark, just a shadow under the trees where my yard
ends and the edge of the forest begins. It *has* to be. Then
that traitor, the thing we call hope, whispers that it was my
Kate I saw, no mistake. Real, alive, not a ghostly vision or
figment of my imagination. If that were true, why wouldn't
she just come home?

I wash my coffee cup and stare out the kitchen window, across the yard to the tree line where Kate seemed to
be standing last night. Now it's just trees; no sign of her
now, if there ever even was. I sigh, turning on the morning
news in the hope that it'll chase this false vision away. It
doesn't help. It fades into indistinguishable background
noise, and I turn again to thoughts of my vanished girl.
It's like a missing tooth that my tongue goes back to probe
again and again, as if something might have miraculously
changed in the last two minutes.

I remember when I finally did meet her. I discovered that fire was her personality too: passionate, quick,
warm, and a temper that could burn you to ash if she was
provoked. I wasn't the only moth drawn to Kate's flame,
and she made it clear from the start that she was a woman
of many loves. I didn't care. Well, I did, but I wanted to
bask in her heat more than I cared whether I was the only
one. We went out on our first date two days later. It lasted
a week, and I was hooked.

When Kate went missing I tried to file a missing

persons report. The deputy who was supposed to take the report dismissed Kate, me, and my concerns for her. His look was cold and full of distaste, and he suggested she'd just gotten tired and moved on to one of her many other lovers.

"You people…" he'd started, and I knew in my bones from his look and tone that by *people* he meant any LGBTQIA freaks in general, and this freak and her missing lover in particular. "You people, well, you're not exactly the most stable or committed, are you? She's probably fine, just hooked up with some other…female."

I imagined all the epithets he was thinking during that pause. Bigots are so predictable, and so divorced from fact. I was angry, but I ignored his looks and his significant pauses, just pushing ahead until he finally took my report. I doubt they bothered much about it. I tried, for a while at least. I called the station to check in, and I posted fliers. I drove around looking, as if she would suddenly appear by the side of the road and apologize for losing track of time. I know I should have kept following up, kept pushing, but I finally sank into this hopeless depression and barely had the energy to get out of bed most days.

"…believed to be the man responsible for the dis-appearances of several women in Selma and surrounding communities." The voice of the anchor on the morning news breaks through the grey wall of depression and my thoughts about Kate. I never listen to the news, and didn't know this had been going on. The anchor continues in a practiced, neutral tone. There is just the slightest hint of concern around their eyes, the way reporters are trained to show.

"Police say the investigation is ongoing, but he allegedly abducted at least four local women that we know of so far. One source inside the department says they believe he kept them alive for about three months…" I switch the TV off, scrambling for the phone. I didn't catch the man's name in the broadcast, but I'm sure that he's the one. He's the reason my Kate disappeared, the reason why she's been gone two months.

Maybe she's still alive! Maybe they just need to find her, or maybe she's been found but her name was withheld from the press. Don't they do that with victims to protect their privacy? Maybe she's giving a statement, or at the hospital, or…I exert some willpower, forcing myself to stop grasping at straws. What I need to do is talk to the Sheriff, or at least someone else involved in the investigation.

My hands are shaking so hard that it takes me three tries to dial, and my urgency makes hours out of the four rings it takes for my call to be answered. Finally, a voice on the line says, "Josephine County Sherr - " A great, broken sob bursts from me, cutting her off. I haven't cried, not once, since Kate vanished. Throwing hope on top of the brittle sticks of my despair and dry-eyed mourning shatters it all, the final stone that brings the whole crushing weight down. Now the tears come hot and fast, and I can't speak. All I can do is shake and make these noises of grief that sound barely human into the mouthpiece of the phone.

I fight to push it down, to put a lid on it. I come to realize that the voice at the other end of the line has been trying her best to calm me down, but I can't hear her over my own sobs and the turmoil inside me. In the end the concern in the voice on the phone helps me to regain control. As the violence of my sobbing dies I can finally start to make out what she's saying.

"Ma'am? Ma'am, are you okay? Ma'am, do you need me to send someone? Do you need help?" The concern in the woman's voice gets stronger with every question, and I know I have to get myself under control. I take a few slow, deep breaths, my sobs growing quieter. The questions keep coming, but the speed and urgency diminishes a little.

"S-s-sorry. Sorry. I'm o-okay. Sorry…" That's all I can manage for a moment. I take another deep breath, try to find some calm, and attempt speaking again. "Okay. I th-think I'm okay. I saw on the news, the guy…the killer in Selma. The m-missing women. Can you tell me if any were alive? It's just…my Kate…Kate Sommers, I mean… she went missing two months ago, and the news said…" I trail off as my emotions threaten to get free of my tenuous control again.

There's a pause, and then, "Kate Sommers? Is this Melissa? Melissa Satterfield?" Professionalism has now completely disappeared, replaced by shock.

She sounds so surprised. I bet that means that bigot never did anything about the report I tried to file, comes my unbidden thought. It's so detached from my feelings right this moment that it could have come from someone else.

Then another thought on the heels of the first: *Or maybe because she knows they found Kate's body…* Suddenly I no longer feel detached, and a renewed sob threatens. Shoving the reaction down hard, I manage to say aloud, "Yes, this is Melissa." The tone of voice I automatically fall into sounds like I'm answering some business call, but the formality helps me keep control of myself.

"Kate was a really close friend. She talked about you all the time." The woman's voice is lower now, as if she's trying to avoid being heard by anyone else in the station. "I shouldn't be talking about this. It could mean my job. But…we haven't found any sign of Kate in the cave with the other victims' remains. I'll call you if something comes up."

"But the guy's house is in Selma?" That's all I can think about right now, the house in Selma, not far from here in Wonder.

"No. Nothing there. He took them to a cave…" She trails off, and I can hear other voices in the background. "Look, I can't talk now. I just started here, and I can't afford to lose this job already. I'll call." She hangs up before I can say more, leaving me in the same limbo I was in before I called. Is Kate gone? Is she still alive somewhere in the forest?

But no, she did give me one bit of information, didn't she? A cave. Presumably a small one somewhere in the forest, nothing that would be remarked on or remembered, nothing that would draw attention. He wouldn't want to be found. That doesn't help me much, since the Rogue

River Siskiyou National Forest is huge. Short of finding law enforcement and following them to the site, I'll never know where the cave is. Besides, no one was found alive there. The friend of Kate's - and I realize now I never got her name - only mentioned remains. Kate, if she still lives, isn't going to pop out of a shadowy nook and shout, "Here I am!"

I wander through the house to our bedroom and open the closet door. Amid the more prosaic, everyday clothing are Kate's dance costumes. I run my hand over the shining metal of the one I first saw her in. Even in daylight it's still glittering flame, all golds and reds. I remember her telling me she got it from an artisan not that far away, a man she called Troll. She said he lived and worked somewhere in Cave Junction, ironically enough with that nickname.

He wasn't far from Wonder at all. I suddenly re-member now that he and some fellow artisans call their business Fae Built, Inc. It's appropriate. The outfit could easily have been spun from fairy magic, with the way it looks in motion. So shining and vivid, like Kate was.

There it is. "Kate was." This thought, this start on accepting that Kate's gone and isn't coming back, is simul-taneously terrible and relief. Hope can keep you going, but it also keeps the hurt alive.

I run my hand over the scales again, watching them move and catch the light. But what about what I saw last night? Kate, at the edge of the forest? I wondered why she didn't come in then. I've never believed in ghosts, but now I have to wonder. That Kate was so pale silver and dark, not anything like the vital flame she always was, not like this fiery metal.

I have to know. I have to find this ghostly thing, and see what it really is. Tonight I'll have a flashlight ready, and I'll wait for the specter of Kate to appear. Maybe it's all in my imagination, and she won't show up. Maybe she's just shadow and moonlight. Or maybe Kate will be at the edge of the forest tonight, and I'll at least have a chance to say goodbye, if nothing else.

Whether the vision last night was a ghost or not, I've been haunted by Kate every moment of every day since she disappeared.

...

The moon is near full when it rises, flooding my back-yard with light and leaving deep, jet shadows under the trees at the edge of my property. It's frustratingly difficult to see if that pale, still version of my fiery Kate is there. I stare out my kitchen window for so long that it all starts to become a single, monochromatic blur as my attention begins to drift.

Movement calls me back. She's there, *she's there*, just stepping out of a shadow beneath the trees. She comes fur-ther out into the light tonight than she did last night. She's still wan and pale, and even now I can't tell if she's alive or a ghost, or even some kind of hallucination dreamed up by my deep need to see her again. I can see her amid the undergrowth at the edge of the tree line, looking sadly toward the home we shared.

I shiver as her gaze passes blankly over the kitchen window, where I stand with the lights out as I watch her. Seeing her like this chills me to the bone, and I'm frozen in place. It's only when she turns and begins to drift slowly back into the forest that I break my paralysis. I grab my flashlight off the counter and hurry to the door.

By the time I'm out on our small, rear deck the phantasm of Kate has begun vanishing into the shadows beneath the trees. "Kate!" I call to her, but it's like she doesn't hear or see me, like I'm the one who's barely connected to the world now. I run down the stairs and across the yard to the tree line, too late to catch her before she melts into the silver and black zebra stripes of tree shadow and moonbeam.

It's colder in the tree shadows. I shiver as I switch on my flashlight, calling her name as I search for her. There's no answer, but I hear the snap and crackle of the twig and leaf litter from the forest floor off to my left, so I head that way. I stumble over roots, nearly falling a couple times, but I keep going. Real Kate or phantom, I have to know. I feel like I'll lose my mind if I don't.

The sounds only come occasionally, just enough to draw me on. Once or twice I catch a glimpse of movement, which must be the phantom I'm chasing. I think she has a limp. Do ghosts limp? I don't think I've ever heard of one that did. A wind begins as I work my way through the trees. It isn't strong, but now I'm thoroughly chilled. Goose flesh ripples down my arms, and the hiss of the wind through the leaves sounds almost like someone whispering. I can almost hear my name in it, calling me onward. I lose track of how long I'm in pursuit, or how far I've gone. I stay focused on just keeping after the sounds and short glimpses I get.

A flood of moonlight ahead, bright after so much time in the shadows of the trees, breaks me out of the spell. I look around and quickly realize that I'm lost. I make my slow way toward the brightness ahead, shivering and scared now. I can't be all that deep into the forest, but it's far enough that I recognize nothing. I make my way towards the moonlight, and soon find myself at the edge of a small clearing. I peer into the light, and gasp.

Kate stands on the far side of the clearing. She still doesn't acknowledge me; instead she's staring off to one side of the clearing. I see her in achingly beautiful profile, moon-silvered skin and hair a waving, ethereal shine as it catches the light. I call her name, then blunder through the last bit of the trees into the clearing.

But the clearing is empty; there's only me and the cold light. No Kate. She's vanished, as if she was never here, and I can't find any hint of her among the shadows circling the brightness of the open space.

"Kate! Where are you?" My voice sounds a little panicky, but I keep trying. "Kate, it's me! It's Melissa!"

The wind picks up as I listen for any response. I hear something at last, the sound almost lost amid the rustle of the leaves.

"Meliiissssaaaaaa. Meliiiisssaaaaa!"

It's coming from the same direction I thought the vision of Kate was looking. Recklessly I plunge back into the shadows, chasing the phantom sound like I did the ghostly sight.

Abruptly I reach a break in the trees. Before me is a wall of natural stone, and in it is the blackness of a cave mouth. Kate's ghost has brought me here; the place, I think now, that she probably died. I take a cautious step forward, shining my flashlight around the opening. A scraping sound echoes from somewhere inside, and then, unexpectedly, yellow light shines from somewhere in the cave's depths. My heart leaps into my throat. What ghost needs light? Kate must be alive! I run into the cave, but I don't get far.

Around a slight bend I trip over something in my blind rush. There's a brief, sharp pain as my head hits the stone of the cave floor, and then blackness.

...

My head hurts, and ridges of stone press painfully into my side. These are what I notice first, then I hear movement and I remember where I am and why I'm here. I open my eyes, and there she is. Here's the same profile I saw in the clearing, without the ghostly hues of the chase through the woods. The dim candle Kate lit has restored the flush of life to her skin and the shining gold to her hair. She is alive, and she's here now! I want to leap up and throw my arms around her and never let go, but I discover I can't. I struggle, realizing that, while I was unconscious, Kate had firmly bound my arms behind me.

"Kate? What's going on? Why? Why did you - "

The sound of laughter cuts me off, though it's not the

joyful laugh I knew. This is different, a gruff almost-growl of a laugh. It barely sounds like something that could come from Kate's mouth. Her body shakes with it, and it grows from the growl-like laugh into something more like a roar. It's insane. That's when I realize *she* is insane.

Whatever that monster from Selma did to her, however she survived, it pushed her over the edge. It explains everything. I see why she just stood in the woods instead of coming home now, why she acted as if she didn't know I was there when I was following her. It explains why, when I finally found my girl, I wound up bound and helpless on a cave floor in the middle of the forest. If I could just get her to untie me, to come with me out of the cave and back to civilization, we can find her some help. We can fix this, together.

"Honey, whatever happened to you, whatever he *did* to you, we'll get through this. I'm here for you, and we'll figure this out. Just…just untie me. Just come home."

The laughter cuts off abruptly, and Kate turns her head to look at me. She's smiling, but it's not a reassuring one. There's no warmth there in my fiery Kate, just a kind of cold amusement at my expense, at what I'm saying, at the whole situation. "Home?" the question is a whisper.

I touched something. I did! If I can just keep going… If I can get her home, maybe that would fix whatever is broken. Or at least start to. My thoughts are rushed, but I try to keep her attention now that I've made some small connection. "Yes, home. You don't have to stay here. You could come home. Get clean, have some hot food and a nice bed. I'll do whatever you need, whatever it takes. Honey, I've missed you so much. Please, just come home with me and we can start to put it all behind us. Everything will be okay aga - "

"Melisssssssaaaaaaaaaaa..." Kate says my name, cutting me off. She draws it out like she did in the forest, and it reverberates from the cave walls, giving it a dark tone that I don't like. Her voice also seems weirdly accented, not like herself at all. It sounds vaguely Hispanic, maybe.

"Melissa, you did not look around, did you." It's a statement, still delivered with that accent. She turns to face me, and I let out a small, involuntary shriek of surprise. She's missing a leg, and in place of it she has a wooden one. It's narrower at the hem of her skirt, then it widens into a large, slightly flattened ball with fancy notches carved into it. She limps closer to me, and even though this is my Kate I shrink back, trying to avoid her touch. My skin crawls with revulsion as she reaches toward me. She grabs hold of my t-shirt anyway, lifting me partly off the cave floor with a strength she never had before. Before I can react any further she turns me to face back toward the cave mouth.

There's the bend I came around, and the thing that must have tripped me. It's a pile of bone with a few shreds of raw, red flesh still clinging to them. And beside them, partially open eyes cloudy in death and mouth frozen in a silent scream, is Kate's head. Most of the flesh has been left intact, so she's still recognizable. I stare uncomprehending for a moment, then I realize what it is I'm seeing.

I scream, trying to push myself back against the cave wall. I think I'd force my way through the cave wall if it would get me further away. The thing, whatever it is that looks like Kate, laughs its growling laugh at my terror.

"You people. You forget your old stories. You put all your faith in your machines and your science. Back home in Ecuador, or in Colombia, some still remember the lore. They know there is more than your science has found. So, when people disappear into the forest, they know. They say *La Tunda* is hunting, and they come to drive my kind off. Finally I came here, where the hunting is rich and no one remembers. Even with the *molinillo* that marks the Tunda," she gestures toward the elaborate wooden leg, "you do not know what you face. You people are so accustomed to the monsters being your own kind, you never suspect that there are real monsters."

As she - it - speaks, its features ripple and fold. Kate's likeness melts away. I'm left staring at a hideous thing, skin like the darkened, rotting flesh of an old apple core. The large lips reveal sharp, jagged, triangular teeth like a shark's as it speaks. "And so easy, in spite of all your science, for a shape changer to eat her fill and make sure some man takes the blame."

I moan, "Please. Please just…just let me go. I won't tell anyone. Please. Who would believe me…"

It laughs. "Oh, you will leave this cave. At least, something looking like you will leave this cave. You see, it is time for me to move on to new hunting grounds. Tomorrow you are going to be seen driving north, and then disappear. This will happen conveniently, just before the police find what's left of your girlfriend and take an interest in where you went."

I shake my head in denial of everything it says, pushing harder back against the cave wall as it gets nearer. It slowly drinks in my terror, like a fine wine. I can't even beg any longer; the sounds coming uncontrollably from my mouth are whimpers and sobs.

"This Kate, she was delicious. Vital, and full of energy like a flame. Her fire drew me like a moth. I had to have it. I drank her slowly, just a little blood at first. She was too wonderful to waste by gorging. And oh, how she cried and called for you. It was almost as tasty to listen to her as it was to feed! I waited until she was too weak to provide me any dinner entertainment before I began to eat."

The creature watches my face, savoring every reaction I make, every tear I shed. "If it was not time to move on, I might not have hunted again for weeks. But now it is time to go. You are no Kate, but you will do."

The mouth of this thing that calls itself the Tunda opens impossibly wide. It grabs my leg, shredding the denim of my jeans easily with razor-like fingernails. Its slimy tongue comes out and licks delicately at my skin while it keeps its eyes locked on mine. It chuckles low in its throat at my disgust and horror, at my attempts to squirm away. Then it decides to stop toying with me. I scream my throat raw as it begins to feed.

O. SANDER
ABOUT THE AUTHOR

O. Sander is a writer, artist, composer, photographer, crafter, and family caregiver. She is originally from California but has bounced from place to place for most of her life. She finally landed in "25 square miles surrounded by reality" in Michigan, where she spends her time inventing worlds and exploring them through her drawings as well as writing their stories and music. She claims to be a combination of Morticia Addams and Glinda the Good Witch and tends to embarrass her long-suffering spouse into trying to pretend he doesn't know her.

A Pillywiggins For Beau Hensel
Stuart Croskell

My brother Beau and me, we left the pickup truck on the northern edge of the fir plantation. The scent of the fir trees was citrusy-clean, and we breathed in deep as we strolled along the overgrown trail into the forest.

My knapsack, though only half full, lay heavy across my back. As was tradition we held hands, and Beau swallowed heavily. He was doing a lot of swallowing, and he kept glancing at me when he thought I wasn't looking.

I said, "You okay, Beau?" I was two years older than his sixteen, and it was my job to look after him.

"A little nervous, Daisy," he said. "Truth be told."

"Me too," I said.

"But you've done it before, haven't you? It's not your first time."

I waved my free arm toward the forest, towards the toothy peaks of the White Mountains that towered in the distance some twenty miles south of Jefferson. "I ain't counting or bragging, Beau, but you're number five."

"So it's true, there've been others?"

"Mr. Beau Hensel," I said, letting go of him as I folded my arms, all coquettish-like. "You *know* there has."

"Yeah, I guess. Dale sorta hinted it was gonna be you who...you know. And Boone, he straight-up told me, 'Beau, my friend, Daisy's the one who's gonna do me.'"

"That Boone," I said, laughing. "Ugly as a mud fence. I liked him, though."

"Always knew where you stood with Boone," he said.

"You okay with that, little brother?" I gently grabbed hold of his thin shoulders with both hands, looking him right in the eyes. "That you ain't my first?"

My brother thought for a while, stroking his chin like some old-timey philosopher. "Yeah," he said slowly. "I reckon. I kinda like the idea that...other folks have gone before me."

"Well, if it makes you feel any better, Ledger's one of mine. Dalton, too. All nice boys." I tugged his nose with my thumb and forefinger. "But you, Beau, you're as cute as a bug's ear." Beau smiled at that. It was true too. With his angular features, and dreamy blue peepers, my brother was a looker.

I grabbed his hand again, and we moved deeper into the forest.

After a while, he said, "You know what Momma told me?"

"Not until you tell *me*, Beau."

"She said that I was gonna be your last one. That

true?"

I wished Momma had kept her trap shut. "It is, Beau."

"But why?"

I shrugged. "I don't want to do it anymore. I've done my part, and when I've done you that's the end of it."

Beau chewed this over. I knew what he was thinking, and I was thinking it too. "I don't have to do this, do I sis?"

"No, you don't."

"But I want to. I mean, it's what I'm for. Ain't it?"

"That's what Momma told us."

"What *all* the Mommas told us," Beau said. "Over and over."

I nodded.

Beau halted, looked around. "Can you hear 'em, Daisy? The *young'uns*?"

I lifted my chin, trying to tune into the forest's secret language, but all I heard was the wind caught in the pine branches. "Yeah, they're here, Beau," I lied. "With us."

"Any pillywiggins out there?"

"I can't hear any right now, Beau. But they're comin'."

"For me?"

"Of course, Beau."

"I wish *I* could hear 'em."

We walked another half mile or so, and then I led him off the trail, into the forest's hidden places. We were about five minutes in when my brother stopped again. He removed his hand from mine, and walked up to the nearest fir, patting its trunk. "These trees, they're gonna be chopped down soon?"

I nodded. "Couple of weeks, Momma said."

"How old are these ones?"

I studied the pines. "Thirty years, give or take."

Beau shook his head in disgust. "That ain't no age, Daisy. No age to die. Not for a tree." He put his arms around the tree's trunk, embracing it, resting his forehead on its bark. "If these trees were folks," he said, "it'd be like killing little kids."

"That's why we do what we do, Beau," I said, hating the irony of his logic. Beau turned his head, so he faced me, closing his eyes. "You sound just like Momma."

I moved over to him and pulled him gently off the tree. "Come on, brother. We've got promises to keep."

"As long as I bag me a pillywiggins," he whispered, almost to himself, "I'll be happy."

We moved further into the woods, and after a few minutes Beau said, "What about here?"

We were standing in a small glade; thirty-foot diameter, I reckoned. Glades were something of a rarity in plantation forest, since the regimented, straight-lined planting tended to hinder deviation. It was as right a place as any. Besides, I think Beau wanted to see the sky, even if that sky was lowering and wintery or was spitting out occasional sheets of rain.

"If you like, Beau," I said.

He sat down in the middle of the clearing, looking up at me expectantly. "I'm all yours, sis," he said. Kind of nervously.

"Yeah, you are."

I shrugged off my knapsack, opened the flap, and rummaged around inside.

"Do you think it's true, about Ricky and Fern? " Beau asked. "That when they went into *their* forest, they decided against it. Just lit out?"

"Yeah, that's exactly what they did." I found my cell phone, checked for a signal, and placed it on the mossy pine-needled carpet next to Beau. "Ricky and Fern, they were supposed to do *this* forest. That's why *we're* here. According to Momma, Fern and Ricky walked clean through these trees until they came out the other end. Found a highway and thumbed it, got as far as they could get. Left the Mommas all holding their dicks."

"Mommas don't have dicks, Daisy."

"Yeah, but you know what I mean," I said, retrieving the oily, cloth bundle from my knapsack.

Beau chuckled. "I wish I coulda saw that. Oh boy, the Mommas' faces. Can you imagine? When they realized what Fern and Ricky had done?" He chuckled some more.

Beau eyed the bundle in my hands, hovering on the edge of apprehension. "Can't believe this is happening, Daisy," he said. "It's kinda unreal."

"I know," I said.

"So what're you gonna do? You know, after…I'm over?"

"I dunno, Beau. Maybe New Mexico. Find a place in the desert, away from any damn pines. Grow big fat peaches. Eat 'em all day long, juice running down my chin. And my kids, when I have them, lots of them, they're gonna be tanned peachy-brown, bones big and strong."

"That sounds nice," said Beau.

"I'm tired of being cold and damp. No more winters for me."

"Bet Momma's angry."

"You can come, too," I said. "Doesn't matter what Momma thinks."

"Like Fern and Ricky?"

"Like them, yeah."

"But what about the forest? What about the *young'uns?*"

I shrugged.

"No, we gotta do this, sis. *I* gotta do it. I gotta play pretty, I got *responsibilities.*"

I sighed. "Beau, are you sure? I mean, really, *really?*"

"Really, really, sis. I've made my mind up, and I don't chew cabbage twice." He stood up, buoyed by his own certainty, and removed his jacket. He folded it up neatly on the ground. Next came his t-shirt, shoes, and socks. When it came to his understuff he shyly turned away. After he'd removed that, he faced me once more, eyes down.

"Jeez, Beau. You're as skinny as a toothpick."

"Feels weird, being like this."

"Lie down, Beau," I said. "And close your eyes."

He did what he was told, his back on the forest floor, hands covering his privates. He was already shivering. I slid the knife from its cloth sheath, holding it up to the pale light, hating and loving its deadly glint.

"I'm gonna start now, Beau," I said. "You'll feel a coupla pricks, maybe, nothing else. There's no pain."

He nodded, eyes still closed.

I kissed him on the forehead. "I love you, brother," I whispered.

He nodded again. "You, too, sis."

I took the knife and cut the right places on Beau's body, the way Momma had taught me; the way all the Mommas taught their girls. As Beau started to bleed out I stood up and called Momma on the cell. I told her Beau was doing okay, and that the young'uns were already sniffing around.

Momma started to say something, but I broke the connection. I was done listening to her. Instead, I sat down next to my brother and held his hand. "How you doing, Beau?"

"I'm doing good," he said, his voice small. He was afraid, I could tell.

"Are they coming, the young'uns?"

I listened to the woods, to the wind in the pines, to the *caw* and *kraa* of overhead crows.

"Yeah, they're coming, Beau. They're coming to you, and they know you're here for 'em. That you're gonna take 'em to their new home."

"Any pillywiggins?"

I stroked his forehead. It was clammy, cold. "Well, let me see." I paused, playing along as if I actually could see the forest's children. "Well, they kind of all look same-ish, on account of their early years. But as far as I can tell we got dryads, green boys, brown ones too; wood maidens, moss girls, a coupla woodwose, and a whole bunch of faerie. You got yourself quite the collection, Beau."

He smiled, his blood now pooling around him. "And pillywiggins? Have I nabbed me one of those?"

"Not yet, Beau, but they're awful rare."

"Did Dale or Dalton, any of the others, get a pillywiggins?"

"No, not one."

Of course I *would* give my brother a pillywiggins, but that would be later, just before he lost consciousness. I wanted Beau to go out on a high.

To my left, fallen branches cracked. It was the Mommas. I was glad they were here, and this was all on them now. I could be a child once more. I leaned into Beau's ear. "The Mommas are here," I whispered.

Beau smiled again. "Not long now," he said. "I'm weak as a kitten."

The Mommas were singing softly. They'd sing their song for as long as it took Beau to die. I'd never been able to make out the words to the song, even though Momma had sung it to us kids since forever. Mostly she sang the lullaby to Beau, to sing him to sleep. This time it was for eternity. The words were Old Country words, soft and lilting. Their familiarity, I knew, would comfort Beau. Years ago our Momma had promised me she'd teach me the words when I became such as she, a Momma.

Today there were six Mommas, including our Momma. Six, like pallbearers. Except, in this case, the cargo lived yet. One of them was smoking a hand-rolled-cigarette, and two of them carried lengths of burlap slung over their shoulders. They wore what they always seemed to wear: Blue jeans and boots, with waxed, cotton dusters of varying lengths and colors. But all of them, without fail, wore green-silk gloves. Jeanette, the youngest of the Mommas, was a couple of months older than me. Grand-Momma was the oldest. Nobody knew her age, and nobody dared to ask.

The way they were dressed in their everyday clothes lended a freaky normalcy to the proceedings, like it was the kind of thing regular folks did every day. The first time I took a boy into the woods I was shocked at how they were garbed when the Mommas showed up. I guess I imagined they'd be fitted out in some kind of ceremonial get-up, you know, to underline the moment. A boy's life was being sacrificed so that others could live, and it felt sacrilegious that they could be so matter-of-fact and workaday about it all. Like they were taking out the garbage.

"Keep your eyes closed, Beau," I whispered. "They're here."

He nodded. "Is Momma with 'em?"

"Uh-huh."

He relaxed. I hadn't realized how tense he'd been about that. Me, I'd just assumed she'd be one of the ones carrying him out of the woods. As the Mommas entered the glade I kept my eyes on Beau while they approached. When they stood around my brother and me, Momma said, "Daisy, stand aside now."

I kissed Beau on the lips and stood up, moving away

from the women now surrounding him. Working as one they lifted him up, wrapping the burlap around his limp body, gently enfolding him. Years ago Momma had told me that the cocooning part of it betokened Beau's upcoming rebirth.

"Momma?" Beau said.

"I'm here, Baby," our Momma said, her weather-tanned face expressionless.

"Am I doing alright?"

Momma looked over to me, her too-blue eyes shaking me down to the soul. "He doing alright, Daisy? The young'uns, they come marching two by two? To Beau?"

I nodded.

Momma said to Beau, "Baby, you're doing just fine."

When they finished all I could see of Beau was his head sticking out of one end of the burlap. The Mommas positioned themselves around him, three on either side and facing his feet, Beau's head behind them. I always wondered about this. Was it because they couldn't bear to look at the boys as they died? Were the Mommas, when it came to it, cowards? Or was it that they just didn't care?

From inside their coats they each took out chrome-red hay hooks, snagging them carefully into the tow sack. In near-perfect sync they bent their knees, backs straight, and lifted my brother to thigh-height.

I looked into the Mommas' eyes to find the truth, the *righteousness*, of what we, they, were doing, but all I saw was heavy-lidded weariness. They seemed weighed down by the sheer, inescapable routine of it all.

I wanted to scream out, *Why are we still doing this!?*

"Babe," Momma said to her only son. "You're so heavy, I reckon you musta got all of them."

Outlined in blood, the moss held a Beau-shape where my brother had lain, like one of those ancient crime-scene photos that chalked out the contours of the victim's final, everlasting sleep.

The Mommas trudged off, away from the glade, back toward the forest trail and the waiting vehicles. I brought up the rear, behind the back of Beau's head. Occasionally he opened his eyes, smiling at me. His face was about as pale as pale could get, and his lips were tinged blue.

"Not sure about that Pillywiggins, Daisy," he said. "Not sure I got one."

"He's coming, Beau," I said. "He's biding his time, not far behind."

"Don't you be botherin' the boy," Grand-Momma snapped, breaking off from the lullaby.

"It's alright, Grand-Momma. She's telling me about the pillywiggins," Beau said.

"He's coming, Beau," I whispered, leaning down to him. "Can't you feel him?"

And, as if to emphasize the truth within my lie, a great gust of wind sprang up behind me. Sweeping over all of us, it ceased as quickly as it had started. A shiver and shake of branches, a hiss of swirling movement, then gone.

Just the wind in the trees, I thought.

"Gotcha!" Beau cried out. "I got him, Daisy. I got him."

Like always. It's always just the wind in the trees.

"There you go," Momma said. "I always knew the boy was good for a pillywiggins."

"Well done, you," I said to Beau.

Beau's smile seemed to reach out beyond his face, moving into the forest, into the world. He whispered to himself, "I got me a pillywiggins."

I whispered back, "Yeah, you did. You did."

For the rest of that sad patrol through the firs Beau kept quiet, eyes remaining closed, a silly grin fixed to his increasingly skull-like face. Occasionally I'd rest my palm on his forehead, letting him know I was still there. I could tell that Beau's time was soon, and that the Mommas would have to step on the gas to get him to where he needed to be.

The trees started to thin out, and without their dark, sentinel presence the day grew lighter. Deprived of the firs' protection the rain grew heavy and ice-cold, the trail turning muddy and slippery. Somehow the Mommas managed to carry Beau without dropping him. I'm glad that didn't happen; I wouldn't have liked it.

When we returned to where I'd parked I saw that the Mommas had arrived in two vehicles. One was a rusty, old pickup, and the other was a newish, blue box-truck.

Grand-Momma opened the rear doors of the truck, standing aside while the Mommas slid Beau, feet first, along the metal floor. I kissed him one last time, wondering how it was that I couldn't weep for my own brother. I wondered why none of us were weeping, not even our Momma.

"Goodbye, Beau," I said.

He smiled once more, apparently content. He'd got his pillywiggins, and he was now about to be taken to the Mommas' land, their forest. They'd lay him down among ancient trees, and his blood would seep into the forest floor. It would release the young'uns, setting them free; the ones who'd come to him as he lay bleeding out into the moss.

Three of the Mommas boarded the pickup, while Grand-Momma, Momma, and Jeanette climbed into the box truck. From behind the steering wheel Momma rolled down the window. "You coming, Daisy? See Beau do the thing he was born to?"

"I don't think I will, Momma," I said. "Not this time."

"For your own brother?'

"I can't, Momma. I just can't." And *then* the tears came, flowing down my face. They were hot and angry, my body wracked with convulsions. I bent over to dry heave, my hands shaking violently. After a minute I achieved some degree of control over myself, and I leaned on the truck as I sucked in deep, steadying breaths. Momma stared at me, her expression neutral. Eventually she said, "You felt it, right? When the pillywiggins came to Beau?"

I wiped my mouth. "Momma, it was the wind in the trees."

She shook her head slowly, squinting at me. "You gonna be home when we get back?"

I rested my forehead against the truck, where, inside, my brother lay dying from my own hand. "I don't think so."

"I figured," she said, sighing. "You know, Daisy, the special beings of this world, well, you gotta save 'em." She rubbed her eyes, weary. "When they're gone, they ain't comin' back."

Momma got the truck's engine turning over, slipping it into gear and driving off. She didn't wave, or smile. The pickup with the other Mommas set off after her. They ignored me, too.

I stood in the wind and the rain, shivering. I thought of all the lies I'd told the other dying boys, about the young'uns they carried. About what'd happen when they were taken to the old forest, the one the Mommas protected for all-time.

I had to admit something, though: the sudden wind, back there in the woods that swept toward us...it was fast-dyin' when it reached Beau, and it was strange. It'd never happened before, not like that. I'd never sensed a young'un, and it spooked me, actually. But *good* spooked, the kind that helped me hope against all hope that Beau *had* snagged himself a pillywiggins.

Imagining my brother running happily around the Mommas' woods, with the pillywiggins he'd saved, made me feel a whole lot better.

When I could hardly move, when my feet and hands were properly frozen, I shuffled to my pickup. I slumped behind the wheel, turned on the ignition and turned the temperature control to the hottest it could go.

Later, when I trusted myself to drive, I followed the trail to the highway, turning right toward the sun. To the hot, treeless deserts, and those juicy peaches.

STUART CROSKELL
ABOUT THE AUTHOR

Published Short Stories:

Stuart Croskell lives in the Uk. He is currently trying to write a novel about a haunted house.

'Dave Danvers' Final Foray Into All Things Woo' (Shallow Creek anthology, Storgy Books ebook/print, 2019 UK)

'Pastor Goodman's Five-Spot Onanist' (Crime & Mystery Library, Tell-Tale Press, online, 2019 USA)

'We Manifest When & How We Can' (When the Ride Ends anthology, Owl Canyon Press, print/ebook, Feb 2020 USA)

'Death & Pixels in LA' (Nabu Carnevale anthology, Tell-Tale Press, print/ebook, May 2020 USA)

Enjoyed the Book?

Indie Authors live for reviews and recommendations from their readers. Please take a few moments and review this collection on Amazon or Goodreads.

Don't Miss Out!

Looking for a FREE BOOK?

Sign up for Eerie River Publishing's monthly newsletter and get **Darkness Reclaimed** as our thank you gift!

Sign up for our newsletter
https://mailchi.mp/71e45b6d5880/welcomebook

Here at Eerie River Publishing, we are focused on providing paid writing opportunities for all indie authors. Outside of our limited drabble collections we put out each year, every single written piece that we publish -including short stories featured in this collection have been paid for.

Becoming an exclusive Patreon member gives you a chance to be a part of the action as well as giving you creative content every single month, no matter the tier. Free eBooks, monthly short strories and even paperbacks before they are released.

https://www.patreon.com/EerieRiverPub

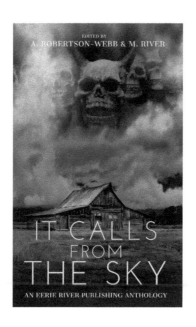

IT CALLS FROM THE SKY
COMING 2020

Lightning Source UK Ltd.
Milton Keynes UK
UKHW022103030920
369323UK00011B/195